UNITY

UNITY

-Mike Dirubio

UNITY

DEDICATION PAGE

To Judi- All good things come to those who wait. I promise to have myself whipped into shape as a decent husband sometime in the next decade.

ACKNOWLDEGEMENTS

All the cool things in this book are from NASA and other people. All the mistakes are mine. Thanks to Dave Zauhar for the fantastic pictures. Thanks to all down at Sabino's coffee for the weekend therapy sessions to keep me sane.

TABLE OF CONTENTS

Chapter 1-Alan Shepard

Chapter 2-Virgil Grissom

Chapter 3-John Glenn

Chapter 4- Scott Carpenter

Chapter 5-Wally Shirra

Chapter 6-Gordon Cooper

Chapter 7-Deke Slayton

Chapter 8-Virgil Grissom, Ed White, Roger Chaffe

Chapter 9- Walter Cunningham, Wally Shirra, Donn Eisele

Chapter 10-Frank Borman, William Anders, James Lovell

Chapter 11-James McDivitt, David Scott, Russell Schweickart

Chapter 12-Gene Cernan, Thomas Stafford, John Young

Chapter 13-Neil Armstrong, Michael Collins, Buzz Aldrin

Chapter 14-Charles Conrad, Richard Gordon, Alan Bean

Chapter 15-Fred Haise, Jack Swigert, James Lovell

Chapter 16-Stuart Roosa, Alan Shepard, Edgar Mitchel

Chapter 17-David Scott, Alfred Worden, James Irwin

Chapter 18-Thomas Mattingly, John Young, Charles Duke

Chapter 19-Harrison Schmitt, Gene Cernan, Ronald Evans

Chapter 20- Yuri Gagarin

Chapter 21-Valentina Tereshkova

Chapter 22- Alexey Leonov, Pavel Belyayev

Chapter 23-Vladimir Komorov

Chapter 24-Sally Ride

Chapter 25-Mark Kelly

Chapter 26- Story Musgrave

Chapter 27-Sunita Williams

Chapter 28-Koichi Wakata

Chapter 29-Robert Thirsk

Chapter 30-Oleg Kotov

Chapter 31-Sergei Krikalev

Chapter 32-Kjell Lindgren

Chapter 33- Koichi Wakata

EPILOG

CHAPTER 1

Launch Day 001 05 Mar 2021 0947 Kennedy Space Center

The assembled dignitaries watched the operation with the fascination of fan boys. The single 5' plastic cube barely fit into the dragon X capsule cargo hold. The technicians swarming on the rocket started attaching the skin panels and buttoning up the capsule. With the cube safely snug, the remote controlled cargo craft perched atop the Falcon 9 rocket on pad 29 at Kennedy Space Center was ready to go. The countdown continued. Just a normal launch, now. SPACE X had been using the launch facilities from NASA for the last five years to run resupply missions to the ISS. Historically, complex 29 and 30 had been the space shuttle launch points for over 134 missions. Now the complex buzzed with a new purpose. The privately owned Dragon and SPACE X had taken over as the supply shuttle for the International Space Station. Dragon was owned and built by Elon Musk of PayPal and Tesla fame. Musk and his team had started SPACE X in a non- descript, El Segundo Ca. warehouse in 2002. The laughable goal was a private commercial space company. What followed was a brilliantly executed series of flights that established Space X with its Falcon 1, Falcon 9 and Falcon Heavy rockets as the preeminent satellite and cargo/crew launch company. Their main competitor was now Antares, not NASA or the European Space Agency. Hell, Branson, Rutan and the team at Scaled Composites had morphed into Virgin Galactic and had hauled 88 tourists into space. The real psychological brake thru came in 2015 when people could start booking space flights on Expedia. The period between 2000 and 2015 had been an exploratory dead period while NASA grappled with declining budgets and interest in Space. The lack of a common goal kept splintering the missions. Several camps had split NASA along a "moon first Mars second" path and other exploratory missions. NASA had successes with Hubble and Kepler searching for extra solar system planets and the mars rovers Curiosity and Spirit. The economic meltdown in 2008 saw the enthusiasm for space exploration wane. However some technological breakthroughs and some long range planning for mars come together very quickly for NASA. 2013 saw a test firing (called a SNORT) at ATK that got NASA serious. Serious about a manned mars mission. ATK made rocket motors. Good ones.

The test of the new rocket motor design increased power quite a bit. NASA appointed the young engineer and program manager who had led the SNORT test as a tiger team leader and started looking at mission plans with capabilities. The working group quickly realized that no single entity- government or commercial could wrap its arms around the 30 billion dollar project. However, a world- wide mission to mars could work. The zealous engineer convinced NASA administrators to allow him to pitch The Obama administration and congress. Aligning the competing interests in the US political system had proven near impossible but slowly, the merits began to be seen. Next step, President Obama got the young man 30 min at a closed door G20 session. At the 57 min mark the meeting broke down with members arguing over the nationality of crew members. The young engineer, Bob Royce, knew he had a chance. Quietly, NASA, The European Space Agency, SPACE X, Antares, the Russians, the Chinese and several large multi- national corporations each set aside 10 million to form exploratory teams. After a series of extraordinary meetings in Feb and March of 2014, Royce had learned several new curse words and the basic framework had been hammered out: A committee from various members was to be formed. Decisions flowed down from the committee with input on feasibility. NASA was the lead technical agency coordinating efforts around the world. All information and tech break-through's developed as a result of the mission would be shared. All proprietary information developed prior to the mission would be available for purchase. Standardization and duplication were to be the norms. National interest came in second to the mission success. Moneys had to be allocated. Easy things to say but tough to follow thru. But in the end objections were overcome, compromises worked out. The Mars mission came at a time when the world was coming out of a long depression. Big ideas and bold steps were needed to kick start the recovery. The project may have looked like a stimulus package to some. A jobs program to others. The typical "how can we waste 30 billion on Mars when we have such poverty in the world" statements came from short sighted people. Space programs did give back for the dollars invested. Personal computers, cell phones, and satellite TV were just some of the off shoots of the space program. Royce envisioned similar benefits for all participants for the Mars mission. Bob Royce was idealist and a visionary and a ruthless manipulator. He quickly lost track of how many times he had been threatened and hauled in front of the committee to answer questions. His looks were unimposing. Short brown hair thinning and greying from the stress. Five ten, 170 lbs., he maintained a tough workout schedule to keep from having the inevitable heart attack this job was going to give him. Pushing, prodding, cajoling, people and agencies, he got designs approved and long lead items procured. Five years working 80 hours a week cost him a marriage and built a space craft. Now they had to get it to Mars.

The cube being loaded into the into the Dragon cargo ship atop the Falcon 9 rocket represented a significant mile stone in both the program schedule and the off shoots of the program benefiting man- kind. The cargo cube was approx. 5 feet on all sides. It weighed 2,000 lbs. fully loaded with fuel, air, food and tools. The cubes sides were made of two separate panels. The panels were put together more for their follow on use than the strength requirements of the cargo container they were now. The panels were made of PLASBOND. The wizards at Scaled Composites had long since moved away from petroleum based plastics. Now they used the emerging field of graphene carbon polymers to mimic other polymers. The plasbond panels were lighter, stronger and more flexible than anything ever produced. Once production lines were optimized the new plasbond sheets would be inexpensive to boot. Cheaper, lighter, stronger. Impervious to rain, termites and cat 1 hurricane winds, the new sheets would soon be on all new homes in the US. If the cube represented a major milestone in the program the way it was being loaded was certainly not a glorious moment for the program. Normally the cargo is loaded well in advance into the hold while the craft is being prepped. Then the craft is mated with the rocket and rolled out to the pad. Can't load the pod if you don't have the pod. Late by 24 days. Actually, 24 days late on a schedule laid down 3 ½ years ago was fantastic in terms of normal military or NASA projects. Not with this. Planetary orbits were setting the timeline not people. Hey, it's possible to remove the rocket fairing, open the cargo hold, slip the cargo in and button it all up. Using helicopters and harnesses, it can be done, it's just risky. Risky to people and equipment. "Winging it" was not NASA's style. And yet here we were. Royce and the rest of the VIP's watching in fascination as the last bolts were torqued into place. SPACE X techs were ready to continue the fueling of the rockets so its nine Merlin engines could blast the cargo into low earth orbit. The tanks just needed to be topped off to ensure a safety margin of fuel prior to lift off. The falcon had a unique launch hold system that kept the rocket pinned to the ground until a sufficient number of engines were working, ensuring a successful liftoff. 47 min later a tech gave Bob the thumbs up sign. Bob quietly moved to the Presidents side and spoke in her ear. "Madam President, the rocket's ready to go, we have about 25 min to liftoff. If you want to make some remarks, now is the time". "I've also promised the French Committee member Mr. Legarde some time for remarks. He won the drawing to represent the committee and be here".

Hillary Clinton looked up from her tablet. She looked every bit her 74 years. Bob hoped he was aging better. He knew the stress was getting to everyone.

Catching her eye he said "The tough part is over. Now it's just a routine resupply mission to the ISS."

"Thanks Bob". She moved to the front center of the NASA VIP Launch Lounge. Natural political instincts kicking in, she stopped just right of dead center of the window with the rocket providing a natural back drop. The President spoke the usual words when reminding people that they could celebrate tonight but the big prize was still ahead. Clinton stepped off to the left and approached Bob as the French committee member Legarde started into his long winded remarks about team work and cooperation while being led by the French.

She smirked just slightly for Bob to see and then said, "Good work Bob. Congratulate your team for me. I'd also like to know who the new crew member is as soon as you know."

"Certainly Madam President, just as soon as the committee informs me."

The committee met and worked in Brussels. Members felt that being in any of the usual capitols would subject them to too much outside interference. Members were regularly being called back home to get yelled at when the committee made a decision that didn't align with the geopolitical interests of the home country. Bob travelled or VTC'd once a week to the committee to get screamed at and be cajoled and be prodded and to actually get decisions made. As the countdown continued Bob looked around the lounge. To be one of the 85 people in here was to be very lucky or very powerful. The lounge itself was paid for by the Northrop Grumman Corporation. Its logo was plastered on everything. Like the SPACE X and Scaled Composite logo's on the rocket. Bob felt like a NASCAR driver sometimes. All the visitors watched eagerly as the rocket lifted off the pad. Normal launch. One down, thirty six launches to go. The numbers clicked over in Royce's head: 37 launches at 250 million each. 9.25 billion. Another 3 billion for current hardware development. 18 billion more was being spent to produce the rest of the hardware and facilities and planning and people right now. 18 separate heads of State and respective congress, 4 Space agencies. 9 prime contractors. 1800 major subcontractors. 150,000 direct report workers. 250 astronauts needed to fly the supply missions, crew the ISS and build the Mars craft in space. He had resources to get it done: NASA and Kennedy led the way. NASA had the SLS heavy lift rocket as well as the Delta IV. The Jet Propulsion Laboratory in Pasadena, Ca. would add its communication and flight control centers. The Johnson Space Center in Houston would also play a large role with training and mission control. But then so would Star City in Russia to oversee the Soyuz heavy lift launches as well as the European Space agency and the Arianne rockets from French Guiana. The newer players in this would be the Chinese and their new Gui Long rockets from their base in the Gobi desert. The private companies included Space X and Antares from Kennedy and Vandenberg. Virgin Galactic would lend its

Mohave facilities as back up for Johnson or Kennedy. Bob had a wall in his office at Alliant Technologies that consisted of the integrated master plan. A twisting maze of milestones and inter dependencies and boxes. Oh, the color coded boxes! Old project managers would wander in and take one look and shudder. Bob would grin. The key was really simple: Tell them what to do, not how to do it. Tell them what the end product had to look like or what function it had to perform and let them go about it. That's where the committee came in. They set the ground rules. They set requirements. They set parameters. The committee didn't re-invent the wheel. These stake holders had been involved in the space program for 70 years. The committee leveraged every lunar requirement and adapted it for Mars. They stole every hard won lesson learned from every blue ribbon panel, feasibility study or think tank in existence. The components and knowledge were out there. Could they wrap their arms around this greasy octopus and wrestle it into submission? As the Program Manager for Mars Flight, Royce was the man in the ring with the octopus. After the President left and the press was spoon fed and the dignitaries stroked, Bob slipped out of the lounge and drove off Kennedy to his office. Highway 528 was jammed at the port junction.

16

Tourists. Space was suddenly cool again. He hoped it remained that way. Bob spent the next three hours reviewing status and making phone calls. The next launch was scheduled for 120 days from now at Kennedy and the real ballet would begin. 2 days later another launch from French Guiana. Then it was a series of launches from various countries on various rockets carrying all sorts of parts and people. That's where the octopus had the upper hand. Bob sighed heavily. Kennedy would be ready. The French were on track. The Chinese on day 250? That was another story. The Chinese were behind schedule. Ideally 250 days from now the Chinese heavy rocket would blast off from their secret base in the Gobi desert carrying the equipment section of the mars craft. Boeing was ready with the equipment section 2 days early. They wanted to ship in 90 days. Boeing had leveraged off its aircraft and satellite design business and broken new ground on the equipment module. The module was designed to be the work horse section of the Mars craft housing the equipment/tools and science gear necessary to complete the mission. The 16foot tall 24 foot diameter section weighed 196,000 empty and was the biggest single piece going into space. The Chinese had been selected because they claimed the Gui long could carry that payload. Einstein was going to be too big. Bob chuckled as he got on the phone. The official government name for the equipment section was: Equipment Module, Crewed. EMC. E=MC2. Einstein. God save us from the Big Bang Theory. Actually the old TV series had made it cool to be a geek. Suddenly astrophysicists and theoretical physicists were solving complex math by day and dating hot blonds at night. NASA was not above basking in the glory. Several scientists and astronauts had been on the show. Astronauts on TV? Advertising on Rockets? Patent sharing on advances? Welcome to the new world of space exploration. Bob would do just about anything to get this mission accomplished. Bob didn't have many friends right now. He checked his watch as he dialed a number. Speaking Cantonese Bob saluted Lu chi Chan head of the Chinese Space Agency.

"Chan my old friend how are you"?

"Tired and cranky as you well know". Chan replied in English. Are you calling to inform me of the zero day launch? No need I've been fully briefed", Chan went on.

"No, Chan, I'm calling about the Day 250 Launch. Boeing wants to ship".

The pause on the line was heavy.

"The Chinese Space Agency is fully committed to meeting its obligations to the mars mission. We remain confident that the Gui long will be ready to launch the equipment module up to the International Space Station".

Bob smoothly replied, "NASA is just as firmly committed to the Gui long as the preferred launch vehicle for the equipment module launch. However NASA is concerned about certain aspects of the program testing data". Royce waited. "Is it still the weight"? He spoke softly.

"Of course it is the weight. The EMC is the heaviest object lifted off the earth' surface. 196,000 lbs. The Gui long was never designed for this lift. The modifications are very involved", Chan grumped.

"How did last week's test firing go? You kept Ms. Williams and the Boeing techs out of the control center", Royce prodded.

"I'm sure the resourceful and beautiful Ms. Williams used her spy craft to pass on the info", Chan retorted.

She had. Just this morning. Which necessitated this call. Whatever modifications the Chinese had made to the solid rocket engines of the second stage had not been enough.

"Perhaps the test would pass if we had access to the ATK

engine mods"? Chan trailed off.

Bob carefully weighed this last sentence. Typical Chinese opaqueness. Chan knew full well that ATK had made the break thru years before the mars mission was announced. The new packing method had allowed a Solid Rocket Propellant motor to get a 25% increase in thrust and the resultant increase in payload weights. Solid Rocket Propellant was packed into the rocket motor. Most people assumed that the propellant was just packed in solid, but that was not the case. If you cut a cross section out of a rocket motor there would be a hollow spot in the middle and a pattern on the interior surface. This allowed the igniter to get more of the propellant involved in the initial burn. As more and more of the propellant burns the limiting factor becomes how much gasses can be passed out of the bottle neck on the motor. You could increase the size of the opening but that drops the pressure and you don't get as much thrust. There is a pressure/thrust curve and you tweaked it to find the sweet spot given the size of the rocket motor and the burn rate. Then the cross coupled idea: how do you get soda out of a 2 liter bottle faster? If you just turned it upside down it chugged out slowly. However, if you spin the liquid inside the bottle it causes less interference as it exits and you get the liquid out faster. Could you spin the escaping gasses in a solid rocket motor during a burn? Well yeah. Not initially but if you put baffles inside a motor that became exposed as more and more of the propellant is burned away you could start the gasses swirling. Then it was just a matter of various opening sizes, and baffle patterns to achieve the thrust increase. Bob remembered the smiles after the static test he had witnessed as the NASA rep at ATK. The mars mission info sharing agreement called for all advances made as part of the program would be shared by all. Like the PLASBOND material. Anything prior would be paid for. Companies and agencies had looked pretty hard at the tech being offered. CEO's and Directors took some technology and passed on others. ATK had sold the SRP mod to Teledyne and SPACE X while the Chinese had passed. ATK had also bought Motorola's Comms Software/Hardware suite for a nice chunk of change. Most of these exchanges had worked out without one company being too hurt or helped. After the Chinese had passed, Bob dispatched his deputy program manager, the aforementioned Ms. Williams to be a technical liaison with the Chinese. Tech Liaison, Spy. Tomato, Tomotto. Now Chan was on the line dropping hints. He was angling to get the tech for free. They didn't want to pony up the 2 billion ATK was charging. So he staged some tests

he knew would fail and then stall until the schedule demands made

any other route prohibitive. If the Chinese walked Bob knew that

might bring down the program. Chinese hardball. Bob was no

stranger.

"Chan that suggestion is a nonstarter. The Russians and French

have agreed to pick up your launches in exchange for some other

considerations. Even the SLS is nearly there if we allow the liquid

first stage to go up a little light on fuel. The safety margin is

compromised but within tolerance. As the program Manager I have

to make a GO/No go decision in the next two weeks. In the

absence of verified positive test data on the engines, I will shift

D250 to the Russians, D 430 to the French and prepare for the

Chinese exit from the program". He waited.

"Bob... My government has already announced the launch as the

major accomplishment of the Chinese Space Agency. It announces

our coming out as a major launch player. The loss of respect

would be... devastating", Chan choked out.

Royce suppressed a flash of anger. "As I recall I urged you

strongly not to make that announcement. Now you must live

with the consequences".

A 10 count of silence. Royce played his trump.

"Perhaps a strategic withdrawal from the Tiger fund in the First bank of the Caymans is in order. Account number 72012QxxCH7788888 has 6.25 billion as of the first of the month. As luck would have it ATK has an account at the same bank. Specs and drawings could be to you via courier within an hour of transfer. ATK will say nothing. Le Quan must be made to see the right path". Le Quan was the Deputy Space Minister and the Premier's brother.

Heavy breathing on the other end. Bob waited stomach in knots.

"I think that will be acceptable to my superior, Chan relented. I will make him see the path".

"Thank you my friend. You are a true steely eyed missile man".

Bob granted the old boon. He wondered how much of the 2 billion would come from Chan's personal account. Well the stick had worked, now the carrot.

"Ah... forgive me, one more item. The committee has decided to remove the African crew member. China will get one more slot". He waited.

Chan mumbled a prayer. "Thank you my friend. The chairman

will be most pleased with this news. Most pleased".

"I need 20 more applicants for initial testing. I have a good idea who they will pick, but send them anyway".

"I will send them". "Godspeed Bob Royce".

"Be well", He hung up. As he cradled the phone he penned a quick note on his tablet to his assistant to draft orders sending Ms. Williams back to Cape Canaveral. With the motor tech knowledge all but transferred, her talents were needed elsewhere.

Royce then went to his office safe and opened it. Removing a cell phone he dialed a number from memory. A series of clicks and tones answered the phone. He waited 2 seconds. "This is RA authentication is Xray Alpha 117. I need to get a message to Raven: I had to use the Chinese Cayman bank information. You may want to pull your guy out or whatever it is you guys do…

Silence. Thanks Bye".

Thanks Bye. Real James Bond shit right there Bob mused. Bob was less than pleased to have to use the best info he had on the Chinese. Information was power and he had just exercised a large amount. Dropping the now useless phone in the waste basket, Bob picked up the next file folder waiting to boil over. He knew a new phone and a visit from Raven was forthcoming. Raven was a

present? Tool? From President Clinton. Royce hated spooks.

Reading the file he soon forgot Raven. The French needed a visit

in Guiana.

CHAPTER 2

Launch Day 002 06 Mar 2021 1147 Washington, DC

Dr. Janice Lincoln moved from the work station table back the computer to input the test results. She was looking at the micro biology of the latest GMO alfalfa. The plant had been genetically modified by Monsanto to withstand the pesticide Round up. It sounded kind of counter intuitive: Why would you make a plant able to withstand a new pesticide when it could already withstand two? When the two current pesticides didn't kill weeds as well and were pretty bad for the environment, that's when. Round up worked better on weeds but it also killed the old alfalfa as well. Dairy farmers paid more for weed free alfalfa than stuff that had weeds in it. So; design a plant that could withstand round up and reap the profits right? Monsanto had been doing just that. It was Janice' job to ensure that the GMO food was able to be eaten safely by the cows and then by humans drinking the milk and

26

eating the cheese. Janice had worked for the FDA for the past three years. She had left a job with the CDC after the crash had killed her husband and son. At 36 she was really overqualified for this job. PHD's in Biology, Micro biology and Computer Science from UC Berkeley as well as a Medical Degree. Janice never considered herself a "genius" or a savant or a prodigy. She simply liked to be busy. She had natural gifts that were helpful: an eidetic memory, natural hand eye coordination and curly brown hair. Janice was really good at prioritizing and focusing. High school taught that she could handle a hard work load. She started college classes as a junior in high school. She learned to size up the syllabus from a class and break it down into manageable bites. Then she would set her schedule and stick to it. She was one of 13 triple majors at Berkeley. She had as normal a child hood and college life as possible. Her parents regretted that Janice was an only child. She did study most nights but she also went to parties, football games, and concerts. She had met Charles at Berkeley. Charles Bennet was not intimidated by the reputation or the reality of interacting with someone that smart. Janice thought he was interesting and was amused when he asked her to pencil him in the schedule for a date. Zachary's for some pesto pizza and red wine. She actually was 22 min over schedule for the date when he dropped her off. Lost a few minutes kissing. The tenuous nature of time made manifest. She smiled at the thought. So the schedule got adjusted to have Charles at the parties or the game or just time alone. They got married as he finished his MBA and she completed the Triple Crown as Charles called it. Offers had been coming in for the last 18 months. Bio tech, universities, government agencies all came sniffing. Don't worry about the money Charles had advised, just make sure it's something that can hold your interest for 5 or 6 years. Besides we will just have to make do with the six figure signing bonus he chided. CDC and Coke got themselves some new young talent to dazzle the world. They moved to Atlanta. Janice dug in with both hands. CDC put her in a lab and then started asking her questions. How did this flu strain mutate and can you predict what the next strain might look like? I don't know let me see... 13 months later she looked up and published the paper on influenza strain mutation and the predictive course for future mutations. The HHS Secretary and the President just stared at her while she made her presentation. It really hit her when Charles took her face in his hands in bed that night. Honey you just saved millions of lives today. Kids that would have died from the flu will now live because of you. Him beaming down at her was better than any accolade from the President. Tougher questions followed. Hey Janice, dementia seems to be linked to this gene but it can take a slow path or fast path to actual cell break down. Is there a trigger mechanism and could there be a blocking agent? 22 months passed in a blink. She had proved the genetic link for the fast path dementia and the test that would allow early detection. She could see how the blocking agent could be laid in the path with the right genetic treatment.

The design of the genetic modification and the testing would take another 2 years. She gave birth as the testing wound down. She and Charles had a long talk about the schedule. Charles had moved over to Ryder Capitol management. They decided that Charles would raise Danny. Janice never got the Charles in Charge joke. Three good years working, raising a family, trying to schedule a second child. The phone call to the lab put aside many things. Gone, both of them, just like that. Traffic accident. Janice would never again take a phone call without thinking of that moment. She tried not to schedule into the future. She tried to ignore the gaping holes in her life but she could not. She left CDC. She took the job and moved to DC at FDA because she thought the supervisor understood. Janice should have been supervising an entire section of the FDA testing group instead of being a researcher. Two years in she realized that she was lonely. That was actually progress. Feeling nothing to feeling something, even loneliness was progress. She filled out the NASA application because a colleague had suggested she would be a good fit for the program. A trip to Mars might be fun right? She took over the FDA's computer hardware/software upgrade. Alfalfa was a stopgap until something, anything else came along. Opportunity had an iPhone 6 bell tower ring tone. She hung up from NASA's call with a sudden realization. Did I just commit to a tip to Mars? That's 3 years! Never mind that the only offer was a trip to Florida for the second round of testing and qualifications for the Mars crew. The thought that she would not be accepted, never occurred to her. Of course they would offer Mars. Did she really want to go? That required some thought. She would go to Florida and see.

The lanky Russian paused to look at his cards. Pair of Aces. Top pair. He scanned the other 4 players at the Bellagio Texas hold em table. Cards, odds, chip counts and player ticks all passed thru the computer in his head. He raised 400. 2 calls and 2 folds. He looked at the man on his right. The guy should have folded. Sergei Ivanovitch processed him. Bad bluff. The flop came King Ten nine. The bluffer raised 1000 on top of Sergei's 500, repping top pair. Sergei called. The other player called. Sergei focused on the man across from him now. He had good cards. The turn came up six. Bluffer went 1,000. Player called. He raised to 5,000. Player called, and bluffer finally folded. Sergei focused. The room froze, achieving the zone. The zone was his secret weapon. In the zone time slowed. Sergei was able to notice things at an almost atomic level. He studied the opponent. Jeans, button down shirt. Unkempt hair, stubble. Relaxed face. Why would he be relaxed? He couldn't have aces. Unless. The river came up Ace. Sergei looked at the player. He quietly folded without betting. Sometimes the only play is to cut your losses. Player looked at him. How did you know, he asked turning over the eight seven to complete the straight. Sergei stacked up his remaining chips.

"You were too calm he said. No reaction at all to the Ace. You were set from the flop."

72,050. Up over 22,000. Not bad for 4 hours work. The

game ended and Sergei cashed out and went to the bar. The large Russian was classically handsome with short blond hair and a square jaw. He walked to the table with every bit of grace and swagger a trained fighter pilot could muster. Vegas was as far as possible from Vladivostok. Or Moscow or Baikanour or Kennedy. Sergei was running. Running from the government. Running from his past, his future, and present. Fuck em he thought. They can't make me go. I'll play nice, but I'm not going. He sipped his drink and tried to pin point where it had gone wrong. Every action seemed right at the time. Sometimes you can play every situation correctly and you just had to cut your losses. He didn't regret sleeping with the Minister's daughter. She was over 21. Barely but over. He was only 22 at the time. 17 years is a long time to hold a grudge. Who knew she would grow up to run Russia's Space Agency? Well when Daddy was Putin's hand-picked successor, baby gets what she wants. Besides by all accounts Tatiana was good at her job. Cool, competent, and professional. She had dogged him his whole career. Ruined the Sukoi job. Ran him out of Star City. Now she was bugging NASA. Royce told him so himself. Now she wanted to meet. He had gone to Vegas to avoid her visit. With any luck he would gamble for a few days spend some time with quality booze and hookers and slink back to NASA to continue the development program.

Development only. Royce had agreed to that. Good man that Royce. Royce could use some time in Vegas himself, Sergei thought.

He spotted them as they started across the bar towards him. One American and one Russian. FBI and CKE. Both ex- military. Professional. They blocked both avenues of escape without getting in each other's way. Sergei figured his odds. As the American approached the table he stopped short and spoke to him, "Sergei Ivanovich, it is time to quit playing childish games and do your duty. She wants to see you upstairs".

Sergei assessed the situation. He could take the two of them. They would do some damage, but he could beat them and get out. He started shifting his weight slowly preparing for the move. "Tovaritch". The Russian agent spoke softly. He nodded to his left and behind Sergei. Sergei slowly turned his head. Seated at a back table was another CKE agent. Two more FBI appeared at the bar entrance. Five. Sergei weighed the odds. In the zone he might, might be able to beat them. Fighting five men at once was actually not as hard as it sounds. 5 men attacking individually

had no coordination. They often blocked each other's movements, allowing for the one opponent to exploit that advantage. However, if they were professional they could come at him in a two, two, one formation and wipe the floor with him. Did Sergei want to go thru that? On the other hand he didn't want to see Tatiana. Their last meeting six months ago had been... eventful for him. The bruises were barely healed. He had signed the application to go on the Mars mission at the point of a gun. Sergei promptly went in and faked some medical data that indicated he had epilepsy. He was a little disappointed that she had figured that out as quickly as she had. Royce was still convinced he was not a candidate. It had taken a little fancy footwork to convince Royce to let him stay.
You know what? No. Wrong tactic with Tats. Running only made her chase. Time to anger her. Then she would kill him or let him go. Either way, Sergei didn't go to Mars. He eased to his feet. Setting himself he said: "lead on Mc Duff."
The agents exchanged a glance and the formation formed up for the trip across the lobby to the elevators. Sergei relaxed now that he had a plan. The trip to the penthouse was in silence. As they approached the door to the room, the US agent warned him "no tricks we have every angle covered here". Sergei smiled. He

doubted that. As he entered the suite, he told the agent "don't wait up, we are going to be at it all night".

The CKE agent smiled grimly. "I don't think that would be in your best interest, she's mad at you".

Entering the empty living room Sergei moved to the bar and poured two drinks. He stood at the window looking over the Vegas strip. He heard her enter the room. He held the drink out behind him without looking at her. She took the glass silently. They both stared out. This had to be done delicately. Finesse. He turned to look her up and down. At 21 she had been all skinny planes and angles. Beautiful, but not yet mature. Now Tatiana had come into her beauty and power with a vengeance. She did look fantastic with her hair that red color. Sergei made his play. He turned and hurled the glass across the room smashing it. He took both her shoulders in his hands and stared down into her blue eyes. Voice loud, hard, he said, "Let me make this as plain as I can. I don't care how much money daddy has or how much power you have, I'm not going to Mars. I don't care about the glory or the science or the honor for the old country. You can only kill me once. We had an affair 15 years ago. It's over. Deal with it. Quit hounding me you bitch"!

He shifted her back towards the window and moved his hip over to keep her from kneeing him in the crotch. He took a deep breath to continue the planned tirade and looked back at her face. Amusement.

Not fear, not anger, amusement. He focused in and achieved the zone. Her breath hitched in. Uh oh. She casually moved her hand behind his head running her hand thru his hair. Now her hips shifted and he was turned with his back to the window.

She moved her head in close to his ear as the zone shattered. "Poor Sergei Ivanovitch. The sacrifices you must make. The burdens you must carry. To be asked to lead the most important space mission the earth has ever undertaken. To be the most famous cosmonaut since Armstrong. To be the first human to set foot on another planet. It is just too much. We have wronged you", she nuzzled into his neck kissing him softly.

Wait what?

She entrapped him. Arms legs lips eyes hair everywhere as Sergei tried to regain the upper hand.

"Well I appreciate the status of this mission, Tatiana, but I really only want to design and fly, this is too much command. Too much responsibility".

"Of course it is too much", she purred, maneuvering him to the couch. He was way too aroused as she wriggled on top of him.

"I'm not committing to anything, Tats".

Kissing her feeling her tugging off clothes and one last defiant,"

This doesn't mean anything…   "

"Of course not, Serge" she whispered as she took him.

Many hours later in bed Tatiana looked over at him. His drowsy eyes half closed.

"Sergei, look at me".

He did, starting to apologize and object.

"No, here me out; It is simple. This mission is going to require the best we can muster. You are the best. I know it; The committee knows it, and so does Royce. Without you this mission might fail and people could die. People might still die but the mission can succeed with you. So you are out of your comfort zone, commanding. Deal with it, as someone recently told me".

Sergei was silent. She had a point. Sergei knew the myriad of things that could go wrong on a space flight. What was the lesson on the US Space shuttle Challenger disaster? If you have 10 million parts on a space craft and 10% are critical how many critical parts is that? 1 million. How many parts on the Mars craft? How many on the site base?

He told her his fears. "How could I possibly look over the 2 million parts"?

She gazed at him with confidence. "Look at it this way; Watkins gets the nod without you. Watkins could only look over 800,000 parts. That left God to look over 1.2 million. You can look over 1.4 million parts. That reduces God's work load by 50%. You are doing God a favor". He contemplated that.

"Okay. I'll do it. As a favor for God, no other reason".

She smiled at him, reaching out to stroke his chest.

"Hey, I'm not a circus performer. I can't just perform on que. Besides I need to convince Royce I am suddenly cured of epilepsy".

"Royce"? Tatiana laughed throatily. "Who do you think sent me"?

Tyler Watkins eased the wrench down to better fit the bolt. These small bolts were tricky. Too much torque snapped the heads off, while too little just caused the heads to strip. Bracing his right foot on the platform, he switched the wrench to on. The bolt resisted a little and the wrench slipped on the head for a turn. Watkins adjusted on the fly and the bolt started to back out. 10 seconds later he reported last screw out step 17 completed. The step was dutifully checked off by Edminton. Zhou then moved onto the platform to install the handles. The three astronauts were in Houston at the NASA weightless training pool. They were developing the procedures that would allow the Mars mission astronauts to assemble the craft and for in-flight refueling using the attached plasbond cubes. The pool was featured as the training ground for NASA astronauts on spacewalks. During the famous Hubble Space telescope maintenance missions NASA legends like Story Musgrave and Tom Akers had spent hours in the pool honing skills and procedures. Of course what NASA never highlighted was the amount problems those spacewalks had to overcome. EVA suit problems, comms issues, tool malfunctions. Astronauts learned to adapt and fix on the fly. But they proved that 8 hrs of complex work could be done in space. Mars mission was the next logical step. They had fixed Hubble and repaired the ISS now they would assemble the Mars craft. Now they had to build the thing in space. Time in the pool was precious. With 250 astronauts needing certification on all types of procedures and tools, wet time was gold. NASA was monitoring and coordination the 4 agencies as they certified astronauts. Almost half, like Watkins, had previous ISS EVA on their resumes. Jack Edminton and Lui Zhou were new. Watkins was leading them on the qual walk.

 Tyler and Zhou acknowledged the next step from Edminton and shifted to remove the panel. As Tyler handed off the panel to Zhou he lectured: When you get the panel in space you need to be very aware of tool placement and handling the panel. If you leave that wrench attached on too long a tether, it can become trapped between your suit and the panel. That tends to put pressure on parts of the EVA suits that they weren't really designed for. The wrench end tends to break the small wires of the telemetry links internal to the suit. Then we have to do maintenance on the suits and that leads to less space time. Zhou acknowledged curtly.

 Watkins tended to pontificate vs teach. But they needed his signature on the sign off sheet or they had to do this again. Once the panel was stowed on the truss bracket, they proceeded to retrieve the fuel bladder from the cube and restore the panel. It took longer than some but it was done correctly. Zhou and Edminton were new but competent. Watkins knew that they would be in the mix for the final crew. Edminton was a no, but Zhou had a chance at the Chinese slot. The US had three crew members out of 8. China had one. Russia, Europe, South America, and Africa had one each also. An earth representative crew. Watkins was a favorite to be an American crew member. He wanted more. Mission Commander. The first man to set foot on another planet. He had the speech all planned out: "I take this step to advance all mankind" It was his for the taking. Ivanovitch had turned chicken. He didn't want it. And there were no serious contenders among the European, Chinese or South Americans. Other Americans like Grace Adler or Michael Keith were contenders but not really in his league. Rumor was that the mars crew finalists were heading to Florida soon. He just had to play the game for a little while longer. Growing up poor in Henderson, Nevada Watkins never had much. He was a natural mechanic and had an uncanny ability to see things in 3 dimensions. He had worked on the math and science to escape the bad family situation. He joined the military straight out of high school. The Air Force saw potential right away. They sent him to school and made him an officer. He was a wiry five feet eleven inches. Brown suntan and a scowl smirk that seemed to be his go to facial expression. He flew jets in combat and had earned medals and citations but no friends. A loner by nature he signed up for and got astronaut training. He had been in space 4 times to the ISS. Now he had Mars in his sights. As he signed off the qual letter and changed back into his flight jumpsuit (more patches than open space) an envelope was taped to his locker. Opening it he smiled as he read. Orders to Florida for "special training".

Slipping the envelope into his flight suit he went to pack. It was time to blow this popsicle stand. Nobel Prize? Time's Man of the Year? Either would be fine. It was only his due.

CHAPTER 3

Launch Day 006 11 Mar 2021 0957 Kennedy Space Center

The NASA commercial came on. The first commercial break of the NCAA March Madness coverage: $1.3 million to tell the world: Footage of Obama announcing the mission. The conference where the committee was announced and the primes selected. Glorious launches from all over the world. Cut to a woman wiring electronics board in India. Voice over: I'm making the electronics for the radar system that will warn the astronauts of anything incoming to endanger the spacecraft. Cut to a male engineer working at a computer. I'm writing the software that will allow the astronauts to fly the craft out of danger. Cut to a team testing a pipe. We're building the mars spacecraft itself!! I made that. I made that. I made that. Mars spacecraft: built on earth. Ready for the stars.

The briefing room was the largest at NASA. The video screen displayed the Dragon x Capsule landing in the Pacific Ocean and retrieval. All 52 people in the room watched with interest. 48 candidates plus Royce, Kat Williams, John Scanlon the NASA Director and Tatiana Medvedev. The candidates watched them and each other with more interest. Many of them knew others very well. Watkins saw James Andrews AKA Digger. He also saw Ivanovitch, which surprised him. There was Lui Zhou from Houston and Elkington. He had spaced with Brad Elkington before. They nodded at each other. They all eyed each other sizing up the competition. Some were wide eyed and nervous. Others blasé, hiding it. Janice Lincoln committed the briefing material to memory. All quieted when Royce moved to the front of the room as the video display cutoff.

"Welcome to you all. As I'm sure you've guessed, this starts phase 2 Mars mission, Crew testing and qualification. The Mars Mission crew will be selected from the people in this room. The selection process will be long, complicated and fraught with political wrangling and a bunch of hurt feelings".

Several chuckled at that. Oh. Royce was going to tell the truth was he?

Royce continued. "The crew breakdown is as follows: 3 Americans. 2 Chinese. 1 each South American, Russian and European. That's eight total". Some buzzing at the omission of the African crew person. More internal racking and stacking.

Royce plowed on. "We need a Mission Commander, Flight Lead, a Comms lead, a Geology Expert, a Computer Expert, Biology, Medical and Physicist. Everyone on board will be an engineer. The engineers are the fix it crew. You are here because you represent the best in those fields. You have all passed the basic psychological tests and the physical requirements. You are all smart, competitive and goal oriented. You do the math. Any one person who is qualified on multiple fronts stands the better chance of going. Each one of the fields will have more knowledge testing, practical tests and scenario driven faulted operational tests given. Don't worry about the space flight. You will be sick of the ISS and your space suits by the time this is over. Each one of you will get a minimum of three flights to the ISS. Anyone who is uncomfortable in space will be discovered and removed. Some of you have been to the ISS before. That puts you in the flight driver seat. But someone who has flight experience as well as computer expertise or comms knowledge is going ahead of the flyboy. Lastly a large chunk of your scores are going to be on how you help others in the testing period. This is about mission over self. We are putting together a team not a collection of fighter pilots. Egos are checked at the door. Anyone who doesn't want to play nicely will be asked to leave. The committee has delegated broad authority to me in this area. I'm choosing three from among the Americans here. The 2 Chinese I will give a recommendation to but the Chinese will get their choices. Same going forward for the European Space Agency and the Russian group. The South American candidate will be picked by committee. You could be the best American physicist but if the best Chinese or South American is a physicist you are out of luck. Make yourself indispensable. If I need to I can take circumstances back to the committee and tell them I have to have more European geology experts for example. We are not above removing all of you and starting over if need be. I fully expect you to be up to speed on all of the material you have been given. Everyone reach under your seat. Pull out the goodie box. You'll find a color coded card

RED GOLD BLUE WHITE. Those correspond to your group. Find a tablet. That tablet is classified Secret. It will now be with you every second of every day. You will sleep with those tablets. You will notice that they are very special. Please turn them on. Royce paused while 48 tablets got booted up. These are the latest from IBM. Ultra high def flex fold screen. 4096 parallel A7 processors. 400 terabytes of storage. New Polymer lithium batteries from Sadoway. You should have 26 hours continuous use from the batteries with a 45 min charge time. You will note that every bit of information is already loaded on this tablet. Full Mars craft specs and tech manuals. All procedures, every photo ever taken of Mars. Every technical spec of the equipment you will use. It also has your schedule and a can be used to text and send messages as well as a camera. I expect that each of you will be fully versed in this tablet tomorrow. Where you are supposed to be and when you are supposed to be there is on the tablet. Be there. You will be expected to know the day one material tomorrow morning. There will be a test. If you think I won't send you home after one day, please try me on this. If that tablet says to be in a specific bathroom at a specific time you better be there grunting. Titters in the crowd. By the end of the week we expect to have four operational groups ready to start training for various ISS launches. Last thing. This is no place to have a secret. If you know something you better tell me. Secrets get people killed. See you at the Day 6 second event. Dismissed".

Janice sat in the crowd looking at the tablet. It was remarkable. 1.3 lbs. About 8 by 12 with a small bevel around the screen. She reached to the screen and folded it out. The screen was now 16 by 12. She touched icons on the screen. One was marked Register me first. She registered her name and info into the tab. A new icon appeared; Daily schedule: Dr. Janice Lincoln. Gold Group. Barracks room 142 A. The room number was hyperlinked. She clicked and a map of the Kennedy Space Center came up with a flashing triangle indicating where she was and where her room was. She memorized the directions. She noted a section marked required tasks: 1) attend orientation brief 0700 Aldrin Auditorium. 2) Register Laptop 3) Barracks room move in 4) Gold group meeting conf rm 6D Mcallister Hall 1030 5) Make video log entry 6) attend astronaut social 1900 Green house. Again hyperlinks led to maps or additional information. She marked the first two items on her schedule as completed and started on the third. She noticed others milling about or talking. No one seemed interested in the laptops. She slipped out of the auditorium into her car and followed the road around to her barrack room. Spartan but clean. She walked into a small shared kitchenette with a sink, small fridge, microwave and table. Beyond was a couch entertainment center with a TV, one small window and two doors off either side of the lounge area leading to the bedrooms. Two bunks in each room. On the bunks were sheets, blanket, pillow and case plus three pairs of blue running shorts with a NASA logo. Three women's medium short sleeve shirts in gold with the Mars mission logo. Dresser with a small closet. Two desks with chairs in the bedrooms. The left side bunk had her name over it. Janice stowed her clothes quickly in the bottom two drawers with the rest hung up in the closet. In the closet were eight jumpsuits- 4 with her name on them and 4 with Gonsolvo on them. She stowed a small toiletries bag in the left bottom side of the bathroom cubby holds. She moved her note books and some journals and another laptop into the desk. She sat at the desk looking more closely at the apps on the tablet. Apps were not the right word. The laptops contained an extraordinary amount of information. It had13 distinct modules: 1) Laptop 2) Schedule 3) Training presentations 4) Procedures 5) Ships schematics 6) Equipment Schematics

7) Mars information 8) Video blog 9) Comms 10) Navigation 11) Flight 12) Testing 13) Science. She tabbed 2 open. It had several subheadings: Personal Physical Classroom Practical Testing Medical Flight. She tapped personal. Her schedule was laid out for the week. Janice expanded it out to the month. Wow. She closed out her personal and opened the classroom portion. She closed that back and reopened her personal schedule. The classroom was group and individual specific for the whole group. Likewise the Practical schedule. Her personal schedule grabbed those items and coalesced them into her personal schedule. But she could look at anyone's schedule in the program. Up to and including Royce. Ditto her instructors. She closed the personal schedule down to a week. She started tomorrow at 0600 with Physical training (uhgg) with gold group at the gym (Physical training gear was listed as the uniform). She then had a group breakfast followed by group classroom training session 1 (Hadenfeld) (Flight suit) (Allen Hall classroom 2). The session 1 item was hyper linked: Clicking on it she saw NASA Mars Flight Orientation power point presentation slides come up. She perused them. Clicking on the professor's name she saw his NASA bio and some links to newspaper articles: "Canadian astronaut wows

earth followers with photos and Davis Bowie songs". She clicked

the You tube link. Space Odessy. Not bad. Tomorrow had

continued with a Baseline medical test for hearing sight and blood

work. She had an individual training session at 1400 with Williams

at the flight mock up lab in the VAB. She then joined her group

for dinner and an EVA suit fitting and training session. It ended at

2000 with, no shit, a test back in the auditorium with all four

groups. The test hyper link stated that the testing materials would

be provided at the session. Okay. NASA was pretty serious about

this. They were just going to fire hose the info at them and see

who could cope. Janice tabbed open 8 for the video blog and

started to record. The instructions had been pretty clear: record

your thoughts about the mars mission and your personal reactions.

For the first session answer this question: Why do you want to go

to Mars? Janice adjusted the camera and closed her eyes

composing her thoughts. She started recording:

Video log of Janice Lincoln on 11 March 2021 0819

I'm in my new dorm room getting ready for my next group

session. The room is adequate and the laptop is fabulous. Mr.

Royce you said no secrets so here are some I know: The

hyperlink to the map of Kennedy Space Center brings up an out of date map. The Kennedy website has the current one. The Power point slides for session one by Astronaut Hadenfeld are misnumbered. They go 1 thru 6 but then 8, 9 then 11 thru 27. We have a swim session listed as our physical training for Tuesday but no swim suits were provided in our rooms. Could you please indicate in our session this evening if the suits are at the pool facility or if I need to get one? The list of items we were required to bring did not include a swimsuit. I'm assuming you are monitoring these blogs and tracking us thru the laptops. Why do I want to go to Mars? I'd like to know if life existed once or even still exists on Mars. Thank you. Lincoln out.

She switched off. A little smile on her lips as she continued to peruse the laptops and got deeper into the slides for session one. As she studied the door to the barracks room opened. A short dark compact woman entered the bedroom. "! Hola Chica!" She sang. "I'm Rosario Gonsolvo. It looks like we are going to be roomies".

Janice stared. The woman was bursting with energy. It crackled off her eyes and hips. Slinging her bags down she dropped onto the bed.

"Whoo! They are grim out there. Everyone is very serious today. No one has been cut yet. What's your story- Janice, is it"? She asked reading the name tag. Janice gave her the NASA bio version of who she was. Rosario was impressed. "Well if you can stomach the flight and EVA stuff you should be a shoe in. I'm a comms tech as well as RADAR and flight back up. I also have an Astronomy back ground".

"Have you been to the International Space Station"? Janice asked her, while Rosario unpacked.

"Yes, once, two years ago". "We installed the new Motorola gear on the ISS. That was actually fun. Worried about the flights? Well don't sweat it. I'll help you with the Space woman stuff. I might need a little help on some of the science items", Rosario bargained.

"Deal", said Janice smiling. Janice liked this little bundle.

"Have you looked over the laptop"?

Rosario frowned. "Just a glance, why"?

"I think they are real serious about us sleeping with the laptops. I think the laptops are how they track us and grade us on things. Look here". She helped Rosario boot up and register, then showed her the schedule and hyperlinks. The Argentinian woman frowned down at the computer.

"Aiy Mommy you are right. Royce is a bastard. A cute one but he would cut his mother to get to Mars. Who is in gold group"? As she said this the door opened again and two men entered the kitchen area. The tall skinny blond man grinned down at them. "Hello ladies. I'm James Andrews. You can call me Digger. I'll explain later. This is Qyuhn Le from the People's Republic of China". Introductions all around. Janice warned them "You guys have about an hour before gold group meets for our session".

"We should go together", said James. "We can keep Qyuhn from getting lost".

Qyuhn bristled. "I have the highest IQ ever measured in China, I think I can read a map".

Janice left Rosario making her blog entry and the men arguing as they unpacked. She went out onto the walkway in front of the barracks building. There were four buildings around a central courtyard. Gaps between the four story buildings showed other structures. Janice called up a mental picture of the map. Southeast was the main classroom Mcallester hall. The galley was kitty-corner to that. To the North east was the VAB in the distance with the view of launch complex 29 and 30 blocked by the

54

buildings. The Northwest corner led to the Auditorium with the gym and flight mock up buildings beyond that. Kennedy was a huge sprawling massive complex. A good description of this mission Janice thought. She watched men and women move into and out of barracks rooms. Well we shall see.

The small office was buried deep in the bowls of the Mcallester hall. Royce sat at a three screen console with Katherine Williams his deputy just back from China. One display showed an aerial map view of Kennedy with small numbered triangles blinking. The vast majority of the 48 were clustered in the 4 low slung buildings around the quad. He looked at the list correlating names and numbers. Watkins had his three roommates up and running. So did Sergei although his blog entry was a long string of profanities directed at Royce over Tatiana. Kat smiled at that. A surprising number had figured the laptops quickly. Watkins, Lincoln, Ivonavitch, Adler. Even trigging to the monitoring and who would be behind it. He started calling up video blogs and most were pretty honest. Watkins sounded like a NASA commercial: "carrying the honor of mankind into the stars". Kat inputted times and tasks accomplished into the algorithm that would come up with the ideal crew. It wasn't just a matter of could someone get their own tasks performed but would they or could they do to help others? As the training progressed, individual scores would matter less and less. Group scores would start to weigh more heavily. Sighing, Royce looked at the screen display. Two laptops unregistered. Dr. Hoffman and Dr. Xiling. It looked as though Hoffman had left his laptop in his car and Dr Xiling had his in his room but had yet to turn it on. Why hadn't someone in the group helped them? Royce called up a list of phone numbers. He called the number listed for Xiling. "Dr? Are you okay?" Royce asked. "I see."

"Dr., I cannot stress enough how important those laptops are. I know you had a long flight in and are tired. Please complete your items and then you can get a good nights' sleep. Thank you sir". Checking his list again he dialed another number. "Officer Jenkins? Royce. I need to you to go to room 132 south of Apollo barracks and find a Dr. Hoffman. Georg Hoffman. German geologist. "His laptop is in his car. Please impress upon Dr. Hoffman how important we think classified laptops are. He has a meeting at 1030 so you have about 20 min to read him the riot act okay? Thank you".

He went back to monitoring. "I want you to head down to the classrooms and observe the small groups", he told Williams.

Sergei sat in room 6 E of McAllester Hall. He studied the blue group of 12 people in detail. 7 men and 5 women from around the globe. A nice mixture of scientists and astronauts. He had started with himself in introductions around the table.

"Hello, I am Sergei Ivanovitch, obviously a mad Russian. Flight Command candidate. I've been in space 4 times. I'm qualified on flight, 67 actual EVA hours, certified on every space tool, comms, radar, rover, and all systems on the ISS. I have been involved lately in the Mars craft design and production. I have helped develop all the procedures we will use on the mission. I have advanced degrees in mechanical and electrical engineering as well as geology and computer science. I'm a Taurus and I like to collect Staffordshire pottery". He waited a beat while the joke sank in. Not much reaction. After the intros were done (no one even came close to his qualifications) Sergei looked at all of them. "I have been thru this rodeo before. Please let me give you some advice: No one knows everything. We have to work together if we want to get to Mars. Every action we take is going to be graded.

Dave, Phuong, could you explain what you are wearing"? Both of the named scientists looked bewildered. Jeans and a tee shirt came the reply. "Why aren't you in your flight suits? Didn't you see them in the closet? Do you have your laptops"?

Both produced them. "Let me show you". He went thru the schedule highlighting time place and uniform. Several people had startled looks as he called up the session 1 training slides.

"Every single action we take is being graded. Someone will note your lack of the correct uniform and mark you down. Small details make a huge difference in space".

Sergei also noted a smug smile on another face. "Dr. Atkinson, you are perhaps a little pleased to see a competitor get marked down a grade"?

Atkinson quickly replied "no, of course not."

Sergei waved away the protest. "Understand the entire group got a grade on this session. We all got marked down because they are not in the right uniform. As your potential flight and mission commander, I am especially marked down because two of my people were not correct. Harsh? Maybe. There is an old science fiction book called "The Moon is a Harsh Mistress". "Mars? Well Mars is just a stone cold bitch. 50 percent of the missions we have ever undertaken to Mars have failed. Dave and Phuong need not worry. It's just one point on a scale of thousands". "But enough that attention to detail is what separates who makes it and who doesn't. Now let's talk about tomorrow. Does anyone anticipate problems with the physical training"? Four hands went up. "Other than you don't like it", Sergei laughed. Three hands went down.

"I don't have running shoes, Dr Jones stated. I just forgot them. I'll pick some up at the base exchange after lunch".

"Good. Does anyone know Dr Tyson our training lecturer? No? Too bad". Sergei went thru the process of leading his group. He suggested they all eat lunch together to go thru some of the laptop modules in preps. The American flight candidate Kelly Johnson was suspicious at first. But she came around. The group was talking animatedly about the mission when Sergei noted Ms. Williams at the doorway. She nodded to him and slipped out. He missed that caramel skinned exotic beauty while she was in China. He hoped she liked his video blog entry.

The chow hall was crowded at 1200 when the blue group arrived. Watkins had the Red group all standing at the table while the last few gathered drinks and napkins and such. Once they were all around the table they sat with a big "Go Red" chant.

"Wow, Watkins, Sergei mumbled under his breath. "You managed to get a group of 11 of the smartest humans on the planet to recognize their colors". Two women behind him laughed in response. Sergei turned, embarrassed. He saw Rosario Gonsolvo with another woman. He quickly embraced Rosario.

"Hey Rose, how are you", he said happy to see her. Rosario stood on tiptoe to kiss his cheek. "Hey Serg. I thought you had decided against this beauty pageant".

"Well, I heard you needed me. "Gold huh", he added. "Too bad. I enjoyed the ISS 72 mission".

"Not as much as I did", Rosario leered. This is Janice Lincoln my teammate. Rosario introduced them. Sergei shook hands with Janice.

"Dr. Lincoln your paper on quantum computers was groundbreaking and helped put me to sleep three nights running", Sergei teased. Janice blushed. She murmured hello. Rosario rolled her eyes and slapped Sergei on the arm. "Hey you're supposed to be swooning over me! Why don't you bump Elkington and join the gold team"?

"Nah", Sergei said as they moved to thru the chow line. "The blues are the good group. We are going 8 for 8. Sorry guys. Rose let's catch up at the social. I want to pick your brain on something for the Mars craft".

"Sure Sergei", Rosario lit up. They passed thru the chow line debating cafeteria food.

A quick "see you" as he went to join the rest of the blues eating at a nearby table. Rosario and Janice joined the goldies. Janice asked if she and Sergei knew each other well. Rosario sighed.

"Not as well as I would like. Sergei was the commander on the ISS mission I went on. We trained together for 4 ½ months. Sweat and strain and no relief for Rose. "Cool and professional. Then after the mission at the landing party he ghosts into the party, grabs my hand and the next thing I know we were doing it in the VAB Shuttle mockup". "I get horny just walking into that building. I could never lock him down though" she frumped.

"Elkington is good", she said nodding to the Gold team Flight/Command candidate, "but Sergei just has this knack for calmly getting things done that make you trust him". "I'll take Serg every time I can get him". Janice looked at the tall Russian as he sat conversing with his team. He did have certain X factor.

Janice had felt it even with their brief conversation. Enough to make her want to go to Mars? She felt the weight of the decision. Elkington broke into her reverie.

"Dr. Lincoln? Kat Williams wanted me to pass on a message to you and anyone else who might have been wondering: swim suits will be provided at your locker at the pool. "Tool and equipment packs are also located at other training stations". Elk nodded at her.

"That's a good question. Sharp to anticipate the need. Anybody else have any questions about the setup here"?

James "digger" Andrews raised a hand. "Can we request extra training in a weak area"?

Elkington paused considering. "I would say a qualified yes. Qualified by the availability of personnel and trainers. That being said, I think you could squeeze some extra time in". "This is a broad spectrum training setup. Lecturing now, Elk got on a roll. "We are going to get a lot of info in a short amount of time. Likewise we are going be performing a variety of tasks some of you may not be good at. Both in a lab, then in a mock up. Then progressing to the pool, perhaps even on the Virgin galactic space ship. Simple things like loosening screws. In space it's different than on earth. NASA has a whole room setup just to practice loosening captive screws, connectors, wire locked nuts, switches and the like. The scientists will have trouble with those tasks while the military trained flight jocks will have trouble with the hard science experiments we will use both on the ship and at the site. "I suggest Dr. Lincoln and her colleagues spend some time turning wrenches while digger, I think you need to spend some time with Dr. Lincoln talking about the computer and the experiments she might use to id life on Mars. I need help with geology Dr. Leon. Look around the table and around the room. Everyone here is an expert on something. Rosario helped design build test and field the communications units we will use on the flight". Elkington paused to let that sink in. "She knows everything there is to know on the relay satellite we will deploy. Talk to her about it. Why do you think James is called digger? The bobcat/rover is his baby. I propose to setup evening sessions where each one of us will go thru our respective specialties and help each other". Nods around the table as people could see the merits of his plan. Everyone quickly agreed to meet tomorrow at 2030 to have Rosario go over the comms laptop module with them. Dr. Leon tentatively raised a hand. "What about the physical training"? He asked. The portly Frenchman was certainly no stranger to fine wine. Elkington smiled. "Yep. It's going to suck. The flight crew is going to spend 8 hrs in an EVA suit assembling the mars craft. That amount of concentration requires a body up to the task". "The pure physical demands of a 141 day out bound flight plus a 330 day planetary mission with a 121 day return flight is killer".

"But why all the push-ups and sit ups", Leon asked.

Janice answered for Elkington. "Every single one us will set records for space endurance. The low gee and no gee environment will deteriorate our muscles and weaken our bones. We have to start from a fit point in order to survive the breakdown of our bodies". She went on.

Elkington took over again. "We are going to get more space time than the Apollo guys ever dreamed of. That takes a toll on the body. The whole group will go thru the physical training. This group of 48 is just the Mars Craft crew". The gold group was staring at Elkington taking in the info.

"There are 200 more people who will fly rockets and turn wrenches with us without ever getting the honor of going to Mars". Janice felt that weight get a little heavier. Elkington then requested they each go over the next weeks' schedule to see what was upcoming. Qyuhn Le from China asked about an individual session with Bob Royce tomorrow at 1030. Rosario was not surprised. "We all have meetings individually with Royce or his deputy over the next few days", she said.

"Hey- has anyone really looked ahead at the schedule?" Abromovich the navigation and computer expert asked.

Just the next month or so was the general reply. Abromovich pointed to the day 120 SLS bobcat launch. Gold group was highlighted for that mission.

"There is our intermediate term goal", Elkington said. "In 4 months the members of the gold group will participate in the bobcat/rover launch and mate mission". "Our short term goal; getting thru tomorrow mornings' three mile run"! Several people laughed. Some didn't laugh at all.

"See you tonight at the Green house at 1900 in flight suits with laptops", Digger reminded them. They broke up as people bused trays and left to get a jump start on the training. Janice and Rose looked on in amusement as the Reds almost marched out with Watkins leading them.

Janice joined Rosario, James and Qyuhn in an impromptu

driving tour of Kennedy. They went past the launch complex, VAB and flight buildings. The training centers and simulators were housed on the same side of the base as the classrooms. Janice returned to her room to spend perhaps the last two hours of free time she was likely to get for a while before the social.

CHAPTER 4

Launch Day 006 11 Mar 2021 1735 Kennedy Space Center

Bob Royce gently let down the receiver. 15 straight minutes of ass chewing by the President. Yes, he had withheld the new crew member from her. He needed to protect his source on the committee. No, it was not his habit to piss her off. He needed to bargain off the crew member for the Chinese money for the ATK technology to get their rockets up to speed. Yes, he had read the polls showing 48 % approval of the Mars project. No, the successful launch of the POD had not budged the polls. The people wanted manned missions not remote controlled supply missions. Yes, he appreciated the position she was in. He was right on that ledge with her. So was his boss, John Scanlon NASA's Director. Yes, the crews were assembled. Yes, he felt some publicity with the brave mars crew could be arranged. Yes, mission commander would be an American. Yes, he was slated to brief the congress on flight status later this week. Yes, he would see her in Washington. Thank you, Madam President. What a successful phone call. Only one lie and only a minor ass chewing. No where near his record when talking to the President. Royce made some notations and closed out the briefing slides. The French were ready in Guiana. Kennedy was 1 day ahead in the pad clean up from the dragon launch and ready to prep 30 for the SLS. Bobcat/Rover prep was underway. Now that the astronauts were in place they could begin the serious training for the mission. He needed Kat to get to mission planning and see if they had nailed down landing sites. He made more notations and pocketed the laptop. He had to brief the committee in three days' time. He wanted them to give NASA the GO decision for the D120 launch at that meeting. Wandering out of his office and over to Kat's. She was concentrating on her screen a slight frown on her face. She looked up. "Have you seen this request from the sub- committee"? He had. Congress wanted NASA to summarize the in -flight threats to the space craft and delineate the mitigating actions NASA had taken. The same request was made for the landing site and the return flight. Did some congressman just now realize that this was dangerous? In- flight threats? Well they could lose power and freeze to death. Some rouge asteroid could pulverize them. A burst of radiation could fry them. And so on. Mitigating factors? Does prayer count? "Volley it back to the subcommittee and ask for clarifications as to what threats they mean". That should buy us a year".

He paused. "I want you to make sure the Chinese candidates are relaxed. They know you and will open up about what they need".

"Will do boss". "Ready"?

"Yep". They drove over to the Green House which was technically located on the Air Force Station. As they entered the bar they heard a distinctive roar. A US Ohio class fleet ballistic missile submarine was docked at Port Canaveral. Her crew was blowing off steam in what was likely the first liberty they had seen in months. As Royce watched the sailors cheer on a crew mate chugging a beer, he thought that they looked awfully young.

 Working his way to the back room where his group was gathered he was accosted by Dr. Leon.

"Doctor how are you? Enjoying your last night of freedom"?

"Yes, replied the geologist, but why this place"? "This bar is not at all clean and the food is horrid".

Royce grinned, "well yes the old girl has seen better days, but I like the nostalgia of this place. Generations of Sailors, Pilots, Astronauts have all mingled together in here before embarking on their individual trials. The walls are lined with memorabilia from shuttle launches, submarine exercises, and air force flights. Ask any US submarine sailor if he or she has been to the green house and they will say yes. Same goes for the British boomer sailors. And shuttle pilots. 70 years of people accomplishing great things have drunk in this place and tonight you join them". He raised a glass.

"I salute you".

Dr. Leon seemed mollified as Royce turned. He noticed Dr. Lincoln and Rosario Gonsolvo watching him. He prepared to give that same speech but Janice stopped him.

"This is place is really a dive bar where lots of people have spilled a beer", she told him.

"Also true, he said, but why ruin a good story with facts". Janice smiled as Rosario spotted Sergei and went over to him. Royce stopped Janice from joining them.

"Dr. Lincoln a moment, please. How are you adjusting?" he asked.

"Fine", she told him.

"I would really appreciate it if you gave this your full attention, he said,you must be on this crew".

"Why"? she asked puzzled.

"You have a unique skill set that would bring successful goal conclusion for this mission", Royce answered.

"Can you try that again without the buzzwords", she asked sardonically.

"If life exists or did exist on Mars you are uniquely qualified to make that determination", Royce said. "The President herself is asking for updates on your training progress and crew placement", Royce informed her.

"Just so long as there is no pressure", Janice complained.

Royce laughed.

"Dr. You have no idea of pressure. I get to brief the committee in three days. I have a to- do list that would kill someone half my age. I know you are waffling on the decision to go. Don't. I need you 100% fully committed on this. We can change the world with this flight. I firmly believe that. We stand a better chance of accomplishing those changes with you on board. The world needs you and I'm asking you; 614 days from now, be on that ship". He walked away without waiting for her answer. Janice stared after him for a long time.

Over at the bar Watkins took a long pull of his drink. He watched Sergei and Rosario talking. He noted Royce in serious conversation with Lincoln. He saw Adler and Elkington working on Kat Williams. Everyone lobbying. Watkins didn't feel the need. He knew the Chinese would give the nod to Zhou and perhaps Qyuhn Le. That there would be two had not concerned him. The other crew members unimportant. Only Mission Commander mattered. Why was the Russian here? He had thought Sergei was out of it. Was he just marking time until Royce named him to some technical post? Watkins eased over to interrupt Ivanovitch and Gonsolvo. Something about the EVA suit and the comms gear.

"Hey Sergei I was surprised to see you here. I thought you were going to JPL to continue design and fab work", Watkins mused.

Sergei regarded Watkins with hooded eyes. "Royce told me you needed help Tyler", so here I am ready to save you". Sergei put the needle in.

Tyler stiffened. "You need to face facts, Ivanovitch, you might be Royce' fair haired boy, but I've got a little more clout backing me this time".

"Tyler, Sergei said sadly, the thing you don't understand is that I don't compete with you. I'm only worried about the team mission and how to make it succeed. "It won't matter how much clout is backing you. I know that you will do just fine for a while, but then things will get tight". Sergei held his eyes locked to Watkins mesmerizing him with his voice. "Some situation will come up and you will get wound so tight you can't handle it and poof, your scores will dip. The strange thing is, if you worked less hard you would actually get better scores. He leaned in ready for the swing if it came. "If you learned to relax and let your team do their jobs without micromanaging them, you would score better". Tyler Watkins looked ready to go at it. Rosario stepped in between the two. "Let's put aside the testosterone for a little bit okay", she said nervously. Watkins immediately regained his mask of cool. "Serg, this time is for the real prize. Nothing gets in my way. Nothing". Watkins left them moving off thru the crowd. Rosario watched him go with a bad feeling. She said, "I'd watch my back with that one". Sergei shrugged. "His pattern is set. He has no other hand to play". He felt, what, sorry for Watkins? Watkins would try something but he was as subtle as a sledgehammer. He ceased worrying about Watkins as Janice Lincoln walked up to

73

reclaim Rosario. "Ladies, he said, I have an EVA suit fitting after our run tomorrow and then some more medical testing. Someone got the crazy idea I have epilepsy. I have to get that fixed. See you soon", he waved at them as he left. Janice and Rosario went back to their barracks room discussing Sergei and Watkins' not fight and the next day's run. "Those two alpha males are going to butt heads sometime soon", Rosario predicted. Janice was disgusted by the display but she had a hard time believing that Sergei would let himself be drawn into a confrontation. He impressed her as being in control and always smooth when trouble hit.

"I can't worry about them, I've got to get thru this run without puking", Janice admitted. Rose' advice was to concentrate on something else as Janice did the run to keep her mind off the discomfort. Janice doubted that would help.

Video log of Fong Li 11 Mar 2021 2104

Hello Dr. Royce and Ms. Williams. Thank you for welcoming us so warmly. My colleagues have all gotten here in good shape and we are ready to train for the mars mission. I would request a more aggressive physical training regimen. We will need it with the long flight and mission profile. The question of the day;

why do I want to go to Mars? I would like to participate in an

expedition that expands the knowledge base of science. Thank

you.

   The next morning she finished off the three mile run in 25 min

and 6 seconds. 18 min was the goal. Janice was pleased to even

get thru the whole three miles without barfing. She knew she

would feel it the rest of the day until her physical conditioning got

better. Showered and dressing quickly for the gold group

breakfast. That was followed by the group's first training session.

The Mars flight overview with Dr Hadenfeld was a very thorough

look at the mission.

   The darkened classroom showed the power point slides as they

came up. The seemingly disembodied voice of the instructor loud.

Mars Flight is actually a whole earth attempt to put a team on

Mars, build a site base and return them safely. Serious mission

planning had begun almost 4 years ago. The operating concept

was to launch components up to the ISS and assemble the craft in

low earth orbit. Food, fuel, equipment and supplies would be

attached to the lander in PODS. The PODS themselves then

would become the building materials for the landing site. Each POD cube was made up of 12 panels and 8 pole/channel assemblies. 20 such PODS would be attached to the lander. The Mars Craft itself consisted of 4 separate sections: The Command Module. The Equipment Section. The Cleanroom and the Airlock made up the lower two sections. The overall size was 43 feet tall with a 24 foot diameter. The weight was 793,000 lbs nominal, empty. There were 4 re-enforced portions of the Equipment section where 4 landing struts angled out 6 feet from the walls of the craft and 19 feet from landing pad to the top of the angle. Each strut would have a main engine attached and 3 small thruster/maneuvering engine mounted orthogonally from each other. The landing struts contained the pipes and umbilical attachments to transport fuel and commands to each of the engines and thrusters. The top of the landing struts also contained brackets to facilitate the attachment of the supply cubes. Each strut would stack 5 cubes in a two/ three configuration. As the cubes were attached to the strut brackets and the umbilical and fuel pipes, they became defacto fuel tanks. Pipes running from strut to strut would allow fuel transfer to the different main engines. The maneuvering thrusters were of the new solid rocket motor design. The motors were designed to be small enough that it was supposed to be possible to EVA outside the ship and remove one of the thrusters and bring it back inside the equipment section to replace the SRP.

The Command Module was the most recognizable as a space craft. The nominal "front" of the craft was designated by 4 small windows set high up on the 16 foot section. The windows formed a bank of light above the command console. The console ran the curved length of the module from one side approx. 16 feet wide. Display screens in a group of four sat in the command console just under the windows. The console flattened out as a typical desk setup with a keypad input device and other switches. The bottom half of the console was given over to displays and cabinets housing the circuit boards and computers for the craft. Instead of chairs or couches at the four stations, the backs of the first of two rows of four acceleration pods came within 3 feet of the console. The back had a recessed panel that folded out to become a chair with a restrain harness. The Accel couches themselves were Approx. 8 feet tall and 4 feet in diameter. The couches were attached to the floor and they could be moved forward or side to side. Each of the couches was identical. A padded couch/chair was configurable to lie flat at a 45 degree angle. A full restraint system was in place. The chair adjusted to full sitting and even a stowed position where the couch was vertical and against the back of the unit allowing max interior space for the occupant. The accel couches and the rest of the Command Module had been made by Lockheed Martin.

The huge US defense contractor had installed its new quantum computer as the centerpiece of the Mars craft. The Mars Craft now had essentially a supercomputer installed. The comparison to the computer in the Apollo capsules was Model A to Ferrari. Each side port and starboard of the command module had small porthole type windows in a row of three. Further aft along the centerline was a small hatch and ladder leading down. The computer animation of the module layout they had been watching now flew down the stairs. The forward lower section was comprised of eight workstations and storage lockers. Mid ships saw the two toilet shower stations flanking either side of the galley area. The lower aft section was given over to 8 bunks. Stacked two high the two most outboard port were built into the wall of the space craft. Each bunk was 7 feet by 3 feet with a thin mattress. Personal storage and lockers were underneath the mattresses. The end of the bunk held a small desk with a molded chair as a workstation. That left a small 3 foot isle to the next row of bunks. The centerline bulkhead contained an airtight hatch to the Equipment Module. The stbd side was a mirror image of the port in the bunk arrangements. The only difference was just forward of the bunk rack high up on the bulkhead was a crew access hatch. The Royce hatch it was called. Much debate and angst over this hatch. Why came from Qyuhn Le? What operational need did it serve? The current operational scenario for crew and supply loading called for EVA from the ISS and the cycling of the aft (lower) airlock to allow access. Royce had fought hard to have an egress point into and out of the CMD module. Royce had felt that it was asking too much of the crew to work their way thru the craft to the airlock in an emergency. The Apollo Three fire had weighed on Royce's mind while he worked thru the emergency scenarios. Royce had felt that the hatch might not be necessary in an everyday scenario but god help them if they needed to get out in a hurry. The video continued with the operational concepts portion. The in flight crew concept now looked like this: 6 hour shifts. 2 on flight duty (one in an EVA suit). 2 designated as work/science crew. The other 4 would be "off", designated for eating sleeping or personal tasks (working out). The rotation would be: Work to Flight to Unassigned to

Off. That way the work science crew rotated to flight having been awake for 6 hours and fully aware of the ships condition or status and knowing what evolutions were upcoming. The section just coming on to work would be rested and ready to perform whatever science or ships functions as required. The flight crew coming off could then relax and have 6 hours to do whatever they wanted and then 6 hours of sleep. The flight person in the EVA was the mitigation against a fire or loss of compression. He or she was the fireman on duty against whatever came up. Hadenfeld then continued with the description of the rest of the mars craft. The lower centerline airtight hatch led aft to the lower section of the Equipment module. The Equipment module was divided into two 8 foot "tall" floors. The 02 level contained the fwd hatch and the aft hatch directly in line. With both hatches open this comprised the longest sightline in space: with the 6 feet from the galley station the full length of the equipment module the 22 foot sightline was longer than the ISS center cabin at 20 feet. The 02 level was divided centerline by a work alley. Either side contained numerous pieces of equipment. Medical storage lockers and mounted light packs. Fuel transfer system pumps and pressurized tanks. 4 dedicated science stations contained brackets and

mounting areas to attach instruments. The lockers for those were
mounted in any open space. Air scrubbers, battery cells, heaters,
ventilation fans, water tanks, air compressor and vacuum pumps.
Two solar arrays were folded and stored in lockers down here.
The electrical generator and distribution panels were located aft
port side outboard high. Waste water and the recycling plant were
opposite on the stbd side high. A trash compactor was neatly
stored port side forward low. Tools supplies and fuel and water
were all stored in various lockers, and tanks. All were color coded
and stenciled. The 01 level was accessed by the ladder that led
from below to above by a square ceiling opening. The ladder was
sided with handrails. 01 level port side forward were the main
EVA suit lockers (12) near the EVA airlock. That airlock was
meant to allow access to the attached storage cube PODS should it
be necessary. The astronauts could also evacuate the ship or bring
items back into the ship from mars if they could muscle them into
the airlock. Rigging equipment was stored in the airlock section
but it would be an improvised rig to get anything into the upper
hatch. The 01 level was more open with three workstations
dominating the space. An 8 foot by 4 foot table with lockers
underneath was located centerline about four feet from the

bulkhead. The ladder opening was located 3 feet aft of the table with another station 3 feet further aft. This 2 by 6 foot table was 4 feet high with the flex tunnel storage locker underneath. The aft stbd corner contained the third station at 5 wide by three deep and 4 feet high. These stations had tablet docking stations on the surface. Various electrical and mechanical attachments could be added to perform whatever task was at hand. Several hooks and bars mounted top the ceiling would allow the equipment to be rigged in and held aloft while being worked on. In a weight less environment the rigging mounts would serve as anchor points. A variety of air powered or electric tools were available to be attached and mounted to the table to allow easy working conditions. The forward large table could also serve as the medical operating table. More lockers and storage containers and equipment were mounted throughout the compartment.

The animation video continued. The students fought the urge to nod off as the session dragged on. The clean room was a new concept for a space craft. NASA anticipated a large amount of Martian dirt and dust entering the spacecraft while the astronauts setup the landing site. The dirt and dust was thought to be beyond the capacity of the air filtration system. A cleanroom was located forward (above) the main airlock. The small 7 foot tall room was dominated by several lockers containing floor pads and vacuums. The room was large enough that four of them could be eggressing or entering the ship as required. The landing ladders were also stored here mounted underneath the lockers. The 5 foot ladders could be combined to form the ladder that would be lowered when the airlock door was opened to access the surface. The lockers would hold the EVA suits while they cycled thru a cleaning process. Small hand held vacuums were also provided to clean up the room itself. Dustbusters anyone? Black and Decker had been pounding the airwaves with the advertising for them for weeks now. The last section was the main airlock. Two more ladders were mounted as well as the controls/status displays for the airlock. The airlock was again large enough to accommodate four people.

The training video ended with a brutal series of 143 pictures of each major section and piece of equipment onboard. At the end CDR Hedenfeld announced that the test would be at 2030 in the auditorium over the identification by name purpose and nomenclature of the equipment shown. Groans accompanied this announcement. The flight personnel had an advantage in this. They had been practicing on the mock ups for a while now. They would struggle with the individual science pieces but overall they were more versed in the rest of the equipment. Janice had her memory of course. Two times thru and she could rattle them off without error. That wouldn't help Rosario or Qyuhn Le, though. As she gathered her tablet and notes she saw Sergei and the rest of the goldies file into the classroom across the hall. He smiled and waved hello. She waved back. "Oh that's how it starts, an innocent wave and a smile", said a voice behind her. A casual "how's it going", followed by an innocent "I can help you with that training problem" and boom! "The next thing you know you're in the VAB trying to find your bra". Rosario teased. Janice recoiled shocked. Was she flirting? No. There had been no one since Charles and she missed him terribly. She stared hard at Rosario. "Ayi mommy, sorry. No need to give me the death stare, just kidding".

Janice softened and asked if Rose wanted to go over the slides before her medical appointment. "I only have 25 min before I have to meet Royce at the mock up. I can go thru it twice". They settled in to look over the slides and pictures. "I'll skip any I'm really comfortable with like the comms units. Elkington wants everyone back at the dorm for a stretching session and test prep before dinner. He wants us at the rooms at 1600. Start in Chica".

Rosario entered the Mars flight mockup at 1025. Royce was waiting to see her holding one of his file folders. He smiled as they kissed hello. "How are you getting along with Elkington", he asked? Rosario waggled her hand. "I'd rather be a blue team ranger," she said.

"We can't afford the damage to the VAB mock up", he replied dryly.

Rosario blushed. Royce opened the file.

"You are clearly the top South American candidate, Rose. "Are you up to mars"?

"Hell yes!" she said. "I want you to get good at flight he directed. "The more you know about the ship and procedures the better".

"Ayi". "Who else?" she probed. Sergei would be my choice".

Royce frowned. "The Mission Commander has to be an American."

Rosario stared at him. "Watkins?!?" she said incredulous.

"Why not, Watkins?" Royce asked.

"He doesn't have it".

"What do you mean he doesn't have it? He has led three ISS missions with 50 EVA hours. He is qualified flight, comms and rover. He grades out at 96% in almost every category. He never puts a foot wrong with the press, why not Watkins"?

"I missed the cutoff for ISS 71 Rosario explained. I'm glad I missed it. The way I hear it if it wasn't for Adler, Watkins would have been drummed out of NASA".

"You believe the rumor mill over the data tapes", Royce countered.

"I don't believe a data package that Watkins was in charge of. You know he designed those systems".

Royce frowned. The incident in question had come down to his word and the tapes vs hers.

"He can't adapt under pressure", Rosario complained.

"He does well on every scenario we give him, Royce countered.

"Yeah because it is a planned scenario. Give him something off the books and see how well he does", she said.

"If it comes down to it would you take Mars and Watkins vs Sergei and earth, Royce asked earnestly. Rosario considered for a long time. "Mars I guess. But I wouldn't sleep well for 691 days. Oh, by the way. I'll get Lincoln up to speed on the flight stuff ", she said casually.

Royce looked at her sharply for a second. "After you get back from mars I'm going to need a new deputy program manager for crew training. Johnny is calling it quits after this. Interested"? Ayi, she cooed.

"You know people", he said. Too well he thought. He waved her off as the next trainee entered.

Sergei finished his test at 2049 and submitted it for grading. 98%. He had confused the mass spectrometer with the gravitational measurement unit. Okay. He spent 5 min reading over both units and went to the front. The test scores were being displayed on the large front screen. His was on top. Several 90's were displayed but a large number of 80's were evident. A little sound went up as a 100 was posted. He went over to Janice.

"Dr. Lincoln, no fair. Eidetic memory is cheating".

"Maybe I'll try for mission commander and not science geek," she said.

Sergei looked at her. "Don't make me have to kill you" he said in his best Ivan Drago voice. Janice was speechless. Sergei laughed spoiling it.

"I think you would make an excellent mission commander", he complimented. Now who's flirting, Janice wondered? Rosario came up gushing with her 92. "That's the best I have done on these thanks to your help", she said. They both congratulated her as Watkins posted his 94. No one failed. One 70 was posted by Dr. Xiling. He could be seen as everyone left talking earnestly with Kat Williams.

CHAPTER 5

Video log of James Andrews 15 Mar 2021 2207.

I'm bushed but I need to make this log entry. Thanks for the training program Mr. Royce. It's not possible to make a person an astronaut in one week but you are trying. I got my finale EVA suit fitting today. The EVA suit is the coolest thing about this mission. The new suits are a generation lighter and more flexible than anything we have used to date. When do we break them out for real? Being able to mount the tablet in them and have the screen displayed on the helmet is genius. It makes spacewalking much more efficient. We ganged three suits together via the data link up feature and I had three displays going: One with the step by step procedure, one with the pictures of the equipment and one with the video of the procedure being done in the pool. Any trained monkey could follow that. The science nerds had the procedure up and the tool video to reinforce how to use the wrenches. That alone makes them usable as wrench turners. The little asides from the experts like Story Musgrave are outstanding! The fact that I'm wearing an EVA suit watching a video of me as the rover expert delivering a little tip on how to unpack it from the crate is mind blowing. I think we need about two more weeks of normal training scenarios and then two weeks of group normal scenarios. Then spring the faulted stuff. I'm hating the physical training. Wow you guys are pushing hard. No one busted out yet huh? Are you happy about that or mad? I'm betting mad. I know you wanted some decisions to be taken out of your hands. That's why you get paid the big bucks Bob. Let's see what todays question is: Who do you think is the best candidate for Mission Commander. Whew. I got to go with Tyler. Sergei is a friend and he's great but Tyler is American and the USA is number one. Andrews out.

Bob Royce stood before the VTC camera and screen scanning the members of the committee. The 24 members were arrayed in an arc around on one side of a large table. He finished the slide and went to the next: The KSC PAD 29 clean up proceeds on schedule. The Bob cat rover arrives next week for prep and loading in the VAB. The pad 30 preps were one day behind schedule but they still had 9 days of float. The French were slightly behind the day 124 launch preps but still had a week of float. The Russians were ahead of schedule on the 128 engine launch. Royce was skeptical of the Russians. The Soyuz and the dragon would bring everyone back. Next slide Crew status:

Gold crew scores were posted. The five on top would go to the ISS with the bobcat: Elkington Gonsolvo Lincoln Andrews and Jones (J).

Red crew scores: The top five would launch with the French from Guiana with the engine: Watkins, Fong, Zhou, and Jones (D) Hoffman.

Blue crew scores: The top four would launch from Star City in Russia with tools and fuel: Ivanovitch, Nyguen, Keith, and Sanger.

White crew: scores at the 23 April meeting.

All of the crews are performing magnificently, Royce briefed. All space agencies are to be complemented. The candidates are outstanding. Almost any combination would be a great crew for Mars.

These launches would see the first use of the new EVA suits if approved today: Do we have permission from the committee to use the new EVA suits?

Royce paused for questions. "Pro's?" said the member from

Northrop Grumman. 1) More efficiency in the suits. The old suits were projected to need 240 man days to complete the mate and launch. 84 man days had been projected for the new suits. 2) The suits were actual Mars hardware getting close to earth testing. 3) Great publicity to show actual progress on the mars mission.

Royce reminded them that Nova was scheduling a near real time inclusion of the footage for the 20 July anniversary of the moon landing. They wanted to juxtapose the new suits in space against the bulky old suits.

"Cons?" called the rep from France.

"The suits are unproven hardware", stated the rep from China. The rep from the Taiwanese SingTech company exploded. "The technology has been extensively tested as the member knows full well"!

Of course the Chinese are going to be prickly about the Taiwanese getting publicity for the suits. The civil war was still being fought 80 years later. "Peace my friend", said the representative from the European Space Agency. "We know the suits have been tested in your labs but not in actual space. If they fail, the mission will have to be put on hold. It could mean the cancelation of the mission". Royce said into the silence, "you have all seen the test data.

The suits have to have an operational test. The ISS has several of the older suits. If a problem arises we can fix the suits and use the older suits to mate the engine to the rover cube. There are no more cons worth dealing with. Members I call for a vote does the committee approve the three launches and the use of the new space suits for the upcoming missions"? Approved 22-2. China and the rep from the Chinese company China Telcom voting no. "Thank you".

Launch day 21 26 Mar 2021 1027 Houston Space Center

Janice adjusted the EVA suit headgear and positioned the wrench on the captive screw. The EVA suit dexterity was a little difficult to get used to. Elkington read the step for her: Worker three will loosen the 12 captive screws on the panel and remove. All workers acknowledged. As Janice loosened the screws she was watching a small video on her display that showed the position of the workers on the platform as avatars. There were small differences between the video and the reality of the trainer. Elkington stood off to the stbd side while Janice was on the outboard side of the engine cube. Rosario and Andrews were aft and on the port side holding tethers for the cube. Jones held a tether ready for the engine. As the last screw loosened, Janice moved the wrench/powered screwdriver to the stow position at her hip and grabbed both panel handles that had been installed. She was booted into the platform hard point and had limited mobility. As she lifted the panel clear, Jones stepped in and tethered the engine. Janice stowed the panel underneath the platform in the bracket. The first 2 1/2 hours of this procedure had been spent prepping the brackets, installing handles, getting work boxes into position. Elkington served as team leader watching Lincoln, Gonsolvo, Andrews, and Jones work thru the procedure. Leon was on the far side of the platform acting as the ISS safety observer. NASA had three other safety divers in the pool with them. Given the size of the platform and the number of workers this was a crowded pool. Now the tricky part. Elkington read out the workers new designations and the who was responsible for what. Janice became worker 1 and the actual focus shifted to Digger. Since he was closer to the Rover cube it made sense to have him actually install the engine. But he had to shift his tether to Janice and get his torque wrench into position. While he moved to the new hard point and removed the 8 bolts from the engine cube molded

Styrofoam holders, he and Elkington discussed the procedure. He had the video playing on his display. "Ready" he announced. "Okay. ISS arm attached to engine and lift positioning on the rover POD mounting rig", Workers 1 and two, tether to engine and POD Janice and Rosario watched as the mockup of the robotic arm came in and grabbed the engine and lifted it out of the POD. The arm positioned it over the mounting rig. James moved in and started installing the bolts. The first 6 went in easily. The last two were harder. They were in the middle and the engine bulged out. When the wrench was on the bolt head the 90 degree angle distance between the bolt head and the outside top edge of the wrench impacted the mounting rig strut. He could get the socket on the head but not cleanly. They discussed it for a few minutes. As he started to tighten the bolt heads were getting chewed up by the wrench. Digger stopped. He asked the NASA rep if there were a minimum number of bolts that had to be installed. "Is six okay"? "Not known now, keep working", was the reply. He got them in but it wasn't pretty. The last part of the procedure went smoother but they finished almost 18 min behind schedule. 5 hrs and 52 min in the water. 1 hr 22 min to suit up and gear up before the actual EVA. At the debrief it was revealed that the spec called for all 8 bolts. It was discussed if the torque wrenched were all the same? Are there slight differences? Were they standard from one manufacturer to the next? Could we use an old fashioned box wrench? Has anyone else encountered this? Nearly 2 hrs to discuss what happened and get their grade (86). That made for a long day. The gold team had arrived in Houston two days earlier and had received an orientation run thru in the pool without water the day before. No suits were worn. Just walking thru the blocking like a theater production. After the debrief, Elkington had signed off all the qualification cards. Abromovitch, Adler, Leon, Helmut, and Rodriguez had all performed the procedure last night. Adler had not had the problem with the bolts. NASA had purposely kept their sleep at 4 hours. Janice' team had spent the 4 hours while Adler's group finished up suited up in the aux pool working on tool quals. Now they all regrouped for the second and "real" debrief. They had 1 hour before their flight back to Kennedy. The officers club on the base was adjacent to the airfield. They wouldn't be the first to roll from a barstool to a jump seat in a Military Air Transport flight. Elkington smiled as the group kidded each other about the evolution. They were really bonding nicely. Rosario was teasing Digger about his reporting the bolt problem to NASA. "Houston, I think I screwed up these bolts. That's what you said? I screwed up these bolts? The single perfect time to use the Houston we have a problem line and you screw it up".

Everyone giggled as Digger looked abashed. Grace Adler said, "I thought all you men spoke in movie lines all the time? My husband quotes Monty Python at me like I'm supposed to know a 40 year old television show. He can't remember my birthday but an obscure line from a stupid movie? Suddenly he's like Janice over there.

Janice took her round in the barrel over her prodigious memory. Elkington rescued her as a thought occurred to him: I could have 3 or maybe even 4 members of the mars crew right here. Janice, Digger and Rosario for sure. Maybe Leon. As he processed crew and mission goals he silenced the kidding as he said to Rosario, "You do realize you are going to be the second person to set foot on mars don't you"?

Dead silence greeted this as all eyes swiveled to Rose. She looked at Elk and asked how he figured that.

"Well you are the top South American candidate. Sorry Rod. You are going to be the comms tech on board. The first mission objective after landing will be to setup that comms relay unit.

That's you. Voila, second person on Mars". Rosario objected:

You know mission commander has discretion in that. He could

lead two or three recon landings before the comms unit. You know

Watkins. He's going to land and start giving speeches then take

out his backup".

"What if Sergei is mission commander"? Elk asked. "He's not

going to worry about speeches. He knows how important that

relay is going to be. He's going to take you right out".

"You think Clinton is going to let a Russian be the mission

commander over an American"? Rose countered. "She will pick

you first".

Elk just smiled. "Don't count that out. And if I am Mission

Commander I would take you out second as well".

Now Rosario was in the barrel: What are you going to say? Hey

how can you give a speech with that accent? Has anyone ever

fallen off the landing ladder? Elkington sat back and looked again

over his group. Good people. He knew this mission was out of his

reach. But what about number two? He was only 33. The current

mission profile ended with the mars craft docked back at the ISS.

The landing site would be sealed up. There was already talk of the number two mission. Perhaps a yearlong stay. A close look at Phoebes. Who knows? Grace going was a distinct possibility as well.

Janice smiled as Rosario grabbed Elk and took him off for discussion. That's when it struck home for her. She was committed. She wanted to go to Mars with these people. She wanted to set foot on another planet. That's all- just to share that experience with Rosario and James and Sergei. Not loneliness, not glory. Not the honor or love of country. Just to share with fellow travelers. As they headed out to the plane she motioned to Elk. "Hey could I get some time with you when we get back on the flight sim? I need to be better at flight".

"You bet. You and Rosario can get it together".

"Mr. Royce: I'm 100%". That's the only thing she put in her video blog on the plane ride back to Kennedy.

Watkins prepped the flight sim for a normal take off. Fong and Zhou needed the sim time. All three sat at the command console setting the systems switches for the takeoff. Zhou and Fong setting with Watkins supervising. They looked to be the Chinese

picks. Both were scoring acceptably and both had several fields of

expertise. Watkins was not pleased to see them chatting away in

mandarin while they went thru the preflight. Both had been

perfectly willing to do what he said but they set their own agenda

when it came to the mission. Watkins could not allow that. As he

watched them he reached out and took two switches back to an off

position. He hid the movement from the NASA camera with his

body. He knew where the camera was. He had positioned it.

Subtle. Effective. The Chinese flight candidates had missed the

same two switches on an earlier sim flight. The position of the

switches for the backup reference data routing changed based on

ships profile as it took off. Depending on what type of reference

data was available the switches would be on or off as necessary.

For the earlier sim flight the data had been available on the normal

channel and so had not been needed. The missed position had

caused an alarm 7 min into flight when the two reference sources

competed to give the ship the data it needed. The ship alarmed

telling the humans to tell it what it wanted to know. Fong and

Zhou had schooled themselves on the flight modes and data

routing and had the system down cold now. To miss this now

would be to repeat a mistake. That would be devastating to their scores. But Watkins didn't want their scores to suffer. He wanted them in his debt and he wanted NASA to think he was the leader.

As Fong announced that they were ready for flight her voice excited. Watkins casually put his hand over the camera but did not cut off his mike.

"Guys look at the R4 reference panel switches", he whispered. Fong and Zhou immediately looked at the two offending switches. Hi ya. As they started to argue about who had missed them Watkins held up a hand. They cutoff speaking. He repositioned the switches and loudly announced an Amen and moved his hand away from the camera. Zhou and Fong immediately looked grateful. Watkins shook his head. He announced jovially- Let's light the big rocket! He knew NASA would pick up the audio and try to figure it out during the debrief. "Were the switches out of position" I don't remember. Fong and Zhou positioned the switches as part of the preflight. Did he prompt them? I just said a prayer. I thought the flight went well. Dr. Fong and CMDR Zhou are valuable members of the mars team and I would be proud to go into space with either one of them. Or both, he said. NASA had to accept the answers and now Fong and Zhou owed him. Your move Serg. I'm just going to keep piling up points.

   Sergei had Dr. Hoffman into his third run thru of the EVA tool room. He needed all the help he could get. The German scientist was a brilliant geologist, computer expert, and was a pioneer in hydroponics. Georg Hoffman was 44, tall, balding and less pudgy now than what he had been. NASA desperately needed him up to speed as the European candidate. He had to be able to do more than just geology to justify his spot. Sergei had volunteered to run him thru while Watkins was busy in the flight sim. Georg was a decent engineer. He could fix things but he was dodgy on EVA. He just didn't like the environment. Put the item on a work bench and he was your man. Put it out in space and he tended to look at the view too much. Sergei contemplated him for a moment.

"Georg how do you like cars", he asked?

"Cars, Hoffman looked up blinking. I like cars fine. I rebuilt mine several times as a kid in Munich".

"Have you looked at the Rover"?

"Rover, said Georg, I thought that was Andrews's baby".

"Of course but he's going to need help. We have to transition the bobcat from a tunnel digging device to an earth mover back to a full-fledged science rover". "What happens when the digging is done? The rover is going to take the geologist out to explore mars, Sergei explained. "The planetologists are going to want evidence of any volcanic activity. They need to understand what the core of the planet is doing. It's going to be up to you to find the aquifer bearing rocks, or the tectonic plate boundaries."

That had Georg' attention. "If I got qualed on the rover I could be on all those expeditions.

"Yeah but the tools to fix the rover are little more exotic and require some training".

Hoffman turned back to the tool sim with renewed vigor. "Okay I think I'm better at the wrench but the tether carbine is fairly small. Am I holding it right"? Sergei moved in to give him pointers.

They ran long on the session. They never saw Kat Williams as she left the trainer control room for Royce's office. He would want the update on this.

CHAPTER 6

Launch Day 035 05April 1154 2021 Kennedy Space Center

Mars Commercial: Dramatic video of a man walking on the surface of a planet. Driving on the rover kicking up dust in a turn. Bounding across the moon swirling dirt as he went. Cut to an interior of an industrial looking room while the space suited man opened a locker. Removing his helmet the dark haired handsome man with the square jaw reached in and pulled out a Black and Dekker dust buster. He started to vacuum off the dirt. The tag line: Look ladies he even does chores! Dust buster. Even good on Mars!

Time! Janice looked up from her test. 200 questions over procedures used on every tool. Open book. Timed. She hadn't finished. As she submitted her test for grading she thought that she had done well. She was tired. Next week was going to be a little bit of a break physically but a little ramp up on the practical evolutions. They were going to move the SLS upright in preps to mate the crew capsule and the payload next week. Once it was

mated then it would be rolled out. NASA had a very efficient crew

for this but the Mars team needed to understand how it worked. So

they were going to help. Janice waited while her score was posted.

89. She waited while the goldies gathered to see grades. The

teams tended to stay in their groups now. Elk, Rosario and Grace

had all tied at 90. Janice saw Sergei saunter over to the red team.

Did he never just walk over? Did he have to glide like that she

mused. She saw him put a hand on the German geologist

Hoffman's back. Hoffman turned beaming. 92. Wow. He

pumped Sergei's hand and thanked him while Watkins looked on

with disdain. The whole room stopped as a score went up Xiling-

68. The man quietly got up and went to the front. Kat and Royce

walked him out. That was it. They had lost the second member of

the group. Alesworth went down due to appendicitis. No fault of

his, just bad luck. Janice saw Watkins mutter something and

Hoffman react pulling back. Sergei said something to Watkins and

walked away. Janice walked over to Rose and said goodnight.

She was due for a 16 hour equalizer. Sleep. Tomorrow saw them

break off the top five people and start some specialized training for

the mission to the ISS. That started in the VAB. But now she needed sleep.

Kat Williams watched Janice Lincoln walk to her barracks room. Kat knew she needed the rack time. Kat angled over to intercept Sergei. She fell in step as he went back to the barracks. "What did Watkins say"? She asked.

"Fuck Watkins", Sergei said dully.

"What's up Serg? Watkins bugging you"?

"I'm still not worried about him", Sergei said. "I'll admit his scores are better than ever and he seems to have made some allies here. That's new for him. But underneath it all he is still Watkins: a narcissistic asshole".

"Don't sugar coat it tell me how you really feel", Kat laughed. As they approached his room Kat leaned in. "Is there something I could do to lift your spirits"? Sergei looked at her with eyes wide.

"I think I just need to wallow in it for a little while. Sorry Kat". She smiled at him. "If you change your mind, let me know", she said as she leaned in for a little peck on his cheek. She left him. Later Sergei would not remember what woke him up. He just woke up. He knew it was late. Or early depending on your definition. He put on some shorts and walked outside into the night as he moved into the courtyard he could see the stars out. It was

0135. He paused and looked to his left. Janice Lincoln was looking at him from a few feet away, sitting on a table in her jammies. He walked over. "Dr. I'm sorry to disturb you. I just failed open and came out to stretch".

"What does failed open mean"?

"It's a submarine term he said moving onto the table. Sometimes when something fails you want it to be in a certain configuration. Like if you have a fire hydrant. If there is a valve that supplies water to the fire hydrant and it fails and you can't move it again, you want it to fail in the position that supplies water to the hydrant. Open. If your eyelids fail you want them to fail open so you can see. So I failed open".

"How do you know so much about submarines"? she asked.

Sergei smiled grimly. "The Russian air force has a sure fire way to see if you are serious about cosmonaut training. They stick you in a big steel pipe called a submarine with 130 other smelly guys and drop you under the ocean for 125 days. If you survive you learn about eyelids failing open and can become a cosmonaut". "Eyelids can't fail", Janice said stubbornly.

Well Dr. It's very technical I could explain it but you couldn't really keep up".

UNITY

"Oh I can keep up with you, Mr. Smooth".

"Oh can you now"? He asked looking at her. She looked pretty good. "I don't know I'm pretty fast when I want to be".

"I'm pretty fast myself", she said making no sense.

"Are we still talking about eyelids" he asked?

Sergei achieved the zone. She was trembling and looked a little lost. Ripe for the plucking. He knew she was a widow. And that there had been a child lost. She was interested but it was layered in a lot of other emotions. He slowly, gently, reached over and kissed her. "Mr. Smooth" he asked? "Really? Seriously"?

She laughed. "I'm not good at the whole international seductress thing".

He laughed uproariously at that. "International seductress? Wow. That fits you perfectly". He put his arms around her. "Oh you got me Sofia Lauren. Let's go back to your room and I'll let you school me in the ways of an International seductress.

"Okay, yes. I think Rosario got a better offer for the night". They moved into her room and shut the door on the world.

Sergei was gone when Janice got up at 0630. She felt pretty good. He called her Sophy. She smiled remembering. He was patient

109

and more than a little skilled. She hadn't felt guilty or ashamed or anything. She just went with it. She knew he had just as tough a schedule as she did. Well I know where he'll be every hour of every day for the next two years. Just relax and let it come to you. Play it cool international seductress.

The Vehicle Assembly Building or VAB at Kennedy is enormous. The building can be seen from the highway miles from the launch complex. When the tour bus drives up to it they liked to point out that the stripes on the flag painted on the side are wide enough for the bus to drive on. After the huge bay door closes after it had been opened for a while, clouds would sometimes form high up in the building. Then it rained inside the building. Built for Apollo, adapted for the shuttle, the SPACE X folks now it was used for the Mars and SLS rockets. The primary bay contained the SLS launch vehicle. On its side the rocket was 320 feet long with two solid rocket boosters. This configuration was the 70 ton personnel config. The Orion crew capsule and the rover pod would fit nicely. The Orion was sitting in its bay ready for the mate with its ride. As was the Rover. The VAB crew was starting the evolution safety brief when the 5 mars crew showed up. They quickly found their assigned buddy to shadow for the day. Janice was assigned

Robert Gunderson. A huge bear of a rigger who would be

strapping the rocket to the crane for its ride into the cradle. Rosario

got to ride up to the hoist crane to watch from the cab. Safety brief

complete the crew of 33 riggers, engineers and safety people

started in. The collar strap was rigged around the upper end of the

second stage. The collar provides a lift point for the rocket. Janice

would glimpse others of her team while she went under and around

the rocket with Gunderson. Finally the main hook was attached to

the collar and all was ready. The rocket came off the blocks and

was checked for deformity. None noted. It was set back down and

checked again. Clean as well. Slowly the rocket went vertical.

Janice had a nice discussion with one of the safety engineers over

pivot points and cross coupled stresses. Sometimes the job really

was rocket science. The whole process took over three hours for

the final mate to the cradle. Now that the rocket was vertical they

could grasp how big it was. The SLS actually was very similar in

design to the Soyuz and the Gui long. The French Ares and the

falcon 9 were different types. A large first stage with multiple

liquid fueled engines, followed by a SRP second stage and the final

stage with a single engine SRP motor to get to final altitude.

Elkington and the rest of the Goldie's went back to the Orion bay and went thru the Orion crew module for orientation purposes. They had time in the simulator tomorrow. They also stopped in for a look at the clean room where the rover was stored before being crated. James had promised them some hands on special time with his baby. A second full version of the rover was available for training. They finished and left with some free time. Janice was getting in her car to head to the gym when Rosario stopped her. "All right spill, she said. Who was it? Andrews? You know he's married right"? Janice looked at her. How would an international seductress handle this? Probably a lot better than she was about to. "Rose, it was Sergei", she said simply.

Rosario stared at her. "What"?

"It was Sergei. We didn't mean for it to happen". She went on.

"Oh, I'm sure you didn't mean for it but he is another matter", she said huffing. She muttered something. Then looked at her.

"You like him don't you"? She rolled her eyes as Janice smiled.

"Aiy, don't let him see that smile, he'll take advantage. Don't get burned. Sergei is a great guy but no one has tied him down". She smiled at Janice. "You used that helpless science geek thing on him didn't you? Men go crazy for that naive smart girl type".

"Hey, Janice protested, "I'll have you know I compare with Sofia Lauren".

"Chica you are many things but not Sofia. If anyone is like her it is me, the Latin heart breaker". Rosario climbed in her car.

"Speaking of which, where were you last night"?

"Aiy, mommy, now that is a story"!

Royce stood in his own office with John Scanlon while President Clinton, Madam President they called her, sat at his desk. She liked to pop in unannounced and sit at someone's desk while they had to stand. "Talk to me about the crews".

Bob went into detail about the gold blue reds and whites. He showed her test scores and videos of them performing. Clinton sat back. "The press is hounding me for names Bob. Who is going to be on the crew"?

"If we picked today, it would be Watkins as the mission commander, Ivanovitch as the second seat. Gonsolvo from South America, Zhou and Fong from China. Hoffman and Lincoln. Andrews as the final American". "That's a good crew in any order. Heck even Dr. Lincoln is going to be flight qualed as back up".

The President looked up. "Why can't we take advantage? After they go up on the first round of mate launches we spring them on the Today Show with footage of them working on the ISS. In the new suits right"?

"Yes Madam President".

"Bob how come every time you say "yes Madam President" it sounds to me like Madam President I'll do any damn fool thing I like and you can't stop me!"

"My mouth earned me more than one whipping from my mom", he acknowledged.

"You don't want to be whipped by me Bob", she said. Royce bit down hard on the Vince Foster comment that wanted to come out. "Madam President, he said, I have not had a visit from Raven. Is he alright"? Clinton looked at him. "Raven is busy right now. We have more than one thing going on right now".

"Tatiana says the Chechens are stirring. Royce was concerned. "Is there any chatter about the mars launches"?

"Not as such. We all know what a high value target these launches would be". Clinton looked at him. "After this is over you might as well come to DC. I think you might work as the new UN ambassador".

"Yes Madam President". Clinton saw the twinkle as he said it.

CHAPTER 7

Video log of Fong Li 10 April 2021 1922

Mr. Royce I must use this blog to protest the actions of CMDR Watkins. His behavior is increasingly antagonistic. He is actively working to lower our scores. I understand how competitive this is but to alter our data! He cannot be allowed on the mission! One more incident and we walk. Out.

Royce sat back and blew out slowly. He looked at Kat. Slap

him down hard.

Launch day 40 12 April 2021 0845 French Guiana

   Guiana is hot and humid. The French launch facilities were utilitarian. Watkins was in a non-descript building at a small table with a laptop. He looked up startled as the door opened and Kat Williams walked in. He sat back and regarded her. She waited a beat and softly asked him why she shouldn't remove him from the Mars crew right now. He smiled at her. "Because that would make a certain female politician very angry", he said haughtily.

Kat regarded him with disdain. "Do you really think Clinton cares whether it's you or Elkington? I'll just have to explain to her that your hacking and switch manipulation to down grade the Chinese candidates is responsible for the Chinese pulling out of the program". "If the Chinese drop out, the program ends. You think she is going to cover you in a scandal"?

Watkins looked murder at her. Kat held his gaze coolly. "Do you know my back ground"? she asked. Tyler blinked. "You are Royce's bitch girl", he said with a sneer.

"Well I am that now but I started life in the CIA. I performed functions for them that I had a certain aptitude for. When I got tired of that I asked to work with NASA. Given the international nature that space flight had become Royce and Scanlon thought I might have some value. You call me a bitch girl. I prefer the term trouble shooter. Royce sends me to fix a problem. How I do that is up to me". She smiled at him. "My tool box is wide open. So this is how this situation gets fixed; "You have kidney stones. 6 weeks on the side lines. Your training is much too valuable to totally throw away. You quietly come back and do the supply missions and wrench turning but Mars is out. Or I leave you dead on this floor".

Watkins stiffened. He looked at her. "A) You could never explain the death and B) you couldn't kill me".

The knife flashed by so quickly Tyler barely saw her move. It had nicked his ear before embedding in the wall board. He screamed and ducked back holding his bleeding ear. Kat casually walked over and retrieved the knife. "The CIA is good at killing people and covering it up. You and I have a plane to catch to Kennedy. I want you within knife range".

He stumbled out of the building, Kat following. Watkins spent the plane ride alternating between terror and rage. In the end he decided to wait. His shot would come. And when it did he was going to make some people pay.

Launch day 41 13 April 2021 1549Kennedy Space Center

Royce had called the White team over out of the flight mock up to inform them that Grace Adler was going to the red team to replace Tyler Watkins who was down with kidney stones. She left for Guiana within the hour. Hugs and hoots followed her and Royce out the door. The gold team watched this announcement with interest from the flight observation room. They all looked at Elkington. He looked stunned. He was now Flight second seat if all held steady. Rosario just smiled and whispered in his ear; "If you bump me out of being the second person on Mars, I'll kill you in your sleep". Elk turned to see her smiling at him. He thought she was joking. Thought. Rosario now looked at him in earnest. "It wasn't real for me until the other night when you mentioned it. Now I think it's real for you too eh poppi"? Brad Elkington settled down and got them all back into the sim. Training took on a whole new sense of urgency.

Sergei had his group running thru the mechanical systems of the mars craft in the equipment section mock up. The Blues had been heavy on EVA for two 1/2 weeks but now they needed to get into the space craft systems for engineer quals. Today they were looking at the O2 generation system. The main oxygen generator on the mars craft was an upgraded version of the same Russian built Elektron system used on the ISS. The Elektron worked the same way submarines had been making oxygen for years; Electrolysis. Take pure water. Add an electrical conducting agent. Run an electrical current thru the water. The H2O splits into H and O2. The Hydrogen is pumped overboard while the O2 is either stored in a tank or released into the craft. The total air system then had cleaners to scrub the Co and Co2 and other harmful gasses out.

There was a monitoring system to look at the various levels of gasses in the atmosphere. They had been thru the monitor and the scrubbers and were now looking at the grey cylindrical generator unit. The pumps and motors in the unit were the standard motor and pumps that were in so many of the units on board. The upgrade mainly came in the weight and capacity of the unit. A hand went up. "Dr. Zapata a question? Sergei said.

"We have talked extensively about the ships systems, but we

have not spoken of the landing site or its systems. "How will the oxygen get generated on the surface"? "Good question. I have no idea". Stunned silence greeted this. Sergei cracked up. "You should see your faces. Of course I know how we are going to generate O2 on the planet. The mission profile has us launching the air plant in a POD to the surface to land separately. It should land near the rover. Which is where we plan to land".

"Why the rover and the air plant separately? This again from Zapata. The NASA technician in the mock up took over smoothly; "Royce and Sergei and the rest of the design folks had to wrestle with a lot of problems. The mars craft has to have duplicate systems for the landing site or it has to be able to use its systems to augment the landing site. Take heat for example; the mars craft has double the heaters it really needs. Same with batteries". "All of those will be off loaded into the landing site for use on the surface. Some items were either too big to fit into the mars craft like the rover. Or they couldn't be broken down into component parts that could be put back together in space. So the air plant for the landing site is one big generator scrubber monitoring and storage unit all combined". He called up the unit on the training display. It's a big bulky 54"by 48" by 51" unit. Even the remote sensors and some cables are going to be carried in the cube". The tech finished off showing them the site layout on the screen.

"What happens if the cube never makes it to mars"? This from Akitoma the Japanese scientist.

"The mars craft has extra sensors and fans. It's also carrying compressed air cylinders in the storage cubes. There should be enough to pressurize and fill the landing site three times. The scrubbers and vent fans can ramp up to clean the air. For a short time", the tech cautioned. "There could be a need for EVA suits. The hydroponics setup will provide a small amount of air and scrubbing capability". Suddenly the thoughts of air on an essentially airless surface loomed large in the teams mind. More questions followed; "How are we going to refill the EVA suits"?

"The suit lockers contain a small compressor that will draw air from the ship to refill the suits". This from Sergei

"The air banks the ship will carry have an enormous amount of air. The air will be at extremely high pressure (5,000) psi. so it will expand greatly to fill the ship at need. The mars craft was different from a submarine in that a submarine used compressed air to work some of its mechanical systems. So it was necessary for the sub

121

to replenish its air from the outside. The mars ship was mostly electrical with small self- contained hydraulic tanks or even compressed air used in isolated cases.

"But won't we need to refill the suits many, many times"?

Sergei smiled. Sometimes training re enforced itself; "What did we learn about the EVA suits he asked? "The new suits real advance is that the underlining fabric had new graphene nano carbon filters". Sergei replayed the suit overview from the training lecture. The Co and Co2 were blocked as the suit recaptured used air and recycled it. There was no need to carry a scuba pack on your back anymore. There was a small pack but nothing like the old suitcase that used to be there. A small emergency supply was compressed back there. Batteries and umbilical connections as well. The front was now devoted to the tablet dock and comms/data unit. The cooling and heating systems were woven into the material. "That gives us a huge advantage", Sergei finished. Oh yeah.

Sergei looked out at the group. "We have been force feed many individual facts about individual components. We need to start thinking about how these systems interrelate. That's what gets you in trouble. You do something on one system without knowing what the effects are on the other systems. That's why the ship will have two command personnel with the 2 maint/science people on watch to prevent bad things from happening. Gospel from the book of Sergei Ivanovitch. "Now let's get back to the O2 gen unit. We have to leave for Russia next week and I want to get into more systems before we go".

Later that evening Sergei approached the barracks with some uncertainty. He knocked loudly. Elkington answered looking at him in surprise. "Hey Serg". "Elk. How you doin"? Elkington smiled. Sergei heard a door open a little behind him down the hall a ways. "A little gob smacked", Elkington said.
"Well sometimes things happen outside of our control and we just have to roll with it". Sergei heard a snort of derision behind him but did not turn. Elk held his tongue. Sergei started in again. "I just wanted to say congratulations and I think you deserved the shot in the first place". Elk grinned, "maybe I'm ready for a shot at you", he said.
"Junior I think you better concentrate on Mars 2 for that".
"Keep on your toes, pop".
"You too Elk". Sergei casually turned to see Rosario and

Janice watching him. "Hello, ladies"! he said jauntily. Rosario snorted again. She looked ready to lay into him when Janice said; "Rose aren't you going over to the flight sim for a few hours"?

"I am if you are going to be okay"? she said looking at Janice.

Now it was Sergei's turn to snort. "You should be worried about me. I barely survived our last encounter". He maneuvered Janice into the room and shut the door in Rosario's outraged face. Sergei grabbed Janice and kissed her passionately.

"We only have two hours and I'm leaving soon".

Janice started to protest and Sergei stopped that with a kiss. When they broke apart Janice was no longer protesting. He looked at her.

"Tomorrow we will be serious. Tonight is for fun". Laying her on the bed, Sergei started to unbutton her shirt while kissing her neck. Janice moaned a little and pulled him into an embrace. He had her shirt off and worked at the clasp of her bra. It unsnapped and she gasped as he roughly grabbed her breasts and started sucking her nipples. His head worked down her now flatter stomach kissing her as he went. His hands worked at her jeans and got the buttons undone. He pulled her pants and panties down and then off in one motion. He then went back to kissing down her stomach. As he worked to her pussy Janice was moaning and arching her back to meet his tongue. Her initial orgasm was small and satisfying but she wanted more. Grabbing his shoulders she pulled off his shirt. Pants and underwear followed suit. Sergei was erect and ready. She took him in her mouth and slowly licked the shaft. Sergei' breath came quicker as she worked. He stopped her before he came and reached out fumbling for his pants. He removed the silver foil package breathing heavily. Tearing open the package he rolled on the condom. He returned to the bed and levered down on top of her. She reached down and put him in. He groaned and slowly started rocking. Janice was amazed by the build in her pleasure and the intensity. Minutes later the release brought a small cry. Sergei finished a few moments later and collapsed against her. As his breathing slowed and he softened inside her Sergei pulled out and removed the condom. He went to the bathroom and flushed it down. Coming back he looked at Janice slick with sweat and a small smile on her face. He laughed. Struggling on the small bed he lay on his left side against her. Janice was quiet coming down from the pleasure high. She looked up at him with a question in her eyes.

"I know, I know" he said. "Not good enough. I'll do better next time I swear".

She laughed. "Yeah. Work on that condom move, it's not smooth enough. There might have been one wasted motion".

Sergei looked at her seriously. "Was it in the pants find area or the package tear or maybe the actual condom roll on? I need to know for my notes". She chuckled again. "I absolutely believe you keep notes. Mr. Smooth. Are you scoring these sessions"?

"A gentleman never kisses and tells".

"Find me a gentleman in here and we'll ask".

"You wound me madam".

"Commie bastard".

"Oh now we are going there huh"? He laughed. "It's been thirty years. I was 8. My family were Cossacks". "Hey where were you born"?

She snuggled up to him and began to find out those things about each other that couples learn. Sergei chatted happily about the Crimea and University in Moscow. He talked about his older sister and her love of all things American. She had forced him to watch reruns of old TV shows that were just available to them. Likewise music. You didn't have to be born in the USA to appreciate when Springsteen sang about wanting to get out of a dead end town he told her. She knew he glanced over some women and other

126

aspects. Janice was pretty sanguine about her relationship with Sergei. No one had tied him down and she didn't think she could either. She had faced a reality. Her husband and child were gone but she lived. She was going to Mars and try to grab some life as it came at her. Janice reached down and grabbed a hold of Sergei. They went back for more.

CHAPTER 8

Launch day 068 12 May 0922 2021

Royce, Kat and Scanlon watched the gold group in the VAB. They were suited in the clean room working thru the rover. Allowing the actual rover to be put thru its paces by a training crew was a big item in Scanlon's book. As NASA director he had tried to run interference and allow Royce a free hand. He thought they were a team: Scanlon did the back room dealing and arm twisting with Congress and Royce ran the mars flight. They had discussed this evolution over several beers in the green house, Why take the chance? They had a full mock up that they could practice on. Why risk damaging the actual hardware before it went into space. For Royce it came down to trust and he had none. He didn't trust that the company who made the bobcat had done enough testing. He had voiced several objections to the committee and had been slapped down. The Consolidated British Design (CBD) company rep had aligned the British government and got the European Space Agency to bring in the Russians against him. Several reps that had lost other battles had come down on him over this. Royce simply went around them now. He told Scanlon what he was going to do to allow him to get clear politically.

The rover bobcat was packed into the crate for the next two days prior to loading it into the SLS and Orion hold. No one said that they couldn't remove it and run it around. Then remove the blade digger and transform it into the full science rover. Several times.

He had Digger down there now with the CBD team. They were calmly and rationally debating the merits of Royce's plan. The word mutherfucker came up several times. Loudly. Digger ended it with the best argument there was: the truth. He asked the company engineer if he thought the testing plan was good enough to go to mars. The engineer paused. He slowly looked down. "We didn't have time to really put the stress to it. It passed some basic things but we never got a full 5 days 12 hours a day running under mars conditions. How could we test that? We ran it in the cold and a vacuum. We then tested the digger under earth conditions for some stress tests. I'm concerned you may have to look at the wheel housing and mounts. Digger and the engineer bent to look at the parts. "Do we spare those parts", he asked? "No, the rep replied. "That's what worries me. Not the parts themselves. You have the three D printer to make anything you need but the special stand and pull unit are not going". The engineer stopped and looked up where Royce and Scanlon were standing. "NASA weight limited it. We can't get it in the crate. The cat and the digging blades barely fit. Based on some of the testing data it was considered so unlikely to fail that it wasn't included in the tool load out". The older man looked at Digger. "The puller is relatively flat and about 5 lbs. Complicated. The stand is pretty basic. It's about two lbs. but really bulky". "It's a tri pod assembly. If a fellow was to cut that assembly at the base into three pieces it would lie pretty flat. If that same fellow had a roll of duct tape he could reassemble that stand where it would work. Wouldn't be pretty but it'll do". He looked at Digger. "I could get you one. 7 lbs out of a personal 50 lb allowance is asking a lot I know". Digger laughed. "Is that all Billy? Hell, I'm taking 40 lbs of scotch". Royce looked at Scanlon as the men below laughed and shook hands. Royce looked at Scanlon who looked shocked. "John, remember your ship is always built by the lowest bidder".

As Digger rejoined the team Elkington looked at him. "Everything good Digger"? "You bet", James replied. Abromovitch was using his laptop to run the unfolding command program for the rover. Like an origami magic trick the wheels came up out around and down before lifting the body of the rover clear of the ground. The front portion where the digger blades would be attached came initially back towards the back then up out and forward to settle in front. The seats popped up and came forward. Various antennas, cameras jutted skyward while displays seemed to come from no- where to land above and just forward of the seats. The ever present docking station for the tablet was imbedded on the main dashboard. Typical British design with a right hand drivers seat. The team now installed the battery packs on the back deck platform. Janice seated herself next to Dr. Hoffman. He had begged to be included in this special session, even flying in from Guiana. He brought the rover to life from the tablet and started the systems check. All nominal. He and Janice then started driving the rover around the room. Easy Peezy Lemon Squeezy. Janice was sure mars would be a different animal. Rosario took her turn with Jones while everyone else went over the attachments. The new rock boring drill was a generation above what was installed on Curiosity. The tunnel auger was especially weird with the adaptors and extenders you could add. The plan called for a 7 foot deep initial tunnel with a 30 foot horizontal tunnel 7 feet underground. The tunnel would lead from the bottom of the airlock down 7 feet and then 30 feet from the lander to the airlock door on the landing site. The tunnels would be lined with a flexible ribbed material. It looked like a huge cloth covered slinky.

The trainees packed back up the bobcat/rover. The CBD reps promised to take good care of her and they headed out of the VAB. Janice wondered over to where Kat, Rosario, James, Elk, Royce and Scanlon were standing talking. Scanlon was proposing to take them all to dinner. Janice was about to back out when Kat came up and murmured: "when the boss says go to dinner, you should go". They all adjourned to Rusty's seafood. Janice quickly objected. "What is it with you NASA types and these horrible places"? "Isn't there a place you go that doesn't involve dead animal decorating? she said, eying the alligator on the wall.

 Scanlon seated her right next to him. "Dr. Lincoln I know you are probably one of the 10 smartest people in the world, but when it comes to good food I'm your man. Rosario started in. "Mr. Scanlon you don't know good food. You think salad is the lettuce they use to line the basket of popcorn shrimp". A round of drinks came and Royce rescued his boss by proposing a toast: To the brave men and women of the Mars program. Scanlon quickly got to the business of the dinner. "Elk I need a favor from your team". Elkington paused in the middle of slurping an oyster. Uh oh. "Sure thing boss whatever you need".

"I need you guys to do a round of press". Groans from Elkington, Digger and Rose. Janice looked bewildered. "We get to talk to the press"? She was kind of excited. Scanlon took pity on her. "I need some of the more camera ready personnel on the mars team to do some work on the Today Show. They are coming down to Florida soon to cover the launches". They are going to want to meet with you. I thought you should start out with the local guys to level the playing field". Rosario looked at Scanlon. "Could you explain what camera ready means"? Royce stepped in. "Rose you know perfectly well that every time you appear on TV we get a 2 fold increase in astronaut applications". Scanlon went on; "You guys have gantry evac training tomorrow right? Well local channel Five wants to film you. "You answer some puffball questions and maybe we let the reporters take the slide. What do you say"? Elk answered for them all; "yeah sure. What the hell right"?

Gantry evac training sounded innocuous enough. Just stand in this basket while it plunges towards the earth at 232 miles per hour. Well not quite but the rappel basket did rely on gravity to move the astronauts from the launch gantry to the earth in event of some catastrophe. Just what that catastrophe was and how they were supposed to get from the capsule to the gantry was not explained. Elkington told Janice on the way up to the evac point that the evac drill is a "momma" drill. It was there to make your mom feel like everything was safe. Submarines have a similar drill. Every submariner is required to undergo yearly "escape training". The theory is that there are escape hatches on the sub. So if they are trapped on the bottom then the sailors could get into the hatch and escape to the surface. One slight problem. The max depth that you can survive the ascent from is 400 feet. Subs spend about .1% of their time in waters under 400 feet in depth. So the odds were even if the sub is in shallow enough water to not get crushed like a beer can, it would be so deep that you would die on the ascent. Same thing with gantry training. The system would be used only while the astronauts were being loaded into the capsule. Once they were sealed in the odds of them being able to get out and then down the basket during a fire or other problem were very small. But the ride was fun and it made for great footage so they played along. Standing on the top of the gantry waiting her turn to go down Janice talked to the local TV reporter. The reporter was asking about the dangers of mars. Radiation exposure being the first. Janice stepped up to answer. "Well, we have been told that the radiation exposure is equivalent to a full body cat scan every week. That increases our cancer risk by 3 %. We have talked extensively about what we might be able to do to increase the safety of the landing site." First and foremost the site will be effectively underground, so that should lessen the exposure.

Second we are going to be working with the RADAR unit to see if we can set up a radio wave magnetic shield if you will to steer some of the radiation away from the craft. That doesn't work on all types of radiation but it will help." The reporter asked Elkington about meteorites and potential impacts. "We have very little we can do about those kinds of risks, he said sincerely. "The idea is that anything large enough to detect we will be able to fly around. Anything smaller we won't see and can do nothing about."

The space between the planets in our solar system is relatively empty so the risk is considered small. What about the physical effects of being in space that long? Rose took that one. "The main risk is muscle and bone loss. The body can adapt. Long missions on the space station have shown us that we can endure it." In fact I will grow 2-3 inches taller during this mission, she concluded.

What about spinning the spacecraft to impart some gravity? Elk took over again smoothly. "That is something that mission control is studying. It may be possible to spin the whole spacecraft and get some gravity in the craft. However there would be a zone down the center of the spin line that would be weightless. We would be moving into and out of a weightless zone in a few feet. If we only get 5 or 6 % gravity it may not be enough to justify the fuel burns. Again,that may be something we try underway." Thank you very much said the reporter. Lets slide down the big ride!

Janice was next to load in for the trip down when she noticed who was loading them into the basket: Tyler Watkins. He looked blank. Utterly emotionless. He stared at the crew while loading Elkington into the basket. Elk for his part was none too pleased to see him. He double checked everything Watkins touched. He had eyes locked on him even after the basket began to drop away. Watkins was motioning to Janice to come forward. He ran thru the evac procedure with her roughly. She just nodded when he asked if she was good to go. Why would he be involved with this? Janice had thought he was back in Houston or even working with the build teams on all the mars equipment. As she started downward she realized that her stomach hadn't dropped when she started the slide. It had dropped when she saw Watkins. Her trip down was smooth and uneventful but she couldn't help shaking the feeling that she had been in danger. She said as much to Elk. He nodded. Watkins had been assigned to the drop as part of the publicity push. Elkington was sure he was up to something but just what that was he didn't know. He told her to always check over equipment twice even if she had just done so with Watkins around. Janice suddenly felt lonely. Sergei was in Russia and wouldn't be back for three more days. They had 22 more days until they launched for the ISS. Janice wouldn't feel good until they got away. The next two days would be landing site orientation and operations. Then it was three weeks of launch prep and procedure rehearsal. Then she would be in space. She would be there a total of 19 days. A least 6 EVA walks had her listed as part of the crew. She would actually overlap Sergei by eighteen days when he came up on the Soyuz. This would be a huge test for the program. In the space of three days there would be four crew dockings for the ISS. The SLS Orion capsule. The Soyuz. The French Ares and the Dragon from Space X. Elkington commanding the Orion team. Sergei leading the Soyuz group.

Grace Adler now leading the Ares team with Zhou heading up the Dragon crew with parts and supplies. The work list called for them to assemble the truss system that would house the work platform where they would mount the engine on the rover pod. They had to test the engine and finally launch the rover to mars. Janice' own responsibilities were pretty minor. She would help bolt on the trusses, Install brackets and hand holds for the work to come. She would be part of the engine removal team as she had practiced that operation three times. She would get at least one more run thru and maybe more. She was getting good at the EVA suits. However space was another animal. As the gold team left the evac landing area back to the auditorium for another round of tests, Janice and Rosario exchanged notes on their trips. They agreed that presence of Watkins had creeped them out and would bear watching.

Video log Brad Elkington 14 May 2057 2021

We had an outstanding day at the site trainer. I'm really looking forward to tomorrow's practical period. My whole team was amazed at the plasbond panels and the sealant properties. One minor issue: the dirt you used in the training area doesn't say mars enough. May I suggest the red clay of Georgia? If you used that as the top layer it would convey the red planet and it would help the realism of the airlock scenarios. That fine Georgia dirt gets everywhere. Just a suggestion. The question of the day? What am I going to miss most while I'm gone? Well my family of course. Five and two year old kids tend to grow quickly. I think I'll also miss the trees. I like sitting under a shady tree listening to the wind and lazing around. I'll look forward to planting a tree on mars.

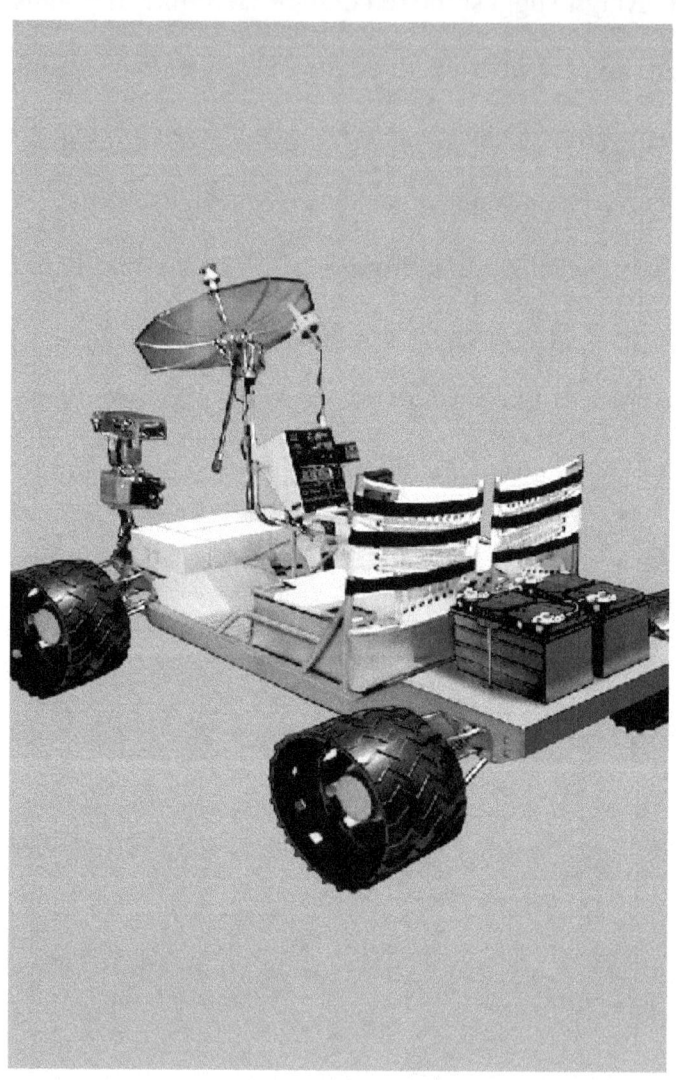

CHAPTER 9

Launch day 071, 0843 15 June 2021 Kennedy Space Center

Rosario pounded the pole into the ground with short sharp raps with the hammer. She kept at it doggedly. The pole was located in the interior of the landing site mock up. Gold team had descended early ready to set up the panels which made up the landing site. The plasbond panels that made up the supply cubes would be used to become the panels in the landing site. The panels were 5 feet on each side. They have premade holes which lined up with the connecting channels. The panels came in 4 different types. The most basic is the plain panel with just the premade holes. These six panels made up the outside set of the cube. The interior had different versions of the panels: One was a "window" type which had a rectangular window set in the middle. These were planned for the second level and the roof of the structure. The third type had an umbilical port on them. The small square had standard receptacles for air, water/hydraulics, electrical, and data. Rosario and Janice had shared a laugh over Sergei's lament that the umbilical could not pick up cable TV. The fourth type was highly specialized with an airlock/airtight door. There would be 12 of these panels. 12 for the umbilical's. 50 with windows and 76 plain panels making up the 240 panels available. Connecting channels and support pillars with hardware for securing them made up the rest of the system.

The landing site was the most ambitious portion of the mission. It had never been tried before and was perhaps the key to man's expansion onto permanent moon or mars bases. The bobcat would be mated with its various digging tools to prep the site. The bobcat would excavate 7 feet down into the soil. The site was being buried to help limit radiation exposure. A 35 by 25 foot area would be cleared. The geologists indicated that large rock formations were liable to be an issue. However the chosen landing site had been deemed the best available option. After the heavy machinery cleared the site, a liner would be laid down. Then a channel of footers followed by the panels. The panels would be set two high in a 10 by 30 foot section with a "porch" branching off at 10 by 10. The interior would be portioned off into basically four 10 by 10 rooms in a T formation. The roof panels would span the distance to a supporting pole in the center. Window panels would be spaced around the second tier and the roof to allow sunlight to enter. Dirt would be carefully moved back around the bottom of the walls up to the windows. The astronauts would have to maneuver the air plant into the structure prior to setting up the last walls. Two solar arrays had been provided to power the site. They would be set up on either end of the site and connected thru the umbilicals. The site would be connected to the ships airlock thru a flex tunnel. The first room going into the structure was to serve as an airlock/clean room. If time permitted and the Mars team felt they could accomplish it, a second structure would be made and connected with a 10 foot flexible tunnel. Then it was a process of making the whole shebang air tight. The rubberized silicone spray was key for this. The whole interior would be sprayed to seal it. It had worked in testing and in mock ups but not the cold punishing terrain of mars. After that a few pillows and some curtains and you had a cozy pied a terre. Pied a Mars. The mission had the flexibility to succeed if the landing site was not constructed. It just wouldn't be fun to spend 330 days on mars on the ship. To actually remove an EVA suit and work at a task would be a powerful image back on earth. The goal for the second structure was a greenhouse section. Earth plants growing on mars said "we were going to be back". That is if Rosario could get this pole run into the ground. The final whacks got the seal disc at the three foot mark flush with the liner. Attaching the second and third sections of the pole brought it to the full 7 foot height. Rosario then attached the top channel dish to which the panels would be inserted. This was the tricky part; Rosario guided the first three panels into the support relatively easily. The fourth panel didn't want to cooperate. She called up the tip video on her EVA helmet screen. The Astronaut (Watkins) recommended lifting the support pole a little to allow extra room for the panels. She tried this, careful to keep the panels in the channels between the four panels. Shifting the support pole back and forth and calling to Janice and Digger and Elk to shove the various sides of the structure itself she managed to get the panels installed and started screwing it down. She repeated the process with the last support pole and the final four roof panels. It took considerable "encouragement" to get the panels to line up correctly. Sometimes you just had to use a bigger hammer. As she drove home the last screw, the rest of the team entered thru the faux airlock door. The work box they carried contained the spray sealant. Each bottle had a self-pump up to allow the sealant to be applied. Working slowly but methodically they sprayed the interior of the rooms. They paid particular attention to the airlock doors and the panel joint seems. Elk reminded them to make sure they periodically pushed on the panels to ensure that the sealant penetrated into areas that were not previously accessible. They called on Dr Leon to push on the walls from the outside to see if all areas remained sealed. When they finished Janice and Elk attached the hose to the vac pump and the umbilical. On the Mars site the air would be evacuated back to the ship. They ran the pump up and took a 2 atm suction on the space. The seal held despite some small leaks. The easiest way to detect the leaks was to throw talc into the air. The fine powder got sucked into the leaks. The team moved around sealing the six pin hole leaks. The final step was to have Dr. Leon connect the umbilical from the ship to the site and start pumping air into the structure. It held at 3 atmospheres. When it was holding the NASA engineers pushed on different sides to see if the seal held. It did.

"That's not bad work," Elk complimented them during the debrief. "Mission profile calls for 20 build days. That's twenty days to erect panels. 8 for the dig and prep. 2 days to set the liner. 20 build and 8 seal and move equipment. He looked over the team." I think we could do it in 16 or so. We are limited to 4 workers at a time so we may be able to get into a good rhythm setting the panels." I would love to be able to get that greenhouse setup going in the second building". Janice smiled at that.

"What about serious leaks", Abromovitch asked? Elk moved to the second work box. He removed a leak bag. The flexible rubber sheets with an epoxy sealant to rigidly set the patch in place. Different sizes of hard plasbond sheets were included. Janice asked about the time they would have in the event of a leak. The NASA engineer started in on hole size and cleanliness of the hole and the shape. If a panel gave way the decompression would be explosive. No airbags were going to drop from the overhead compartment. It boiled down to precious little time. Mission profile called for one person suited, helmet off. The airlock doors would remain closed when not in use. The theory being that if they could isolate one compartment, the leak wouldn't be so bad. A pin hole leak they might have 2-3 days. A pencil size hole one day. A golf ball size, 6 hours. If a panel gave way, they might have 15 seconds, but nothing to patch it with. Not everyone would be in the landing site at all times. One or two would remain with the ship. What worried NASA and Royce was what they didn't know. In risk management there knowns, and known unknowns, but by far the biggest area of concern was unknown unknowns. How do you plan for something you didn't know you didn't know? Gasses leaking up from the ground? The heat from the structure melting the Martian permafrost. Mars quakes? Microbes? Aliens? Its what you didn't know that got you killed.

Royce was dealing with the knowns and unknowns right at that same moment. He sat at the secure VTC room in his offices. Kat sat beside him with a stack of folders and a laptop open. The screen in front of them showed the Brussels conference room for the committee. All 24 members had folders open in front of them and were following. Royce went thru it point by point: 4 launch teams were graded and rated as ready in all aspects. Barring last minute illness the crews were ready. Even that would be not issue as backups were assigned to each member. Equipment: Rover and engine were packed and stacked on their launch vehicles. The tools and supplies were ready on the French Rocket. Dragon X showed all ready with the tech crew. Even the ISS had completed its prep already. The extra toilet shower and sleeping racks had been installed. With 8 crew already up and 27 more coming up the facilities in the old station needed an upgrade. The 35 people in space would be the most away from the mother planet in history. The first 12 days of the project would see the most activity. Peaking with a day 5 event involving 29 astronauts in EVA around the ISS. NASA was drooling for those pictures. The crews would mostly sleep and eat in their respective vehicles but they needed to use the shower and toilet on the space station. The crew on the ISS had done the dirty unglamorous work of making the space necessary to give this a go. They had even made a short EVA to stage some of the work boxes early. They noticed this when installing the new module for the Mars project. The trusses and platform and cube were taking up more space than they had anticipated. Royce went over the approved sequencing document. They discussed in detail the hard linear sequential items and the items that could be worked in parallel. Johnson Space Center in Houston had the overall control of the mission with each craft reporting back thru its own control network. Again Johnson would just give a task to a unit: i.e.- Dragon crew commence 8 hr crew rest period. Then they dropped off the net to allow the Dragon crew to coordinate with the ISS for whatever they needed in the way of facilities. Same with the other vessels. Ares: establish line to move trusses out of the ISS storage brackets thru the airlock

148

and onto the ISS shell. The Russian Representative Tatiana Medvedev asked if the remote control arm would be the limiting factor in moving the trusses or capsules around. Royce looked at her. That was a sharp question and one of Royce's' biggest headaches at the moment. No one had used the remote control arm so often and for so much. They had three fully qualified operators on the ISS and had conducted extensive tests, but if the arm glitched then the schedule was screwed. Royce admitted as much. The rep from Canada, the robotic arm maker, quickly reassured everyone that the arm was fully vetted and ready for this assignment. After all the bigger tests were ahead with the craft pieces themselves. Royce wasn't so sure. The arm would actually get more use during this period then during the craft assembly periods. The arm would just lift and hold in place while the pieces were assembled. Here the arm would be moving trusses and the platform around and moving people to various work platforms. And it would be going round the clock. Royce cautioned them to ensure they didn't use past success to imprint future success. Look at the testing data: The arm was 3 sigma's towards good. In risk management parlance that meant that there was a 93.75 percent chance that the arm would perform nominally. That was outside the 5 sigma goal of 98 percent. However it was not possible to get to 5 let alone 6 sigma's without a major overhaul of equipment. The ISS crew had done what they could with the new motors and control boards. It remained a risk. Royce reminded them that he needed a verbal agreement to accept this risk. The vote was taken and it was agreed to allow the mission to continue. It was close at 16 to 8. Royce also got agreement to move the launches one day to the left. It was a symbolic gesture to assure the public and the politicians that the project was moving forward rapidly. It meant that the crews would be up in space swarming over the ISS before the July 20th anniversary of the Apollo landing. Oh, NOVA was going to get that video, Mars rocket be damned.

Hours later Royce sat at the counter of a burger joint in Coco Beach. He slowly ate a cheese burger and went over his to list in his head. He barely noticed when a man sat next to him at the counter. The guy was average looking. Anywhere from 30-45 years old. Skinny. Average height. Average hair. Average clothes. He looked like three quarters of the people Bob saw every day. Which was the point. Raven ordered a shake and waited while it came to him. He casually glanced at Bob. Then down. Bob noticed a briefcase at his feet. He knew Raven would leave it for him. A thousand questions ran thru his mind. One glance at Raven shook that off. He returned to eating his cheese burger.

Raven finished his shake and left some money on the counter. He left without a word or a backward glance. Bob followed Raven thru his reflection in the mirror behind the counter. Raven slipped out the door and seemed to be swallowed up by the few cars and people outside. Bob knew if he ever attempted to follow him for real, Raven would just lose him immediately. He sighed and took the brief case in hand and left. He never noticed the woman in the back watching him leave. Returning to his office, he sat the briefcase on the desk then opened it. He removed a letter, a file folder, and a phone. The letter gave him detailed contact instructions which he memorized. The hand written note on the bottom: "Thanks for the heads up. Watch your back." He burned the letter. Opening the file folder he read slowly. Nothing on the Chinese or Russians per se. However, it seemed the French rep for the Ares program was seeing a mistress. Big deal. However, the French rep was unaware that that mistress was working for the MEDEX Corp and the Russian billionaire Dimitry Lubshenko. Legarde was also taking some sweet kickbacks from MEDEX. Lubshenko was a direct rival for Medvedev. Okay, he could leverage that info. He put the phone and the file folder into his safe. He ran a hair thin black thread across the lower right corner of the safe and taped it in place. It was nearly invisible. His safe was alarmed but Royce was getting paranoid. Low tech but effective. Raven had taught him.

CHAPTER 10

NASA commercial; Vintage grainy footage of Neil Armstrong pausing at the foot of the ladder leading from the Eagle to the surface of the moon. The audio captures the exchange: Okay I'm going to step off now. He sets foot on the moon and the iconic "That's one small step for man…"   audio is heard. Cut to the video montage of the Mars astronauts training, the mock ups of the mars craft and the landing site. 52 years later, Earth is ready to take that next step. Cut to a picture of Mars up close.

WWW.marsmission.com.

Video log Sergei Ivanovitch 25 June 2021 2203

Greetings from Baikanour Space Center Star City Russia. The
Blue crew is fully ready for Launch in 8 days' time. We have
wrapped up our engine mate demate training and are concentrating
on the SOYUS procedures along with the ISS mockup. I've even
got some time on the robotic arm trainer here. The Canadians have
a winner if they can teach me to operate that thing. My crew mates
are ready to go and chomping at the bit. I must admit even I was
feeling a little anxious last week. Thank you Mister Royce for
allowing me to come back to Kennedy and consult with my Gold
crew colleagues for that day. I know that the fruitful and intense
discussions we had will lead to increased performance for myself
and another. I know Tatiana is looking forward to her visit with
you next week. What's the question of the day? What feature of
mars are you most anxious to explore? Well without a doubt it is
the famous canals of Mars for me. I'd like to see for myself what
all the fuss is about. Sergei out!

Launch day 84 28 June 2021 1222 Kennedy Space Center

Janice had her tray and was just sitting with the rest of the golden five (Gonsolvo, Elkington, Andrews, Lincoln, and Jones) when she noticed Bob Royce and John Scanlon sitting with a tall beautiful woman. "Who's that with Royce", she asked Rosario.
"Aiy that's Tatiana Medvedev, the head of the Russian Space agency. She's over here lining things up with Bob and Kat for the launches next week".
It still didn't seem quite real to Janice, in 5 days they would be in space. They would be starting the real work for the Mars project. Lost in her thoughts she almost missed Jonsey's comment: No wonder Sergei decided to come back into the flight program. I would have too. "What"? Janice asked going pale. Rosario took pity on her. "Hey it's just rumor okay". The rumor is that Sergei has had an on-going affair with her for the last 15 years".
The men in the group started in on the likely hood of surviving a 15 year relationship with Medvedev. Janice felt sick. She knew about some of the other women in Sergei's life (Rosario included) but Medvedev was another story. Beautiful, rich, powerful and a Russian to boot. The unexpected pang of jealousy caught her

completely by surprise. Rose looked at her and quietly said, "Chica

you knew this from the beginning, right? Didn't you have a good

time the other night"? Sergei was sure smiling when he left".

Janice nodded yes and then quickly murmured her goodbye's, and

left the dining hall. She needed some room. She luckily had a

simple test this afternoon and she could then take it easy. She was

scheduled to go over the life science station with Royce of all

people. Since she had been familiar with all the gear and the test

protocols all her life she wasn't sweating the test. Arriving at the

classroom at 1300 for a 1315 test period she saw the same four

from lunch waiting for her at the science station mock up. Royce

broke away and had her sit at a desk and call up the testing

materials. He simply told her to begin the test, as the other three

watched. Janice felt uneasy but whipped thru the 50 questions in

14 min. The 100 was dutifully posted to her grades. Moving over

to the science station itself Royce ran thru the practical in routine

tones. Power up the station, bring the microscope on line and prep

and read a geology sample for life signs. The subject rock and

tools were laid out. Janice powered up her laptop and ran thru the

startup sequence for the machine in 7 min. While she was in the 5

min wait/stabilization period, she prepped the slide by slicing off a thin wafer of the rock. At this point Royce substituted a pre made sample. All she had to do was stain it, mount it and read it. As she adjusted the slide in the mount Janice was conscious of everyone watching her intently. She focused in and started to adjust the knobs. She smiled faintly as the image came in clear. The engineers at IBM had mounted individual carbon atoms on the silica rock surface and had made a picture. It looked like ET. When she had stained the sample it came out green. A she submitted the sample for grading Scanlon took over. "Dr. Lincoln, he said, we were all impressed by your handling of the life science's station. You certainly are qualified for this mars mission". He paused a moment. "Dr. you must be wondering what we are doing here monitoring a routine test. I took this opportunity to sound you out about something. Have you given any thought about what it means to discover life on mars"? Janice paused considering how to answer. She went with a version of the truth, avoiding looking at Tatiana the whole time she spoke. "I suppose I have given it some thought. The existence of life on mars will be a clearly defined before and after point for both science and mankind. Knowing that we are not alone in the universe is essential to bonding the whole human race to the

157

single purpose of discovering what else is out there".

"That's an interesting turn of phrase Dr.", Tatiana said. "Before and after life on mars. Have you given any thought to the religious repercussions of finding life on another planet"? Janice now looked at her ice cool blue eyes, and repressed the urge to hit her.

"I haven't given it much thought. I suppose that the earth's religions are going to have to rethink a lot of things".

Scanlon started in again. "Dr. You need to think about this seriously. Millions of people in this country feel that every word in the bible is literally true. If we discover life, that rips the very foundation from them. If the bible is not true then God might not exist and then why should I follow a set of behavioral norms that don't mean anything"?

"Are suggesting that if we discover life on mars there will be rioting on Earth", Janice gasped.

Royce weighed in. "We've had exactly those kinds of discussions Janice. If there is other life out there then we have to have the next step figured out or people will start to get nervous and they may riot". "Also, if we don't find life a small group of people are going to take that as a sign the bible is 100% perfect and must be followed to the exclusion of all else. Tensions rise and rioting".

"And then again another group is going to be convinced that we in fact discovered life but are withholding it as part of a cover up.

And they will use that to stir up antigovernment feelings about the cost of this mission and there could be rioting", he finished gloomily. Janice gaped at all of them.

"Do you believe in God Dr. Lincoln"?, Tatiana asked quietly. Janice whipped her head to stare at her. "I do not", she said flatly.

Where was god when my husband and child were taken from me? Did Danny deserve to die because he was wicked"?

"Of course not Dr. I just asked".

Scanlon joined in. "Janice we need you to think about this.

Anything you discover out there needs to be verified here as well. We can't have you going off making announcements about life on Mars without running it by us first. We need to prep people. Over the next several months you may be asked as part of your publicity duties about God and his role in this mission. About your beliefs.

About the meaning of what you discover and how it will affect mankind. You need to think about your answers and we need to go over them with you. We are having this same discussion with all the potential Mars crew members. You and Dr. Fong are the most important though. Kat slightly rolled her eyes at this. "Dr.

Fong will announce that the discovery of life is a great achievement for the communist Party and the people of china, she said flatly. "She might as well trumpet that god is dead. I know you are not old enough to know this but google John Lennon and see how that worked out for the Beatles". Janice balked. "I think that any discovery should first be credited at the whole Mars Crew not just one individual. After all I may not even dig up the rock. That might be any of us. Also, if you are scared about these riots because people are afraid or don't understand, then we need to educate them. We could hold some forums and discuss this with rational people with rational points of view. I'm not going to get into a shouting match with a TV talking head". She finished up breathing heavily. Scanlon smiled grimly. "I hope so Dr. "Kat is going to download some information for you over the next couple of days. Then we can go over the potential answers to questions and how to deflect some of the more incendiary ones". Janice nodded. And got up to go as the others moved off on to the next crises point. She heard Tatiana move back to her desk. Looking up Tatiana was giving her an appraising look. "Well, you are pretty enough but I always thought Sergei would go for the starlet type. Of course he has that weakness for brainy women and

160

you certainly fit that mold". Janice remained cool and aloof just looking at her. "Sergei wanted me to pass on a message Tatiana said calmly: He said to tell you and I quote: "Stop thinking of ways to poison Ms. Medvedev and start trying to figure out how we can sneak off on the Space station." He wants to be the first person to have sex in space Tatiana said bluntly. "He is an overgrown boy," she grumped. "Well he's your problem now. Keep him in line Dr. Lincoln". She turned without a further word and rejoined Scanlon Kat and Royce as they left the building. Janice sat there steaming and feeling relieved. He sent her a message. That was nice. But he sent it thru her. Not nice. He wanted to have sex in space with her. Nice. But he sent an old girlfriend to tell her, not nice. She had been surprised and gratified to see him last week. He did drive her crazy in some ways. Wasn't that a good thing? Didn't it mean she had a passion for him? Did he have a passion for her? That was another question. Sergei had displayed no jealousy of Charles when she spoke of her marriage. Only sympathy. He seemed to be genuine in that emotion. Janice hurried outside and caught up the four. "Ms. Medvedev, can I have a word please"? Tatiana separated from the three and regarded Janice with sharp eyes.

"Did you have a relationship with Sergei" she asked bluntly?

"We did", Tatiana replied.

"Did he ever lie to you"?

"Lie? No never lie. Sergei is many things but never a liar".

"Listen, Dr. Lincoln, I meant what I said before. Someone needs to keep the overgrown child in line. That seems to be you. Royce and I share a goal: we want the mars mission to succeed". "I'll be honest in that the successful completion will have great benefits for my personal career. She paused then continued. "The eight of you we talked about tonight have separated themselves from the rest. That's good for you. However, now you have obvious targets on your backs". "In some ways it gets harder and more dangerous from here on in. Think about the Mercury 7 astronauts. They were world famous in the 60's. But that was pre internet". No google, snapr, facebook, twitter, Tumblr, Buaidu, and Growler to let the entire world know every foible. She looked at Janice again with the cool blue eyes. "You better get used to seeing pictures of your deceased child on TV". Janice stiffened.

"Do you really think no one is going to mention your husband and child? You need to be prepared. The whole world will be watching the next six weeks. We just clued you in about the god questions. You need to be prepared for your personal peccadilloes to be aired in public. The sessions will be difficult if you are not willing to listen. As for Sergei, you know how he is. He will flash that smile and charm and the next thing you know you are having zero gee sex. If you are seen as romantically involved with him, you will be eviscerated in the press. A wonton woman throwing away a dead child and husband for a thrill". Janice flared in anger. "That's enough. My relationship is my business"!

Tatiana said sadly, "that's funny. The American people, when they spend 20 billion dollars on a project, have a curious way of thinking that they get to know all about the person that benefits from that money. Russians are not quite that bad but the official government apparatus will try to use that for advantages. Just like I will". Janice felt disgusted. She said as much.

Tatiana smiled, "well we could cancel the program and you and Sergei can live happily ever after. Or you could not go to Mars. But then the mission might not be successful and Royce and I would have to step in. So you get to make a choice: end it with Sergei, and everyone goes to Mars for glory, or continue and face the scrutiny when it comes your way. Less glory for you and Sergei, but the mission succeeds".

Janice ran all of it thru her mind. She made a snap decision. "Give Sergei a message from me: This ends here. Thank you. It was sweet but no more".

Medvedev nodded in sympathy. "Dr. you are a remarkable woman. Watch your back around Fong". Tatiana walked back to the others.

Janice blinked. Fong, the Chinese woman? She was the medical doctor and flight back up for the Whites in Guiana. Grace had gone down there to replace Watkins. Janice had not exchanged more than 10 words with the woman in the whole time she had been here. She supposed there would be more interaction in the upcoming weeks as they completed the rover pod engine mate sessions. Janice felt weary. She had some issues with her going to space and they were wearing her down. She thought her time as an international seductress was at an end.

The next three days passed in the strange way that time had: It seemed to stretch out and slow down when she was alone but contracted and speed up when she was with the crew performing a training evolution. Two nights before the launch they had dinner with a bunch of government and NASA dignitaries. Janice felt uncomfortable schmoosing a crowd. She stuck close to Rosario and Elk and let them take the lead. Digger took pity on her when she was stuck with the local congressional rep from the Florida 15th district. He launched into several funny stories of their training and the crew members. Digger and the congressman walked off to the buffet table like the best of friends. "Let me guess, you want them to move up the launch to tonight about three minutes from now right"? Guessing correctly, Rosario said, coming up beside her.

"Yes please", said Janice.

"Another hour and I'll give Elk the high sign and he will tell everyone we have to get up early and it's his job as flight commander to crack the whip and get everyone to bed early.

"Let's get some more food", Rose directed. "You are going to be just as sick as me of MRE's and toothpaste tube food soon enough".

While they waited for more shrimp, Janice noticed a worried buzz in the room. The general consensus was that people didn't seem to think the mission could succeed. They needed to be reassured.

Elkington was surrounded by worried administrators. Janice thought that Sergei should be here. He'd have them eating out of his hand, throwing out some story and some little speech that would reassure them all. Janice missed him badly at that moment. Can't worry about that, it's over she reminded herself. 59 hrs to launch. Make it come quickly!

CHAPTER 11

Launch day 089 03 July 2021 0557 Baikanour Siberia, Star City Russia

Strapped into the SOYUZ capsule, Sergei was with his crew waiting for the launch hold to complete. Things had gone smoothly for a Russian space flight. That meant that the rocket hadn't exploded on the pad during fueling. They were actually ready. The Soyuz would be the first off the ground and the first to dock. Then the SLS from Kennedy followed by the French.

166

The Dragon would follow the next day. Just getting the crafts docked would be challenging. They all simply maneuvered close and then the robotic arm would grab and drag them into position. Once the universal airlock was opened the capsule and cargo holds became a functioning part of the space station. The Ares and the Orion capsules would be on opposite sides of the space station's new work/docking module. They had the engine and the rover. They were closer to the platform. The Dragon and the SOYUS would be on the forward end of the older part of the station port and starboard. That was the parking plan anyway.

Sergei checked with mission control as the time ticked down. The checklist called for full crew verbal assertion for launch. Mission control this is Orel. Launch checklist step 7 time 0600. Ivanovitch, yes, Nyguen, yes, Sanger, yes, Keith, yes, Larionov, yes, Datsuyk, yes. The latter two part of the SOYUZ regular crews. They would look after the SOYUZ while the other four did the mars work. The launch resumed countdown. At T minus 6 seconds the three huge liquid fueled main stage engines roared to life. With the sun well up this far north the day got even brighter when the rocket lifted off the pad in a huge cloud of smoke. He hated this part. This time even more than normal. He was nominally the mission commander but Larionov was the man in the flight seat for this show. Since the computer controlled the commands to the engines, it was simply his job to monitor and report when things happened. That and get his skull rattled as the rocket shook around. Sergei couldn't see his companions but he could see heart rates on the monitors and all were elevated.

Lighting off a big firework tended to get the old heart racing. 8 min later the bang lurch of the stage separating shook them. The roar from the solid rocket second stage single engine was almost muted. They were 200,000 feet up and 36 miles down range. The second stage lasted 44 minutes and as they separated the familiar weightlessness hit Sergei. Now they actually had something to do as the radar was brought on line and systems checks were performed. The three small solid rocket maneuvering engines on the Orel capsule now engaged as they started the slow catch up process to the space station. All looked nominal. The pressure switched on the cargo holds said the PODS had not moved. Sergei risked a glance out the window and saw the edge of the earth as it curved away. They were over the Pacific Ocean as they made contact with Hawaii and then Houston in turn. Houston reported that the French had a small delay but it was within parameters.

All others on schedule. Sergei spared a thought for Janice. She would be suiting up right now getting ready for her flight. This ends now. That was her message. Oh, really. Nyet. Sergei had to be pissed to think in Russian. A strange thought hit him: Maybe that's why Tatiana saw thru him so quickly in Vegas. He was shouting in English. She knew he would revert to Russian when really mad. That was his tell. Rookie mistake, he was better than that. He came back to the Janice question. It wasn't ego. It wasn't the thrill of the chase. He liked her and couldn't see why she wanted to end it. Ergo, the relationship continued. That's how he saw it anyway. He was betting he could get it done on the space station. More status and reports flowed in as he initiated the comms check with the ISS. 16 hrs to go until docking. Things were getting interesting.

Elkington had run them all thru the suit process several times in training. Still in the ready room all of them had checked each other several times. Jones had joked that he had spent more time in the EVA suit than his regular clothes. Larson and Pickerell the two NASA astronaut's for the Orion capsule had run thru the check lists again just to do something. Royce entered the room.

169

Everyone ready he asked? All affirmative. It was 1000. They had one hour for crew loading into the capsule. Then 4 hours to wait for the actual launch. The 1500 launch would look real good on the six o'clock east coast news. Royce had a little twinkle in his eye as he led them to the door. He stopped Elk just as he was going thru. "Enjoy this; you've earned it space man". Elkington looked at him quizzically. As the door opened the hall was lined with NASA and contractor techs. They burst into applause as the 7 moved down the corridor to the outside and the crew van that would take them to the launch pad. Janice was stunned. The crowd was deafening. As they broke out of the building even more cheering as the large crowd caught sight of them. Rosario was happily waving and blowing kisses to the crowd. Janice had goose flesh as she waved back at faces she recognized. Piling into the van they were breathless. Wow. "That was awesome" Digger exploded! As the van made its way to the gantry every area the road was lined with people who had come to see them off. NASA did like its spectacle. Janice was sure several cameras had caught the moment. Stay focused Elk warned. "We need to strap in and complete all the check lists. Let the training kick in and let's do this by the numbers".

The crew was composed as they unloaded and headed up in the elevator. It was a practiced 52 min to load them all in and seal the capsule. An immediate launch hold was started to final fuel the rocket. Janice was strapped in and running the checklists from her tablet. The hours passed in a blur. Before she knew it, it was countdown time. She was unprepared for the violence of the launch. She was sure something had gone wrong but no alarm or warning came in. Elk was dealing with an engine that was burning slow. It was possible a piece of debris had clogged the engine and was affecting the performance. Elkington reported the problem and confirmed a set of values to Kennedy. Janice was struggling to see with the jostling but she was keeping up on the status. . Elk asked her for a confirmation of the engine output and assigned her to give readouts every 15 seconds. Janice gave thrust in pounds and a percentage of the nominal output. 190,000 lbs engine 2 at 82 percent. She dutifully ticked it off. She watched Elk command the other two engines to more power to keep them on flight path. At the 4 min mark whatever was blocking the engine suddenly cleared and the ride smoothed a bit. Janice reported the new figures. 225,000 lbs engine 2 at 98 percent. Two more reports and Elk called the blockage clear and suspended her reports. He throttled the other engines down to the computer given values. Janice kept her eyes glued to the screen watching that engine until stage separation. As the solid rocket motors kicked in for the burn, Janice got a good look out the window at the Earth. The Orion craft was arcing over the east coast. The black void loomed over the shrinking earth. Elk called for status and all responded in the green. An hour later they completed second stage separation with the three small maneuvering engines starting normally. Houston had called saying they had good telemetry on the launch anomaly and were starting the investigation. Elkington knew there would be a full sweep of the other engines in NASA's system to see if the problem was just some dirt or a design defect or maybe even a mechanical failure. He concentrated on the task at hand. He ordered Rosario to contact the ISS and try to raise the SOYUZ if she could. Orel had 91/2 hours to get to the ISS while the Orion had 12 to go. Rose reported ISS on line and receiving them clearly. The SOYUZ had not yet responded. Rose tapped her tablet and displayed an animated scene for them all over the suit data net: the relative positions of the two space craft, the ISS and the earth were shown. Different colored dotted lines laid out the paths all were on. The SOYUZ was just coming out of the curve of the earth as far as they were concerned. Rosario reported that she thought it would be another 23 min before the interference from the physical earth and the upper layers of the atmosphere allowed them to communicate. Elk spoke briefly to the ISS reporting all nominal with the launch. Houston echoed the status and reported the SOYUZ trying to raise them. Houston relayed Rose' calculations for the open comms window. 20 min later Elkington returned to trying to raise the Russian craft. Hunter to Orel come in. Hunter to Orel come in. Orel here I have you 4 by 4. Sergei used the old air force code for signal strength and clarity. 5 by 5 being the best. The two ships exchanged greetings and status. The ISS reported being able to hear all from the two crafts. The comms link would be vital to orchestrating the ballet coming up. Hunter committed to staying off the circuit to the ISS except in the event of an emergency. Soyuz would keep clear until 2 hours prior to dock. The crew of Hunter quickly settled in to their assigned tasks as Digger and Jonesey started dock preps for the ship. They would approach in stages finally stopping 15 feet from the docking pod where they would be grappled by the arm and placed in the dock. Once locked down it would be a 25 min cycle to clear the airlock and open the capsule to the space station.

With minor differences all of the four launches would work the same. Technically they didn't need to have pilots. The smaller dragon supply capsules were remotely piloted. Same with the Virgin galactic Ares capsules. Astronauts were finicky about letting machines do what they did. Never mind that the space shuttle had been a rock with wings, they flew when it counted on reentry. Flyboys and Fly girls would always be the same. Rosario continued monitoring comms and running diagnostics. Janice and Elk worked thru a telemetry timeline for the engine glitch and sent that down to NASA. Orel and Hunter settled in.

Bob Royce and John Scanlon addressed the media. Several questions came at him over how much danger the astronauts were in if the engine had failed. Bob patiently explained that it would be nothing like the Challenger. The SLS had two other engines that could have put the crew into a safe orbit. They would not have made it to the ISS but the crew would be intact. The cargo and the rockets would be a total loss however. The Orion spacecraft had a thin shell for a cargo hold. The idea is that the cargo got loaded in and then removed to where ever it was destined. The shell was jettisoned after the cargo was removed. In this case the cargo would not have been off loaded when the shell was released into the atmosphere. That would have been a lot of US taxpayer dollars going up in flames. Both launches today were on track and the preps for tonight and tomorrow were on schedule. The dockings would take place as the French blasted off. Dragon following the next morning. Being near the equator meant that the ARES rocket had a quicker run to orbit and a quicker catch up to the space station. Only two hours quicker but none the less faster. By the time Dragon got up on Thursday, the other two crews would have had two days at the station. The hope was Zhou and his crew would be ready once the initial burst of adrenalin wore off and the Orel and Hunter crews were tired out.

The press interest in the flights had peaked. Several organizations were going to participate in a press conference from the ISS later in the week. Royce worked with the press liaison Matt Reid to coordinate the press conference.

Reid complained that he would not be able to keep someone from saying something stupid if it included twenty astronauts. Kat had suggested that they chose two or three people from the mission and let them do it. Royce wanted Elkington and Sergei to do it with Rosario and Janice. They all looked good and were smart and would play ball. Reid left to get to work.

Kat Williams read the report the technician had dropped on her desk and sat up at her station. She looked over at Bob catching his eye. She gave him a discrete signal. Bob wrapped up his talk at the podium turning the press over to John Scanlon and some flight techs to lead the press thru the mission profile. He made a bee line casually for Kat's station. She handed him the report: he read it and frowned." Do we know who"?

"No. There were no clues in the database and the items in the locker contained no finger prints". Kat replied.

"Who knows about this"?

"You, me, Raven, The President. Whoever ordered it done and whoever carried it out. And the person who found it".

"Who found them", Royce asked worried?

"Bob MacArthur Kat replied. Thank god he told no one. He brought the information straight to me. We haven't removed them yet. Or the plans".

 Royce considered. This was a serious breach. "I need to think".

Kat looked up. "Bob we need to be careful here . We have no proof. We can't just do nothing. We can't remove them without exposing what we know". Bob thought furiously. "Okay here is what we do: I want a camera installed in the equipment section in addition to the ones already installed. You do it. Whoever did this is going to check on them. I want Ravens help on this. I want to know when why and who did the last 3-d printer data base update. "I want to know who has access to the video feeds from the equipment section and who could alter them". "Lastly I want to change the plans in the database to disable the gun without the person knowing about it. We have the regular update in four weeks. We slip the changes in then".

Christ what a mess. Someone had slipped plans into the 3-d printer database for a gun. There was a firing pin and 12 bullets hidden inside the lip of a locker in the equipment section. Who would do this? Why? What would some government or person gain by taking over the mission, killing the crew and destroying the ship? Did they mean to do it during construction? Or after the ship was underway. Terrorists?

Royce looked at Kat, "what else don't we know"? Kat paused considering. "This took considerable knowledge of our operating parameters. Also a lot of computer skill. This was carefully planned. Whoever did this knew we were weighing the equipment after every evolution. They knew we had surveillance and they got around it". She continued grimly, "we need to check everyone again. Families too".

"Can we do it discreetly"?

"We need a good cover story".

"How about a genetic comparison for matriarchal and patriarchal abnormalities. We can get siblings in as well for family traits, Royce said.

"Excellent"!

"Dump the announcement in the release from today. Then get me the President". "She and Scanlon need to be up to speed with our response". Royce concluded.

" What about the committee", Kat asked?

"Fuck them right now. I have zero idea who I can trust".

CHAPTER 12

Launch day 090 1423 04 July 2021 ISS

Aboard the ISS the three crews were holding a ground rules meeting. Sergei was leading the meeting getting input from Elk and the ISS commander Mike Camby. The meeting was in the new mars work bay. The small room was crowded. The ISS contingent consisted of Camby plus the three arm operators. The full Orel and Hunter crews were there. Jonesey was taking pictures with his camera. The Hunter crew was decked out in their standard NASA Khaki colored slip on pants with gold colored polo shirts. The Orel crew had the same pants and Blue shirts. The ISS crew had a mix of blue and red colored shirts. The Dragon crew would be in white while the Ares personnel would be in Red.

Sergei floated in mid space by the docking port near the Orel craft. He called attention and received quiet. "Hello everyone! You are all in your places with bright shiny faces, so let's do this! Our friends on the ISS CMDR Camby and his troops have gotten a jumpstart for us by installing the handholds and brackets id's as steps 1 thru 3 on the Master Schedule tasks. Thank you". "So we are to proceed tomorrow morning at step 4. That occurs after the dock of the French. Both Orel and Hunter crews will suit up and EVA to assemble trusses and the platform. The arm will be used to position the trusses from the stowage on the outside into the perpendicular zero degree azimuth strut to allow the work platform to be built. Sergei tapped in commands to his tablet. "The live camera feed from the ISS is now on your tablets". The assembled troops consulted their tablets. "You can see the hand holds and the trusses with the platform tied to the station. The work boxes are staged as well. The sub steps and diagrams are all contained on your tablet as step 4 tasks. "Crew assignments are as follows: Hunter team A: Elkington, Gonsolvo, and Andrews on the Assembly of trusses. Hunter team B: Lincoln, Jones and Pickerel will be assist/safety. Orel team A consisting of myself, Nyguen, Larionov will be on the arm after it completes the truss work with the platform. Orel B is Keith, Sanger, and Datsuk for assist/safety. EVA order is Hunter A then B then Orel A and B". He paused looking at them all. EVA starts at 0820 for Hunter A. 0900 nominal for Hunter B. That's earlier if airlock is available. Hunter B should monitor A progress and judge when it's best to move into position. Orel A goes EVA at 1145. B follows at 1230 nominal. Elk I'll leave it to you if you want to have your teams ingress at that point or shift to assist us. That gives you 4 ½ hours to get those two trusses installed".

Elkington spoke up, "I know we can do that. We can leave B as assist since they will be out on the trusses at the end point". He continued, "Team A will attempt to retrieve brackets and handholds for the platform to try to get them installed as step 6 tasks".

Sergei grinned. "That leaves nothing for our French crew to accomplish you greedy wrench turner". "I'll leave Orel B as assist out on the platform to help you through that. Theoretical EVA max time is 11 hours. Royce has us limited to 9 hours. I see 8 hours of work out there. If we are short of our assigned tasks at 8 ½ hours I will have everyone get things repacked and pull the plug. Ingress is reverse order unless you are ordered in. Camby, your arm operator ready"?

The ISS station commander nodded. "You will have two on duty. I have 2 others suited as safety observers".

Sergei grimaced. "That's boring, thankless work. I'll buy at the green house when we get back home". Okay standard safety rules apply. Anyone can halt the evolution for any reason. When you hear the halt call, immediately stop and put whatever you are doing into a safe mode or condition. We will then discuss what's going on and get concurrence before we proceed". "Houston is not in charge of us. I am. To that end I have the final say". However, permission granted to tell me when I'm going to mess up. 6 days from now we have a mandated rest day. I'll leave it to you to get the rest you need. I need you at your best out there"." Now as Royce likes to say: does anyone know a secret? Anyone see any problems".

Janice raised her hand. "CMDR Ivanovitch the hand holds and brackets the ISS crews installed do not match the diagram on the tablet. I'm not sure where the error lies". Dead silence greeted this.

Sergei ordered the ISS camera to hold and zoom on the port side of the station. There were a series of 5 hand holds and 6 clip hooks where the astronauts would attach tethers or grab hold while they maneuvered around the station to both retrieve and position the trusses for installation. The installation was relatively simple; two prefabricated trusses would be attached to two separate points on the station side and they would meet and be bolted together. A platform would be added to the top. A third truss would be bolted on in the coming days. A fourth and fifth truss would extend out from the mid section into a much larger workspace which would hold the mars craft. Right now the attention was on the hand holds. Janice was calling up the diagram from the tablet. All regarded it. Then they looked at the camera feed.

Janice pointed to two hand holds and three hooks. "If you look at the landmarks you can see that the two hand holds on the left side of the screen are bolted on the wrong longitude marks". Like the lines on a map, the pattern of tapped holes made lines on the station. The hand holds could be bolted anywhere. They had reference marks. As Janice pointed out they were on the right "North" axis but were too far "west". Of course those references were just local and really meant nothing unless you looked at the station.

Sergei's eyes bored in on Janice. "Let me ask you this, if we left them alone would it interfere with our work"?

"Not today, she answered, but the arm operator is going to position the rover cube between those two hand holds on work day three while we maneuver the engine pod onto the platform". "At that point we won't be able to get the engine pod by the rover cube. We would have to tether hold one of them while the other got positioned. Basically the PODS would have to be held in bare hands while the other was moved". Not safe. Or they would have to figure another way on the fly. The hooks won't interfere and can be left in place", she concluded.

 Sergei tried to visualize the hooks and hand holds with what he knew of the procedures. "You're sure"?

"Positive".

Sergei turned to Camby. "CMDR, Dr. Lincoln has a remarkable memory. I believe her. Let's look at the diagram you guys worked under to see if there is any difference from ours. Elk, Dr. Lincoln, you two go with Camby and compare the two diagrams. Meet me back in Orel in 10 min. Rose lets go talk to Houston and tell them what's going on. Everyone else back to your ships. We meet back here in 30 min to go over the new plan".

 The call from the ISS to Houston had techs scrambling. Royce let his flight team work thru the issue. The problem was relatively benign: the diagram had been updated but the changes had not been included in the update for the ISS. Flight lead contacted Camby and Ivanovitch and relayed the findings. The diagram loaded on the tablet was the most up to date. Houston recommended fixing the hand holds prior to the truss work and concurred with leaving the hooks in place. Royce called flight lead. Make sure the French had the right diagram for the hand holds they were installing for the cubes. The headaches began in earnest.

Janice returned from the second meeting to prep her suit. The major difference from the original plan was that Hunter A would no longer try to install the brackets on the platform; they would move the two handholds after the trusses were installed. They and Orel B would ingress as soon as they finished. If things worked to plan all would finish in 6 hours. Sergei had accepted the recommendations from Houston and complimented her on the attention to detail. She had blushed under the praise and attention in front of the whole assembly. Sergei had grinned at her the whole time. She had made her video entry that day from the command deck on the Hunter. She kept gazing out the windows at the earth. Stunning. The view stunned her. The detail you could make out in the clouds. The way lightning lit up the dark storms. The utter blackness of space. She ended with a question for the Houston team: What would the earth look like from mars? Would it look like a bright star? A small moon? Would Jupiter look bigger from that perspective? She had a six hour sleep period coming up. The French were due to dock during that period. She wanted to see that. Well maybe not this one. She would be awake for the Dragon later in the day. Sergei was right. She needed to figure her rest or she would be exhausted. She saw Rosario coming back from Orel. They got some toothpaste food and went to snuggle into their sleep sacks. Weightlessness made for some weird sleep spots. Any wall you could anchor yourself to, served as a bed. She refrained from asking Rosario too many questions about Sergei. She hadn't seen him since they had that one night together three weeks ago. They had exchanged messages thru that woman. The relationship was over. The relationship was over but the scar was raw. Rose put the needle in a little. "It was magnificent how Sergei had taken control of the meeting and very decisive when the problem had come up, and gee, didn't he look cute in his little pajama pants"? "Shut it, Rose". "Hey if you want to throw him away, I'll be happy to pick him up". "Rose," she warned. "Okay, okay. Sisters before misters. Get some sleep. Loads to do tomorrow".

Janice stepped out of the airlock at 0842 behind Pickerel and Jonesey. She could see Hunter A arranged on the side of the

Space Station in a triangle formation. The robotic arm of the station had the first truss in its claw and was positioning it perpendicular to the station with a plate on the end closest to the station. The Ares capsule Argo was docked aft port back behind her. She twisted to see the ship and the rest of the station. The momentary wave went thru her as she saw the earth and up no longer was up. Janice snapped her vision back to the station as a reference point. The comm net in her helmet was fairly quiet with chatter coordinated for Elk and his team as they started to remove the four bolts from each offending hand hold. Janice and Jonsey took up positions above Hunter A with tethers to the hooks and access to the attached work box. Janice spared a glance for Pickerel as he had the most visually precarious spot. Working his way up the robotic arm he anchored his boots into the work station attached to the end of the arm by the claw. Elk called a safety check and all reported safe tethered or attached. Elk was booted in to the footholds slightly below the plate where the truss would be bolted in. Calling up the step by step procedures he projected the steps to the whole team thru the data link. Janice could call up the video from his camera and project that on her helmet display. Elk now called in the truss from the robotic arm operator. As the truss plate came into contact with the station hull plate the operator then rotated the truss to line up the holes. Elk called out the rotation needed in port or starboard and degrees of a circle. Port 20. Port 10. Stbd 2. Hold. Elk ordered Janice and Jonesey to tether to the truss and get ready to rock it to align it perfectly. Rosario and Digger now passed Elk the eight bolts that would hold the truss. The first four went in with no problems the next two had slight binding indicating they might be slightly cross threaded. Elk reported this and called no issue. Sergei and Houston quickly concurred. The final two went in with minimal issues. As the final torque spec was reached, Elkington called for a time check. 0930. Janice was startled. She was so focused on the procedure that she barely noticed the time. She realized she was a little uncomfortable holding on to the station and slightly adjusted her grip. Now the action shifted to the ISS and the arm operators. Pick made sure he was untethered from the installed truss and called in clear. Radio silence was maintained while the arm swung with the astronaut attached. The four trusses stored on brackets on the station were neatly lined up. The anodized hardened alloy gleamed in the sunlight as the arm approached. Larry Pickerell moved back down the arm to the truss brackets on the one end. Jonesey approached from the other end via the stations hand holds. Both called out clear and tethered when they reached position. Elk gave the go ahead for the arm to attach to the new truss. The operator fumbled for a few minutes but got the claw into a locked position on the truss support rail. Clear signal and an acknowledgement from all that the arm was swinging. This was no spot for an industrial accident. Eyes watched intently as the arm swung. Not just the space station and the astronauts but Houston, Kennedy, Russia, Guyana and all over. Silence on the comm net. None of the normal chatter that Sergei was accustomed to when they worked together on an evolution. People seemed very tense. Very. Sergei called a halt. The arm stopped swinging and everyone held their breaths. What? Why? Sergei went private on the net to Elk, Camby and the arm operator.

"Guys, I can hear the assholes puckering from inside Orel. Bobby what kind of music do you like", Sergei asked the ISS arm operator?

"Music", Robert Halderson asked? "I like both kinds, Country and Western".

Sergei laughed. "Okay, going full net again".

Sergei addressed the crews. "Okay, all clear I just thought we were missing something. Houston, request a little Tennessee Ernie Ford"?

"Roger, Station. Coming up".

As the truss arm swung out the deep voice of the old country standard started in softly. "I…   was born one morning when the sun didn't shine". 16 tons by Tennessee Ernie Ford. Grins appeared on faces all over the world.

Sergei said, "I just thought if NASA was going to work us this hard we should have the appropriate sound track. Carry on smartly".

A collective "oh rah" from the crews.

   4 hours later, Elk had called for the motorize wrench from the work box that was not part of his pre staged work tools for this space walk. Jonesey removed it and handed it off to Janice who in turn got it to Rosario who got it to Elk. He started to remove the bolts in turn. As they came out the bolts went up the chain back to the work box. Slowly, steadily Elk removed the four bolts and passed them down the chain. As the hand hold came out the tether to it was reeled in by Digger. Elk moved to extract the second handhold. Again the four bolts slid out and went up the chain.

Elk asked for a time check. 1343. Back on the chain gang from

Chrissy Hynde and the Pretenders played in the back ground.

Digger grabbed the hand hold and positioned it on the lines of bolt

holes. Elk called for verification from Sergei and Houston. Both

answered aye.

Elk looked over at Janice. "Do you agree?"

 Janice checked the handholds. "Perfect."

"Great, commencing." The chain gang got the bolts back to him

one at a time and the handholds were changed just that easily. Elk

paused and looked at the platform they had set up. The two trusses

looked a little odd without their third tripod cousin but that would

come. Two were plenty of support for the rover pod and its

engine. The 7 by 10 foot platform just begged for someone to stand

on it with the station in the back ground. Elkington hoped Jonesey

had got that picture when Orel A was up there. Elk looked back at

the airlock as the last of the Orel team entered. He was tempted to

try to convince Sergei to let him work on those brackets and hand

holds for the PODS on the platform. This was not delicate Hubble

space telescope repair work. This was true garage mechanic in

space action. Still. It was pretty fun. Elk called for a wrap up and

safety account. All tools accounted for and verified by

Houston. All tethers accounted for and verified. This walk was slightly abnormal because the pattern usually called for them to prep for the next evolution. Not so here. Just pack up and go in.
As they waited to enter the airlock, Janice called his attention over towards the earth side of the station. Technically below them. It made Elk dizzy when he lingered on that view. But now he could see the Dragon capsule and crew approaching the station low and behind. Catching up slowly. Elk had been monitoring the comms as they tried not to interfere with the on going work. Now the line was all theirs as they approached. Last man in called Elk as he cycled thru the air lock. Removing and storing his suit was fairly easy. He removed the tablet. God where would they be without them? Hanging the suit up in the temp locker in the Mars work bay, Elk turned to see most of the crews reassembled. Debrief. Good he thought let's get this over so we can get some chow and relax before doing this again. Sergei called them to quiet. "Okay comments"?

"The new suits are fantastic"! Rose called.

Cheers and agreements.

"Agreed. We never could have pulled that off with the old suits."

"How are the gloves for you Elk"?, the commander asked.

"Great, he answered. I have a degree of fine motor movements I have never had before and still have complete comfort. The info from the heads up displays is great as well".

Sergei called a cautionary note, "you can't have 5 separate data feeds going in for everyone. As much as it is improved there are still bandwidth limitations and info overload if you let all the pretty pictures distract you". "By all means if you need video help on a step or you want someone to take a look at what you're seeing go ahead. Just use some restraint". "Other items"?

"Can someone call times out"? This from Sanger.

Yes. No! It just puts pressure on the person doing the work to meet some schedule. It takes what it takes right?

"Yes but people are gauging follow on jobs and decision points based on time remaining", put in Elkington. Sergei paused. "Elk you got the time when you called for it right"? He nodded. "Why don't we keep that system Sergei continued. "If you want it and don't want to dig into the suit display just call for it". Camby, Elk and Serg all exchanged glances. Crap. That was a NASA mistake. The time should be pretty prominent on the heads up display inside their helmets on anything they did.

Sergei said, "I'll raise it with NASA. I'm debriefing Houston in

15. "Elk, Mike get the Ares crew in and settled. Their walk is pretty easy but I want to go over it with them. Say 1 hour"? "I need chow and a quick shower. Then I want both of you off your feet. 4 hours minimum". "Grace will be chomping at the bit".

As they moved off into the station Sergei was telling Elk how nice it would be to get a professional astronaut like Grace Adler in here to replace the screw ups he had to work with.

"Fuck you Sergei, you just wish you were as young as me and as pretty."

Royce signed off from Sergei's debrief and looked at the training lead. "How come this never came up as an issue in training"? "We spent a billion dollars on mockups and we get an issue right out of the gate"? The lead tech looked baffled. A small cough from another tech on the sides of the conference table. Royce swiveled. "Something to say"?

"The clock", came an awfully young female voice.

"What clock", barked Royce?

"In the pool. The Safety people made us put a huge clock with red numbers so the divers and the safety people are constantly aware of the remaining time for air. The astronauts got used to seeing

194

it during training". Uh oh. That sounded right.

"Well, Royce demanded, what is your recommendation to fix this"?

"We can move it so the safety people and trainer staff can see it but the Astronauts can't. That way it will be more like reality", she said.

"Okay. Make it happen. Then check every other mock up for other clocks and assorted anomalies. If it's not in space get it out of there. If it is in Space make sure we have one in the trainer"! Next get me the suit heads up display people. "Why in hell isn't the time displayed all the time"? "Go". Technicians started to scatter. "Not you". Royce pinned the female trainer tech to her seat with a gaze. Everyone else filed out of the room.

"What's your name?

Sara Faith DeAntonio. Royce blinked. "I know Johnny is short time but he will listen if you speak up. Talk to him. He will do what's right. How long have you been with us"?

"Two years", came the soft reply. "Where from"?

"Georgia Tech".

"With a name like DeAntonio"? "Were you lost"? Royce listened to her answer thinking that pairing this young woman with

Rosario's people skills would work well. "Well I just wanted to say well done and keep up the good work"!

Royce' Kat and Scanlon peered at the screen while the President conferred with someone off screen. "Sorry. I'm back. Bob, John, it looked good. I saw NASA TV actually had some viewers over the last two days. My granddaughter showed me the viral video of Ivanovitch playing Tennessee Ernie Ford. How does a Russian know about a 68 year old song from America"?

Royce paused. "Madam President that is why Sergei is the mission lead. He calmed those crews down with a song and moved us back on track when it got tight. It's hard to explain just what the mood was before he called for that song. Tense ,expectant, suffocating. Then he played that song and everyone relaxed and did their jobs. That's why it's him and not Watkins". "God save us If Tyler had been in charge. The job would have gotten done but the crews would have been exhausted and made mistakes down the road". He paused before sparking on another topic. "On the other hand look how well Elkington performed! Smooth and confident. He is a rising star. I'm telling you Mars 2 he will be a natural. A national hero".

"I guess you are going to gloat over Dr. Lincoln as well", the President asked.

"Well ma'am, you pay me to be right all the time not just some of the time. Speaking of which we need to discuss something else". Royce brought her up to speed on the stashed items. "I don't get it. Why not just hide a gun"?

"It wouldn't work, Scanlon explained. "We are x raying everything and weighing every item brought on board. We would have discovered them. The lip of that locker is actually solid so the bullets take up space and replace the weight with their own". Royce continued for him, "The gun can be made at anytime with the three d printer and some alone time". Three hours would be enough. If you were making something else it would be easy to get this job inputted".

"But who and why? Terrorists"?

"Ma'am anything I offer would just be speculation. This seems a little sophisticated"? "For terrorists. I mean they would have to disrupt the manufacturing process for the cabinet to get the lip hollow. Or come in after words and remove the lip without anyone noticing. After the locker was installed". Kat spoke up cutting off Scanlon with a look. "They would have to alter the 3-d database without us knowing and without leaving evidence of the attack. That points to a persistent state sponsored threat".

"China", President Clinton asked? "Why, Royce answered? "What do they have to gain"?

"I don't know. Maybe they can't stand to see us succeed and want to do this on their own. I don't know. Too many unknowns for my taste. "I am committing every resource at my disposal. I need you to ask the CIA and NSA if there has been terrorist chatter about an attack".

"We are looking at the workers and astronauts and the families again. We need some time to look into this", Royce informed her.

"This is the number 1 priority Bob, Clinton said. Getting that space craft built and launched safely is impossible without figuring this out. Now are you all set for the 8th"?

Yes, the press conference was going to go smoothly. He had to work out logistics with the Today show and the ISS but the link had been tested this day and seemed to work fine.

"Excellent. I expect an update ASAP". She broke the VTC connection without a second glance. John Scanlon looked at Bob and Kat. "Let me work on this. I have some contacts that may prove useful in getting this resolved. We will find the group

responsible". He left quietly.

Kat was the next to leave. "I think it's going to be more difficult

than that. This feels very personal to me. A gun in a space craft is

pretty close in and specific on who you hit".

"If it's a suicide pact then why not explosives? Bob agreed. "Kat,

they left some tracks somewhere. Find them. Quickly".

CHAPTER 13

Video log of Lui Zhou 07 July 2021 2219

Hello to Mr. Royce and the rest of the world. I am coming to you from the International Space Station. We have completed our third round of space walks to attach the rover with its engine and launch it towards Mars. The truss system is complete as well as the intermediate work platform. This is my second time on the ISS and the differences in the EVA suits and the data flow is stunning. We are significantly ahead of schedule and we are performing well together. The sight of all those suited figures crawling around the station and the work platform really makes me feel like we are making progress on the program. Perhaps for the first time I can see mars in focus. Not that we don't have hurdles ahead. We have to assemble and test the craft itself and then actually get to mars. But still, it is pleasing to be so involved in this great undertaking. The question of the day? What bugs me the most about space flight? When the toilet is clogged! Zhou departing.

Launch day 094, 08 Jul 2021 0435 aboard the ISS

Jon Jones aka Jonesey stepped from the airlock to the surface of the ISS carefully. He was heading up the side to the truss that held one of the huge solar arrays. He slowly worked his way out along the girder shifting the safety tether as he went. Reaching his desired spot he turned and faced the station. Awesome! The ISS was spread out slightly below him with the earth as the back ground. All over the surface of the ISS space suited figures worked. There were 28 people outside of the ISS performing some kind of work on the rover pod or engine. The comms net hummed with Sergei's voice calling out tasks and names. By the second EVA it became obvious they needed some way to ID themselves. They started with arm bands and quickly progressed to low tech tape. There were scarves tied around thighs, colored leggings, bits of yarn. Anyway to allow Sergei to keep track of who was where. Sergei and his newly appointed assistant Janice. Her memory was just too good to have her turning wrenches. She knew the procedures so well she could get a step status and give Sergei estimates on when they were likely to finish. Jonesey had to admit they were making outstanding progress. Both PODs were unloaded from the cargo holds and on the work platform. The engine rig was even now being attached by Grace Adler and Atlas A. The rig would hold the engine away and centered on what was a flat sided object. The rig attached at the four points and came to a circular hoop about 6 feet from the POD. The engine would ride in this hoop. Along the four sides the crews were also installing the electronics packages that would control the engine. A comms unit and control unit with a battery pack made up the bulk of the assemblies. Two teams worked on either side that made nine total astronauts on the platform and working. The engine was still in its crate, getting a check out by Sergei's own B team from Orel. Orel A team minus Sergei was serving as safety monitors. Dragon A and B had completed their assigned tasks as safety and assistants on the robotic arm and the trusses and they were now slowly making their way back to the airlock. They were at the end of their work day. That was why Jonesey was out there now taking pictures. He was the last of Hunter to go out the airlock. Digger and Rosario were now on the other end of the Rover Pod from Grace attaching the heat shield and the parachute packs. The shield and parachutes came as a package and attached on a frame work on the top of the POD. After protecting the POD from the heat of reentry, the shield would pop off exposing the parachutes which would deploy and gently set the rover down on mars. At least that's what they thought was going to happen.

As the team connected the data sensor line/command signal cable down to the electronics package that Atlas B was working on. That was about it for today. Tomorrow would see the engine attached and then a few days of testing. Assuming the testing went well, the teams would then start prepping the platform for the air plant and engine POD work which would be done in 50 days. The major issue was the turnaround time on the big launch systems. Kennedy had to turn the SLS in 62 days. The Russians had claimed they would be ready. Sergei had hoped to give them some extra time. It looked like the timelines NASA had developed had some extra float in them. They just couldn't believe the capabilities of the new suits. The data flow combined with the ease of use made the new space suits the highlight. Just the comms flow alone was a whole level above what NASA had struggled with in the 90's. The fact that the hardware had all been put together on the ground tested and then repacked had ensured that at least all the pieces would be there. These two POD/Engine mates were the ideal testing ground to evaluate what worked and what didn't. So far it was working. As Grace and Keith brought their teams from the engine and the rover PODS back to the airlock, Jonesey chimed in to Sergei to see if there was anything he wanted filmed. Sergei requested he work his way out to the platform as the others exited to get close ups of the engine rig and the parachutes. NASA had the ISS cameras trained on the work but some closer better resolution shots would always be welcomed. Jonesey rogered up and started "down". Camby and the ISS crew passed him on the way to the airlock. It was close to where Sergei and Janice were standing. Janice would follow Camby's group into the lock. Then Sergei. And Jonesey would be last out last in. Jonesey got a good close up of Sergei and Janice with the solar array behind them. They were talking on the net just between themselves and there was a look of respect and rapport between them that Jonesey instantly recognized. So, it's like that eh, he thought. Cool.

Later in the debrief, Sergei had Elk, Adler, Zhou, Camby, Keith, Digger, Edminton, Lincoln and Laurent the ISS arm operator all in the work bay. They had found that trying to get everyone in for the debrief was unworkable. The team leads had the responsibility to get the info out.

Digger was telling Sergei about a potential problem with the data command cable from the parachute pack. "I think it got pinched when the plasbond panel edge came down. I just can't tell if it's good or not". Jonesey had spoken up. Pulling up the video he had taken on his tablet he digitally zoomed in on the cable. It clearly showed the crease in the cable insulation. Okay.

"Houston are you seeing this, Sergei queried? Do we have another cable up here? Does it make sense to try to repair it"? Should we test first or remove and test outside the system? Do we let it alone"?

Houston answered back. "ISS, we see the cable. There is a second complete electronics rig in Dragon. It is supposed to stay there after being tested sat to be used on the Air plant POD. Don't test it in place now. Remove and replace prior to beginning the testing. Bring the cable back in and leave with the ISS guys. Cherbotsky is a fiber optic repair qualified tech. He can fix it at his leisure".

Camby rogered. Houston had been monitoring the work and had seen the possible damage.

Sergei spoke softly. "Digger why are we having this conversation in here and not out there? Houston for that matter why didn't you guys say something"?

Silence greeted this. James Andrews looked Ivanovitch in the eye and said "because we have four separate teams working on separate work packages up here. It doesn't make sense to stop

205

all work on all items just for a possible problem on one cable. I made a call to install and bring it up out here. I figured that the single cable could get repaired or replaced while other testing and the engine install were going on. I think Houston didn't say anything because they weren't going to stop us in the middle either. You saw how quickly they came back with the plan when you brought it up. They obviously had been monitoring and would have said something to you if I didn't". The team leads all looked at Sergei.

Affirmative was all Houston said.

"Sergei we are going to make some calls up here. We all are. You can't manage everything everywhere", Digger concluded.

Sergei nodded. He muttered something that sounded to James like "God's parts…   ". Huh? Must be a Russian thing.

"Okay Digger. Sorry. I do trust you. Sorry Houston, wound pretty tight here today".

"ISS, Royce here, roger that Orel, no need. Every one of you is to be congratulated. Today was one of the finest performances of precision engineering under extraordinary circumstances that I have ever seen. I speak for the committee and the whole world when I tell you no one else could have performed better and we are proud of you. Orel, it's up to you but you can bring the day 102 event forward to tomorrow if you wish". Royce was giving him the option to take a day off. Sergei looked at Digger and the rest. Some tired faces out there. "Houston that's a big roger. I got a ton of laundry to do". Smiles spread around. "Thank you Houston. We will contact you an hour prior to today's press conference". "Roger, Houston out".

Sergei blew out a breath he had been holding. "Okay anything else"? "Remember it is me, Lincoln, Elk and Rosario for the press conference but anyone can drop by if they want to wave. Jonesey you have the video? Good. I got the feeling NASA and the NBC folks would be happy to show a crowded space station. Other than that, everyone is down for 24 plus hours. Brief of the next EVA's is at 0620 on day 096. Thank you." The crew scattered.

Janice watched as everyone turned for their respective ships and a little down time. Eat sleep shower sleep eat sleep. Sleep some more. That sounded good. It was physically exhausting doing all this mental work. Janice watched Sergei go to the Orel capsule with a heavy heart. She knew he was hurting and exhausted. The strain of keeping track of every facet was a weight on him. He had always seemed to be smooth and in control, but Janice knew he sweated stuff just like the rest of them. She wanted to go to him and wrap her arms around him but that wasn't happening.

Working together so closely over the last three days had been exquisitely painful. She had balked when he asked her to help him but even she had seen the need. She was good at the traffic cop thing while he kept an eye on the big picture. But he couldn't keep an eye on every picture. Hence the discussion with James. She made her way back to Hunter. She had one hour before they came to get her for the press conference. She hoped Sergei was resting as well.

The hour flew by for Rose. She had taken advantage to shower quickly when she hit the airlock. Got to look my best for the spotlight. She got a quick bite and was updating her video blog when Takeshima, the first female Japanese astronaut came to get them. Her, Janice, Elk and Digger made their way to the ISS VTC area. It was indeed crowded. Sergei and Camby were already there. Jonesey was conversing with someone on screen. Six other crew members from the station or the ships just happened to be in the back ground. Rosario saw Digger go up to Sergei and put an arm on his shoulder.

Sergei said something and Digger laughed. "I'll hold you to that", was what he said and moved off. Camby had them line up Janice, Elk and Digger in the back with Sergei and Rose sitting in the front. Well it was hard to say sitting when weightless and floating was a better description. The ISS screen was split showing the NBC feed and NASA Houston. Royce, Kat Williams, and surprise Tatiana Medvedev were sitting waiting on the NBC producer.

When they noticed the crew members on screen Royce said hello they were looking well. They all affirmed and cut off when the NBC producer, a harried looking man came on screen. "We just got this video feed uploaded into our system. We have chopped it down to around seven minutes." CMDR Ivanovitch can you id what we are seeing as it comes up." "Certainly."

The screen showed the first shot of the space station as seen from one of the approaching ships. Sergei guessed the Dragon capsule Wyvern because the other three ships were visible on approach. The producer chimed in: "can you talk about how this is the first time there have been four ships docked at the station. The most before were two during the 90's and later when a resupply mission was underway." "Then we go back to the widest possible shot of the interior of the space station. CMDR you will have those guys stay in position right?"

Sergei affirmed. Camby flew off to lock them down.

"Next we go to the working shots." Various shots of astronauts unpacking workboxes, installing brackets and handholds, appeared on the screen. Sergei described it all. Then the money shot of all 28 astronauts working as the camera panned the station and the platform. Impressive said the producer. Next came a series of launches from Kennedy, Russia, Guyana and the Chinese base. The producer stated that the hosts would talk about the international flavor of the mission. Sergei and Rosario beamed. Lastly was an artist's rendition of the mars landing site with the craft upright on the surface next to it. The producer was pleased.

 This was three segments long. The first was an introductory shot of both Houston and the ISS while the host Rachel Maddow introduced them all. Rachel was filling in for Savannah Guthrie while she did the news that was normally Rachel's. Job swap. Joining Ms. Maddow would be Natalie Morales and Travis Stork. Everyone got that? Then Rachel would start with Houston and Royce and ask questions. Switching to the ISS Natalie Morales would lead Sergei thru the video after he introduced the team.

They might get one question in then commercial. Once they were back the video would run on a back drop while they fielded questions. Sample questions: Are you conscience of the legacy of Neil Armstrong? Why Mars? What benefits do we get? Dangers of the missions. Dr. Lincoln you might want that one. Last segment would go back to Houston for an update on the next steps. There would be an offer for Royce to make history and announce the Mars crew today. Royce politely declined. For the ISS team he told them anyone who said they were a lock to go to mars would instantly find themselves on the bottom of the list. Groans. The producer told them there would be two teases where the video from the ISS would be live while the hosts went to commercial. If anyone needed to pick their nose now was the time. More groans.

"We are back, said Rachel Maddow. "Joining ne now via the miracle of technology is Dr. Robert Royce from NASA. Dr. Hello and thank you for talking to us today, I know you are busy".

"My pleasure Rachel", Royce said smiling brightly.

"Who is with you, please introduce them".

"Certainly this is my deputy Katherine Williams and we are

pleased to have with us the Director of the Russian Space Agency Ms. Tatiana Medvedev". Tatiana said hello.

"Hello again to you all and welcome. Dr. Royce let me start with you. The host started in. "The nation and the world have been riveted to the shots of the astronauts working on the mars mission on the International Space Station. Can you give us an update on that work"?

"Rachel I am pleased to say the work is ahead of schedule and going very well. We have begun to realize that we can be even more aggressive with the schedule and perhaps we will be complete before the 19th. We need to get these capsules on the ground and recovered to give the next round of launches the maximum time to prepare".

"That sounds fantastic Dr. Ms. Medvedev how confident are you in the ability to turn around the launch facilities"? "After all you have never done two launches in 60 days."

"Ms. Maddow we have the utmost confidence in our cosmonauts and in the ground crews supporting them. I heard a phrase today that I will repeat. Today was one of the finest performances of precision engineering under extraordinary circumstances that I have ever seen. Our facilities personnel will do no less".

Natalie Morales knew a que when she heard one: "Thank you Director Medvedev lets meet the people who performed those precision engineering feats today. Hello International Space Station". There was a 3 second delay.

"Hello Natalie this is Sergei Ivanovitch from the Mars team. CMDR Ivanovitch thank you for joining us. Who is with you there"?

"Natalie, Sergei said confidently "I am pleased to be joined by the finest crewmates a person could wish for. This is CMDR. Rosario Gonsolvo. Behind me is Dr. James Andrews, Dr. Janice Lincoln and CMDR Brad Elkington".

Ms. Morales waited an extra beat before she segued into the video. "CMDR Ivanovitch, I think we have some exclusive video of some of the work you are doing could you lead us thru it.

"Certainly." Sergei got thru the opening shot of Wyvern approaching the ISS and then the various shots of them working when Natalie cut in.

"CMDR can I hold you right there while we go to commercial". "Of course". "We will be right back". 240 seconds of commercials passed very quickly. "And we are back on Today. 11 past the hour on the 8th of July 2021. I'm Natalie Morales and with me is part of the crews working on the Mars mission parts and we are going thru some remarkable exclusive footage. "As you can see joining us from the ISS is CMDR Sergei Ivanovitch Dr. Rosario Gonsolvo, Dr. Janice Lincoln, and CMDR Brad Elkington. Who did I forget? Dr James Andrews forgive me please. There you are".

"No worries".

"CMDR Ivanovitch you were leading us thru this video please continue".

"Yes you can see here several of us working on the platform. Our task has been to construct the truss system which holds the work platform away from the body of the ISS. That is similar to the way the solar arrays are held out away from the station. The assembled astronauts bobbed in place. "Once the platform was built the PODS carrying the rover and the engine were placed by the stations robotic arm. Today has been the busiest day in space ever recorded. 29 astronauts. Here you can see all of us crawling around".

Natalie interrupted. "Do you get in each others way"?

Sergei laughed, "sometimes. We have things pretty scripted and we have split into teams so we are not all in the airlock at one time. But I have a pretty capable traffic cop in Dr. Lincoln. I apologize for using the one of the smartest women in the world as a traffic cop but her eidetic memory means she can grasp the whole much better than I and tell me what to do. I'm really the beauty part of this operation".

Natalie laughed. "Well speaking of beauty I know that CMDR Gonsolvo has a pretty extensive fan club. CMDR. are you aware of the you tube clips and the Facebook followers you have?

Rosario shrugged it off. "I'm just a glorified mechanic, but I appreciate the support".

"Travis do you have some questions for the crew"?

"Yes. Thank you Natalie. Dr. Lincoln what would be the major danger you would face on the mars mission? Janice was at least prepared to talk to Dr. Stork. "I believe it will be radiation exposure".

"Are you worried about the risks"? She went thru the standard spiel about trying to lessen the exposure. "In the end it represents a 3% increased risk. I think we can live with that".

"Is the crew prepared for a medical emergency in space? Well, Dr. Fong and I are both medical doctors but not surgeons. The mars crew would have the equipment available but not the

215

experience to use most of it".

Brad Elkington bailed her out. "NASA has done an extremely good job of weeding out potential risks. Even now we are undergoing genetic screenings for cancer risks and other potential problems". "CMDR are you concerned as an African American that there might be a genetic weakness such as sickle cell that would disqualify you"? "No that one is pretty easy. I've been tested long ago for that".

Travis persisted. "CMDR Ivanovitch I have heard rumors that you had an epileptic incident"?

Sergei frowned. "No, I have never had epilepsy. Someone must be pulling a fast one on you", he said.

Rachel Maddow again took over. "When we come back we will talk again to NASA and the ISS crews about where we go next. Stay tuned".

Sergei and Elk shared a look. Royce was completely blank. When Rachel popped back on the screen she started back with Royce.

"Dr. Royce how much is this costing in terms of current outlays"?

"18 billion so far with 12 or so to go", Royce answered smoothly.

"What did the Apollo project cost"?

"200 billion in today's dollars. 10 years of effort. We are 6 in with two to go for 30-40 billion".

"What do we gain by that effort"? Royce stepped onto the soap box. "Rachel look at your screen. Those space suits. 5 years from now that technology will allow firemen who are limited to 30 min timeframes in their suits to go for 90 min. That makes a big difference when you take into account how many men you need to put out the average house fire". "That filtering technology will allow dirt cheap desalinization to be realized. How much is it worth if Los Angeles could pump water from the ocean to irrigate crops and provide drinking water without taking it from the Colorado river"? "And its here now. We are using that technology in our own filtration systems on the ISS and the mars craft. There is a revolution in computing taking place with these quantum computers. How much is it worth in increased productivity to silicon valley if a program that allows the computer to tag every car and driver in the bay area and integrate that with instantaneous highway data to understanding where you are commuting to and when you are going to do it"? You can then synchronizing every traffic light across the region to decrease traffic jams. Same with air traffic".

Royce paused inhaling to pound home his arguments. "If the

system can keep track as a whole of everything going on at once it allows the computer flexibility to make changes on the fly and alleviate bottlenecks as they occur". Cars and planes go faster with fewer delays. Productivity increases". "Those are just technological items. The biggest question is are we alone out here and is there life on mars can be answered. Are there obstacles? Certainly. But the whole world benefits. This is not NASA's show. This is a total earth effort".

Maddow shifted gears, "Director Medvedev, we have noted a general thaw in some fairly thorny relationships, notably Russia and China. Do you credit the Mars Program with that new closeness"?

Tatiana smiled brightly for the camera. "The Mars Program was founded on the basic principle that all would contribute and all would benefit. We have found willing partners throughout the Mars program. The French have been outstanding in providing expertise on some aspects of program management that we have previously had problems with. The Chinese are newer to the Space Race than some of us but that doesn't mean we can't learn from them. In the end this is a structure of relationships. Mine with Dr Royce. She smiled. Director Chan with Minster Legarde, and so forth. We have been working together showing what is possible." I know that I have helped some small way in some trade disputes and some patent enforcement actions, so the cooperation does seem to be spilling over as we get more comfortable with each other. What is the saying? Travel is the enemy of bigotry".

Picking her que with dexterity, Rachel cut back to a shot of the astronauts. "Well my friends it seems as if you have a long journey ahead of you. Thank you everyone! Good luck and Godspeed. We'll be back".

The connection broke and everyone scattered, chattering. Houston signed off. Janice waited a moment with Rose. "How do you think it went?"

We will know when we get back. If Royce yells at us then we know it was bad". "What are you going to do with 35 hours of free time"?

"Workout, shower, sleep, eat. Repeat as necessary", Janice answered.

Rose laughed. "Me too. Maybe some video games later"?

"No that junk rots your brain"! "Aiy, you would say that and ruin it for me. Your loss. See you".

Janice went and changed into some clean pants and went for the treadmill. Dr. Hoffman was just finishing. The treadmill was that in name only. It had resistance bands on both legs to keep the occupant strapped in. Janice got a good 20 min in while people piled up behind her waiting to use the machine. They played zero gee games while waiting: human arrow, gymnastics, and air swimming. She finished and took a crazy shower which consisted of zipping herself into a plastic bag and putting water inside. After wetting herself she soaped up and then rinsed as best as possible. Lots of weird gyrations to get water applied and soap off. The shower was more of a workout than the machine. Dinner consisted of more toothpaste tube food. Janice missed the food at the port restaurants in Coco Beach. Even gator tail. She wandered thru the station and the other ships. That seemed to be the main object of people. Most had not had a chance to see the actual hardware for the Atlas or the Wyvern capsules. She took it all in while talking shop with the other mars program astronauts not in the Gold group. Like wise she gave tours of Hunter for Li Fong and Dr. Leon.

After an initial burst of activity people drifted off to get some rack time. The station had a quiet hum that seemed to lull her off. Janice found herself in the Mars Bay with CMDR Camby.

The one port window had a pretty decent view as the earth rotated. The best view was in the viewing station forward of the ISS, but that was crowded. CMDR Camby made his good bye's and she was alone for a little while. She literally smelled him first. Janice spun seeing Sergei in the opening between Orel and the bay. She must have looked startled because Sergei moved to go back inside Orel. "Wait". He turned. "Sorry, didn't know you were here. I'll give you your space".

"No I just…   "

"Didn't want to deal with me I get it. Look I said sorry for grabbing you up to do the evolution check off but you were the only one capable of it".

"No I just…   "

Didn't want to work with me I get it. You're not mad about the comment on the interview are you? I was just teasing".

"No, I just…   "

"Didn't want to see me. You made that plain when you sent that message thru Tatiana". They had been drifting towards each other in the zero gee and Sergei immediately knew he had made a mistake with Tatiana. Janice face suffused with blood and anger. She reached him and grabbed his shirt front to steady herself.

221

She slapped him as hard as she could. The effect was muted as they both spun off and apart. A zero gee experiment in action reaction.

"Don't you ever mention her name to me again! Didn't you know how humiliated I was"?

"No, I just..."

"Thought you could order me around like any one of your girlfriends, huh"?

"No, I just …   "

Sent me a message thru that bitch? Besides this can never work. Did you forget we were going to be subject to a million prying eyes about our relationship?"

"No, I just…   "

"Thought with your balls as usual. The great Sergei Ivanovitch Russia's answer to Don Juan". Oops that one might have been a little over the line. Now it was Sergei's turn to grab her. "Now you listen here. Giving that message to ta…   "   He held up as she balled her fist and tried to kill him. "That woman was the only way to get a private message to you". I know you don't trust her but I do. And I didn't forget a thing about us. I know what we are in for and I don't care. I kind of…   love you". "I don't know

222

why but you just work for me. Yes we have some obstacles but I know you love me so we can work thru the rest. Tell me I'm wrong".

From an objective observer's point of view they were now 180 degees turned to the floor from where they started. Upside down in effect. They had drifted into the corner of the bay opposite the window.

Janice's eyes were filled with tears. "You hitched a little on the L word Mr. Smooth".

Sergei grinned as he moved to kiss her. "First time I ever meant it".

They kissed passionately. Janice broke them apart.

"We are not having sex in zero gee".

"Yes we are".

"No we are not".

"Come on! Please!

"No."

"How about some zero gee heavy petting"?

"No!"

"Don't you know how tightly I'm wound up? I need some help over here".

"You're fine. No dice".

"Man you are tough. More kissing followed the wheedling. "How about first base"?

"No".

"Prude".

"Hey you don't have a bet with Elkington about this do you"?

"I… "

"I swear I will skin you alive if I find out there was ever a wager on me putting out in space".

"Are we talking just near earth space or the whole vastness of the cosmos. Ow, ow. That hurt. Stop. Okay I give".

UNITY

CHAPTER 14

Launch day 102 16 July 2021 0400 aboard the ISS

Dr. Li Fong was awakened slowly. She had about an hour to the next brief. Today would see the launch of the Rover POD to Mars. The launch would be really anticlimactic. Just a brief burst from the engine and the POD slowly moving away. The major work of these launches had been accomplished. The dragon crew and Wyvern had left the station yesterday. Her comrade CMDR Zhou had left. That freed her to accomplish the mission from the Chinese command. She was not looking forward to it. She had no choice in the matter. Command had been insistent. She had been receiving instructions in the family video exchanges they had been receiving on the station. She really only had today to do it. Atlas was scheduled to disembark on the 18th. With Orel and Hunter following the next day. She knew early would be the time to accomplish it. Their pattern was early. Li wriggled out of her sleep sack. It always reminded her of the hammock in the small room she had shared as a child. She was used to small spaces. She dressed and slipped the camera into the waistband of her pants. Slowly she left the Atlas capsule and floated down to the Mars work bay. Approaching obliquely from the side of the passageway she peered around the corner. There. Taking the camera out she snapped pictures as quickly as she could. She took a few seconds to orient and allow the auto focus to work before the next series. The camera worked silently. She crept back and went down the passage towards the ISS main work bay. She passed CMDR Camby going the other way. Nodding at each other, Li got her chow. Well it was done. The guilt pangs started. She pushed them down. The mission was all. Anything was worth a trip to mars.

Camby floated down to the Mars work bay. He needed to initiate the data vid link to Houston for the launch brief. As he entered he saw that Sergei and Janice were already in the bay. He started to ask how they were when he noticed the flustered look on Janice face. "Uh,,. Everything okay"?

"Yes CMDR I'm fine, just discussing procedures with CMDR Ivanovitch. He is very stubborn about wanting things his way". Sergei flashed out, "and Dr. Lincoln is well known for her flexibility in certain areas".

Camby was at a loss. "Okay. I need to initiate the vid link to Houston. Why don't you guys get some chow before the show"?

"That's a fine idea", said Dr. Lincoln. She propelled herself out of the bay with one big push off. Camby watched her go. "Serg, he said, I always thought Tatiana or Kat was the most dangerous woman you were ever with". "But that woman don't play. She will flat kill you. She's not the put on a diaper and drive cross country to shoot someone kind of crazy, but she will just flat kill you, if you mess with her".

Sergei agreed. "Yeah, I'm out of my weight class with her. On the other hand, I do love her".

Camby looked shocked. "Did I hear that? Love from the Russian Romancer"?

Sergei looked abashed. "Hey could we hold off on those nicknames please".

"This is big news but you need to be careful my friend. Cool it until after the mission. NASA will tolerate a certain amount but once it starts getting them negative publicity they will come down like a ton of bricks".

"Yeah I know. I'm trying but it's hard".

Camby agreed. "Yeah certain parts of you is hard".

"Shut up! What are we in grade 5"?

Camby laughed as Houston came on the line. "Houston come in
ISS Camby here. What a beautiful day"!

 "Roger ISS, that it is. We have good data and vid quality.
 Confirming brief at 0505".

'Roger". He nodded at Sergei, "chow down hound then come back
for the debrief. Three days and I can go back to peace and quiet".

A little over two hours later at precisely 0720 the robotic arm
grasped the rover pod by the installed grappling eye. The ungangly
POD lifted easily in the weightless vacuum. Swinging it away
from the station the arm operator acknowledged that Houston had
control of the POD. Getting the affirmative from Houston he
released the pod to space. It slowly, slowly, floated away from the
station and above it. It took 15 min for it to get 300 meters away.
 The countdown from Houston started. 60 seconds later the engine
flared for approx. 5 seconds. The pod accelerated then steadily
pulled away. It was so small it dwindled quickly. Houston
reported good control and comms signals from the POD. JPL
reported the same. In two days the POD would be in the best

position to start a longer burn. JPL would control the craft from there to touch down. Once the POD got to mars the craft would communicate with both The radar mapping satellite around mars called mPOS and the Curiosity rover on the surface already to establish the PODS exact position. Then the vectored nozzles of the engine would project the POD down into the atmosphere. The heat shield would protect the parachutes which would deploy to slow the decent down to a small level and then a soft touch down next to the main landing site. JPL was promising within 100 meters. Heavy betting was already underway. Sergei briefed out the teams: NASA was pleased. The world was pleased. 10 days early. They should be proud. Loads of lessons learned but the concept of assembly in space had been proven. One more walk to set out work boxes and brackets for the air plant and its engine POD. Let's not mess up now. A mostly new group of astronauts would be up to do that work. That schedule was even now getting ripped up in favor of a more aggressive one. Sergei thought they would have a few problems, but Elk was going to lead them. He would get it done. To that end Elkington was doing the walk brief and would lead the 9 space walkers on the final walk. Then it was button up, say good bye and head home.

Launch day 108 22 July 2021 1003 Kennedy Space Center

The assembled group consisted of the mars flight candidates, all 43 remaining, another 150 or so astronauts from various agencies around the world plus the relevant project managers from the contractors and the associated government agencies. The crowd of 600 people were the drivers of this project and they were in the VAB auditorium to here from Bob Royce. The four crews had returned safely to a hero's welcome. Mars had seemed to take on a reality in the people's imagination. Royce was there to congratulate them.

Bob stepped to the podium. "Ladies and gentlemen I am uploading onto the Livelnk contractor website and the NASA info link site, the debrief of the recently concluded Rover POD mission. Flight candidates can access it on the tablets. The report contains 25 mission critical findings. It has 35 immediate changes to the operating procedures changing the way we do business. 35 ways we can be safer, better. And better we have to be. The crowd stirred a bit at this. Who can forget the majestic site of 29

UNITY

astronauts working in unison on the space station to get the mission accomplished? Who can forget the majestic site of astronauts with bits of colored yarn tied around themselves as identification? We looked like the luggage conveyor carousel at Dulles. Grumbling. We had three instances of equipment damage during lift or assembly or test that could have scrubbed the mission. More grumbling. We had to create a new position of assistant team leader on the fly to get thru the procedures. We never thought of that. We get paid to think of those things. We have to do better. You thought you were coming here for a victory lap? Think again. That was milestone eight on a 35 item list. Victory lap? Save that nonsense for day 1122. We don't celebrate doing our jobs. I expect you to be outstanding. The day we have a debrief that has zero findings or areas for improvement I will fire the evaluation team and start over. Bits of yarn tied to a 4 million dollar EVA suit? Royce was red in the face and rolling. You all better do better than that. Someone is going to get killed if we don't perform better. Not on my watch. I want every project manager to have a detailed explanation of why the particular finding came in their area. I want a concrete recommendation for what you are going to do about it by Thursday. Anyone who misses that deadline is fired. Astronauts. This project is not your play toy. 2 broken bolt wrenches? You're lucky I don't dock your pay to recompense the world's peoples for their hard earned money. Think I'm being unreasonable? The door is that way. I want full reports from each of you per the tablet instructions by Thursday. If I get fired by the committee during my debrief next week its nothing more than what I deserve for allowing you to run roughshod over the world's most important project. Anyone have any questions? If I still have a job Friday I will be speaking to you. Dismissed.

"Calm down". Sergei, Elk, Rose Janice and Digger were all in Janice and Rose' room in the kitchenette. Janice was fuming. "That was totally unfair. We preformed outstandingly! He has no right to lambast us like that! We were 10 days early! We got the rover mated and launched without a hitch"! She grumped. Sergei smiled down at her. "What's Bob Royce's biggest fear"?
"That we die on mars", she answered.
"Not necessarily. What if we get to mars and a meteor hits the landing site and kills us all"? Bob won't really sweat that", he reasoned with her.

"Gee, Sergei thanks for the visual", came from Elk.

Janice objected. Why not? We'd still be dead".

"Soldier's chance", Rose put in.

"Yep. That's it. The meteor is a risk we can accept", Sergei went on. "It sucks and it's bad but Bob has looked at that risk and accepted it. If it happens well tough luck you took a soldiers chance. The same chance a soldier takes when he or she goes into battle. If that bullet has your name on it there is nothing you can do". Sergei shrugged. "No. What keeps him and I up at night is the .99 part. That some small inconsequential part will fail and doom us all". We get paid to think about those things. We broke 2 wrenches on the station. How many spares did we have," he asked her?

"Plenty, we had eight others", Janice came right back.

"How many of those wrenches are we taking to Mars"?

"Three".

"So we broke two in 13 days. In 330 days on mars how many will we brake"?

"Uh. More obviously".

"Could we have fixed the two we broke"?

"Maybe, I don't know".

236

"One I think yes one I think no, Sergei went on sipping on his water bottle. "So what would the effect be if we had no wrenches on the surface of mars"?

"Well if we need to open a food POD because we are starving, then that wrench becomes pretty important. So how do we work around that"? Standard risk mitigation right?" Procedures, equipment design, and training. "We are all qualified on the wrenches, which means we know how to use them properly". We can fix small issues and we can repair major ones. "If need be we could print one out that would work well enough to get into the POD". Plus we have spares onboard". He paused a little to let that sink in. "But now we have some data that suggests that the number of spares might not be enough. "We have some failure rate data on different parts of the wrenches. What are we going to do with that data? Is there a manufacturing problem? A use problem? A procedural problem? All that needs to be looked at before the air plant mate launches in 53 days". Royce won't be happier until that series of launches is over and no wrenches brake. Then some small part that he didn't think of will not be responsible for killing us all", Sergei concluded .

Elk took over. "Look at his problem with your position up there. You did a marvelous job up there. Why didn't we discover that communications problem in training"? Think about it. How many training evolutions in the pool did we have with 29 people involved"?

"None that I participated in.

"Why"?

"I don't know." Janice finished. "Can the pool handle that number"?, she asked interested now.

"Nope. 13 max astronauts", he answered. "So we broke down the tasks into A and B team units and practiced separately. Now it is plainly clear we need to practice en mass. You can bet your ass that the first thing tomorrow I'm going into Royce's office and demand the full Air plant team in Houston for three days of en mass pool training".

"But the pool can't take that many people, she objected.

"Not my problem. That's what Royce demanded. Fixes. Well that's the fix". "If he can't figure it out, then he deserves to be fired", Elk said with a certain amount of malice.

"You have a fix in mind don't you", Janice said.

"I have a thought. I want to run it by Sergei first. The point is we will be working with better realism and that will be better for all of us". Sergei and Elk broke off and went outside to talk.

Janice felt marginally better. But Royce was not her favorite person right now. He has it easy. A few briefs and a few press conferences and he's good to go. They had to do the actual work.

Bob had just completed his debrief of the committee. They had come to sing his praises but Tatiana nailed him. She had grilled him mercilessly on the yarn problem and the wrenches. The cable repair was pretty simple and not deemed to be a tough fix. The yarn? Bob would have a specific plan of action to go over with for the committee next week. He had some preliminary thoughts but didn't want to articulate them until his team had had a chance to go over the findings. What about ramifications for the next series of launches? Couldn't they just use the same teams to do the air plant as well? No the idea was to give all the flight candidates some time up. They needed to revamp all of the procedures based on the new model of running items thru a secondary person. It seemed to work but they needed to formalize it. It was also tougher than Janice Lincoln had made it seem. They were working on ways to ease some of the administrative burdens on the assistant. Checking off steps was a good way to keep track but it could get confusing.

Royce commented that the best person on the Air plant team going

up was Li Fong. She also had an eidetic memory. The Chinese

rep had stiffened at this. They didn't think that Royce had figured

that out yet. Oh Royce was fully up to speed on Li Fong. Three

hours of punches from Tatiana was enough to drag anyone down.

Thank god she had e-mailed her questions to him last night. He

had even fed her some questions. That had allowed him to steer

the committee in some directions he wanted to go. So. He had

retained his job without much trouble. The speech to the ops

group was a slight exaggeration and he had won the right to

explore some new training spots to overcome the comms issues.

 Sergei and Elk stepped into the office.

Royce looked up. "What do you two fuck ups want"?

Elk sat on the couch. "I'm here to rescue your ass so be nice".

Royce waited. Elk plowed ahead. "I formally request that the air

plant mate team practice the en mass portion of the day 163 space

walks together in Houston for a minimum of three days".

 Royce rolled his eyes. "That is beyond the capacity of the pool.

Request denied."

Sergei looked at Royce. "What if Elk had a spot we could all fit into the pool"?

Bob stopped and looked at him. "Where"?

"Chile. San Alphonso ser mer. Largest pool in the world. It has 66 billion gallons of water. 2 miles long by 1 mile wide. It so big we could go sailing. Whats more it's got hotel rooms we can grab up. Its 45 feet deep in the one corner where they go sailing and it's got power running around it. All we need are the mockups put down there. Oh, yeah bring the airlock mock up. Getting people in and out efficiently is harder than it looks. We don't really need the actual tools. We use Houston and the A and B team concept for that. Chile is just for the whole team to practice in and talk thru the procedures". Elk wound down and waited on Royce.

Royce grabbed the phone. "Kat. I need you in Chile, come in and we'll go over what I need". Royce hung up. "You two gen up a preliminary list of what mockups and equipment we need", he directed Ivanovitch and Elkington. Talk to Johnny and the other tech they got there, De Antonio. I want her on this. "Where's Rosario? We need a friendly latin American face to smooth this over with the Chileans. What else? Transport. "We have the C-17 do we need to go up to the C-5? That galaxy is so big it's going to scare the tourists. Well what are you looking at me for? Make this happen"! They passed Kat going into Royce's office. Busy couple of weeks ahead.

CHAPTER 15

Launch day 120 04 August 2021 2200 Kennedy

Ten o'clock at night and the temp was still 86 degrees. Shitty. That's a tad unfair. It was the 90 % humidity that was the real back breaker. Royce stepped out of the bathroom attached to his office to find RAVEN sitting on his couch.

"Shit! Stop that! Are you here to kill me"?

"Not yet, Raven said. "I've got something you are going to want to see". He handed the folder over to Royce. Bob looked at the pictures. Several were blurred but three were good enough to make out Sergei and Janice doing just that- making out. Royce was not surprised and said so.

 Raven regarded him. "Well you know who was surprised. President Clinton. She sent me down here to warn you and ask if there was something else you weren't telling her".

"Shit I've got a lot on my plate. What does she want to know? I can't figure out who put the bullets in the equipment section and the plans for the gun in the printer data base. I've got status' for four upcoming launches I'm trying to coordinate plus the equipment involved and I think my car battery is dying and it's brand new, so what else would she like to know.

The agent perked up. "What about your car"?

"Hey I was kidding about the battery that's not her concern. I'm sure it's just a bad battery".

"New you said"?

 "Yes less than a month".

"How old was the old one"?

"5 years at least. "Yeah it just went bad, but this one has had problems the last few nights. Left me stranded and I have that switch that turns off the lights when the car is off".

Raven rose and went outside. Bob followed. They went to his car. Raven started a preliminary check around and under. He ordered Bob in to pop the hood. Peering in he showed Bob the unit taped to the side behind the windshield wiper fluid container. "What is that? "Transponder and a recorder. See the separate line going down to the battery? It's supposed to turn off if the car hasn't moved or no one has spoken in 10 min. That's why your car is dying". Raven removed it. "I'll take care of it".

"Who's is that"? Royce asked.

"Off hand I would say the Chinese. They sent the pictures".

"Shit. Are they still mad at the rocket motor buy"?

"Yes and no, Raven told him. This really has to do with control. If they think they have a hook in you they feel better and stop trying so hard". "Why", Royce asked. They aren't trying to sabotage the mission are they? The printer data base was hacked from China. We know that".

"Do we? How do we know that"? "It was in the report the NSA analyst gave us", Royce reported.

"That would fit in with them. No doubt they can control what happens on that space ship if they have a gun on board. But that doesn't seem quite right", Raven thought out loud.

"Kat says the same thing. She thinks it's someone else".

"Let me see that report". They went back to Bob's office. Bob retrieved it from the safe. "What am I going to do about the pictures".

"Oh. That's simple. Blackmail only works of the knowledge is secret and you don't want to let it get out. My advice is to have her go on an interview and let it slip that they are an item. Put it out there and they have no control over you", Raven lectured. "If you get out ahead of the story you can frame it anyway you want. The pictures are being leaked for petty personal reasons. Meanwhile you can wrench the Chinese for spying on the crew members and trying crude blackmail. Cockroaches hate light". He turned to the folder. "Let me look into this report". He read thru several times frowning. Royce waited silently. "There's something wrong about this. I need to talk to some experts on this. Meanwhile watch your back. Now that we have the transponder I can only fool the people who put it in for a few days. They are going to twig to the fact that you are endlessly repeating a pattern with your car and speech. Try not to go out of town for a while", Raven directed.

"Great I have to be in Houston tomorrow, Royce said. "French Guiana three days after that, then Russia, then Chile, then the Gobi desert and the Chinese. That's just the next two weeks". "Tell President Clinton I'm going to leak that some of the new composite fiber skin panels on the equipment section are showing signs of staining. I've pre sold this idea to the people at Scaled Composites. They'll say it's reacting to some gas in the VAB. That gives me the excuse to move the equipment section and tear it apart. I need to ensure that nothing else is hidden away".

Raven grunted. "What's in Chile"?

"A big ass swimming pool".

Launch day 138 18 Aug 2021 1001 Alphonso Ser Mer, Chile

It was cold and wind swept out on the beach. The thin strip of sand separating the huge pool and the ocean was not large at all. At the north end of the giant resort complex Scanlon, Kat Royce, and Rosario stood on the ocean side corner edge of the pool.

Several officials of the Chilean government, Military as well as the resort complex managers all were arrayed watching the cranes lower the mockups into the pool. At 45 feet deep the depth was barely enough to accommodate the robotic arm mock up. A scant three feet of water remained on top of the fully extended arm when an astronaut was secured onto the work station. The roar of diesel engines was deafening. Rosario was explaining to the Chileans the process they would go thru to run communication and air lines to the various portable generators NASA had transported down there. The resort hotel manager snapped pictures and had a full video crew filming the entire operation. NASA had commandeered over 50 rooms on the last hotel closest to where they would be training. The space flight teams arrived in just two days. They had been at Houston working on their individual team A and B assignments going over procedures. Now Elk and Li Fong would be bringing them all down to work thru the complicated mass EVA evolution. August below the equator was winter. They had most of the place to themselves. However, that much action tended to attract attention. They had to setup a barrier around their end of the pool to keep out the tourists. Even now sailboats that people could rent for a day on the "sea" were tacking back and forth beside the barrier. The tourists were going to get an eyeful. And the resort was going to be able to trumpet their unique status as the go to pool for NASA. They had been pretty generous on the room rates. Royce spotted Johnny and De Antonio going over the lay out plans with the crane operators. He motioned Kat over to him. Go tell De Antonio to make sure the safety clock isn't visible to the astronauts, only the divers. Roger. He looked at the Chilean Air Force general who had opened up the air base so the giant C-5 Galaxy transport could land and disgorge the huge amount of materiel they needed to make this simulation work. He was listening to Rosario with rapt attention. Royce didn't blame him. Rose had that effect on people. Scanlon approached and asked about the proposed reflective tape with names on them. "It should solve the problem," Bob said. "The visibility in this pool is going to be worse than what would be experienced in space so if they can see the identification marks in here we should be good."

"How are the launch preps going?"

"Fine. I'm taking some flak from the Chinese about Tyler Watkins going up," Royce relayed to Scanlon.

"Watkins? I thought he was grounded." John was surprised.

"I can't have a trained flight qualed astronaut with his

experience sitting on the evac gantry for the next three years, Royce reasoned with him. "I spoke to him he understands the mistakes he has made and is apologetic. And I think sincere. The other members of the red team aren't so forgiving, but we don't have much choice."

Royce paused for a moment laying out the revised schedule. "The day 250 launch is now on day 240. If the air plant goes smoothly it might even be day 235. The Chinese are howling over the shift left". Everyone is. The bottle neck is launch facilities. I have these four coming up and then we start the supply launches with PODS." Scanlon nodded. "5 pods will be up soon. I have had all the fittings quadruple checked and the PODS are holding fuel and air and water just fine. The design teams have done a fantastic job on this craft. The Mars crew will be announced somewhere after day 350. That's about 6 months from now." Royce broke off.

"Around Christmas or New Years Scanlon asked.

"Yeah, New Years' sounds about right, Royce confirmed.

"We could do it live, Scanlon mused. "We could have the ball drop and on its trip down it would light up the names as it drops!" he said thinking out loud.

Royce looked at him. "John maybe we just should hold a press conference?"

"Bob you got to think big!" I've got to get you the last round of funding." Wait till you see the commercial we are going to do showing this training event!"

Royce winced, and told him he would get with him to go over the crew announcement. The committee would have some say in the matter. Royce excused himself from Scanlon and broke Rosario out of the enamored grasp of General Ruiz to whisper in her ear quietly. Rosario looked at him. "You sure?"

"Yeah. It's the only way to play it. Tell Sergei. He'll get it done", Royce told her

"You ready to face the back lash?" Rose asked him

"Yeah, why not? Whats a few more people mad at me?."

CHAPTER 16

Launch Day 164 13 Sept 2021 0535 New York City

Janice stretched and bounced in the lobby of the Belvedere Hotel. The fine old art Deco hotel was near Times Square and the theater district. The predawn lightening sky promised blue skies and mid 80's. Nice. The elevator dinged and Sergei, Ernesto Zapata, and Georg Hoffman stepped out to join her. Muted hello's from all with a wicked look from Sergei. More stretching. "Ready?" Sergei asked. Nods all around, saving breath. "Lets go." Turning left out the door the group headed east on 48th jogging at a slow pace. As they approached the avenue of the America's Sergei increased the pace as he pointed out Rock Center where they would be in a few hours. Very little car traffic but lots of trucks and early workers were out getting the city that never sleeps ready for its daily grind. Dodging cars and people the group hit 1st ave and the UN plaza. Turning right they continued down to 42nd street before turning away from the east river and back west. Past Grand Central Station the group ticked off tourist sites without slowing. At Times Square all were winded and straining. Turning right on 8th Sergei led them back to the Hotel. Left on 48th was a full sprint. The finish line at the Belvedere couldn't have come sooner for most of the group.

"We have a breakfast meeting with the producers of the show at 0700. 0645 in the lobby. Flightsuits. Bring a change of clothes. Suits/dresses. They are sending a car", Sergei told them. The others continued the cooldown stretching. "They want us at the UN at 1530. The UN people will pick us up at Rock Center. I have no idea how long at the UN. Dinner is with the IBM people. 1900 at the hotel churascarria. Everyone okay with Steak"? Nods. "They have a selection of salads and lighter stuff. We work out in the hotel fitness room tomorrow at 0600. Our flight back to Orlando is at 1035. Ernesto you head to Houston at 1105, so you won't have to hang around JFK too long. Sergei consulted his watch. "You have 37 min". "Get cracking"!

They all chatted on the elevator. Janice was amazed. Every American should have a NASA astronaut workout regimen.

She no longer sweated the runs. They had just done 3 ½ miles at under an 8 min/mile pace. Dr. Hoffman was 44 years old. He was holding up. She marveled at how much the man wanted to go to Mars. He and Sergei seemed to have a close bond. She wasn't exactly jealous. Everyone had a bond with Sergei. Going to her room she stripped off the jogging clothes, putting on a towel she wasn't surprised by the knock on the door. She opened it a crack to see Sergei with a grin on his face.

"Excuse me ma'am. I'm with the hotels water conservation board. I was wondering if you would mind showering with me to protect our vital national water supply".

"No".

"No? It makes me sad you don't care about the environment".

"Tell the bad idea bears that you showering with me is a sure fire way to be late. You have 32 min".

Sergei looked wounded.

"Janice, we will have Kentucky Derby sex, I promise".

"What's Kentucky Derby sex"?

"The most exciting two minutes in sports"!! Janice smiled in spite of herself.

"Two min Mr. Smooth"?

"I promise it won't take me more".

Squeezing in the door. He talked and walked her to the bathroom.

"What about my orgasm"?

"Hey I thought that since Hilary, every woman was responsible for her own orgasm". "Besides what about last night, he reminded her"? "That was the super bowl of sex. Three hours with a long halftime".

"More like 3 min of action with lots of needless commercial breaks"!

"Ouch! That hurt a little".

"You'll get over it". Stepping into the shower she dropped the towel and wrapped her arms around him. The horses are at the starting gate!

Rachel Maddow looked at the camera. "We are back thank you for joining us on this special Mars mission coverage. "We are fortunate to be joined by four of NASA's and the world's finest for our coverage of these space walks. We have Dr Janice Lincoln, CMDR Sergei Ivanovitch, Dr. Ernesto Zapata, and Dr. Georg Hoffman. Welcome all. "All were members of the crews who performed the Rover POD engine mate a few months ago, she informed the audience. "No one is more qualified to lead us thru the space walks as they continue the mission to build the mars craft. As a special treat we have arranged with NASA to get a direct feed of the raw video coming down from the ISS. We are not necessarily live. The screen showed the video switching between the space station and the live astronauts in the studio. "There is a 10 second or so delay. But that has mostly to do with the way the video is being bounced around the world. NASA can cut us off if they deem something too sensitive to see. We don't anticipate that happening". CMDR Ivanovitch, hello again. I think the world was riveted by your direction of the crews two months ago on the ISS. Can you set the stage for what we are seeing here. Your monitor should have it".

"Thank you Rachel, I do have it, Sergei said. "On behalf of the whole NASA mars team I want to thank you for being such a champion for our mission. If you look closely you can see a wide screen shot from an astronaut who is up on the ISS solar array girder".

"Can you show us on this model approximately where the astronaut who is filming this would be stationed?", She asked gesturing.

"Sure". Sergei used a pointer to show the spot. "Normally the video down to NASA would have a timestamp and a data link telling who's camera it was. Who is filming from Vlad crew Janice"?

"Edminton is scheduled", she replied. Rachel interrupted. "That was exactly how the rover mission was for most Americans. CMDR, you would be directing everyone passing out orders and then there would be a question or a request for information and this calm and cool voice would come in and answer without hesitation". "Dr. Lincoln that was you correct"?

"Well Rachel I was just keeping track of things while Sergei gave out the assignments. Ernesto and Georg actually had to do the work. We were a team". Janice answered.

Maddow turned back to Sergei. "Indeed CMDR Ivanovitch you worked very closely with Dr. Lincoln and others. Have you developed a rapport with her"?

"Certainly we have become close. Very close. As we all have". Janice shot him a guarded look. Maddow went on "What else are we seeing". Sergei went on to describe the 28 Astronauts who were out on that mission, and what they were doing. The air plant POD was on the work platform and the engine rig was going on. It was virtually a carbon copy of their mission. Elk had them working well. The new tape name strips could be seen on the video but unless there was a close shot the names were not evident. Dr. Hoffman was brought in as they went to a close up of the engine pod and the engine removal. Georg had performed the work under the supervision of Grace Adler. Now it was Tyler Watkins directing Abromovitch in the work. "Based on what you can see can you tell where they are in the procedure and what do they have left"? Hoffman explained that the engine rig was mounted as was the electronics. The parachute pack was installed. There had been no issue with the cables or the wrenches this time. The robotic arm was going to come down and remove the engine from its crate and slide it into the rig. It would be bolted on from there. Then it was a matter of testing. If there was time there was talk of them installing the final three trusses and as many of the work platform panels as they could. This was in preps for the equipment section mission. Ernesto and Georg walked everyone thru the engine mate as it occurred in front of them. It was a free wheeling two and a half hours. There was plenty of footage from their own missions plus renditions of what the mars craft would look like. They spoke again of the closeness of the crew during the long mission. Sergei this time admitted that he and Janice had a relationship that was more than professional. Ernesto and Georg had heard the rumors but now there was confirmation! Janice was livid. She was drawn into a discussion of the possibility of life on mars. She went into non committal mode saying that the search continued but there was no definite proof. At the end of the show the inevitable question came about who was to be the actual mars crew. They all made history by proclaiming themselves to be dead solid locks to make the final mars crew. Royce had blessed this. If all 40 of them went around proclaiming themselves to be locks then all drew attention equally. After the show wrapped up Janice was just looking for a quiet place where she could kill a Russian astronaut, when a rep from Fallon came in. She had heard that the Mars crew was in the building and they would like to film a quick musical segment. The four of them ended up singing Major Tom and Rocket Man with Jimmy and the Roots and the last Singing Idol champ Sandy Gleason. Sandy had the number one album out right now. Pictures and autographs and a quick late lunch with a change of clothes. The UN was a total blur. More pictures and speeches and plaques and handshakes. Suddenly they were at a reception with the UN Secretary General and Scanlon. Where had he come from? Janice thought he appeared like a magician's trick. The US ambassador to the UN, Michelle Obama, insisted on introducing them around. Scanlon took the heat and got them out of there just in time for the dinner. The president of IBM was there. Since they all had their tablets with them there were pleased smiles all around as more pictures were taken. Scanlon smoozed the suits, allowing the crew some time to eat in peace. Thank god the restaurant was in the hotel. At 2130 Sergei reminded them that they had an early morning work out to work off all this rich food. Scanlon took up his queue adroitly giving a small speech that extolled the long industry NASA partnership and how now it was taking them to the stars. Janice thought that was speech 5 C in Scanlon's arsenal. Later in bed she was too tired to kill Sergei she just asked him why he had admitted they were having an affair.

"Royce told me to drop it in the interview. I guess there are rumors about us and he said to tell you that if you wouldn't stay away then admitting it was the best course of action", he said tiredly.

"He's still a dead man".

"You are very violent".

"Just with that manipulative bastard". "And that woman, she

admitted.

"Don't forget Jimmy Fallon. I thought you were going to hit him when he said you were not a natural singing talent".

"Him too, she agreed, snuggling".

"Am I on that list"?

"Oh yeah. As soon as I recover from this publicity tour you are finished". 330 days of this on Mars. Joy.

Launch day 175 24 Sep 2021 1622 Kennedy

Royce wrapped up with Scanlon and Kat in his office. "That was smooth", he told them. "They finished on time but accomplished all of their evolutions and all of mission 196 events. We can actually eliminate the launch". Mission 196 had been the mission to build the mars craft platform. Elk and his crew had installed the third tripod truss to the station and extended truss 4 and 5 together to get a full 60 feet from the station. At the end of the truss there were 9 one foot thick, 5' by 7' panel sections joined together. The 15 by 21 foot work area was actually not as big as the equipment section was at 24 feet in diameter. The mars craft actually would sit with the landing struts extending below the work platform. Special braces would hold the equipment section landing struts to the work area. As more sections were added to both the top and bottom of the equipment section the craft would be adjusted. The crews Elk led had not been able to install the braces. Royce was not all that upset at that. He thought the braces would need some "coaxing" to bridge the distance between the landing struts and the work platform. Better to work those as required during the equipment section install. Royce and Scanlon went over the three separate supply launches that were to be held in the next two weeks. Space X had the Wyveryn capsule ready in their facility in the Mohave ready to hoist up the two cargo pods. The Atlas capsule was ready from Vandenberg, while the French were ready in Guyana to launch the landing struts and braces for the equipment section. Royce could feel the program achieving critical mass. At some point with all large projects they stopped being designs and plans and boxes to be ticked off and became hardware and people and actuality.

Launch day 183 18 Sep 2021 1102 Kennedy

Ten days later the same three were still hard at work in Royce's office. Royce and Scanlon went over the debrief of launches with Kat. "You babied them this time", she said.

"The team changed on a dime and rethought training, procedures, equipment. We shaved four days off the mission and still completed a 122 percent of goals. I'll start yelling again when we are at 99 percent.

"Any word on Watkins performance", asked Scanlon. Kat snorted. Royce ignored her. "By all accounts he performed magnificently. Even the Chinese complimented him. He apparently apologized to Li Fong and Zhou. Elk said he bailed him out two or three times", Royce answered.

Kat said, "I don't care what he showed. He's angling to get back on the mars team".

"Of course he's trying to get back on the mars team. Look if I grounded every astronaut who tried to get an advantage I would be awful lonely". Royce raised his hand as Kat started to object. "Yes, I know what he did. He isn't on the team. And he won't be. We just use him on these missions and get the most out of his skills while we watch". "Now, you said you had some thoughts on the planted gun and bullets", he asked.

Kat took a breath and started in. "I think the Chechens tried to get a person in the gantry crew. I think the gun was meant for him. The printer was to be used before the liftoff. A political statement by killing the mars crew", she concluded. Royce stared at her. "How do we know this"?

"A second source looked at the computer trace". Royce knew she was talking about Raven but said nothing. "Since the Lisbon Protocols the large scale hacking events have dwindled to a much smaller problem. It still happens but the penalties are now pretty sever. Kat laid out her evidence. "It appears that the Chinese computer used to hack into the printer company database was in a public domain. It looks like the perpetrator physically went to China and hacked into the database in Salt Lake City. He emulated a NASA computer and inserted the gun plans into the printer database". She went on. "Three hundred fifty two people have left the program in the last 3 months. One was a computer expert named Isa Busola, who was an ethnic Chechen".

Scanlon looked sick. "That in and of itself doesn't prove anything".

"No, but he had travelled to Uzbekistan about four years ago, and attended some radical speeches and social events. He also got married to a woman who we think is the illegitimate daughter of Mohmad Duadov", Kat piled on.

Royce knew that name was on the Russian Most Wanted list for terrorist activities.

"Busola worked for us for three and a half years before quitting 5 months ago. The hack was done one month later", Kat told them.

We also had a Loma Zovra, employed as a seal tech on the gantry crew. Nothing much on him. Just that he came here 14 years ago, studied and was a good worker. Passed every test, well liked, but a loner". "He died six weeks ago of a gun shot from a home invasion burglary". Kat paused. "Busola had moved back to Uzbekistan four months ago but came back to the US for a visit. Care to guess when he arrived and left"?

Royce grunted. "That tracks but I'm not sure". "Zovra was with us for three or four months and then suddenly stopped coming to work. His apartment was abandoned. We found Islamic literature for jihadists in his room. Zovra could go into the Mars craft before any one of a dozen launches, but most likely the final launch with the crew. He prints out the gun, gets the bullets and kills as many as he can. Relatively simple if the gun specs are in place. I think Busola killed him to cover up his tracks when we found out." I think we dodged a bullet. Literally", Kat concluded.

Royce nodded. "Okay. Package up what we have and I'll brief the President". Kat handed him a thick folder. "Good work".

"What about Busola"? John asked. Royce looked out the window at the huge white clouds in the clear Florida sky. "That sounds like a job for Tatiana Medvedev. I'll talk to her. For now we get the supply pods up and then worry about the equipment module". Royce handed out a sheet of paper. This is my thoughts on the crew make up for the supply missions and the equipment section". Scanlon looked it over. Looks good.

As Scanlon and Kat left the office, Royce was dialing a secure number on the STU V secure line. Clinton needed to be brought up to speed

Video log Janice Lincoln 18 Sep 2021 2035

Day 184. We are coming up on my 6 month mark on the

assignment. Thanks to you I now know how to bleed hydraulic lines and run an air plant. I can also run 5 miles without puking. You still suck, Royce but thanks. I see my next two space missions have up loaded. Out to the Mohave to run a supply mission and then the big launch from Kennedy for the equipment section. I'm pretty excited. Nice to have Rosario along on both. We seem to be a team. Looks like all the heavy hitters are on this mission. Sergei, Digger, Elk, Grace, Zhou even Watkins. I guess I should be grateful a little old scientist is going along with all that flyboy and flygirl attitude. The day I develop that strut I want you to kill me. The days question who is my hero? George Washington. Not for the military stuff or even the presidency. It's what he did at the end of his second term. He walked away from power. People were begging him to be the defacto king in America. He was offered president for life. And yet he walked away and let someone else lead. He was a hard act to follow but he knew that if the country started depending on him for every situation it would never survive. My name is Lincoln and Washington is still my favorite president. Lincoln out!

CHAPTER 17

Launch day 186 20 Sep 2021 0922 Mohave desert

Rosario ran from the car into the air conditioned building. 104. But it's a dry heat they said. Yah, so was an oven, no one wanted to be in an oven. The space X facilities were a little spartan after Kennedy. But they did have good tech and logistics people. Rosario and Janice were in looking over the two pods being loaded into the dragon X capsule. Wyvern was making its third run up to the ISS. So far it had performed flawlessly. The Virgin Atlas guys were doing fine as well. Janice thought the competition was making both teams the equal of NASA. The first of the two PODs contained the spare parts for the life sciences station and the comms unit. The second contained fuel and compressed air and food. That POD check out was easy. Tank full no leaks? Great. Food piled up until nothing else could be crammed in? Great. Done. Seal it up. The spare parts had to be inventoried and tested. Not that they hadn't been before but Royce was paranoid. It took 5 hours to complete the inventory. The tablet had marked it all down while attaching the spare parts to PODs 102A8. The numbers actually meant something. The 1 meant that the POD was attached to landing strut closest to the airlock from the equipment section. They were numbered clockwise around to four. So 1 and three were 180 degrees from each other. Ditto 2 and 4. The 02 meant that is was on the second level of PODs. Since there was a letter designation it was not on the out board stack of three high. The 08 meant the type of supplies. So this little pod would be stowed outboard on strut 1 with a pod on top and bottom. The fuel POD was 101A01. In effect the first fuel tank to be emptied as it was drained by the engines as they thrust into space. The fuel POD held approximately 200 gallons of the new JP 8 fuel mixture. The joke was the new fuel was rocket fuel on rocket fuel. There were only 8 of the fuel PODs on the ship. The equipment section skin was doing double duty as a giant fuel tank as well. The internal bladder in the POD was very similar to the bladder inside the Einstein Module. Fuel was of course going to be critical. The concept was to have the pods linked up to transfer back into the ships tank as needed. The back- up plan called for NASA to shoot seven or eight pods at them while they were on mars. They needed 1200 gallons to make it back to earth. Janice was skeptical. She remembered the huge space shuttle boosters and the giant

269

liquid center tank. Rosario went over it with her again. 1) if the space shuttle had had JP 8 available, the center tank could have been 1/2 the size it was. And 2) they had already escaped earth's gravity well. Essentially they were weightless. The mars craft would never need the huge amount of thrust that Apollo or the shuttle had needed. The mars craft would get by on a small steady burn that would use about 30 gallons in three days. In that time they would go from zero to 2,000 miles an hour. They would do another stronger burn with to get them to approximately 28,000 miles an hour. It would take 600 gallons to slow them down and then land. The return trip was even easier. Just run the engines until they used 1/2 the fuel then flip and slow to zero right at the ISS. That would do it unless they had to maneuver. NASA figured they could avoid something big twice if they saw it early enough. They hoped. Hey, everyone knew the risks. Even Janice had come to grips with it. That didn't mean she had to like it. As they buttoned up they spent time with the Mohave crew. They were a little stir crazy out in the heat and sand and boredom of the desert. Rosario commiserated. She told them the rumor was that the Chinese secret launch facility in the Gobi was even worse. Royce told her you couldn't even get good Chinese food there. The

Space X techs laughed. They knew the drill. They shipped the dragon capsule to Kennedy in the morning. Then the mate onto the falcon and off she went. All Janice and Rosario had to do was set these down on the intermediate platform on the ISS. Easy Peezy Lemon Squeezy.

Launch day 190 14 Oct 2021 1305 Guiana

The by now familiar roar and violent shaking of the space craft were old hat to Sergei. The crew was strapped in tight for an easy supply mission. The struts, braces and PODs would not take the most sophisticated work to tie them down to the work platform and to the ISS. The more critical work would come in 45 days or so, on the equipment section launches. With him were a mixture of the original mars candidate groups. He had Watkins and Hoffman as his workers. The Space X crew was Rosario, Janice and Jonsey. The Atlas crew was Zhou, Thompson and Edminton. Pure wrench turning trips. Sergei was betting they could do it in two busy days. Again it would fall on Laurent and the rest of the arm operators on the ISS to do the real work. Sergei thought they were getting a raw deal: He was on the TV getting famous while they were stuck away from their families for months. Well he could start repaying a little. Camby was due to ride down with them as he completed his mission commanding the ISS. Edminton was replacing him. Sergei owed him some cold ones at the Green House. Sergei was a little apprehensive about this mission with Watkins, but Tyler had been a perfect underling. Maybe the severe encounter with Kat Williams had changed him. That was the rumor anyway. Sergei was still suspicious but couldn't spare Watkins more than a cursory thought. These dockings were all scheduled within 2 hours of each other. They needed to get into contact with each other and coordinate the dockings. The French crew of two astronauts, Martin and Bernard, were handling the launch duties leaving Sergei free to coordinate the dockings. 15 hours later, the soft shake that indicated the arm had them came thru the craft. As they went thru the air lock into the station the arm was just capturing the Dragon capsule Wyvern. Janice would be in here in a short hour. Sergei had Watkins setup for a brief to prep the cargo holds to transfer the PODS in the arranged order. They would have to open the cargo hold to allow the struts and braces to be grappled by the arm. Camby greeted them warmly as he came into the Mars work bay. Luarent joined them and the four of them worked out the sequence. Watkins added some surprisingly cogent points about the swing radius of the struts vs the available work area. Sergei had to admit they were important. He had Watkins go over the order with Houston while the other two crews came in. Sergei spared a quick smile for Janice as she and Rosario came in.

Atlas arrived last with Zhou leading the way. Sergei had Watkins go thru the brief with Camby and Laurent providing input. Pretty Simple: Struts came first, then braces and then the pods. Watkins had them go thru the team leads and the airlock order. Sergei was about to say something when Watkins spoke up. "I know this is pretty simple and it's easy to be complacent when we have practiced this ad nausaem. But that's when people get hurt. Complacency gets people killed. People drive cars every day but they still get killed". "Let's stay focused and get this accomplished". Everyone rogered up and then broke off and went to get suited up.

Janice and Rosario floated up to Sergei as he left Camby and Watkins. Rosario graced the latter with a look. "What's that asshole thinking"? "Suddenly he's Mr. Safety and esprit de corps"?

Sergei flatly said, "I was just going to say the same thing as he did. He's right in all aspects. You know I don't like Tyler Watkins but he is a good astronaut when he wants to be".

Janice grunted noncommittally.

"Ladies, biases and ego's get left on earth. Here we focus on mission over self. Now go get some rest. You have six hours to your airlock time".

Wrangling the landing struts turned out to be tougher than anyone thought. They started in on the original plan and abandoned it after two hours. The large curved piece was approx. 6 feet long and almost 6 feet wide when the curve was laid flat. The strut was in the shape of an elongated v with the single piece of round aluminum towards the ship. The v was approx. 18 inches providing for an interior space that allowed for the fuel line pipes and data lines to be run. All the pipes had isolation valves on the ends and fittings attached. When the strut was bolted to the equipment section a small section of flexible hose would be attached to the end of the pipe and then to the fitting on the outside of the hull. From there the fuel would go into the tank on the ship. The data connections had similar connection ports to allow the lines to fit onto the ports on the hull. Where the data line connected on the bottom of the strut there was a capped plug that tapped into the lines to allow a testing unit to be connected. The testing unit would then run standard electronic test to make sure the fiber optic lines were operating. The trouble with the struts was the length of piece sticking up when the strut was attached to its brackets on the ISS. The almost 6 feet jutting upward from the station interfered with the swing of the robotic arm as it removed the pods from the docked space ships. They tried flipping it but the brackets would only hold 2 of struts that way with the wide side down. Houston weighed in and suggested alternating struts but they would have to have more brackets. Very serious consideration was given to duct taping the struts together curve down with two bolted in. That would have put the ubiquitous silver tape to 1002 uses but the idea was rejected due to the cold. In the end a young engineer at JPL suggested bolting the trusses on the solar array girders. The clamps they used to put the arrays on the girders could be adjusted to hold the slimmer aluminum round pieces of the strut as well. Heads conferred. Brows furrowed. Shoes and socks were removed to allow for easier number crunching. The arrays moved on the girders to keep them pointed at the sun. Was there enough clearance? Uh, yes? Okay that might work. Give it a try. Sergei and Watkins tethered out to the girders with all hands on deck assisting. Even Camby had suited up and came out to help. 6 hours later they had the last strut in place. NASA was scrambling to adjust all of their drawings to show where the struts were now stored. They also had to revise the equipment section procedures to allow for the extra time that would be needed to retrieve the struts. As Sergei and Watkins led the debrief, Camby was looking out the porthole window at the station. Janice was floating nearby and asked what was wrong.

Camby turned and looked at her. "Well those struts just ruin the sleek look of the station! She was always an ungangly thing. Modules stuck together haphazardly. Pieces added as older bays wore out. And now all this Mars work. Those struts make her look like a floating junk yard".

Looking at the newly installed second platform and the truss system, Janice soothed him as best she could. "Hey in 12 short months or so we will all be out of your hair. No person will ever set foot on Mars without this station giving it its blessing".

"Yeah well number two head is down again. And the shower station is clogged. And we get tube food again. Man. I'm going to miss this"!

Janice laughed outright. "You sir need to get back to earth".

"Tell me something I don't know".

Launch day 195 19 Oct 2021 1925 Kennedy

Bob Royce grimly hung onto the phone and said what he had to say: "Madam President you are perfectly correct that Tyler Watkins performed in an outstanding manner on the last mission. Without his leadership and technical expertise the mission itself was in doubt. He certainly seems to have accepted responsibility for what he had done and was now greatly contributing to the team. Even the Chinese were mollified somewhat. However having said all that, CMDR Elkington was still his choice as second in command with Ivanovitch as commander. Madam President you can fire me if you want but that is my decision". He plowed on. " I will not insert Watkins as the mission commander". The famous Clinton temper started to boil. "Don't think we are too far down the road of this project to make you indispensable. Kat Williams can take over for you. If I didn't receive two calls a week from committee members praising you and vilifying you I would can you right now".

"Madam President I will have a resignation letter on your desk in the morning citing a family emergency if you wish it". He waited. Silence on the other end. It stretched for 30 seconds or more.

"No, Bob I'm sorry. I'm looking at the political angle and you are looking at the mission".

"Madam President this is a hard choice. I promise you. Sergei Ivanovitch will do something to make you proud to be a human being before this is all said and done".

"He better".

Breathing heavily he had barely set the receiver in the cradle when it rang again. Kat. "Bob, are you sitting? There's been a car accident. Brad Elkington is dead".

"Oh my god where"?

"Just outside gate 2. He went into the lagoon on the intracoastal side . He must have lost control of his car".

"Drinking"? Royce hated to ask that but he had to.

"Unknown right now. The base police have the car and the body. They said they couldn't smell alcohol but that doesn't prove anything. A bunch of them were with Mike Camby tonight at the Green House welcoming him home".

"Okay Kat here's what I need. Call Scanlon and bring him up to speed tell him to please come to my office. Then get over to the Green House and get everyone connected to the Mars program from there to my office. Don't let them drive. You drive them. I'll call the base police and have them get the local cops over here to take everyone's statement. The cops are going to want that. I also need to inform the President and the committee. ASAP on those astronauts Kat". "Got it".

Royce hung up. Oh man what a mess. He pulled up Elk's personal file for his home number. Wife and two kids. Living in Coco Beach. He knew them a little, had met them. Did they know? Maybe he had the duty. He dialed the number. A pleasant voice answered hello. "Ruthie. It's Bob Royce". He proceeded to rip her world apart. She was so calm. Staying strong for her daughter. Ruthie had thanked him for all he had done for Brad. Brad knew Bob had been a real supporter. Royce couldn't take it. By the end she was comforting him. He called base police and told them to come to his office as he was gathering everyone who had been with CMDR Elkington at the Green House there. He told them to call the cops and have them come as well. He had just finished breaking the news to the President when Scanlon arrived. He looked pole axed. Kat led the solemn procession into his office. Sergei, Janice, Digger, Rosario, Camby, Jonesey. No Watkins. No one was drunk. They had all literally shared one beer as a symbol. It was all Camby would allow. They had gotten greasy burgers and fries and started playing pool when Elk said he needed to get on home. They swore he was stone cold sober. Kat looked at Scanlon and Royce. The Green House staff confirms that. She had names and numbers for the police as they arrived.

Six days later the funeral was attended by dignitaries from around the world. The sight of Ruthie holding her daughter's hand proud, dry eyed ramrod straight holding the American flag while the bugler played taps became an iconic image. Her son saluting brought back images of a young JFK jr. Cause of death had been determined to have been accidental drowning. Janice was devastated. She held Elk's daughter Samantha like a life preserver after the funeral. The little 5 year old had crawled into Janice's lap as she sat forlornly on the couch. Later Sergei had gotten her and Rosario out of there and they had helped Kat Williams pack up Elks things from his room on base. Just clothes and some books. His real life was elsewhere. Now he was gone. Rosario was putting his clothes in the box when she suddenly said, "you know it's just like Watkins said last week, complacency is dangerous. We drive cars every day but people still get into accidents.

Man that was prophetic". Sergei and Kat shared a significant look. Neither one of them believed in coincidences.

Launch day 203 27 Oct 2021 1425 Gobi desert China

Time to grieve was a luxury they couldn't afford. The launch of the equipment section had been scheduled for day 240. 37 days. Janice, Rosario and Digger went to China with Zhou and Fong. The Chinese base in the Gobi was secret and sterile and depressing. Apparently the architectural genius that was on display for the 2008 games in Beijing was not involved in the design of the base. Squat drab cinder block buildings. The launch complex at the far end from the gate was barely visible. The Launch prep building was the largest in sight but still only about 30 stories. That meant more of it was underground. Three huge square buildings surrounded the taller prep building. The prep building was where the mate would take place. The other buildings all had huge roll up doors that made up 8 of their 10 stories. Presumably the crawler machine that would move the rocket from the assembly prep area to the launch pad was kept in one of the buildings. As they

drove up Rosario could see the seams in the prep building where

the door moved up to allow the rocket to be mated with the

crawler. The desert was surprisingly cold for late October. Zhou

and Fong had been no help in giving them a clue as to what to

expect. As they drove up to a small cluster of buildings several

officials waited to greet them. Zhou and Fong handled the

introductions a Mr. Chan beamed at them and gave them the tour

of their quarters. Cinder block chic. A small dining facility was

located in the northern most building. Each Astronaut had a room.

The two other Chinese crewmembers Liu and Piepi met them and

were happily chatting away with Zhou. Fong led them to a

meeting room to go over the mating sequence. A computer

projector was set up to go thru a presentation. Fong and Mr. Chan

the project manager for the Gui Long rocket alternated. The

equipment section was in building 2 right now. That was a

cleanroom environment. They would be going thru the checklists

from NASA in the morning. Each fitting and connection would be

inspected prior to the loading into the cargo hold of the Xi Fang

Bai Hu capsule. The White Tiger of the west. An ancient name for

the symbol of the Emperors power. Fang was the western

name they had decided on. Rosario declared the name fitting and that was that. The presentation went over the mockup training they would go thru in two of the three square buildings. The third was indeed the crawler house. The other held the cleanroom and the test/prep areas while the third was a dedicated training facility. It was 7 miles to the gantry cranes and launch pads. Great more escape training. Didn't the Chinese have a caviler attitude about personal safety? Digger muttered a small amen when Janice objected to more pointless escape training. Chan was having none of it. He went over their schedule. Physical training started at 0530. 5 miles followed by stretching. Janice wondered when they would hit the "easier" part of the schedule. She missed Sergei and the comfort of familiar surroundings. Well she would just have to push thru. Sergei was getting ready to go to Vandenburg for the Atlas launch that would bring up him, Watkins, Hoffman, Sanger and Keith as workers. Pickerell and Larson had drawn the duty to fly up the capsule up to the station. The Dragon would use the small crew module and bring up Adler, Jonsey, Zapata, Hopkins and Leon. Thompson and Larionov got to be the bus drivers for them on the Wyvern.

Three miserable days later the team sat in the clean room going over endless prints, schematics, and diagrams showing what went where on the equipment module. The section sat in a cradle on its side with both airlock doors open. Scaffolding allowed them access to every external part. The skin gleamed white with gaudy advertising logos painted all over it. Corporate symbols for almost every major company on the earth. Some familiar to Janice and rest some not. Several hooks on the side were evident. These hooks would allow them to attach tethers and move around externally if necessary. The bulkier plates where the landing struts would be attached shown silver. The external connection points for the fuel and data lines were visible. The upper outside airlock door was closed. Likewise the radar panel and the comms antenna ports. The internal spaces were available thru the airlock door in the middle of the bottom section. This door would normally allow access to and from the clean room. The inside was gray, industrial and crowded. The lower level housed the majority of the equipment they would be taking with them. A lot of items like food and fuel would actually be coming later. Even with 196,000 lb cargo lift capacity the Gui Long was limited. They were right at that limit. Fuel, food and water would come up on later supply missions. The nominal stairwell to the upper level showed the open airlock door that would lead to the crew module when they attached it. The crew module was even now at Kennedy. The upper level contained the three work stations in addition to the storage lockers and other equipment. Zhou led them thru the check out of every locker and station in the upper level. Others had done it before but they did have 5 of the mars crew on board if the current scores held true. Or no one else died, Janice thought. She was scanning the bar codes on the circuit boards stored in a small locker out board port. The circuit boards were multi- purpose and could go in the radar, navigation or comms units. She checked against the manifest on the tablet. All accounted for. She buttoned up the locker and tied the sealed tag to the latch mechanism. She signed it and dated it. She took a picture of the locker number and the tag and uploaded it to the inventory data base. It accepted the locker number and annotated the picture and stored it away. 100 % accountability. She moved on to the next locker out board above her head. Three more days of this and then we seal it and mate it. Then down to the launch pad and off we go. Could she survive five more weeks of this?

The next night Janice and Rosario were prowling the corridors of the barracks building looking for any kind of snack vending machine. And came up empty. The Chinese philosophy being "if you didn't eat it at a meal you didn't need it". They rounded a corner and went outside to see if there was anything edible in the offing. Chocolate wise speaking. As soon as they hit the ground they heard the voices speaking Chinese loudly. Zhou and Fong were in a heated discussion. Zhou was mostly calm but Fong was as agitated as Janice had ever seen her. She looked on the verge of tears. Janice and Rosario immediately went back around the side of the building. "I don't think they saw us", Janice said. I've never heard Fong angry, Rosario replied. Hell, I've never really interfaced with her at all".

"Me neither, Janice said. Do you speak Mandarin"?

"Only a few words", Rose said. "Me too, said Janice glancing around the building to where the couple were still gesticulating. Fong was now crying. Zhou relented and was soon soothing her and embraced her, rocking slightly. Janice ducked back and went back into the building with Rosario. "I wonder what that was all about", she asked.

"A lovers spat", said Rosario.

"Those two would have to be the best actors in the world if they were involved together", Janice reasoned. "We need to spend a little more time getting to know Zhou and Fong," she said.

Raven picked his way thru the car yard carefully. He consulted a slip of paper and a map of the Broward County police impound lot. He had just reached Brad Elkington's wrecked car when Kat stepped out from behind it. "Hello Raven".

"Jesus Sunshine, I hate that. How'd you get here"?

"Great minds think alike. This doesn't figure", she said gesturing to the car.

"Accidents do happen".

"I don't like the smell of this. Beside if you think it's an accident what are you doing here"?

Raven grinned. "Just my job. As are you. Did you find anything'?

"No".

"Nothing"?

"I said no. Let me ask you something, Raven. How would you do this? If you needed to stage a car wreck how would you do it"?

"I put a tiny amount of C-4 right on the inside edge of his

passenger side tire. Right next to the wheel housing on the tire.
Then I'd remote detonate it when he was going around a curve.
When the tire blows he proceeds straight into whatever is coming
up around the bend. When the police look at it they think the
deformity in the wheel is a rock which caused the flat and it goes
down as an accident".

They looked at the front passenger tire and found it full. "Well
that lets you off the hook", Kat said. Raven snorted. "How would
the great Sunshine do it? Knife in the tire as he passed"?

"No I would have a way to control the steering column".

Raven thought hard. "Yeah that would work but you'd need
access to the car for hours". "Yes but that can be arranged. People
around here are always flying into space or off to another country
for training or a flight".

"Let's look". It took them four hours. The collar bearing as the
steering column went thru the engine fire wall had been modified.
An electro hydraulic trigger- very tiny- had been installed on the
collar. Two rods came out and passed into holes in the steering
column. The rods locked it down and then they retracted
automatically after 60 seconds. It looked like it had been there for
weeks.

"Shit," Kat said. "I need to get to Royce".

"Hold on. We need more evidence. And we need to know who put this in there. We can't just have Royce announce that Elkington was killed", Raven reasoned. "We have to be firm before we go after whoever this is. Especially if it is the Chechens".

"That doesn't make sense", Kat parried. They both started walking back out of the junkyard/impound lot. "Why would the Chechens kill Brad like this? It's not big or flashy. It doesn't stop the mission". "It's like the pictures of Janice and Sergei or the radio transmitter in Bob's car". Or even the gun". Even though we think we know who did the gun there is no evidence that the Chechens did the other items. These aren't adding up for me" Kat said.

Raven agreed. "Whoever did this is methodical and willing to wait for the perfect time to deploy. I suspect that the gun may have been a ruse to throw us off. "Neither Zulova nor Bursola ever come back to check the bullets or the printer, that says methodical and patient", Raven said stepping out of the junkyard into the street.

"Perhaps they thought the weapon safe", Kat said. "We have torn the four sections apart looking for the first sign of anything else stowed away".

"What about the PODS", Raven asked. A chill went thru Kat.

"Shit, shit, shit, no! We didn't think about that. We figured the person would want access to the gun on the flight".

"Maybe, Maybe not".

:There are 7 of them out of our reach. Two in flight and 5 more in storage up on the ISS". "Could you get into those"?

"I don't know. We might come up with some excuse to open them , but I doubt the gun is going to be sitting on the top in the open". It's most likely concealed in a container" she finished.

"Can you Xray the rest"?

"Yes. We can call it a radiation test or a seam check on the plasbond panels". "Okay. You do that. Brief Royce but tell him it doesn't go to Scanlon or the President. Next we need to get to Elkington's wife and see if she took his car in for service in the last six months. We also need to check every other candidate's car. Lots of stuff going in cars these days," Raven mused.

Kat smiled at him.

"Is this going to be like Prague"? Raven brightened up. "I enjoyed Prague, especially the end".

"Yeah but you worried on the job for days. I slept with you just to calm you down".

"What about the next three months"?

Sunshine blushed. "It's always the non- descript quiet ones that have the biggest hardware".

Raven grinned at her. "Good to be working with you again Kat".

"You too, Mike".

CHAPTER 18

Video log of Georg Hoffman 16 Nov 2021 2150

Hello Mr. Royce and I guess the entire world. Today is launch day 222 16 Nov 2021 at about 2200 at night. Great to be back at Kennedy. We are ready to go today not 18 days from now. My team is prepped on the mock up and the procedures for moving the equipment section. You know I never thought I had it in me to be an Astronaut. I filled out the application as a mark on my record so I could show my Geology Department Dean I was ambitious. I'm 44 years old and I love rocks. I guess I am the person to tell you about rocks but now I'm much more than that. Even If I don't get to Mars thank you so much! I've been to space two times with a third coming up. I've gotten to drive the rover and stood on top of the robotic arm on the ISS as it moved a POD onto the platform. I did that while looking back at the earth from 220 miles up. Fantastic. I've worked harder at this than anything I've ever done. But you know this? I'm energized. I've never felt better, or more academically astute. I've had an idea running around in my head for the last few years about plate tectonics and the ice ages. It just coalesced for me last week. . It happened while I was on one of those 5 mile fitness runs we all love so much. I wrote it all out just the last two days. I think it's going to make me famous before we even go to Mars. I have discovered that I can do amazing things when I work very hard. Thank you again for this opportunity! The days question? What food to serve on our first day on Mars? Sourbraten with potatoes and a dry Riesling of course! Out!

Launch day 241 05 Dec 2021 1202 Gobi desert

More delays! Janice was frustrated. Two days tracking down a leak. Loading and unloading into the capsule endlessly. Janice had seen Fong embracing an older woman she had found out later was her grandmother before they had loaded into the capsule this last time. So she had some family then. After so many warnings about Fong Janice was actually starting to pay attention to her. She would watch her in the stress of space next. If they ever went there. Let's go! Digger was actually snoring softly in the seat next to her. Rosario was playing solitare on her tablet. Janice was just bored. This time looked a little more promising. They had

actually found and repaired the leak in the rockets liquid fuel tank.
Now they needed to pass a 1 hour drop test where the pressure was
raised and monitored to see if the tank still leaked. Or if there was
a smaller leak in the connections masked by the tank leak. Or if
something else occurred. Atlas and Dragon had already blasted off
and were waiting on them. The pressure to launch was enormous.
The Chinese (specifically Chan) were waffling about trying to
launch. Royce had steadfastly held to the launch criteria. If this
thing blows up, we have lost the entire program he cautioned.
 Several committee members had left. To top it off the weather
was deteriorating. High winds were threatening. Royce kept
reminding people about the Challenger disaster. Launch criteria
were established in cool quiet times so that when the intense heat
of the mission critical crises came the criteria told you what to do.
If the criteria was 35 MPH top sustained winds with gusts to 40
and the readings were 30 with gusts to 45, then the answer was no.
Even if that meant changing flights. Even if that delayed the whole
program. Better to launch two or three days late versus never. The
winds had to drop below 25 mph with gusts under 30 for 30 min
before the window was opened. The winds had been oscillating
around the low limit to allow the timer to start. On top of all

that the window for launch was closing as well. Soon it wouldn't matter what the winds were. If the earth and the ISS were in the wrong positions, the launch had to wait. You simply couldn't get there if you had to chase the ISS around in orbit. They had 10 min left in the drop test, they had had an 18 min period of lower winds, and still 53 min left in the window. The launch had 10 min of countdown left. So they waited and watched and worried.

Astronauts, engineers and politicians. Chinese TV was showing this to the world. Royce had taken a break and went outside. Returning to the launch control room he looked at the monitors. Hum.

Royce cornered Chan and spoke to him quietly. "This desert is simply amazing".

Chan looked at him quizzically. "Well its dry and the winds do play havoc, but it is beautiful in its own way.

Royce nodded agreement. "I also love the way your atmospheric monitoring program works. You can call up instantaneous data and can plot data over time to look for trends". "It's amazing. It's also amazing that the readings for the last 13 min or so exactly match the readings from about 10:30 this morning. My watch may not have the most accurate temperature reading but I'm willing to bet my watch is closer to reality than that monitor", he gestured.

Chan went pale and told him, "the readings are right on the edge. One good gust and we scrub for the day."

Royce looked at him. "The readings are what the readings are. We can stay here two or three weeks if needed". Chan stared at him, saying nothing. He moved and spoke quietly to a technician who nodded. Seconds later the readings on the atmospheric monitoring program jumped. The astronauts inside Fang capsule saw the jump and called launch control. Chan spoke and said that the readings were indeed on the edge but he had confidence God would calm the winds down. Time dragged. 7 min later the winds had indeed dropped by 4 miles an hour and were not gusting as much.

Royce looked at Chan. "Interesting data point".

"What is that my friend"?

"It took 7 min for the winds to die down. You asked God for a favor. It took 7 min for your words to reach Gods ear. Can we calculate the distance to heaven? Assuming God works instantaneously". Chan smiled.

Digger woke to the shove from Rosario. Hey we are lighting

this firework! Cool. The Gui Long rocket roared to life 15 min later. Easy Peezy Lemon Squeezy. 15 hours later they docked with a soft thump. ISS, Fang is showing good connection and holding. Welcome to the ISS, Fang, good to have you join us. We have a brief in the mars bay at 0615 which gives you about an hour to get set up. Roger.

It was old home week in the mars bay. Janice and Sergei had a small reunion. Rosario said hello to Laurent and Cherbatsky the arm operators from the ISS. Edminton and Kelly Johnson were there as was the other two crews from Atlas and Dragon. Watkins, Adler, Keith, Jonsey et all welcomed the Chinese crew. Janice thought that the only person missing was Camby. And Elk. Then it hit her. Brad was never going to be up here again. She felt the unfairness of that down in her bones. The brief was cursory. The first EVA was just to open up the Fang bay and attach the robotic arm to the equipment section. They were supposed to set out work boxes and brackets to allow them to maneuver the huge piece of the Mars craft and the struts and braces. All of this would go on the large secondary platform. That had already been accomplished during the wait for the Fang. As exciting as it was to see the actual space craft they would take to Mars, be in space, the mission was pretty simple. No real challenges. Sergei had the three team captains: Zhou, Watkins, and Adler arrange the workers under them. He co-opted Janice as his assistant again. She didn't mind. Dr Hoffman drew video duty. Thompson, Larinonov, Pickerell, Larson, Lui and Piepi all got tabbed for safety watches at some point. Edminton was in charge of the operators and the inside safety watch. Bobbi was not too happy to be off the Mars program but she loved the ISS. She told Sergei she intended to wander thru the space craft when no one was looking and scribble her name all over it. Chuckles. Okay. First EVA was at 1325. Team two at 1355, followed by team three at 1430. Get some sleep if you can. This was getting to be old hat for Janice. She wriggled into her sleep sack like an old pro.

Stepping out onto the surface of the ISS six hours later Janice could see the bay doors opening on Fang. The equipment section sat gleaming in the bay. Sergei was communicating with Edminton to have the arm operators link up. The special lifting hook was attached midway up the skin of the equipment section. Grace and Ernesto Zapata were on the end of the arm as it swung out to grasp the section. They tethered to the hooks on the equipment section. Dr. Hoffman was busy snapping away as the operators eased the equipment section out of the bay. The 24 ft diameter by 20 foot long section slowly revealed itself. It was big. Hoffman got some amazing shots of the section with the advertising logos featured against the earth backdrop. Janice was sure those shots were pre planned by Royce and the rest of the NASA team. As the bay doors from Fang swung closed Zhou and Rosario and Fong headed out to the ship to complete the closing inspection. As the arm nudged the section closer to the ISS several tethers clipped in between the module and the station. That's where she was going to sit for two days while they attached two landing struts and one brace. Then the plan called for them to swing the section out to the platform and attach the brace to the platform. Then slap on the other two struts and the final three braces. No real testing to this mission, except for a fairly straight forward test. A data/Power line was being routed from the ISS to the module. The line would just hook up to the small power distribution panel and to the computer that ran the power module. It would be the first time they had communicated with the Mars craft. Discussions were underway to see if they could open and close the two airlock doors and see if they achieved a seal. They had seven full work days up here. Sergei intended to use them. They finished the prep EVA in 7 hrs. Next on tap was to install the handholds and the tether hooks on the platform.

The debrief was pretty simple. Hoffman was busy downloading the video and the stills to Houston. The ISS crew went back to their bays to ensure the station was ready to support the next few days of operations. Janice was just considering dinner when a voice caused her to turn. "Dr. Lincoln can I check something with you"? Tyler Watkins floated up to her holding his tablet.

"Sure', she said neutrally.

"This is the procedure tomorrow to remove the struts using the robotic arm and swing them over to attach them to the equipment section. Here is the picture they have provided", Watkins showed her on the tablet. "See the serial number clearly on the strut. But if you look at the procedure the serial number called out indicates the inboard strut in this picture".

Janice studied the picture and the procedure. "I know something is not right about that but I can't quite figure it", She said.

"If we take the inboard strut we would have to swing it over the curves of the other struts before moving it away from the solar array, Watkins said. "We should take the outboard strut first." The problem slid into place as Sergei approached.

"That is the outboard strut. Look at the shadow. See the longer range shot. The inboard and outboard designation is always with respect to the long axis of the station. In the long range shot 22A the inboard strut is on the right as you look at them. Note the shadow from the solar array slanting across the tops from upper right to lower left on the diagonal. Now in picture 22B the trailing edge of the shadow you can see at the bottom. If you projected it would run upper left to lower right. Whoever took these photos swung around when they got the close ups to show the serial numbers of the struts". She concluded

Watkins and Sergei blinked at her and studied the pictures. Watkins said slowly, "Yeah. I see that now. Let me check something else". He tapped on the tablet. Scowled. "FUBAR. Look". He had the schematic for the strut positions called up. The serial numbers were clearly shown. The whole entire Mars Craft had been assembled on earth before they ever got to this point. Each strut had an assigned position. Per plan. Like erector sets, it just worked better if you followed the plans. Watkins explained that the struts were out of order. They wouldn't come off the girders 1,2,3,4. It would be 4,1,3,2.

"Is that going to present a problem", Janice asked.

"Well maybe". Sergei and Watkins discussed the clamp system they had used on the struts. If they were clamped individually to the girders it would be no problem, but if they were ganged together then yeah, they would have to juggle struts while they worked. All three tapped furiously on their tablets trying to call up video or pictures of the struts and the clamps they had used to secure them to the solar array girders. There it was plain as day. The struts clamped on to the girders by individual clamps as well as a series of clamps holding them together as one unit. Watkins scowled again while Sergei quipped, "they should have used duct tape. Nice catch Tyler, Janice. Now that we know this we can plan around it".

Sergei detailed Watkins to brief Houston and come up with a plan. He thought it would be no real problem to unbolt the ganged clamp and leave them individually clamped for the short duration of this mission. Watkins concurred and moved off to brief Houston. Janice moved next to Sergei. "I still don't like that guy".

"I don't know Janice. He's been boy scout good and doesn't seem to be wound so tight. Even you have to admit that was a good thing looking out for those little problems. He saved us two hours of back and forth with Houston While we waited fully suited freezing or roasting outside". Sergei reasoned with her.

Janice, stubbornly loyal, said, "I miss Brad".

"So do I. "He didn't deserve that. But Tyler wasn't the reason Brad lost control of his car. It was an accident", Sergei counseled trying to sooth her.

"Still, I guess I have to work with him not like him", Janice admitted sourly.

"Okay thanks. Get some chow and some rack time. Unless you'd like to make history"? He leered.

"Is that a record for you"? "5 whole minutes with thinking about sex while we discussed the struts".

"Nope I was thinking about it the whole time. I only had half my mind on the problem. The other half was picturing you naked".

"Ha ha". Besides maybe Rosario has beaten us to the punch", Janice teased.

 Sergei looked worried. "You think? Ask her and find out". Janice laughed.

 "No, I'm serious. Ask her", Sergei said.

"Why"?

"It's important".

"I say this to you again, if you have some crazy bet going on, I will cut off your balls".

"Ha ha, he said. But seriously ask her".

Three days later the last bolt torqued into place on the last strut. They shifted over to attaching the other three braces from the struts to the platform. When that was done the fourth day the module looked weird. The four struts hung down below the platform about two feet. The bottom of the equipment section was about four feet from the platform. All four struts had braces running about 6 feet from the edge of the platform out to the struts. The only other thing holding the equipment section in place was the power data line. And that wouldn't hold very long in an emergency. Day six of the mission saw Watkins and Adler inside setting the switches for the powering up of the power distribution system and the electrical panels aligned so that the two airlock door monitoring systems had power. The ISS provided the extra 15 amps needed to run the systems. It took 35 min to bring the monitoring system online and shut the doors. Janice was jealous in that Dr. Hoffman was inside taking video as the section was sealed. Both doors had green indications. Test sat, lets go home. Not quite yet but soon enough. They set conditions for the next two supply missions. Fuel and water would be coming up. As well as more PODS. The Mars Crafts solar array would also be making a special journey up. The Chinese design was said to be state of the art in solar power generation. So much so the solar array was 5 times smaller than the arrays on the ISS. The craft would need every drop of that power. The batteries and the fuel cells on the ship would make up a large percentage of the total power generated. But they did have needs. Science stations, pumps, motors, and computers all ate power. The new Sadoway batteries were good at storage and quick charge but they wouldn't last forever. Hoffman came away with stunning video of the astronauts working in space. The group videos were fine for the establishing shots as they built up the craft. More video would come as the other sections were added. Part of the craft was in space! They left on day 8 of the mission Launch day 249. Still ahead of schedule. On budget. Approval rating 58%.

CHAPTER 19

Launch day 267 30 Dec 2021 0922 Brussels

Bob Royce and John Scanlon stepped out of the meeting with the committee and breathed a huge sigh of relief. They had the crew. Ivanovitch Gonsolvo Andrews Hoffman Zhou Fong Watkins and Lincoln. Maybe not everyone they wanted but given the political realities these eight would do. Scanlon was getting off the phone with President Clinton. John grimaced at Bob. "She says you better make them work out". Yeah yeah. We have the crew now we need to start the publicity machine. These eight are going to be world famous not just in America. So the tour is set: New York, Buenos Ares, Brussels, Moscow, Berlin, Beijing. Other places as needed. Let's get to them".

Eight hours in real time later but only 5 on the clock, Scanlon, Kat, Royce and the Mars eight met in the small conference room adjacent to Bob's office. He laid it out for them. "Get ready to have no sleep and no privacy. We have a team ready to start reading and answering your fan mail. Twitter will be handled by the PR team. You stay off of it", he ordered. "Face book accounts as well. We have scrubbed off everything we could. Rose".

Rosario blushed. "Hey, I was young".

"As of this second you represent the world. Every word that comes out of your mouth better be carefully thought out. This tour is vital to introduce you the way we want. Each crew person will lead in his or her country. The three Americans will share New York while the two Chinese will take charge in Beijing. That means lead! When we are in Moscow Tatiana will shepherd you around but I expect Sergei to protect you in case someone starts to make a cultural mistake. Likewise in Buenos Ares with Rose. Dr. Hoffman you okay"? He had tears in his eyes.

"I'm a little overwhelmed".

"That's okay. Honest emotions are fine. Frankly I'm proud as hell of each and every one of you. People in this room have really grown in the last 9 months. You have shouldered more responsibility than you wanted to or even thought that you could. Yet I'm asking for more. Because I know you have more in you. You are a team now. I expect each of you to carry the others. Now let's go show the world what they get for 30 billion".

Launch day 269 01 Jan 2022 0831 New York

The enclosed set of the Today show faced the court yard of Rockefeller Center. Crowds held up signs and cheered in the 20 degree weather. Inside Rachel Maddow beamed at the camera. "I've been teasing this for the last two hours but here it is. Without further ado the Mars eight Astronauts"! James and Tyler led them out of the wings to the eight chairs set in two rows. Applause from the crew in the studio. "We have from Left to right in the front row Dr. Janice Lincoln from the United States. Dr. Georg Hoffman from Germany. CMDR Rosario Gonsolvo from Argentina. And Dr. Li Fong From China. In the back we have CMDR Sergei Ivanovitch from Russia. CMDR Tyler Watkins from the United States. CMDR Lui Zhou from China and Dr. James Andrews from the United States". Roaring applause from the crowds.

"Dr. Lincoln let me start with you. First congratulations". "Thank you, Rachel".

"For an unabashed geek like myself the thought of going to Mars is overwhelming is that your emotion as well".

"Yes certainly, I'm thrilled excited, honored, overwhelmed and scared all at the same time". General laughter. Maddow held for a second and looked at her. "Please tell everyone how many degrees you have". Janice looked a little uncomfortable.

"Well I have three undergraduate degree's, three masters and two doctorates plus my medical degree.

"So nine", as Maddow did the math?

"Well, yes".

Rachel turned to the camera. "So kids, you want to go to mars?, study hard. No less than 13 advanced degrees here. By show of hands raise it when you hear your field. Engineering: Five.

Astrophysics two, Computer sciences: six, medical/biological: two Geology: one.

"Dr. Hoffman you are the geologist, right"?

"Ms. Maddow that is my expertise, yes". "Dr. Georg Hoffman from Munich in Germany studied at the Ruprecht-Karls-

Universität in Berlin. The oldest and finest institution in Germany", she read, stating his academic credentials. "You recently found the spare 15 minutes to submit a paper on ice age plate tectonics that is receiving quite a lot of attention, isn't it". Georg blushed. "I just finally got around to putting down the ideas that had been rolling around in my head". Can you summarize the paper? "Yes, I thought that the ice age pushed down the North American and Icelandic plates and that now the ice age is over and global warming is melting away the ice those plates may spring up again. It has to do with predicting where volcanoes are going to appear. I'd love to make some observations on mars to see if the same events had occurred there".

"I think you are going to get that chance". She turned to focus on Tyler Watkins. "CMDR Tyler Watkins from Henderson Nevada". More cheering. "If you have any free time what do you like to do"? "Sleep," Watkins deadpanned. General laughter. "No I like to watch sports and work on cars', he said.

"Is your family excited'?

"It's just me and my brother. He lives in Florida near me. Of course he's a proud little brother".

"I'll bet! "How many times have you been in space"?

Watkins paused considering. "5 altogether". "Amazing"! "This Dr. Li Fong from Beijing China, Dr. Welcome".

"Thank you Rachel, I'm a big fan".

"Wow, one of the Mars eight is a fan of mine. Well Dr. I think you will have your own fan base soon. Are you prepared for that"?

" I think so. We know that everyone is going to be interested in us. We know that the world has spent a lot of money on our training and building the craft so we expect scrutiny".

"Hum the Mars craft. Let's go to commercial and take that up again when we come back", She cut to commercial. During the break everyone waved at the crowds gathered behind them.

"And we are back at 40 past the hour. I have the high honor and privilege to have with me the Mars eight". Cheering. "These eight earth people will go to mars on a space craft that is currently being built. Built but not named. CMDR Sergei Ivanovitch, from Moscow, that doesn't seem right does it'?

"Of course not Rachel every good space craft needs a name. And NASA wants me to tell every school child around the world to submit names for the space craft and the landing site. NASA will pick the best three and we will hold an on line vote". Then announce the winner".

"What would you pick"?

"I think the Enterprise or the Millenium Falcon is out of the question. So is Eagle. Neil Armstrong, Buzz Aldrin and Mike Collins own that one! Deadline is thirty days from now so get those names in".

Rachel cut in. "Okay kids, you heard the man. We have the website up on the screen. Get that going". "CMDR Zhou, CMDR Ivanovitch reminded us of the Apollo 11 astronauts who were the first to land on the moon. Have you given any thought to the fact that school kids all over the world are going to remember who you are and know what you did"?

"I am honored and overwhelmed as Janice said, Zhou replied. "Neil Armstrong is an American hero as he should be. I hope that we are heroes for the entire world. Every person on earth is making some sacrifice for us to be able to succeed. Those are the names that should be remembered. I merely represent them". Zhou bowed a little from his chair.

"Dr. James Andrews from Kentucky, that's a tough act to follow".

"Can you explain to our audience what your main specialty will be on the trip"?

"Rachel I'll be glad to. First let me say that I think everyone of us feels similar to Lui. Don't know that I could have said it so well, but the feeling's the same. My job is to operate the digger and the rover when we get to mars. We have to do some excavations when we get there to build the site as underground as possible. "As you know my baby was launched some time back and should be touching down in 22 days. Once the excavating is done the digger becomes a rover and Dr. Hoffman and I will use it to explore Mars" James explained.

"Just Dr. Hoffman"?

"No of course not. All of us are qualified to drive the rover, and all of us will be using it. We have several science experiments we will be taking and setting up. Dr. Lincoln and Dr Fong and CMDR Gonsolvo will be doing that type of work".

"CMDR Rosario Gonsolvo from Buenos Ares Argentina".

Catcalls.

"How many times have you been in space"?

 "4 all together", Rose replied.

"What is your specialty'?

"I am the comms, navigation and radar operator and repair technician primarily but I am qualified to be the flight back up for CMDR Watkins or even mission commander for CMDR

Ivanovitch".

"What about spare time on mars will there be any or is it just work"?

"We will have some spare time. We can take 50 lbs of personal items with us. I plan on taking some old fashioned books to read. I'll probably leave them for the next visitors".

"What else are you taking"?

"You know a young girl approached me at Kennedy and asked me to take her goldfish with me to Mars. I had to say no, but it did give me an idea. If you have a small, SMALL! memento you want me to take send a letter and I will chose one to go to mars".

"Okay people another assignment. Get those thoughts to Rosario Gonsolvo, care of NASA".

"I think NASA had one more thought in mind, right Dr. Lincoln", Maddow continued getting to all of them.

"Yes, Rachel. NASA is also pleased to announce that they have about 100 lbs for science experiments. This is open for all colleges or university or even high school jr. high school level classes". "If you have an experiment designed but lack a space ship to blast it into space now is your chance! NASA's website has all the details".

"I love an interview where homework is assigned"! Ladies and Gentleman the mars Eight! We'll be right back".

Eight long days later the eight dragged themselves into Royce's office. Aside from the almost fight between Tatiana and Janice the tour went smoothly. Royce had been smart about one thing: letting the home astronaut take the lead worked out well. The Chinese were insane for Zhou and Fong. Janice thought her ears were still ringing from the roar of the crowd. All the interviews had been basically the same as New York. NASA had feed the interviewer select questions and points where the contests were announced. The website had crashed after China from the number of hits. Approval ratings inched up. Royce gave them two days off. They all slept most of it. The next series of launches were supply missions. They were not going to be involved with those. Now they focused on the crew module. This promised to be the longest stretch on the ISS for the team. The hook up of the two modules was the most complex operation any astronaut had undertaken. If they could do it. True the two sections had been put together on the ground and tested, there was also no guarantee that the harsh environment of space would allow the mating to take place.

They had 31 training days to practice.

Launch day 291 22 Jan 2022 1344 JPL Pasadena Ca.

It was typically beautiful California winter day in Pasadena. 65 degrees and cloudless. It was easy to get lulled by the relentlessly good weather in SoCal. The Jet Propulsion Laboratory was nestled in the hills just off the 210 highway. The control room had been the scene of many tense moments while waiting for various landings. Curiosity, Spirit, Opportunity were all controlled from this facility. JPL had control of the POD carrying the Rover. It had made the long journey to mars with little fanfare. But it was crucial that the rover land softly at the correct site. Or close to it. Define close. That was the sticky point. The point chosen was MC-07 Cebrinea. In general that is. Just north of where Viking 1 had landed on mars decades ago. Near to Mons Elysium and a second volcano called Hecates Thoulus. There were mountains, valleys and canyons in the area. It was close enough to the polar ice cap that an expedition could go up and investigate. Also close enough to Curiosity rover to the south that they might go and retrieve that vehicle. One of the 4th level goals was to retrieve the rover and try to revive it. 1st level goal was obviously to land and return. Secondary goal was to set up the landing site. The tertiary goals were to perform science experiments, in as many disciplines as possible. The fourth level goals involved exploration. Make it to the ice cap. Make it to Curiosity. Try for Mons Olympus. All these secondary and below goals were possible if the rover worked. If it got there safely. If it was close to where it was supposed to be. Digger had a place of honor at a monitor looking at the readings. The 4 min delay in communications with mars was killing him. The rover POD had made contact with the Mpos satellite and tried to but failed with the now stationary rover curiosity. The software installed on the electronics package had triangulated the POD position and adjusted accordingly. The JPL engineers calculated that the rover POD had a 72% chance of landing exactly on the designated latitude and longitude. They had about two hours to find out. In 12 min a retrograde burn would slow the POD plunging it heat shield first into the thin atmosphere of mars. Then Newton was in charge. Janice and Rosario were on chairs in the VIP lounge with Zhou and Fong. Sergei Watkins and Hoffman were standing behind the engineers intently looking at the monitors. Janice had no idea why they were not comfortable with them. They had a repeater of the same information. They would see the deceleration at the same time as the JPL people. They would see the signal indicating chute deployment. They would see the velocity read zero. Then the interminable wait for the Mpos to confirm position and the installed camera to take the self- portrait showing the undamaged POD. They would see those things at the exact same time as Sergei James and the JPL engineers. Rosario and Janice discussed the need to be the first to get information. It's like a game with them. I got the sports score 2 min before you. SO what? Did it change the outcome if you got it 10 min later? Janice shook her head. She asked Zhou if Chinese men were like that. "Are you seriously asking if a group of male astronauts like to discover new information first? I believe it was Confucius who said: "Fish gotta swim, Birds gotta fly". The three women giggled.

"Did Zhou just make a joke", Rosario asked sotto voce. Janice just widened her eyes. A small cheer indicated the burn had started.. It was followed by a larger cheer that indicated the burn had started on profile. Fong observed that the POD was in reality already on the ground and whatever had happened had already happened. 3 min 37 sec later they heard Chute deployment signal. Followed by another cheer. Velocity at 300 ft per second. That indicated the three chutes were deployed fully. 60 tense seconds later the velocity was at zero. Query POD for position trianglerization. 402 ft north 331 ft east of nominal. A muted cheer. It was all for naught if the POD was damaged. 41 tense min later: The shot was from the engine rig it showed the POD on it's side with the parachutes and the heat shield rig attached. The POD was undamaged in the photo. A huge cheer went up. Smiles and handshakes all around. A group of engineers huddled near a monitor. With a large flourish they handed an envelope to a black haired, glasses wearing, thin, young man. He grinned at them.

"Wind speed and direction gentleman. Never bet against the meteorologist."

"Shit, said a young astrophysicist. "My degree is worth less than a guy who know which way the wind blows? Hey is it too late to change my air plant POD bet"?

CHAPTER 20

Launch day 294 25 Jan 2022 1101 Alphonso Ser Mer Chile

The C-5 ride in was crazy. The abrupt weather change was also a little disconcerting. Hot in January in Chile. The intense travel and training schedule had taken their toll. All in all the reasons this particular training session was going south in a hurry were pretty evident. If the mob of tourists outside the barriers could hear the arguing they would not be impressed. There was currently a screaming match underway between Tyler Watkins and Dr. Georg Hoffman. While Digger and Zhou were intensely "discussing" their differences as well. Janice had moved next to Sergei.

"Aren't you going to stop this?"

"Nope."

"Why not?, she asked.

"Cause they need it." Watkins just then screamed FUCK YOU, and started to move off the crew module mock up. At the same time Digger had just shoved Zhou, when Sergei said quietly over the comms net: "Anyone who leaves their station or touches another astronaut will be kicked off this team I promise you."

Watkins stopped and Digger moved back. Dead silence on the net.

"Oh, now you speak up," Watkins sneered. "I recommend we scrub this evolution and try again later."

"NO!" came out harshly from Sergei. "Are we going to be able to just scrub it and start over on mars? Do you think things are going to go smoothly on the ISS or on the mission itself? Why do you think no NASA trainer has said a word to us in over 43 min? Are they asleep? No they are waiting to see how we get out of this mess." We are supposed to be professional astronauts. We are supposed to be the best earth has to offer. This connection is hard. It is absolutely vital that we get this right. Other wise the ship won't ever achieve air tight status. Are you telling me 22 astronauts can't state what is wrong and come up with a plan to fix it?" More silence. "Can someone at least tell me what is wrong?" Three different voices started up at once. "Okay quiet again. One at a time." "Watkins what do you have?"

"Hoffman is on the wrong step of the procedure and he has the wrong tools, Watkins said flatly.

"NO, I don't." immediately came from Hoffman.

"Hang on, Sergei instructed. "Tyler what step do you think he is on and what does he have and what should he have?"

The man went thru it. "He should have the larger wrench and the inspection gage. Step 13 A. 1. "He has the small wrench and no gage."

"Dr. Hoffman what step are you on, Sergei asked. "I'm showing step 12 D. (1) a. Install gage bracket in holes a1 thru a8 as shown in fig 12d1a4. That calls for the small wrench."

Sergei asked the other two connection teams were they were. Step 12 C. (4) came the reply.

"I heard a go," Watkins replied defensively.

"I think that go was for the station 1 team, Sergei told him. "Look people, I know you are tired and it's hard to focus. But that is when you need to slow down the most. This evolution is the most difficult. That's why we are practicing it. Who has a suggestion to make it better?" Slowly Sergei drew out ideas to make it better.

He had them break out of the four team concept and go to a ring of workers around the mockups. The main problem with this connection was that none of the teams could coordinate. They were supposed to go separately until the end. However the whole thing needed to be worked on at the same time. Up above in the monitor shack Johnny Lang and Sara De Antonio exchanged glances.

"I'll tell Royce they worked thru it", she said.

"Yeah I'll have them go thru it slow so we can re write the procedures. The astronauts ran thru that same scenario four different ways over the next five days. In the end they had a good plan of attack. But better yet they had a new appreciation of the group dynamics. That's what training is for. You made mistakes on the ground so that they didn't repeat up in space.

Launch day 300 31 Jan 2022 2245 Kennedy

Video blog of Sergei Ivanovitch. Bob you are killing us. We can not keep up this pace. The training and the publicity together are too much. We must concentrate on the mission before we worry about what Ms. So and So's third grade class wants to call the mars craft. We worked thru it in Chile but that's what happens when tired people make bad decisions. I know we have to tear it down to the bottom to get the team to function, but we are pretty tight right now. Can the flight simulator get a technical glitch for the tomorrow morning? Just until 11:30 or so. We'll do the rest of the schedule, just let folks sleep in for a bit. Too tired to think of the question today Sergei out.

The next morning Janice was blearily getting up when Sergei put the phone back on its base. "Who was that at 0545? Doesn't matter we need to be up anyway. Trainer at 0630. We need to get at it."

"Relax, Sergei said with a smile. Trainers down." "They need four or five hours to fix it. Event one is canexed. Free time to replace. Proceed to event two as previously scheduled." "Whoa. We have four free hours?"

"Yes we do. That's fantastic," she said crawling into bed. God, I'm going to sleep for 3 more hours and then have a big breakfast and then we shall see about science station experiments." "Good for you he murmured wrapping his arms around her. They were asleep in no time.

Raven was having a difficult morning. He could not find the garage for all the GPS and maps he could download. This part of Florida was swampy, buggy, isolated and forgotten. Bordering Georgia, north of I-10 in the lower end of the Okefenokee swamp stood Marysville, Fla. Somewhere in here was a garage that had ordered five different steering wheel collar bearings in the last year. Where as a normal garage would order one every three years they had ordered five. That stood out to Raven and he was going to find it. Kat and he had found two more collar devices on Astronauts cars: Ivanovitch and Sanger. He disabled the devices. The NSA had used PRISM to tell him that a garage had ordered five and that was way out of the ordinary. Bobby's in Marysville. So here he was. Single main street. One stop light on state road 441. 2 liquor stores 3 bars and five churches. Zero strangers. He drove into town and asked for directions back to the interstate. This needed to be approached in a different way. Stood out too much here. Needed a cover story. He favored oil company geologist. That way he could drive around asking to get on people's property. It wasn't out of place to carry an equipment case, and people were willing to talk to someone who was going to strike oil on their lands. None of the stuff was with him now. He would go back and approach again in the morning.

Launch day 315 15 Feb 2022 1015 Brussels

The press conference was heavily attended. After more than 1 billion entries and votes, the name for the mars craft and landing site was upon them. Legarde gave the announcement with the usual speech leaching all joy from the moment. Mars Space craft Unity. Unity to symbolize the total earth dedication to the mission. The landing site would be Zhenge He, after the famous Chinese explorer who may have beaten Columbus to the new world by 70 years. Royce was pretty sure the US press was going to have a field day with the landing site name. A little controversy was good for selling newspapers. Not that there were any more newspapers. Royce tapped out a note to Kat to have the PR folks get with the Mars crew and brief them on Zhenge and his exploits. Be prepared to answer if you think he beat Columbus to the new world. Best answer: "I'm not sure. Whether you approach the new world from China in three small leaky boats or from Europe in three small leaky boats you are still taking chances. Both men should be celebrated for their accomplishments." As Kat read the note from Royce she nodded. Kat also looked at a second note from Raven. "Enjoying Florida. Finally found a place to fix my rental car but guess what? No mechanic. I guess I'll have to wait. Plenty of stuff to see though so not a total loss. Be seeing you soon E. Poe.

Kat prayed Raven came up with something quickly.

Launch Day 345 23 Mar 2022 1454 Baikinor Star City Russia

Sergei patiently waited for the countdown to recommence. Glitches, glitches, glitches kept coming up. Fuel tank leaks. O2 system failures. Batteries beyond counting. They had delayed the SLS launch with the crew module from Kennedy by a week now. The team with Grace Adler in Vandenburg on the Atlas was also held up until they could go. The launch windows were particularly short. They just flat screwed up yesterday. 5 min was wasted waiting for the Orel capsule to acknowledge when they thought mission control was giving the heads up. The wait had bumped them out of the window yesterday. Sergei rarely lost his temper but he had started in on the flight control crew as soon as they were unsealed from the capsule. He was spouting Russian curses not heard since his youth. Even Tatiana was a little scared when he turned on her. Digger had rescued them when he muttered under his breath loud enough for everyone to hear: wow, that guy needs to get laid. Sergei had stopped speechless for a second while the words penetrated. Even he quirked a grin. While the others guffawed.

"Okay he said. "Hot gas venting from the large orifice is complete. "We better go tomorrow or I might have to get really angry." He stalked from the control room with Digger, Zhou and Rosario in his wake. Tatiana soothed Demitriov and Petrakova, the crew for Orel. Now they were just waiting the proscribed 10 min while the pressure on the main engine was topped off. This countdown had gone smoothly. Tatiana had warned them that they program was pushing the rockets and the capsules as hard as they could be pushed. Even the newer Atlas and Dragon systems were revealing problems when turned around as many and as fast as they were attempting. The Soyus program was older. Some of the components were very old. The Soyus and Orel had gone up just 56 days ago with a supply mission. Even this mission was just crew and parts/supplies. They didn't have the crew module like Kennedy. It wasn't too technical, just a certain amount of work had to be done each launch. The turnaround was tighter than they were used to. Engines had to be refurbished. New motors mated to the rocket body. New motors to the capsule. The capsule recovered and gone over and repaired for any damage. Any reconfiguring of the rocket or capsule adaptors had to be installed. The whole thing mated together and then tested and then dragged out to the pad where it was fueled and lit off again. Hey guess what, 62 days until the next launch and that one had the Unity clean room on it. Tatiana watched as the rocket slowly lifted off for the space station. Get the crews to the pad for inspection and clean up. No rest for them either.

Launch day 347 27 Mar 2022 1232 ISS

Rosario was on the far side of the equipment section. Clipped in on a tether she could see Hoffman on her right and Janice on her left. Seven others were strung out around the module including Sergei, Fong Zhou Watkins and Andrews. The Unity crew module was above her attached to the stations robotic arm. This was where the rubber met the road as far as she was concerned. Four astronauts were inside the section at the connection junctions. All of the ships data and electrical hydraulic fuel air and water lines ran to four different junction points. The four junctions corresponded to the landing struts. As the equipment section and the crew module were inched closer. The team on the inside would be connecting the lines. Be it hydraulic or air or water fuel or data. The design was really ingenious. Each connection point came with an isolation valve or circuit breaker and a testing port. So the water line was an easy mechanical hook up. As the lines came together when the sections were mated, the pipes carrying the water from the crew module to the equipment section would theoretically line up perfectly. Close the two isolation valves, connect the pipes. The threaded nut was already in place. All they had to do was wrench it tight. To a torque specification. Then they hooked up a test rig to the two test connections on either side of the connected pipe. Open the isolation valves and a small amount of water came into the pipe under pressure. That pressure was supplied by the test kit. They ran it up to three times the normal 125 lbs of pressure and held it for 30 min checking for leaks. Since everyone at NASA knew there would be none, the teams would move on to the next line be it data or fuel or air. However they could do none of that until the two sections were mated. That was another tricky feat in space. The design of the two section mating rings was also ingenious. Ingenious if it worked. The two sections had two large

flat rings that would be the seating surface when they came

together. An inflatable o ring ran around the smooth 8 inch wide

surface about 3 inches in. there were upper and lower bolt holes

that would align when the sections were properly positioned. A

small inflation port marked where the o-ring would be pressurized.

The bolt holes were spaced every 3 inches around the

circumference. At the landing strut points around the craft four

main beams with larger holes would line up when the sections

were mated. The four ribs gave grater rigidity and strength to the

craft. The ribs laid on the outside of the mating ring. The ribs

would come together and slide into place along side each other as

the sections came together. The ribs would also ensure that the bolt

holes would lie up and not be able to slide around while the arm

jostled the sections. That was the plan anyway. They had made it

work in the pool. Once all the bolts were installed pressure sensors

would be able to tell if the two craft were properly connected. The

o-ring would be inflated for an extra layer of airtight precaution. A

smooth film of silicone lubricant had been applied. Rosario now

watched as the robotic arm lowered the crew module down another

two inches. The ends of the four ribs were sticking up and

down from the sections and were almost touching. Sergei called for a measurement at each rib. Rosario reported 1.35 inches at her rib at the zero degree. Andrews gave 1.20 at the 90 degree rib. 1.33 at the 180 and 1.50 at the 270 rib. The crew module was cocked ever so slightly aft. Sergei ordered the 8 zip ties put in. Janice and the rest of the workers responded and ran a plastic zip tie thru the bolt holes in both sections. Each bolt hole was numbered and corresponded with its mate on the other section. Janice had no trouble getting the zip tie snugged up. Now the crew section couldn't just float off into space. A small spacer was run from the brace to the lower section of the crew module. As the padded end hit the module a hand fitting was turned expanding the spacer slightly. This shifted the crew module slightly. More readings. All within tolerance. Sergei ordered the crew module lowered.

 Contact came four reports. The tips of the ribs were touching their counterparts. The crew module slid down another inch. Reports on alignments followed. More adjusting with the spacer and a second added 90 degrees out from the first. More measurements and adjustments. Down a half inch. Hold. One half inch to go. More measurements. More adjustments. Houston and Kennedy were absolutely silent. "Okay. Down" said Sergei. The crew module slid the last half inch. Reports indicated sat. The ribs were aligned. Bolts were placed in the holes but not tightened. Sergei asked for a status of the lines inside. Grace gave the summary: lines were within tolerance. The internal connections had some give due to the lines ability to flex for expansion and contraction. The pipes were mounted to rubber coated guides that allowed for the movement of the pipes as the heating and cooling expansion and contraction that would occur. The data and electrical lines were very flexible and just needed to be within the vicinity to be connected. Sergei now asked for bolt hole alignment checks. Bolts were again inserted into the ring holes without tightening them. The zip ties were cut free. Some had to be "encouraged" to go into the holes but most went smoothly. The vast majority of the crew module and equipment section of Unity was in the shade here. The metal had contracted in the cold and it made for easier connections. The workers proceeded to tightening the bolts on a very controlled schedule. The opposite ring hole bolts were tightened as the four rib bolts were also snugged down. Once the bots had gotten their initial torque value, the O-ring was inflated. This was a crucial step because if the 0-ring failed to inflate, the bolts all had to come out and try again. The o-ring inflated without any issue however.

 Sergei ordered the bolts all torqued down to the spec. 45 min later

the last bolt reported done. Grace was just beginning her work

attaching the lines. She reported no problems. They had at least

three days inside. Air tightness tomorrow. Sergei looked at his

display to note the time. 10 hours. He felt every moment. Houston

agreed to allow Grace and her team another 4 hours to work. They

had come out last. Sergei ordered all the others in for debrief.

 Some small grins and high fives greeted him. He thought there

might be more in the way of celebration. They had done it. The

crew was exhausted after a grueling day outside.

"We still have the drop test", Digger warned.

"And the connections inside," said Fong.

"Then we have to put the skin panels on and hook up the solar

array, from Watkins

"Then prep for the next series of supply launches followed by the

Clean room," said Janice "This is mile stone 20." Hoffman

"We'll celebrate at milestone 38", lastly from Zhou.

Sergei knew Royce was grinning somewhere. "Okay debrief then

get some chow and some sleep. We have busy days ahead."

12 hrs later Tyler Watkins stepped out of the airlock to proceed

with his assignment. He had to install the solar array stanchion on the port side of the equipment module. The two 8 foot sections were not connected yet. Only the top section had actual solar panels. When fully deployed the panels would be 8 by 16 feet on either side of the stanchion. The two box covers that held the small motors that furled and unfurled the array were mounted perpendicularly on either side of the 4 inch wide square stanchion. The motor that moved the array to follow the sun angle was likewise small. 4 double A batteries could power the whole apparatus. Held in Watkins' hand the top section looked like an 8 foot T with a double top. The bottom section was also 8 feet long with a mounting plate at the base end and the other end beveled to accept the other section end. An interior power line ran from the solar array to the base where it would be connected to power the Unity space craft. Watkins had retrieved the array from the intermediate work platform where it had been staged on an earlier space walk. Zhou and Janice were with him getting tethers and tools connected to work belts on their suits. Together they slipped the two ends together and bolted them in place. The robotic arm then came down and took the array in the claw. Dr. Hoffman was on the end of the arm as it swung down to get the stanchion assembly. Watkins, Lincoln and Zhou now made their way past other workers out to the port side of the Unity craft away from the station. Connecting the power line and bolting the stanchion in was very simple. 30 min later the arm had swung away with the three astronauts clipping guy wires from points on the space craft to the middle of the stanchion. The 1 10th gravity of Mars would not be enough to weigh down the solar array but old habits died hard. Watkins checked with Sergei and Houston and deployed the upper section of the solar array. The upper section only because the lower section would interfere with the robotic arm during the clean room mating. The deployment took a maddening 90 min. The ultra thin film solar array was on a flex frame. The arrays had been built out of a Chinese company SunPower tech. Zhou had raved about the increase in efficiency the arrays represented. Watkins had sneered a little at that. Adler and her team had been inside the Unity for days now making connections and aligning switches. She reported to Sergei that the power available panel was registering green. Sergei requested from Houston permission to bring power into the distribution panel and illuminate some lights in the crew and equipment sections. Houston grudgingly agreed. That was not according to plan. 20 min later 12 individual spot lights came on in the crew and equipment modules. The crew inside had given a little cheer. Normally the space craft would not run lights and other equipment straight from the solar array. The array would charge up the batteries while the batteries ran the transformer which powered the distribution buses and then the individual panels. Now they had the most basic power lineup you could get. The array feeding the transformer, the transformer powering the 60 hz distribution bus and the bus powering the two distribution panel L1 and L2. Only four circuit breakers were connected in the panels themselves. But the ship was alive. Sergei congratulated the team on bringing this small amount of life to the ship. Everyone wanted a quick look at the interior with the actual lights on. Sergei allowed them to cycle thru one at a time. Watkins muttered as everyone praised Grace, "you'd think no one has seen light bulbs turned on before." He was ignored. Outside the work went on. When Janice entered the craft interior airlock door and saw the lights, she was extraordinarily moved. The bulbs shown a little dimmer than the 100 watts they should be providing. Here and there a few panel status bulbs glowed green or red. She could see the two teams of two running the line connections huddled together. Even though she had been in the mockup many,

many, times seeing it anew here was raising goose flesh. The second thought was: man this is a small space to spend a year with seven other people. She shared as much with Rosario as she cycled thru after her. "Oh yeah chica we are going to be sick of each other at the end." Hoffman told them he was sick of them already. Digger was of the opinion that Sergei's mother was certainly sick of him. Which could be taken a great many ways. Those ways were debated robustly while the work went on. The majority of the space walkers were installing the skin panels over the mating ring area. That was making the ship look whole. The cycle of brief, suit up, work, debrief, chow, sleep blurred days for everyone.

Video log of Grace Adler 31 Mar 0235

Space the final frontier. Sorry just kidding. I'm happy to be up here working on the Mars craft. We seem to be making progress. I was a little skeptical of the concept, but the tech advances in the EVA suits and the data links available make anyone an expert. The design is brilliant. Once the sections are joined the interior and exterior lines and connection points are all aligned and just need to be put together. That has proceeded better than expected. I think the crews are working well together. I see my scores are just under Sergei and Watkins. I know I probably won't get to Mars on this trip, unless someone else gets hurt. I both want that to happen and don't want that to happen. Just being honest. Bob, I'm simultaneously bummed out and thrilled to be doing this work. Crazy. Can I ask for a Mars two? Lets see the question of the day. Who inspires you? I'm always impressed by the average person who just comes in and does their job with no fanfare or publicity. Like Ms. Williams. She was my fifth grade science teacher. Shout out Ms. W! She just taught us the basics of science but also to think big and dream big. She inspired me to get good grades and take hard classes and get into astronaut training. Now here I am in space. Ms. Williams taught for 32 years. I just want her to know it didn't go unnoticed. Thank you. Night all.

CHAPTER 21

Launch day 351 01 Apr 2022 1212 Unity space craft

Two days after the drop test was passed satisfactorily, the radar antenna was installed. The comms unit had been powered up after 36 hrs charging the batteries. The battery units were on a slow charge discharge cycle. The advantage of the sadoway batteries were long life, quick charge time and no memory. One of the huge drawbacks of lithium ion batteries was that batteries tended to develop memories over time. It meant that the battery would charge up to a certain point and no more. It was like filling a cup with water. Once it was full the cup would allow a little to trickle out and a little to trickle in to full capacity. If you froze 95 percent of that water in the cup you could still do a trickle leak and fill and think everything was normal. However when you went to fully discharge the battery it only lasted a fraction of what it was supposed to. The term memory stuck to that phenomenon. The new batteries just charged up and discharged fully. And you could reliably get 250 charge discharge cycles. Plus they stored a hell of a lot of power. And because they weren't liquid there was no harmful hydrogen gas output. Now the Unity ship was crowded as 10 astronauts moved thru aligning switches and installing pieces of equipment. Rosario was checking comms with Houston and the rest of the ship. The ship had an announcing circuit that they couldn't check out until they got air ventilation working. Air didn't come until they got the scrubbers working. Those didn't work until the power was supplied and the water systems were supplied. Those didn't happen until the pumps were turned on and tested. First was electrical. The array was providing enough power. It was producing almost 10 kw of power to the batteries. Which could store about 200 hours of full power at say 7kw per hour. They needed to get the rest of the electrical systems up to speed. The ship used a 120 v 60 hz standard US system for AC power and a 110v 50 amp DC nominal to power other systems. For instance the computer ran off the AC system just like you would plug into the wall from home. Likewise it was cooled by a ventilation fan from 60 hz power. However the water pump which moved water thru the vent fan to take away the heat used DC power. The comms unit used 110 v 60 hz ac and then made its own power internally. The unit used ambient air to cool itself and had multiple back up channels. Rosario was testing those back up channels with the ISS and Houston and Kennedy. Just about anybody around the world was getting a call from Unity. The computer was next to come up. They need to get access to the display screens and the monitoring program to allow the program to watch the batteries. If the computer was off-line the ISS would have to send in an astronaut every 8 hrs or so to check the batteries. Janice worked with Fong to align the power and bring up the computer. The four big display panels on the command deck were bright enough to provide all the light the space needed. The interface to the quantum computer was similar to the old silicon models. Commands were still typed in or a mouse clicked on icons but this computer also had enough computing power to run a speech recognition program. Fong and Janice had just spent two hours inputting the status of various systems into the computer operating system and monitor program. The displays were giving the status of the systems in the green yellow red categories. Each system was represented by an icon on the monitoring program main display. The systems could be accessed by a voice command as well. Each mars crew candidates read a prepared script into the computer. They would have to do it again with the EVA helmets off when the heating and cooling systems were on line. Oh and air was available. Not yet. Houston was monitoring everything now that the Unity telemetry was available on the VDT link. The vid link was also being initialized by Rosario. Janice shifted one command display screen to the video link and Jimmy Peoples popped on screen from Houston. He grinned at them as the camera was adjusted to get the best possible picture. They tested several cameras installed to ensure good feed. The equipment section second deck aft camera showed a little static in the feed. That went on the troubleshooting list. That list was growing by the hour. The hardwired video cameras were just one aspect of the video and voice and data communications suite. The Comms VDT unit had become Janice's baby and now she was finally getting to put it thru its paces for real. So the minor glitch went on the list. The source could be any number of problems. The most likely suspect was interference from another RF source. But exactly where that interference was entering the system was another story. The craft was a marvel of design. The connection points linking the two sections together was genius. But there were trade offs. The data line bundle was a plasbond pipe approx 12 inches in diameter. Inside that pipe cables and wires from various units ran to different units and to different end points. At regular intervals

346

smaller diameter pipes branched out and ran up and down the walls of the craft. From those ends of the pipes the individual cable, video, data, power line would emerge. The cables then ran the upper and lower channels in the ribs of the craft until they disappeared into the units they supported. Every single connection had been tested and checked out on the ground at Kennedy Space Center. The most likely candidate for interference in the vid camera was one of the newly made connections that Grace and her team were undertaking. The plan called for them to run the trouble punch list down after the systems had been brought on line.

Days blurred together for the mars team and the ISS crew. The test and checkout had to be 100 percent before they moved on. Watkins Digger Hoffman and Sergei had installed five of the PODS into their positions on the landing struts outside the ship. POD 101A01 was bolted into place near the airlock door. Janice always thought of that as her POD. From the starboard side outboard command station window she could see the edge of the POD and the radar antenna as well below her. They marked a small victory with JPL when the air plant POD touched down softly on Mars approximately 500 feet from the rover. Air was a possibility on mars if they could get the water to the plant. Sergei and rest of the Mars crew spent a nice 4 hours inside Unity conducting an extensive session of interviews with world wide news outlets. Perhaps the most interesting question was posed to Tyler Watkins by a Rueters reporter. "CMDR Watkins, NASA has announced that you are 32 days ahead of schedule on this project. Is that from a generous planning timeline or hard work from the crews?

Watkins looked in to the camera and quietly said: "Well we have worked hard that that is true but the real credit has to go to the design team and the contractors producing this hardware. CMDR Ivanovitch was essential in the design of this spacecraft. If Bob Royce supplied the vision for the Mars Mission, Sergei Ivanovitch was responsible for getting that vision put down on paper and the contractors took those designs and built this beautiful craft. It seems like every day we do something that has never been done before. Or we complete a task that other people have always assumed to be impossible in space." His speech was simple and effective. Janice watched Sergei as he modestly brushed off the attention. He wasn't buying the Watkins act, Janice thought. Ugh. A year in space with Tyler Watkins. She turned back to the camera to announce the winners of the science experiment contest. High schools in China, India, Russia and the US had won. Six colleges were selected: Cambridge, Cal Tech, Russia's Senior institute for Physics, Dr. Hoffman's alma matter Karl Ruprecht Univesity and China's Physics Institute of Beijing. Joining them was a small college in Australia, Adelaide College. All been selected to send up their experiments. The video feed had shown the joy as each campus was announced. Janice was especially touched as she recognized a kindred spirit in the young girl from Adelaide, Zoe Smyth as she gushed over how awesome it was that her experiment would get a chance to study chemical reactions in the low temps and zero oxygen atmosphere of Mars. Rosario took over to announce what she would be taking: Several artists had designed small sculptures meant to catch the wind and sun of mars and move. NASA had chosen one from a young African artist. She was also taking a flat metal plate inscribed with the words of different poems from around the world. A Japanese haiku, a limerick and others were represented. The family of Ray Bradbury the author had saved some of his ashes and some would be spread on the planet he had written about. A multilayer CD was going packed with pictures of people and places of earth. Janice was sure that some of those choices were sure to provoke controversy.

They closed out the interview with some music provided by the Unity speakers in the back ground.

The teams made progress, hour by hour, test by test. Seemingly before they knew it, the work was complete. The final debrief after they had set conditions for the next series of launches was celebratory and sad. The ISS crew promised to take good care of their baby while they were away. Ships dropped off the ISS one by one, back to earth.

Video log of Sergei Ivanovitch 13 Apr 2022 2311

Hello from planet earth! Good to be back on terra firma. I can't believe how much 19 days in a weightless environment ruins my toned taught model body. I'm a little worried about the mission. The long stretch in 1/10 th gee is going to be a killer. I just hope the run back at higher gee will bring us back enough to overcome the real bone loss and muscle problems. The other big worry is the fact we are going to get on each others nerves. It can't be a coincidence that we are mostly single. I think boredom is going to our biggest enemy. I need to start thinking of some activities that can keep 7 genius people entertained. I have some thoughts I want to run by you Bob. The psyche makeup of the crew is improving. We won't kill each other right away. Once we get to mars all bets are off. Question of the day: how will the mission change me? I hope for the better and I hope weirdly not at all. I know that sounds strange but that's how I feel. I don't want to change "me" but I know I will be changed. I hope for the better. I'm scared maybe that long in space will make me weird or crazy or an asshole. Not that I'm not those things now just that every now and then I'm okay. Enough with the psycho babble. Out!

Launch day 367 17 Apr 2022 1456 Brussels

Scanlon Kat and Royce sat on the other side of the table from the committee. They had finished the debrief of the first mate launch. They had a round of five supply launches over the next three weeks. Dragon would lead off and do the fourth launch from its alternant facility in the Mohave. The Atlas crew was also doing double duty on this series. The French were the other launch facility. Due to the larger capacity of the Arianne rocket the total number of PODS was 10 but water fuel and compressed air tanks would all be delivered as well. The committee was impressed with the schedule not so much with the cost. "You're not saving money. In fact this could be costing us money in the long run. We project a huge cost savings if we stop the overtime and slow down". Royce soothed them.

"We project the possibility of adding more crew members to the Soyus and Gui Long launches and eliminating the Atlas launch on the airlock mate round of flights. That's at least 200 million".

"If you don't spend it on more ad hoc training expeditions", the Chinese member complained. Scanlon plugged in his weapons in this fight: Ratings. "The program is garnering huge ratings. We got thousands of applications for the experiments and the mementos. The website crashed twice due to volume during the voting. Over 1.5 billion votes. If we slow the progress we risk losing the momentum that has people interested".

Tatiana speared Royce with a look. "Are you driving your people too hard? There will be no momentum if a rocket crashes or a major engineering problem arises due to sleepy technicians".

Royce considered her. "Yes we are pushing the boundaries of what's possible. We are driving these people, and by them I mean everyone connected to this venture very very hard. Look at yourselves. I see more than one pair of eyes with bags under them. Except for MS. Medvedev of course she always looks exquisite". Chuckles. "But my point is that we have this mission in our grasp. It has proceeded as well as it has because we are all professional and are doing our jobs. What's a few late nights next to space exploration? What's an extra hour or two at night versus the possibility of discovering life on another planet? We launch for Mars as early as day 550. We have to launch by day 621. I've got day 555 in the betting pool. My career and reputation as well as my hard earned 100 dollars are tied up in this program. I have skin in the game as they say. I'll sleep more when they land back safely on earth. Do I have permission to proceed with the supply missions marked as events 374 thru 395"?

He got it. Too late to stop it now.

Launch day 375 25 Apr 2022 2003 Kennedy

Kat Williams was working late in her office. Late being a subjective term. Eight o'clock was late for the average worker but she was used to odd hours. She looked up at the sound of approaching footsteps. Raven entered without knocking and sat in the chair. "You look like hell," she said. Raven grunted. "I can't figure this. I know the garage is the key but I can't figure it. I have never seen the guy. My tap on his phone has recordings of him making phone calls but I have never seen him. I have not been there all the time but enough to have seen him come and go a few times at least. Nothing." Raven shrugged.

"Has he made you?" Kat asked.

"I think that's the only explanation. He keeps real strange hours too."

"What about the records search of the business."

"Weird as well. Owned by Donald Puring, deceased 6 years ago. The will left it to his son Mitchell also deceased, 5 years ago. The son was an alcoholic, divorced, one kid. Ex wife lives in Nevada. However the business is registered to S M enterprises out of Deleware, which pays the taxes. The IRS has some files. I'm working on getting those. Interagency cooperation my ass, he muttered. "It looks like SM enterprises is a shell corporation hiding the owners. But they are not doing anything illegal. SM enterprises has a bank account that was opened by Mitchel Puring 5 years ago after the old man died. 50 K deposit. It writes three checks a year: One to the state for taxes one to the IRS for taxes and one for the business license. The license goes to a PO box in town. I've never seen anyone go to the PO box. But the check was written 3 weeks ago. The PO box was paid for by Mitchell for the next 10 years. They have obviously made me and I have no choice but to bring in some outside people." "Not you," he said to her unasked question. If they know me they know you. Raven wound down to silence. Kat looked at him squarely. "I think we have been missing something crucial here she said. Maybe these events are not all related to each other. The death of Brad Elkington, the pictures of Sergei and Janice, the car monitoring of Royce. The gun I think we know about. They may be a single acts by one or more people or grouped acts by two or more perpetrators. We need to look at each act individually and find out what connects them to see if they are grouped. Meanwhile get some new people to watch Marysville. Use satellites and wire taps remotely if you have to. Clinton will authorize it. I have some ideas on how we can see if someone is tagging you in the mean time."

Raven looked at her. "Brains. That's why you are in this cushy office job and I'm still breaking and entering into places I don't belong. Brains." They put brains together and planned into the night.

CHAPTER 22

Launch day 401 21 May 2022 1700 Kennedy

The Mars eight and Royce met for dinner in a classy upscale

private dining facility. In reality they commandeered the back four

booths at Rusty's while the tourists gawked. Royce explained that

this was one of the last times they would all be together with him

before the mission and he wanted to make sure they were eating

well. Royce really wanted to get a sense of where the crew was at

mentally. So far there was good and bad news. The crew was

exhausted and frayed a bit from the schedule. However they were

getting to understand each other and make accommodations. There

were still deep divisions of trust: The Chinese were still ignoring

Watkins. Janice was distrustful of Fong Li. Watkins hated Sergei.

 Digger was getting on Hoffman's nerves. But hey, everyone

loved Rosario! Sergei asked about the lunar shakedown trip. Initial

planning had the ship rounding the moon for a quick trip to test out

the engines and nav system. Hell the initial plan had them full out

landing on the moon and setting up a base. Maybe the Mars

two guys could do that. Now it was pared down to the trip around the moon and then back to the ISS. Sergei was arguing for no return trip to the ISS. It would save them 8 or 9 days. Days Sergei felt would be better spent on Mars. Royce was letting himself be talked around. Truth was they had been considering truncating the trip around the moon for some time. It would take them 6 full days to get to the moon at the reduced early speeds. They could then sling shot around the moon and head out to Mars with a little more velocity. It also meant that the top off supply missions would not happen. So they had to be 100 percent ready when they went up the last time 20 days prior to launch from the ISS cradle. That sober thought sank in. Planning looked like day 560. 149 days from now. Call it 5 months. 30 days from now they all went up to mate the clean room. More systems would be brought on line as the clean room had the majority of the water they would need for the trip. They planned to get the living quarters situated on the 29 day mission. Enough systems would be operational that they could move into the bunks on Unity. Showers and toilets would be brought on line as well. The three big work stations would be brought on line and start to do actual maintenance. The last priority would be to work on the fix it list. Royce made a mental note to talk to the Atlas and Dragon people about getting two more crewmen up to the ISS for permanent station on board Unity until it left. Bobbi Edminton had suggested this and it was a good idea. Edminton and her crew had been sneaking over to Unity on any pretext to work on her. Give an astronaut a new toy and they would flip switches and push buttons until told to stop. Royce made mental note to ensure more MRE's were included in the load out. If the Mars crew was going to move over to Unity full time they might need the food. He also had to check on the system upgrades to the computer and the data files. The French were right at launch weight limit with the new crewmen but the Russians had some capacity to spare and he needed to utilize all of that. With a start he realized he was talking to himself while the eight others watched. He casually flipped them the finger. "Dealing with you eight numbskulls would drive anyone to talking to himself. Anyway. You're a good crew even if you're a group of overachieving rocket jocks. I wanted to tell you I'm proud of you and that I have faith that each and every one of you will perform outstandingly. To Unity!" The toast was echoed loudly. Applause from the tourists. Kisses from Rose, Janice and Li. Royce thought he was getting better at speechifying. Oh yeah you all have more physicals prior to the flights to Russia and China for the clean room mate launch. Check your tablets. Groans.

Video Log of Tyler Watkins 17 Jun 2022 0807

Hello from cold windy Russia! I am pleased to be on the clean room mate mission for the Mars program. The crew is performing flawlessly with very little personal tensions. It is a testament to NASA's leadership that the crew and systems have performed this well. We launch soon to complete another step on the path to Mars. The question of the day? What is my favorite place to visit? Well it may be corny but I would have to say Mt. Rushmore. Just seeing those faces always reminds me of American greatness. Thank you.

Launch day 429 18 Jun 2022 1423 Star City Biaknour Russia

Sergei could hear the shouting as he approached the conference room. Tatiana and Janice going at it again. He considered not going in the room. A smart man would just keep walking. As he opened the door the cessation of noise was ominous. Both women's heads whipped around at the door and glared at him. They both started talking over each other. "Get out" and "Sergei, would you please leave!" They glared back at each other for accidentally agreeing on something. Sergei gulped. "Ladies. There's no need to fight over me. Plenty to go around. I might need a blue pill but I'll be ready very soon, I promise". He gave them the lecher smile knowing that would provoke them. Tatiana started in on him in Russian while Janice just glared.

"Okay forget the sex for a little while, what's the problem now"? Janice and Tatiana had been stalking around since they had arrived 6 days ago. 8 days until launch. Nine total crew members: Sergei Janice Fong Hoffman with Datsuk and Dimitrov on the Soyus team. Armbrister destined for the ISS crew and Larson and Nyguen as the Unity babysitters. The Gui long crew was held at eight: Zhou Rosario Andrews and Watkins. Pipei and Liu as the Xe Fang capsule crew. Jonesey and Hadenfeld got the ride as the other two Unity workers going up. Eight more days of these two trying to kill each other, Sergei thought. It seemed every time they got alone a problem erupted. This time Tatiana claimed that Janice was not listening to her. Janice snorted. "I may have to listen to you but I don't have to agree or even care what you think. You might get me booted from this crew but everyone would know it was politically motivated. You would be exposed as the petty, vindictive bitch we all know you to be". Tatiana smirked, "vindictive bitch certainly, but petty? Never. Don't say I didn't warn you". Janice looked on the verge of tears. Sergei turned to her and said "Please wait outside for me, I'll be no more than two min, okay"? Janice frowned. "Okay". She suddenly reached up and kissed him full on for 30 seconds or so. Tatiana rolled her eyes. Sergei broke apart a little discombobulated. As she left Sergei achieved the zone and focused on Tatiana. "I want you to leave her alone please".

"Sergei don't be ridiculous. I know we are through. She didn't have to kiss you in front of me. I know you love her. Any fool can see that". She pouted and went on. "Marking her territory like a common ally cat. I was trying to get her to see the danger in Fong Li".

"You keep saying that but what can Fong really do to her? Kill her"? Sergei asked.

" She is capable of that if need be. What about destroying her professionally. Fong Li is smart enough and ruthless enough to sabotage Janice's work and her reputation. I admit that Janice has gotten tougher but she is not in Li's league even still". Sergei was bewildered. I will help if you tell me what you suspect she will do".

"That's the problem. I have no idea. Sergei ,she doesn't even lock up her research", Tatiana said exasperated. "Her tablet has the most rudimentary password. "Sophy" what is that? I bet her room and car are unlocked right now". Sergei smiled at the truth of that. "Grin all you want but when I tell her to fix those things she just snarls at me like a moon struck teenager". Sergei drew breath and Tatiana forestalled him. "No quips about how good you are in the sack. If you truly love her you need to watch her back". "Okay Tats run what you want her to do thru me and I'll suggest it".

"Sergei you stick to Rockets and the flying, Tatiana said. "Let me handle this. If you start suggesting these things she's going to know I put you up to it and then she's going to be pissed at you too. Get out your two min are up". Sergei went. Janice froze him with a look when he reached her. He raised his hands in supplication. "Lets stop this fussin and fightn'" He drawled.

"You are no cowboy".

"Cossack, remember"?

She did. "Just keep her out of my way please".

"Janice she really isn't your enemy. You know I have no feelings for her any more".

Janice looked away. "I can handle most of the other women, but she gets under my skin". Turning back to face him, she said "Tatiana is everything I'm not: tall, rich, beautiful, politically connected. She knows fashion and high finance and glamorous parties on yachts. I know test tubes and computers".

Hey, you are too beautiful, Sergei objected." Besides that she is very jealous of you too".

"Of me"? Janice repeated skeptically.

"Yes you. Beautiful, and very smart, and now the most famous geek in the world. Look at how much the Australians adored you", Sergei reminded her.

"They adored Zoe Smyth the Australian college kid who got her experiment on the mission. I just happened to be in the way" she said sardonically.

"Ah but you handled it perfectly. Focusing on the kid, letting her shine", Sergei responded. "Tatiana could never have done that. Somehow the event would have come back to focusing on her. She can't help it- she's hard wired that way". "You know I'm not interested in anyone but you? Right" he prodded?

"What about Helen Mathews"? Janice asked innocently.

"Helen Mathews"? Sergei laughed. "I talked to her for 3 min in the green room at Conan Obrien's show last week".

"She sure seemed to hang on your every word while you told the story of that plane crash".

"That's cause I tell it so well and I'm the hero in that story" Sergei crowed.

"Did you mention the part where you threw up" Janice teased?

"Hey who told you that? Besides a flat spin in a jet can be very disorienting. I did miss the buildings and put it into the field".

Janice grinned at him. Sergei had her though. "What about you on Fallon with that football player"?

"Hum? Joe Painter? Please, he's just a dumb jock", she said back peddling.

"You sure felt his bicep".

"Come on! That was a bit for the show you know that".

"Maybe I should be lifting weights, he said.

"Maybe I should practicing my breathless pandering: oh CMDR Ivanovitch, you were so brave in the rocket". She batted her eyes.

"Come on Sophy, you know you are the one for me".

She did at that.

Launch day 430 19 Jan 2022. 0435 Star City Baikanour Russia.

The countdown went smoothly. The routine was normal now. This was Janice 5th time in space, ten for Sergei. They docked with the ISS to see the French capsule already there. The Chinese would be along tomorrow. They greeted Bobbi Edminton like an old shipmate. They had two hard days prep to get the platform and the Unity ready to accept the clean room. The two current sections would be freed from the braces and raised up a total of sixteen feet. Two more sections would be added to the struts. Those had been brought on the supply missions. Larger braces would be needed to attach the struts back to the platform. The old braces would be recycled into landing ladders stored in the clean room when it was mated. The struts themselves had a multitude of connections to be made as well. The mating procedure was going to be the same as the first two sections. Ribs and bolt hole aligning. Five days later they were finished. It had been a little more difficult than the first time but not so bad. There had been some "persuading" with a pry bar to get it accomplished. Now they split into four teams. The first team would finish the skin panel installation. Janice got that job with Watkins and Nguyen. The second team would finish the pipe connections on the outside. Sergei, Hoffman and Peipe got that one. A third team to start installing the first of the solid propellant rockets that would be used as maneuvering thrusters. There would be three on each strut arranged orthogonally along the x, y and z axis'. The fourth team would be inside doing the connection work. Day 438 saw them finished outside and making connections. The clean room was now going to be pressed into service as an airlock. They could draw a vacuum on the clean room. The air, water and fuel had been transferred to the ship. The air plant was up and making oxygen. A small compressor was tanking a small surplus as the ship was not yet using o2. The scrubbers and burners were on line. Heaters and ventilation as well. The ship was not at full capacity power wise and they had very little to spare. Don't plug in a razor was the admonition. Sergei had assigned the Unity baby sitters to monitor the power levels as equipment was brought on board and on line. Today started the test. If they could maintain temp, o2 levels and pressure and move water around for 24 hrs they could get 8 people in the Unity space craft and get out of their suits. Houston was worried. 6 hours in the o2 plant went down. It took 22 min to get it restarted. Royce got a full debrief on the problem. Faulty circuit card assembly had had shorted out and tripped the breaker. The plant went into shut down mode as it was expected to do. The ship may have been able to ride thru the power suck but it didn't have the excess power to do it this time. The good news is that the system monitoring the plant alerted as required. The crew followed emergency procedures and would have donned EVA suits but there was no need. The troubleshooting identified the problem quickly and the spare was right where it was supposed to be. After the fix and brief to Houston the test recommenced. Sergei led them in some what if scenarios. What if the spare had not been there? The circuit board is a standard power distribution board and is common to the air plant and the scrubber unit. We could get a spare from there. We could attempt to find the problem and replace some of the more standard issue components on the circuit card assembly (CCA). We might be able to hard wire some of the power inputs using an ac/dc power supply test unit. That from Watkins. Sergei was impressed. That would be some out of the box thinking right there. It might not look pretty but it would work as a last ditch effort. More scenarios on different gear. Everyone had done this in the mock up on earth but nothing like an actual alert coming thru the comm net to make you feel alive. The next day they all waited anxiously. The appointed time came and went. Unity requested permission to strip down. Granted. At the unspoken command they all cracked helmets. The first breath of Unity air was a little strange. Metallic, and faintly oily, the air had an industrial smell. It would take a while before the human smell took over. Grins broke out all around. Houston, Unity here. We're home! Sergei's throw away line was the headline in the New York Times the next day. He told them to store the suits in the lockers assigned forward port of the 02 level in the equipment section. When they opened them a small problem presented itself: suits were already stored there. He had forgotten they were ahead of the program here. Sergei had them store the suits in their individual acceleration PODs. They all had a small bag of personal effects. Toothbrush and underwear to store in the bunk pans. The zero gee was making the orientation of the craft a little difficult. The space ship was designed to lay out with some level of gravity. So there was a deck and an overhead. There was nominally an up and a down. The majority of flight would be done with some gee force being felt. The fuel available made for about a 10 th of earth normal during the trip. That was what they could expect on mars. So the zero gee now had some consequences as things they stored would have to be tied down. The crew sleeping qtrs was pretty spartan. Digger was the first to personalize the underside of his bunk with a Zhenge landing site drawing. Janice, Rosario and Fong Li all took stbd side bunks with Janice and Rosario outboard. Rose was on top by choice. Dr Hoffman was quickly offered a bunk station with Fong. He was the only guy who didn't snore. Plus he was fastidious and kind. Exactly the man they wanted. Sergei pouted a little when he was shown the door figuratively. The American men took port outboard set of racks while Zhou and Sergei got the inner port set. Zhou and Digger on top. They all rigged up sleep sacks chatting away like it was the first day of camp. Larson, Jonesey, Nguyen, and Hadenfeld continued to move about Unity working thru the connection points for data air and fuel. They were fixing some minor leaking but nothing catastrophic. The three big work stations had come on line. One was almost a garage work shop setup. Compressed air, hydraulic power lift and tools. A vise and clamps could be mounted. Special lights were above the seven by five table top as it doubled as an operating table. The team each docked their tablets in the work stations and commanded the various systems. Almost 80 percent of the valves and switches on board Unity could be remotely operated. It made lining up to transfer fuel or water around very simple. The computer allowed the operator to select a tank or POD position and select a destination tank. Then the amount was keyed in and the pump came on and the liquid transferred. The purging of dangerous gases was automatic. The navigation system was up and reading no movement relative to the station. The graphical display could render the planets and the ship in detail to show routes and distances. Houston advised them that 12 hrs had elapsed. Time for sleep. As they cycled the four baby sitters back to the ISS. Larson joked that the secret knock to let them in would be "shave and a haircut." Blank looks from the young members of the crew. Hoffman demonstrated. Du pause du du du longer pause. Du du. Shave and a haircut two bits. What's two bits? Get out.

Houston woke them the next morning with "Good Morning Star Shine", the song from the musical Hair. Digger grumbled "what does glibby glip glibby mean again"? The toilet and shower worked okay. The same setup as the ISS made the shower sacks tolerable. The water went down to the collection tank and started the recycle process. Breakfast was a communal MRE fest. The calorie count on an MRE was over 5000. They would need them. They had a full testing schedule. The ISS crew came in. All four could go thru the clean room pump down and pressurization at the same time. Sergei had asked for a pressure and o2 reading before during and after the cycle. He compared it to the previous night. Houston confirmed that they were recapturing 99.54 percent of the air pumped out of the clean room. Today they also had to transfer water and fuel to and from the storage PODs and the ship. From the command deck Watkins and Zhou ran the water around to various tanks and PODs. They could also use the ships pumps to go from POD to POD. 10 hours of moving water and fuel left them drained. Zhou could not believe that he could be so tired from watching a video screen. Houston was very pleased with the progress in the system testing. Watkins and Zhou were satisfied from a hard days work when Houston reminded them that they needed to repeat the whole series of tank to tank moves using voice commands.

Video log Lui Zhou 15 Feb 2022 1957

Hello to earth from Unity. The spacecraft is performing marvelously. I'm a little tired from the rigors of avoiding the numerous bodies inside the space ship. It gets crowded with so many of us inside now. I'm looking forward to some off time when we get back. Soon we will be back on earth and then quickly we will be back here for good. For the mission. I'm trying to get a mental picture of us on the mission. I have endured some tight quarters and long missions before but this is daunting. I know my crewmates are also worried about this. Li and I have had many discussions of the issues involved in long space flight. I know we can overcome them given some leadership and cooperation. We work together best when we are accomplishing a task. Left to sit and wait we tend to crowd each other. I will work on my suggestions to overcome this with Sergei and Mr. Royce. The days question is who is my favorite movie actor or singer. I am a great fan of Martin Handler the action movie star. His performance in Last Man was outstanding! Out!

CHAPTER 23

Launch day 458 17 Feb 2022 1543 Outer Mongolia Gobi desert

Rosario Gonsolvo hated the reentry part. The violent shaking. The super hot plasma glow that made it seem the ship was on fire. Which it was. Nothing to do but sit there strapped in waiting for the ship to tear itself apart. The Columbia disaster was etched indelibly on the brain of everyone connected with space flight. The peace and quiet of the parachute deployment was a welcome non sound. The white tiger capsule reported three mains deployed. The control station responded by telling them the winds were blowing them east of the intended drop zone. Great Watkins complained. A 60 min wait while they tried to find them. Rose sighed. She wanted out of the capsule out of these clothes and away from these people. NASA had promised them two weeks off. They had agreed to the "suggestion" from the crew, that before the endless training/publicity tour of the actual mars mission got underway, the slaves needed some time off. Royce had told them use it well and don't get hurt. Rosario had a certain Chilean Air Force General lined up to meet her back at St Alphonso Ser Mer. She intended to swim in that pool, not work in it. She asked Zhou and Watkins what they had planned. Home to Chaing Mai and Florida. That sounded peaceful to her. She knew Janice and Sergei were headed to Rome for at least a week. Hoffman was taking the waters in Baden Baden and Andrews was off for England with his family. No one quite knew what Fong was up to. Rosario thought she was an odd one. The thump of touchdown interrupted her thoughts. They had a full mission debrief with the Chinese and Royce. Then playtime. As the Chinese ground team led them out of the capsule Rose noticed a large chunk out of the heat shield. Man she hated that part!

Launch day 460 19 Feb 2022 1821 Coco Beach Florida

Royce sat at the counter quietly eating a burger. He was going over supply mission status reports as well as the debrief on the clean room mate mission for the committee. Raven came in and sat next to him. The briefcase went down between them. Neither spoke. Royce continued eating and reading and didn't consciously notice when Raven left. He put the folders in the briefcase and paid and left. They didn't see the woman watching them. Kat saw her though. Humm. Maybe no one was watching Raven. Only a true spook team could watch him unobserved. However, someone could watch Royce without him noticing. Kat sat in her car watching the woman as she tailed Royce back to his office. Kat followed at a discrete distance. She multitasked to write up a description and take some pictures. Maybe this is the break they needed. Who was the woman?

Launch day 474 04 Mar 2022 0735 Kennedy Space Center

The large auditorium was filled. The Unity crew along with the rest of the remaining mars candidates (all 32 of them) as well as program managers and contractor leads. The government types were there as well as NASA brass, committee people and various space agencies. Royce wanted them all to get this message first hand so everyone is on the same page. Royce stepped up to the podium. "Ladies and gentleman, thank you for coming. The full debrief is available on the live link mission folder on the net. Unity/mars candidates you will find it uploaded to your tablets. The upshot of the brief is that we met 119 percent of mission goals. We only Ided" 3 procedural issues. The mate went well and you should be congratulated". Small applause sounded out. Royce paused. "We have reached the point in the old western where someone points out that it is quiet. Too quiet". The next scene is a mass of natives charging down on the settlers". "Well it is quiet in our program. Too quiet", he looked out at the crowd. "We better be on the lookout for natives. Ask yourself this: what did I not think of. Every program manager is to call in a group of the youngest engineers on the program". "I want you to explain to them what you are doing and why. Then ask them what they would do". I want these sessions video taped and sent to me next week". He let that sink in. "The list of required videos is posted. Lastly, I want you to put yourselves in my shoes. Tell me how you would handle it, or what you would change". "That list is posted as well". He shifted gears. "Okay. Let's talk schedule. We have six more supply launches over the next month and a half". Some of the ISS crew is living in the Unity and they are eating up the food and using up air and oxygen that we didn't plan on". "We need to get more food up there". "The airlock mate mission is slated for day 499. Mars crew goes up day 550 for good". A quiet rustling as the crowd heard the reality in his voice. "They are going to be packed to the gills with food and parts and water. The final science experiments go up with them. Mars crew you have 103 lbs each". A small cheer. "Submit to Freddy what you want to take. Some liquor will be allowed". A whoop from Digger. Laughter. "Remember we plan to send up video programs so you can watch the latest Fillmore Rules episodes". "Launch day for Mars is 556. Janice and Fong please go over the medicinal load out with Freddy". That goes on one of the final supply missions. We still have 9 more milestones to go. Mars crew you have an exciting 66 days of training and publicity ahead". Royce paused knowing what was coming. Horrified groans from the crew, laughter from everyone else. "Okay people we have our tasks. Get at them".

Royce and Scanlon met with Unity crew to set out schedules and see how they had survived the time off. The small conference room was crowded. Royce only had half a mind on the meeting. Raven and Kat had requested a meeting tonight. Not in his office. They were being cryptic. Tatiana was hounding him about Fong Li while every major city mayor in the world wanted all 8 astronauts to spend weeks in their city. Some were no brainers: DC, New York, Paris, Moscow, Beijing, Berlin, Buenos Aries. But San Francisco, and Cape Town had made the list. Sydney was also almost set. It looked like 20 days of training, followed by 21 days of the rubber chicken circuit followed by the last 20 days of training. President Clinton had them at the Whitehouse three days prior to launch. The eight looked reasonably happy. The two weeks away from each other worked wonders. Scanlon had asked Tyler Watkins what he had done on vaca. Drink beers and work on cars with my brother he replied. Relaxing. His place was just north of Kennedy bordering the wildlife refuge. Redneck heaven. Sergei and Janice had spent the time in Rome and Venice. Rosario looked tan and happy. Even Zhou and Fong looked eager and ready. John hoped that would last.

The days rushed by. The training program was more fine tuning on the site prep and build. They formalized the watch stations and duty roster. The concept of flight command, work/science and off was still operative. Sergei, Watkins, Rosario and Zhou were set as Flight leads. They pared them with Janice, Hoffman, Andrews and Fong. They had stuck with 6 hr shifts. The in flight watch bill looked like this

00-06.	06-12.	12-18.	18-24
Unassigned. Sec 2	Sec 1.	Sec4.	Sec 3.
Off/sleep. Sec 3	Sec2.	Sec 1.	Sec 4.
Science/engineering. Sec 4	Sec 3.	Sec 2.	Sec 1.
Flight. Sec 1	Sec 4.	Sec 3.	Sec 2.

Section 1 would be Sergei and Janice. Section 2 Tyler and Georg, section 3 Rosario and James and section 4 with Lui and Li. The unassigned period gave them some flexibility for changes. No one expected the watch bill to last for more than 3 to 4 weeks. They practiced the watch bill in operational scenarios in the flight mock up. They practiced faulted scenarios where they lost air or water pumps, computers, radar, nav units. They flew on low power, bad engines, bad water. Royce made them don EVA suits and work in the dark, like they wouldn't have flashlights. The one real outcome of the video tapes Royce had ordered is that it became clear that the landing site (Zhenge) was totally dependent on the rover bobcat. If the bobcat couldn't dig thru the permafrost there would be no Zhenge He base. Royce seemed not too concerned. The CBD reps and Digger went thru it again and again. Should they take some dynamite or something else? Would the ice be more than the four to six inches the curiosity rover had found. The Viking lander that had touched down near where they would land had no real digging capability. They just didn't know. Digger and the contractors felt positive that they could punch thru the permafrost. Time would tell.

Video log Rosario Gonsolvo 15 Mar 2022 2210
Hola, mu chachos! I'm very honored to be talking to you again from Buenos Ares. The start of this publicity tour was exciting. Everyone has been cheering us and waving flags and wishing us good luck! I know I speak for the whole crew when I say that

as tired and wrung out as we feel, just a few minutes with the people really lifts our spirits. I can feel the mission getting closer and the excitement building. Man setting foot on Mars. It has a whole electric feeling when people say it. As I was saying to my good friend the Chilean General Banos and my fellow astronaut Janice Lincoln, we are now citizens of the world not just of our individual countries. The mission can't come soon enough as far as we are concerned. The days question: What do you fear the most? Oh that's tough. I guess running out of air would head the list. Oh, and spiders! Ciao Bellas.

Launch day 504 04 Apr 2022 1325 San Francisco

The crowd on the embarcadero was huge. Hundreds of thousands had jammed the waterfront of San Francisco to see the crew. The podium was setup near the Gothic space ship sculpture by Gergan. The stainless steel space ship had a bulbous smooth rocket shape with three large struts jutting out to connect rocket to the ground. Sergei eyed the sculpture critically. That's pretty close he thought. Gergan had made the sculpture in 1973 based on old pulp

paper science fiction drawings. Well they came close. Yesterday's

science fiction was today's science fact. Sergei noted his thoughts

to the crowd. He commented that the work going on in silicone

valley made products that 30 years ago were the stuff of vivid

imagination. The road sensors going in to allow the self driving

cars were pipe dreams just 10 years ago. Imagine big today

because it was coming true faster and faster. And could someone

please get those flying cars that George Jetson promised us? The

crowd roared with laughter. Mr. Smooth was at it again. China was

the crowning moment. They stepped on the podium to the

deafening roar of 4 million people packed into Tienemen square.

The last of the crowd was watching them on big screens setup 5

miles from the stage. Lui and Li had the crowd rocking, singing the

latest popular song in china. Who knew Fong could carry a tune?

While the Mars eight were singing and carrying on in China, the

crew performing the airlock mate had a few issues. They had

several aborted attempts to get the ribs and bolt holes aligned.

They also had trouble with the o-ring inflating. It took four tries to

get the ring inflated correctly. Royce corralled Sergei and Tyler to

talk Grace Adler thru the intricacies after the third day working on it. Grace was frustrated. Sergei told her to walk away from it for twelve hours. Take a shower and get some chow and sleep. Start fresh with the whole team. "Grace, Sergei said, "You've turned more wrenches on that ship than anyone connected to the program. The only reason the Unity space ship was in as good a shape as it was is because of you". On this tour I had four million people chanting my name, but I am your biggest fan! I know you can get this done".

"Thanks Sergei that means a lot".

"Now go get some sleep! And don't make me come up there"! Grace snorted and cut the connection. They got it done. It took four extra days but the ship was together. The baby sitters sent up with Grace would complete the connections and the testing.

Launch day 551 27 May 2022 1925 Houston Johnson Space Center

The Unity crew completed the debrief with little fanfare. Janice felt wrung out. The rest of the crew mirrored her. They were done! The training program complete. They were as ready as they could be. Tonight they flew back to Kennedy. Then to the White

House for one last photo op. Then they loaded personal effects onto the Orion capsule. Only the eight of them would be on the Orion. The capsule would take back the last set of baby sitters from the ISS. The Dragon and Atlas would also come up. NASA was concerned about fuel levels. There was even talk of shooting some fuel PODs out ahead of them. NASA had also granted a last min request from Fong Li. A telescope. The 14 inch wide mirror was basically the best amateur telescope you could buy. 10,000 dollars and 190 lbs later, they just needed a spot to store it during launch. They agreed the port side aft window would offer the best view of the moon as they whipped around it on the way to mars. The best spot while they waited for launch was the clean room. Li intended to get some good pictures of the ISS as Unity pulled away. Then she wanted some close ups of the Martian moons. Who knows, she could discover the first extra planetary comet. Then work on the basic planets. Hey she would be closer and with almost zero atmospheric interference. Her talk made them all curious. What would Jupiter look like in the Martian skies? The sun a small ball of light? Would the Martian sky really be pink? It was these kinds of discussions that made Janice certain that they would be successful. In the end they were all curious. They all just wanted to see what was out there. Explorers all.

Launch day 553 29 May 2022 1934 The White House

The official State Dinner for the Unity crew was the most lavish the Clinton 2.0 Administration had ever thrown. 300 guests. Mere Representatives were sent packing. This dinner was for people who mattered. Heads of State, Billionaire CEO's, Senators and Officials all jockeyed for position in the receiving line. The President had ensured that the crew had taken a photo with her daughter and three grand kids. She regretted that her husband had died in 2016. Bill Clinton famously died of a heart attack election night as she was sweeping to victory. The Mars eight were all dolled up. NASA had sent Tatiana and a bevy of stylists to make up the ladies. The men got tuxes or dress uniforms. Sergei had several gaudy medals on his. And a sword. Janice asked if he was ready to repel boarders. Sergei replied with the old joke: what's a pirate's favorite letter of the alphabet. Arrrr! He was handsome in the uniform. Tall and trim with his face tanned with character lines. He caught her staring. Want me to wear the uniform later? Yes, please. He laughed full out. Janice secretly loved that she could make him laugh. The receiving line was a full on Washington power play. The jockeying to get in a picture with the heroes of the day was almost as fierce as the fight to get money out of congress. Royce and Scanlon were very near the end of the line. "You guys should dress up more", Rosario said kissing them on the cheeks. "You guys look good as well", Royce replied.

"Janice was so freaked out she let Tatiana dress her"! Royce chuckled "I'm sure I'll hear about it".

Scanlon said "I think I can double our appropriation if you wear that dress during the next budget meeting". Rose laughed as the next couple came up gushing. The whole evening was capped off by a simple speech from Georg Hoffman. The absentminded professor was gone. The slim scientist summed up the immense honor they all felt. "We don't feel the weight of the responsibility, we feel billions of hands lifting us up. We don't feel the fear of the unknown, we feel the curiosity of the unexplored. We don't feel the pressure of expectations we feel the hope of the whole world coming together. Some have said we represent the best earth has to offer. We disagree. We just represent the best in everyone. Together we reach for the stars. United we find our destiny. Thank you". Tee shirts were being printed with the speech emblazoned on them within the hour.

Launch day 556 01 Jun 2022 0920 Kennedy Space Center

T minus 60 min in a preprogrammed hold. The countdown was proceeding as smooth as possible. As smooth as possible for a giant cluster fuck. Two separate containers were strapped down with tie downs and zip ties. Jesus, they almost forgot one of the science experiments! Royce was livid. He sarcastically asked Freddy if they remembered the food? The crowd was so large and so close it took 45 min to get them from the prep area to the van. It was like a freakin Beatles concert. Christ is that Raven with Kat in the VIP area? Is Raven here to kill him? He was slated to go down there to be with the families. He might as well go down. He was done providing leadership, well yelling at people really.

Kat and Raven grabbed him before he got to the VIP platform. "Who is that man right there"? Kat asked pointing. "That's Tyler Watkins brother, why"? Bob replied eyeing him. "What's his name"? "Mathew Puring, again why"? They are half brothers. "I think Mathew was adopted by Watkins mother in Nevada before they came to Florida" Royce went on. "Oh shit, we have to stop the launch" Kat shouted over the tumalt! "Stop the launch are you kidding me"? Kat asked who the woman was.

"I think that's Mathew's girlfriend. Tyler only has those two so it wasn't tough to get her here". This is the first launch he's asked for so we gladly let her come."

"Why? What's going on"?

Kat and Raven related the woman watching Royce and Raven with the steering column bearing collars that had been ordered to Donald Purings old garage.

"We've been assuming the same person did all of the acts of sabotage. But what if that assumption is wrong", Raven said. "What if The Chinese did the pictures to have a hold on Dr. Lincoln? They desperately want Fong to make the discovery of life on mars". "The gun was the work of the Chechyns", he told Royce flatly. "The plan was to wipe out the astronauts and stop the program". "But what if the tracking device and Brad Elkington's murder were done by a third person"? Who gains by knowing what you are doing and saying and who benefitted by Elkington dying, Raven went on? "Tyler Watkins. Look at the other bearings"?

"Sergei? With him out of the picture Tyler is mission

commander. I think Grace Adler was backup if you found a reason to bypass him after Elkington's death". "My guess is that his brother inserted the collar devices months ago". Watkins waited to see which way he had to go. But Elkington was enough". I think," he wound down. "I have no idea what he is capable of if he gets stymied again. He seems to act when he gets denied something he sees as his due" Raven finished.

"What proof do you have? The collar device? That will never hold up in court", Royce said succinctly.

"This will never see a courtroom," Kat said.

"I can't stop the launch," Royce said quietly.

"You're going to let them go into space with that socio path", Raven asked incredulously.

"We pull him out now we have to insert Grace Adler. It will take 40 days or so to get her integrated. That puts us outside the mars window". "We can't", Royce said softly. We can do a few things though". "Raven, I think Mathew and his girlfriend need to be under intense scrutiny". I want to get a private message to Sergei. We know how the Chinese are communicating with Fong. "Lets set up something similar with Ivanovitch. I need to talk to Tony Larson before he takes off in the Atlas tomorrow. Kat you come with me to setup the one time ciphers for Sergei. We give them to Larson to give to Sergei". Kat nodded.

"We also need to subtly let Watkins know we know". Royce thought furiously. "Come with me. Stay behind the families on the grand stands". Royce led them out. He immediately sought out Puring and the girl. Spotting them he motioned Kat and Raven to the back. Royce went down front and asked the families to line up class picture style and get picture to send up to the astronauts in space the next day. It was the girl who spotted Raven, her face going blank. She whispered furiously to Mathew Puring but they were trapped. They stood with the other families for the photo. Royce made eye contact with a scowling Mathew Puring. The small throat cutting gesture from Royce made him blanch and turn pale. They fled the platform with Raven watching. He started to follow but Royce caught him for a second. "Follow but don't kill them. We need them as hostages for Watkins good behavior". Raven left the platform. Cluster fuck. The launch of the Unity crew was almost an afterthought for Royce. He watched the liftoff from the platform with conflicting thoughts. He had done what he could but had also made mistakes. It was up to them now

CHAPTER 24

Launch day 558 03 Jun 2022. 1002 ISS and Unity

The last min packing was always the most stressful part of the move. After a few days delay, they were finally ready to go. The Unity crew was not taking much beyond standard clothing and "special items". Getting all their personal effects situated was daunting. Each bunk had a pan area underneath for clothes and other storage. A common large locker held items needing to be hanged up. Sweaters and thermal suits. The standard uniform was a thin pair of stretchy pants that tied at the waist and a polo type shirt. Shoes were a slip on vans type loafer. Socks and underwear at your own discretion. Underneath were the ubiquitous pressure skins. It got cold in space so sweaters were the preferred outer wear. The heaters could be cranked up but the electronics preferred colder so cold it was. A steady 64 or so. The galley had some large flat locker panels and these became places to tape up pictures. Discussions with former ISS crew members had made many small additions to what NASA called the "habitability" program. Many little items that went along way to improving crew moral. Want

393

UNITY

a drink while you are standing watch? Sure. You are going to need

a cup. A cup in near zero gee? Really a squeeze bottle. That

squeeze bottle is going to get dirty. There was a small autoclave

like device that sterilized instruments that also served as an ersatz

dish washer. Okay you have a squeeze bottle and it's clean.

Coffee? Brewed? Nope. Instant. Hot water? Again the hot water

was heated by the same unit that served the auto clave, the shower

units and the galley. The shower sacks served as laundry units as

well. Instead of zipping in a human, clothes could be put in and

hand agitated. Dryer? The Unity spaceship was going to look like

Brooklyn in the forties. Laundry on lines hanging to dry. Once that

coffee was made and in your bottle, now you might not want to

hold it in your hand all the time. Cup holders on a spaceship? Zarfs

wouldn't be practical in zero gee. Zarf. Great Words with Friends

word. A zarf was a coffee cup holder usually made out of metal. A

term from the Middle East. The US Navy submarine force has

been pop riveting zarfs to bulkheads and pieces of gear for

decades. NASA kind of frowned on pop rivets on a quantum

computer. Velcro. Did the entire military industrial complex run on

Velcro and duct tape? Yes it did. So the watch stander had his or

her drink and it was velcroed to the command console. It wasn't six hours into the move in when the first "who moved my coffee cup" whine drifted from the command deck down to the galley. Trash was the bigger concern down in the galley. Wrappers seemed to be everywhere. Very few of the spare parts were wrapped. Some of the more sensitive electronics parts were ESD wrapped but mostly it was the MRE packets. The packets contained an outer sleeve where a small amount of water was poured to start the chemical reaction to heat the glop. More water was poured into the inner sleeve to make the edible glop gloppier. The stuff that was supposed to be dry was wrapped in foil and that foil was supposed to be buried along with the rest of the packaging from the MRE. They had a very small trash compactor. The current thought was to pump down the airlock and let the trash cubes drift into space. They could remotely open the door. However there was no way to ensure the trash pockets drifted out. Could a suited person be clipped in the airlock when they opened the door? Maybe. NASA thought they could store the trash until mars. Sergei was going to watch this very closely. He had visions of them wading thru MRE wrappers to get out of the space ship. He had some intense talks with Bobbi Edminton about how much trash they were making and how the galley/toilets/showers were working. He had told her to make sure they stressed those units before they left after the clean room mate. He wanted to know they could handle eight people for an extended period. He also flat out asked her about tampons. Bobbi had laughed uproariously at that. "Sergei you misogynist! NASA has had woman astronauts since the great Sally Ride. Don't you think we have figured out how to handle that"? "Uhh". "If you must know there is a locker in the toilet area that has a supply and there are sanitary bags that will get compacted. Just so you know, 95 percent of women astronauts do not menstruate due to the physical exertions. My guess: one or two tampons the whole time. You're just now worrying about this"? she asked. Sergei left the ISS bay defeated. The loading from Orion and Atlas and the Dragon capsules continued. Food fuel water air and parts. They wanted them as close to 100 percent as possible. Watkins was on the command deck moving liquids. Janice and Fong were down on the second deck of the Einstein mod starting some of the science experiments. They were setting up seedlings in a UV light box. They also just planted some herbs and tomatoes in another box to see how they grew. The mice were next. Fong was waiting for permission to set up her telescope. Georg was setting up some of the long term radiation and other cosmic ray detectors. Rosario had the telemetry vid link with Houston up full. Digger was moving certain delicate personal items from Orion over to the ship. Everyone had something. James had three special glass lined metal containers that had 30 year old scotch in them. McAllam had made them special. Georg had some nice wine. Even Sergei had some vodka and Champaign on board. The ladies tended to more practical food specialties. Janice had a special box of chocolates, while Fong had some noodles made especially from her hometown. The people at Coke had sworn to Rosario that the special containers would work in zero gee and survive the rigors of space. Rose needed that fix bad sometimes. All of them just needed something to remind them of home. Zhou ran thru the departing check list with Houston. All looked on track. Tony Larson called Sergei back over to the ISS for a special present from Bob Royce. Returning to Unity Sergei called them all down to the galley to see Royce's present. The picture was from the launch three days ago. It clearly showed Royce and their families. You could see Janice's mom, and Rosario's beaming parents. Of course Georg's sister had her eyes closed. And some people had not heard the cheese command. Some were notably not smiling.

Sergei and Watkins locked eyes. Watkins turned and went back to the command deck without a word. Janice noticed the tightening of Sergei's grip on the railing to the ladder leading up to the command deck as Watkins left. She put a hand on his shoulder. Later he muttered.

Launch day 560 05 Jun 2022 1702 ISS and Unity

As Janice toured Unity she could see the final shape of the ship in focus. On the command deck and Zhou and Watkins were inserting the final Nav updates. The mission profile for a full turn around the moon and a slingshot rip were being loaded. Digger, Georg and Fong were setting up more science experiments and the work tables. The largest had been completed during the mating runs but the second smaller table was now set up as an electrical work bench. Smaller padded clamps for holding circuit boards and a soldering station was set up. Janice had been bringing the specialized electron microscope on line. Rosario was running trend analysis of some of the air cleaners and realized that the added people and equipment moving in and out had caused more particles to build up more than would normally be expected. Consequently she was pulling and cleaning filters. Sergei himself had the galley clean. Watkins had reported down that the water transfer was complete. That marked the final umbilical attaching Unity to the ISS. The Atlas and Dragon crews had been disconnecting the braces holding Unity to the platform. They were down to two. The two braces had been stored in the airlock and that marked the final piece of gear to come on board. The other two braces would await their return a year from now hooked onto the ISS. There were three PODs on the intermediate platform. That was NASAs back up plan in case they ran out of fuel. 2393 gallons in the ships tank and 1600 on the PODs. Sergei called for them all to get suited. Tony Larson would be there with Pat Nyguen any minute. The ISS had a special dinner planned. Tony and Pat were actually going to stand watch the whole night. The crew was due for an 0300 wake up to start the undock and launch procedure. They wanted a good night's sleep before the start of the mission. But Bobbi wanted them over to the ISS for one last meal before they left. As the Unity crew came into the airlock an hour later the ISS station was decked out in large banners with Buon Voyage on them. English ,

Spanish, German Russian and Chinese banners as well. The table setup as a "buffet" had special dishes. Real food, not reconstituted. Sergei told Bobbi they were going to be picking turkey out of the station corners for weeks. The Unity crew mingled and ate with the dragon, atlas and ISS crews for five full hours. They ate and drank and sang songs to mark the start of the journey. Houston had long since given up on getting them back at a reasonable hour. "Do you really think any of us is going to be able to sleep tonight", Digger asked? Many hugs and kisses later, the Unity crew settled in for what turned out to be three good hours of sleep.

Launch day 561 06 Jun 2022. 0700 ISS and Unity

The 78 th anniversary of the allied invasion of occupied France during WW II, was marked by wreath layings and an eye on the news. The launch was scheduled in prime time in Europe. Late night in China and early morning in the US. Unity was as buttoned up as she could be. The final two braces were removed and the robotic arm was swinging them out as far as possible. Messages of Godspeed and good luck had been coming in from around the world. As the arm now had them away from the station and the cubes were loaded, the ship was fully deploying the solar array. The array was sloooowly unwinding. Twenty min later the computer alerted that the array was fully extended. Sergei called for systems verification. Flight reported first: all computer inputs available. Monitoring was on line. Engine connectivity was good. That meant that the computer had command lines to all twelve thruster engines and the four main engines on the struts. Radar and Navigation was set. Auxiliary systems reported sat. That meant the air banks were topped off, the air monitoring system was working and the fuel, water, hydraulics were functional. The batteries were fully charged and the electrical system was aligned for flight. Science stations reported ready. Comms data and telemetry were sat. 0728. Two min early. Sergei gave the command to the ISS. Arm disengage. The arm gently nudged the ship away from the station and slightly elevated to the plane. Unity floated free by 2 feet. 10 feet. 60 feet. Sergei said confidently, "Houston, Unity, ready for initial burn". "Roger Unity go for burn. Godspeed Unity". "Roger. Computer on my mark maneuvering burn for initial thrust away preset heading, elevation and azimuth set alpha. Mark". The mechanical voice acknowledged. The voice was no where near as good as Majel Barret, Sergei thought. Not even as good as Siri. The burn was kind of anticlimactic. The maneuvering engines came on for about a second. Three of them combined to send the ship away from the station and up at about 2 feet per second. Unity slowly pulled away from the ISS. Telemetry and monitoring data poured from the engines to be mated with the inputs from the ring laser gyros on the nav units. All of that data was being sent to Houston and correlated as well. Watkins and Sergei had the flight plan displayed on the two middle screens of the command deck. Sergei, and Watkins occupied the chairs in the backs of the middle front row accel couches. Rosario and Zhou occupied the outer two. Flight jocks in front, science geeks in the back. Digger, Janice, Fong, and Hoffman arranged in the second level of couches facing forward. The two middle screens showed predicted and actual flight plans. On the left predicted screen, the 3D drawing of the ship showed which three thruster engines the computer had predicted what would be necessary to propel the craft to Sergei's order. It also showed durations, velocities and other variables. The three engines on the model glowed red to show they would be used. The right middle screen showed the actual engines used. The same three glowed green. It showed the actual burn times, the ships velocities, and the ships relative position to the ISS, the earth and the moon. Objects would occasionally come across the screen. Satellites as they were tracked while passing thru the space Unity was operating in. Had there been any deviation between the predicted and the actual an alert would have been sent out. The computer could stop all engines if the situation demanded, however the final say was the human. Sergei had sized it up in a min and reported the burn successful. Three more min while Houston confirmed. The ships position had been compared with GPS. All nominal. "Roger Unity confirm good burn. Proceed with maneuvering plan Alpha". Unity and Sergei now went thru a series of preprogrammed maneuvers designed to test the thrusters. They stopped the ship, then compared data. They rolled the ship and compared. They made it go backwards. They flipped it. All the while comparing the predicted and actual with the GPS as an outside reference source. Had there been any issues, they would have limped back to the ISS but none appeared. The window when Mars was too far away closed in 34 days. They could repair something minor not major. One major test left. One quick burp of the mains and then flip and stop. If that went well it was off to the moon and then Mars. At 1322 Sergei called for the computer to initiate main test Beta two. Mark. This time the thrust was way more substantial. The four mains burned for a full twenty seconds. The crew could hear contents in lockers shifting. There were some hull popping noises. The computer initiated the flip on schedule and the counter burn showed them stopped in space relative to the ISS. Data again poured back and forth. It looked good. Finally at 1545, Houston concurred. "Roger, Houston, Unity is go for sustained 1/10 th burn for lunar orbit". So for the next three days they would have 1/10 th gravity on the ship. That was essentially what gravity mars had. Just enough to keep things on the ground. "Roger Unity go for burn". "On my mark computer preset lunar slingshot burn Charlie one. Mark". The engines kicked in. The gravity was strange after the zero gee. However it was still not enough for real "walking". The burn went off as all the others had. Sergei had the seven others running various systems checks to confirm all greens prior to setting normal watches. As Sergei set underway sec 2 with the rest of the 12-18 watch. Sec 1 had science/engineering watch until 1800 then they took over as flight. That meant Sergei and Janice wouldn't get any sleep till midnight. As Rosé , Zhou, Fong and Digger all went to grab some chow and rack time, Watkins and Hoffman settled into the flight chairs. They only had about two more hours of watch and then they would have 12 off. Sergei asked if he or Janice could get them a cup of coffee or another drink. They were set. Hoffman set comms with Houston while they watched the speed build up with agonizing slowness. As they looked at the display they achieved one mile per hour. Sergei and Janice set off on the post launch engineering check list. They had many items to look in on after the launch to see if the shaking from the maneuvers had disturbed the gear. They weren't near completed when their reliefs came up. Zhou and Fong. They should be able to finish on their watch. Sergei also gave Li permission to install her telescope. The ISS was rapidly dwindling. Sergei and Janice relived Watkins and Hoffman. The latter moving quickly down to get out of his EVA suit. Speed three miles an hour, good vid, comm and data link. Next voice check at 2000. No alerts. Radar clear. Post launch engineering checklist underway. I'm ready to be relieved. I relieve you. Janice had lost the coin flip so she had to be in the suit. "The coin wanted the brains of the operation free to think on his feet".

"Yeah right. Next time we use my coin".

"Did you remember to bring one"?

"No", she said weakly.

"Then we use mine, Sergei said confidently. "Say- do you feel the heat coming off the quantum computer underneath us"?

"No do you"? A note of alarm in Janice's voice.

"Yeah it feels warmer than it should. Can you see anything"? They both dropped down to the deck to check. Sergei moved to kiss her. He silenced her questions by pointing to the camera display. They were hidden from view but not thier voices.

"See feel right here it's definitely warm". She grabbed her hand back and slugged him. Are you 12 years old she mouthed. He grinned at her. I know other places where the cameras can't hear or see he mimed. She rolled her eye and used a quick arm push to float off the floor. "Well thank you for checking Dr. Lincoln we have to remain vigilant". "Dr., maybe we should experiment with these accel couches. We might find a better configuration". Janice ignored him.

As Rosario and Digger relieved Zhou and Fong, who in turned relieved Sergei and Janice, the comms unit began spilling out radio messages for them. Everyone who had called the day before now sent the same well wishes on paper. Sergei mentioned for Rosario to keep an eye on the Chinese. Although they were doing nothing more than playing with the telescope. Exhausted the two went down to shower quickly and sleep. Janice wanted to discuss the problem bugging Sergei but he held her off. We have a long flight. Plenty of worry time.

Launch day 562 07 Jun 2022 1100 Unity in lunar space

"Wake up sleepy head. I thought you might want some food before we came on watch". Sergei was waking up Janice. He looked freshly showered and even shaved. Her mouth felt funky and she had to pee bad. Glaring she moved by him. "Wow, you are not a morning person" he laughed at her. "Remember we have Ms so and so's third grade class at 1300".

Ms. so and so had become their catch all phrase for any extraneous duty they had to perform. More glaring. Sergei laughed. "That's right, keep that expression. Scare the shit out of them and turn them to science"! 45 min later she felt human enough to go with Sergei up to relieve Watkins and Hoffman. They were ready to go. They had worked thru a few items on the science check list and a few less items on the weekly engineering tasks. Hoffman went thru the hydroponics setup for Jaince and told her the key items to watch for. The goal was fresh food with a small herb garden and lettuce and tomato's growing under UV lamps. Janice had it under control. "We have the school thing at 1300", Sergei reminded them. Watkins rolled his eyes. "Are we going anywhere"? Sergei asked. "Do you have plans"? Watkins grunted and moved up to relieve Rosario. Sergei motioned to Hoffman, "let me know if there is any problems getting him to pull his weight". Hoffman responded that there were no issues. Janice was surprised to see Watkins in the EVA suit this time. "Hoffman won't flip a coin. He's a pretty tough guy actually," Sergei told her. Janice turned to and started work. She checked on the seedlings. She fed some mice, she reset the cosmic detection units as they changed position relative to the moon. The real hard science wouldn't start until Mars, but they had some things to do. Sergei checked bus voltages and looked at power production/ consumption levels. All were within predicted norms. The air plant was working to produce air. Sergei didn't want to use up the water this way but once the system was up it liked to be run for a week or so solid. Complex electrical components liked to be up and running with out going up and down all the time. That's what broke things. At 1245 they went up to command deck. Hoffman had the VTC link setup and they could see the kids. Technically Watkins was supposed to lead this discussion with the high school kids from Danville, Ca. Sergei asked if he could do it. "Be my guest," Watkins surly replied. "Ms. Atkinson is that right"? Sergei asked with his most winning smile. "Yes, that's right" came the reply a little breathless. The science teacher at Accalanes High School was 32 and an attractive blond. And she had caught a little case of Space man fever. "CMDR Ivanovitch we are so thrilled to be able to have you and your crew, speak to us today"!

"We are happy as well. Are your kids ready? I know it's a few min early, but if we are all set lets rock and roll", Sergei said brightly. Giggles from the teachers assembled however, the students were fairly silent.

"Okay first, here on Unity we have CMDR Tyler Watkins, Dr Georg Hoffman and Dr Janice Lincoln. I'm CMDR Sergei Ivanovitch but please call me your majesty". That got a little chuckle from the kids.

"We are going to split the VTC screen and show you our flight screen. Dr Hoffman which button do I push? The one marked engine jettison"? More giggles. Oh Mr. Smooth was right in his element. Sergei explained what they were seeing on the screen.

"So we have been blasting away with our engines for 14 hours now, how fast do you think we are going. 10,000 mph? 15,000? Apollo 11 achieved 18,500 mph on its trip to the moon. Any guesses? A young man identified himself as Sumeet and said "you are going 81 miles an hour". "Very good, someone can read the display. "You can see our speed right here", he motioned. With the skill of a fine teacher Sergei led them thru the acceleration vs mass debate. He had them plot out the acceleration curve asking them to figure out when they would hit 100 mph, 1000 and 10,000. He brought in Janice and Georg and even Watkins to illustrate the different math problems they had to overcome. 45 min later they had figured a rough idea of how much of a sling shot effect they could achieve from the moon. The curve that Sumeet and another young man named Adam came up with was 835 extra mph because of the moon. Sergei called Houston into the discussion to ensure Adam and Sumeet got into the pool. Janice explained the almost pathological betting engineers did on things like this. Sergei told Bob Royce he would ensure the boys entry money of $100. Royce had them entered on the clip board. The applause from the kids was pretty good. As they wrapped up Royce cautioned that contributing to the delinquency of a minor was not a thing NASA condoned. Hoffman said he could scratch them all from our next flights. Royce snorted and broke the link.

"I think that went well," Sergei said a few min later. They were back down on the 02 level deck in Einstein. "You are a natural teacher aren't you," Janice said.

"Yeah, I do like it. I would love to teach after all this space junk is over with".

"I expect you could have the pick of any university in the world," Janice said. Harvard, Stanford, Oxford. Anyone would kill to have you".

"Nah, he scoffed. I would like an American high school". "Why"?

"They could use me and I could get the kids young before they become jaded. Danville, Ca. Thats your neck of the woods hum"?

"I wasn't born in that area but I did go to Berkeley, which is close. Danville is nice", Janice replied.

"Yeah that Ms Atkinson seemed nice. I could help her out a little". She slugged him hard.

"Do you realize how much you hit me? This is an abusive relationship. I'm seriously thinking of lodging a complaint".

"I'll batter you again if Ms Atkinson comes up again".

"We have to get this jealous streak under control".

CHAPTER 25

Launch day 567 12 Jun 2022 1322 Unity in lunar space

The moon had been swelling for days. No telescope was needed now. They would pass within 142 miles of the lunar surface. That was about 80 miles closer than the ISS was to Earth. Zhou and Fong had flight watch but everyone was up. Sergei debated having everyone get into flight suits. If something happened what could they really do? He left it up to them. Only Fong was in the suit. She always wore the suit. Sergei intended to talk to Zhou about that. From an outside observes perspective the ship stopped the main engine burn and one min later initiated a thruster burn. The thrusters stopped after 35 seconds. The ship dipped under the moon to ride the gravity well slinging around for three full orbits. Emerging on the other side rising "up" relative to the plane of the elliptical. Mars had the solar systems most eccentric orbit. Not eccentric in terms of odd dress but eccentric in terms of not being a perfect circle. It had the most elongated ellipse of any planet. Outside Pluto. That is if Pluto is a planet. Find three scientists and get five opinions on the matter of whether Pluto is a planet. Mars' orbit was also tilted to the galactic plane. So they had to go "up" to get to Mars. Six hours later the ship was pulling away from the moon and reinstated the 1/10 th burn. They picked up 923 mph from the slingshot. Sergei was out a hundred bucks for Sumeet and Adam. Who won? Unity demanded of Houston. An aero space engineer named Jim Parson from Lockheed in Denver. Well at least it's not the meteorologist from JPL. Fong had 921 in the pool. They commiserated her bad luck and celebrated her amazing pictures as they came from the computer/ camera she had hooked up to the scope. In the haste to leave, the telescope had been an over looked item, consequently there was no data cable that could connect the Commercial off the shelf (COTS) computer and their system. Digger started on that right away. He read thru the tech manual that came with the computer and telescope. IEEE standard echelon three data communications. It uses a 20 pin adaptor. He took copious measurements and figured the cable requirements. Some time with the three d printer and he had the connector shell made from a piece of thin aluminum and another insert of plastic. He used the micro circuitry connector kits that had been provided and viola, the six foot cable necessary to connect Fong's scope and computer with the ships computer and database. Fong sent in the pictures. The ISS photos and the moon close ups made the online Newsweek publication. The crew settled into stations and habits, they would use for the rest of the flight. Everyone soon knew who needed that extra nudge in the morning to wake up. Who sprang out of bed. Who would always find ways out of work and who pulled more than his or her share. The standard patterns since the Phoenicians began going to sea. Human nature is human nature.

Launch day 570 15 Jun 2022 1802 Unity in space

The moon and the earth continued to dwindle in the windows. The Unity crew morphed into a routine. Sergei set a meeting for one week hence to talk about how things were going and switching up the watch bill. Rosario was on flight watch during the first "secret" evolution. Unity was not altogether powerless against radiation and meteorites. A thick antenna was now being extended from the nose of the ship. Rosario and Digger controlled it while Sergei and Watkins watched from the camera mounted outside. The idea was simple and radical. What protected the earth from the radiation of the sun? The magnetic field around the earth. Could they set up a localized field and protect the ship? Would it work? Would it fry the internal components of the ship? Would interfere with the other electronics while it was on? The modeling said no to that. The real question was would it make a difference? Would the field bend the radiation particles around the ship? The only way to know was to try. The antenna stuck out about 30 feet. The powerful magnet on the end would be subjected to an electric current to make the magnetic field even more powerful. They were setting up a faraday cage around the ship. Dr Hoffman took radiation readings as a baseline value for the test. They were being exposed to 12 times the normal background radiation. Rosario reported the electromagnetic shield system deployed. Houston concurred and reported go for the test. Rosario supplied the power to the control unit at its minimum value. The electrical arcs were visible extending around the antenna end about seven or eight feet. The field was coming close to the solar array on the port side forward. Sergei ordered the array tilted more perpendicular to the thrust axis of the ship to move the array out of the way. The efficiency of the array went from 93.5 to 89.3. Everyone began checking the ships equipment for malfunctions. The rest of the crew was up except for section 4 of Li and Lui. The L and L connection they were being called. They were relieving Rose and Digger. A check of the monitoring program on the computer showed no interference of the performance of any equipment. Comms and VDT were good to Houston. There was also no discernible drop in radiation. Power was bumped up two settings. The arcs now came out around 20 feet. They seemed to bend around the projected curve of the ship. The power consumption of the unit plus the ship's equipment was just under what the solar arrays and fuel cells could produce. The comms to Houston had a noticeable digital static quality. You could hear and relate data but the quality was a b plus. However there was a huge drop in the radiation back ground. The reading was now five times background. That was within the OSHA 90 day limits. Bumping power a little more got the optimum: radiation down to two times while maintaining the comms at 80 percent. Some of the science experiments needed to be altered. One shut down altogether. The power consumption was over the power output by 2 percent. They were now draining the batteries. The ship could maintain this for 60 hours before needing a battery charge. They experimented by turning off various pumps and lights to achieve a low power consumption mode, that allowed them to get this level of radiation protection for an indefinite amount of time. The Unity crew and Houston spent some time crunching the numbers of various scenarios trying to get the most protection for the longest time while operation the ship on a reduced power bases. The faraday antenna was reeled in to ensure full recovery of comms VDT. Houston came back on with the increasingly annoying 4 second delay in comms. They were now further away from earth than man had ever been. 400,000 miles away moving at approx 4,000 mph. They had planned for and trained for that delay, but it was becoming more annoying than they thought. They could still have conversations, but it was harder. The faraday antenna was redeployed at the previous power setting that put them within the 90 day OSHA radiation limits. Janice calculated that they now had a 1percent increased risk for cancer. They could accept that. Watkins theorized that the landing site could be protected by the similar system if they could rig some wires and the antenna was tall enough. Sergei assigned him to come up with a parts list using available parts or what would be needed to be manufactured by the printer. They had two solar arrays available for the landing site, so power should not be a problem. They had another magnet unit on board. Hoffman wanted to know why they all hadn't received training on this feature. There was very little "training" to it. Reel it out and turn it on. No one knew if it would work. The committee had only just given permission to test it. Hey there were risks every day. You could get run over crossing the street, but you still did it right? What else is secret Zhou asked? Good question.

4 days later the other shoe dropped. Sergei called them for a test. Tyler and Georg were up for this even though they were missing sleep. Again, no training was necessary. Drop a panel on the command module on port and starboard sides all the way aft by the airlock. A small self contained unit was inside the water tank. The ports on either side were visible a 2 inch diameter opening was visible on the camera. "What are we seeing"? Asked Janice. "The two rail gun units", Sergei said. "Rail guns"? Janice asked quietly. "Why would this ship be armed"?

"It's not really armed", said Sergei. We only have 50 shots. The gun is fully self contained, with the power from its own solar array. It's taken this long to charge the batteries from the dry fire test we did the first day. You guys never even noticed did you"? Much

discussion among the crew about the validity of hiding this

capability. As they waited on test initiation Gorge asked about the

technical details of the rail gun. Sergei explained. "It's a pretty

simple concept. The electro magnetic coils wind around the tube

you see to push the projectile out at very high speeds. There is no

explosion, just kinetic energy transfer. We can charge up the gun

batteries from our solar array or let it take weeks from its own.

NASA and others felt like we might need a way to blast out the

landing site. They didn't want us carrying explosives so the rail

gun was the best solution. It's really a construction tool", he

concluded. "We test it now with a shot. NASA has run the

numbers. We won't hit anything. So here we go". "Computer

initiate project bulldozer authenticate, 110axbae9". The computer

responded with affirmative in its SiRI voice. There was no sound.

No jolt. Just a cold, Test complete sat from the computer. The

camera replay showed the projectile coming out of the barrel. The

2 inch diameter, seven inch long depleted uranium slug came out

of the barrel at 1935 feet per second. Way short of a conventional

bullet. However, the rail gun slug weighed almost two pounds.

Moving at that speed the slug would have the equivalent of five hundred lbs of TNT. They could dial up or down the speed. Shots could move out with only the equivalent energy of one lb of TNT. That should break up any permafrost or rocks that impeded the bobcat. Sergei confessed that this was the last "secret" capability of the ship. Digger had asked if the ship was going to transform into a car or an 18 wheel truck. No such luck. Li and Lui joined them as the test wound down and Sergei suggested they hold the crew meeting now. No objections. First the watch bill. Sergei proposed that the science engineers rotate one section up from the flight leads. Section 1 became Sergei and Li. Section two Tyler and Janice, section three was Rosario and Georg and finally section four was Lui and James. Change to go into effect at 00 two days from now. Okay? Aye. No real grumbling. They had known this was coming and it might be good to stand watch with someone else. They proposed to set the changes on auto pilot every 10 days. With a 141 day flight plan they would rotate thru 14 times. Next item: food. "We are about out of the fresh food we have onboard, Sergei confided. We have a certain amount of frozen, but I suspect we are going to get sick of MREs and the toothpaste stuff." The others nodded.

"We do have a trash problem. The compactor is just too small.

We need to transfer a bunch of the compacted bricks into the airlock and jettison them."

The first time was going to be just open the airlock remotely and see if they would drift out. Then they would cross the bridge of having someone in the lock while the door was open. They discussed ways they thought might force the trash out. None came to mind. Sergei would get Houston to figure this out for them.

Next item power consumption. "We seem to be fine." CMDR Ivanovitch said scanning printouts. "The long term trend analysis shows a battery pack might be going bad. Everyone needed to be on alert for an alarm telling them to replace it. We have had very few mechanical issues so far. We have some more intricate preventative maintenance procedures coming up, so be ready." Again nods from the crew. "If we need to move an expert off the watch bill so they can do the monthly battery or air scrubber maintenance we should be ready for that. Pitch in. Don't let small items build up. If the weekly maint tasks get pushed off then the monthlies are going to be more difficult. The thin skin is the only thing between us and the vacuum. Treat it well."

Next: "Water. We are using too much." We are below the predicted line by 85 gallons. Not critical but worrying. The recycle plant is performing but we need to be vigilant for leaks. I don't want to dry out the ship any more. 30 percent humidity is good. Conserve water." Blank stares.

Next: "Air. That's fine. We have a scheduled maint shut down of the scrubber so we will bleed off some oxygen from the compressed air tanks." Watkins acknowledged that he was handling the work in two days time.

Science: "Janice, Li? Any issues?"

"None. The experiments are going well and the mice are fine. The seedlings have sprouted fine and the tomatoes are growing. We might get some actual fruits", Janice related.

"Great. Li any objects for your scope?"

"I need to run some projections on the computer to see what might be visible. The window provides some distortion but it's clean and I've worked around that. So I'll post what pictures I'm getting next. Good Houston is screaming for more of that kind of thing. We also have more Ms so and so classes coming up. Georg you are on the hot seat. Wow them please. We should start getting messages from home now. Houston wanted 14 days to allow us to settle in so expect to get some well wishes from home soon. Any items for me? Digger? James grinned. "I volunteer to shower with

Rosario to conserve water". Guffaws.

"Denied! You two would break the shower. Janice raised her hand.

"We have scheduled medical tests over the next week. Fong and I will be visiting you on watch so be ready." "Okay, everyone got that? Good thanks. That's it then."

Video Log Fong Li and Sergei Ivanovitch 22 Jun 2022 1807

The video screen showed Sergei and Li with colored plastic tubes having a sword fight. Back and forth they thrust and parried while performing acrobatics. They were making whirring noises when the swords would touch. They broke apart and looked at each other. "Obi Wan has taught you well" Sergei's voice mechanical.

"He taught me enough".

"Did he? Obi Wan never told you about your father."

"He told me that you killed him." Venom dripped.

"No, Luke I am your father."

"That's impossible!" Li's voice frantic.

"Search your feelings you know this to be true. Join me and together we will defeat the Emperor and rule the galaxy as father and son."

"Never! I'll never turn to the dark side!"

"So be it." Sergei slashed Li's hand which retracted into her sleeve. She pushed off from the command deck and "fell" into the galley area. Sergei looked at the tablet and the camera. In his mechanical Vader voice he said "That's what happens when we run out of fresh food".

Launch day 585 30 Jun 2022 1200 Unity in space

Janice and Rosario were not speaking. The consequences of being cooped up together for 36 days now, both on the ISS and Unity were taking their toll on even the best of friends. The fight had started over Janice' remark that Rosario had gained 7 lbs. since heading into space. It was a medical fact but the tone behind it had been bitchy. Rosario responded that she would stay skinny if she were playing slap and tickle with Sergei. Janice was livid. More words were shouted. Something about pudding cups and skinny brainiac bitch. Two days of stony silence followed. Sergei knew the cure for hate and discontent. He waited until Rose and Janice had the midnight watch. They sat at the command console with bored angry expressions. The suddenly whooping of the hull breach alarm was very loud. The computer reported it on the Einstein 02 level starboard side low aft. A piercing whistling sound was ringing throughout the ship. Janice froze. She stared at Rosario. Who was white faced. They fumbled for the emergency repair kit. They both grabbed it simultaneously then dropped it as each let go. The ladder down to the 02 level clipped Janice as she went down. The air lock door into the equipment section was crowded with Zhou and Watkins. The whistling changed pitch as they finally entered the compartment. The klaxon sound continued as the shouting started. Watkins announced he was in command. Rosario overrode him. Janice opened the bag she was holding to find it was the electrical repair kit bag and not the hull breach bag. Another minute passed while the second bag Zhou had brought was opened. As soon as they got the rubber patch out the klaxon cut off and the whistling stopped. Sergei looked at them in silence. Li and Hoffman stepped thru the door.

"5 min 32 seconds to get here" said Sergei. "Computer estimate survive ability of crew with today's time to repair given the size hole in the scenario". The computer emotionlessly stated "All lost".

"Everyone come to the command deck". They trooped out like school kids caught smoking. Sergei called up the outside camera on the port side. He fiddled and brought in the solar array on the forward half towards the outer edge. A dark spot could be seen on the gold of the array. Watkins swore. "Tyler tell them what that is while I zoom in".

"It's a hole made by a micrometeor Watkins said sourly.

"Yep. Happened a few days ago. We came that close. "Review the emergency procedures. We will have more drills. I don't want to die", he said earnestly. "Please do better. So we all stay sharp, everyone will take turns being the drill officer. We only have one a week. It will be up to you when they happen. The computer has the drill scenario. "I'll give the officer the access code. Then you have the week to implement the drill. Understood"? Sullen agreement from everyone. "Dismissed".

As Janice left Sergei caught her arm. "Fix it with Rosario", he said simply. She nodded. Twenty min later she and Rosario were crying and hugging at the command console.

Six hours later Janice found Sergei, on his unassigned period.

"You guys good", he inquired? "Yes we are", she said sounding down. "You okay" he asked her? "No".

426

"What can I do to improve your morale"? He massaged her shoulders and neck.

"You mentioned a spot where the cameras couldn't see us", Janice asked intently? He laughed and kissed her. They went all the way forward in the upper level of the equipment section. The outboard starboard side had a dead spot behind the navigation equipment rack. They wormed their way back. Reduced gravity made it easier. Janice held on to Sergei. "This is harder than I thought" she said holding him. "It's not the physical. It's the mental. I'm bored to tears and then scared to death. I got into a stupid, pointless fight with the best friend I've ever had".

"Cut yourself some slack", he told her. "This is what happens when the hard push to get launched gets accomplished and then the slack time hits. Leave it to old Sergei. I have some tricks up my sleeve to combat the hate and discontent". Clothes began piling up. He maneuvered next to her. "Ow! Careful. I bruised that hip on the ladder". "Want me to kiss it make it better"? "Kind of", she said wrapping arms and legs around him. Oh that does feel better. Ohh. Remember I get a cut of the winnings from the bet" she said breathlessly. "Hush".

Sergei was true to his word. He played games with them. He hid a 100 dollar bill somewhere on the ship and left clues as to its location. Zhou won that. They had a poetry contest. Haiku and true Shakespearean sonnets. 14 lines of rhyming couplets. Digger displayed a stunning depth with his MRE sonnet. They had a drawing contest and played huge games of night vision goggle assassin. They masked all lights and divided into two person teams. Each player got a nerf gun. Then teams stocked each other. Tyler and Hoffman won big. Hoffman won by wedging himself into the overhead in a maneuver that would be impossible in normal gravity. Team after team walked right beneath him and paid for it. Perhaps not the intended use of the night vision goggles but Kennedy was millions of miles away. Sergei organized a poker tournament. People could only bet personal items. Sergei played conservatively losing a few hands and getting them hooked. He knew what he wanted. The item came out four hands later. Digger had some small bottles of Tabasco sauce. Sergei had him drawing dead on a filled inside straight that Digger could not figure out. Sergei kept baiting him and baiting him until the bottle made its appearance. Mcilhenney Tabasco sauce was the only thing that could kill the taste of MRE's. It's value rivaled gold out here.

The sweet look of shock on James face was enough to make all that crappy food taste great when he turned over the straight to beat his cowboys. Sergei donated the bottle of hot sauce to the galley so everyone could partake. It must have worked. A box of chocolates showed up with a note for all to enjoy. Some fantastic noodles were enjoyed a week later. Someone produced chips and salsa. Little victories.

CHAPTER 26

Launch day 622 05 Aug 2022 1456 Unity in Space

The last compacted brick of trash went into the airlock. The vacuum pump cycled to bring the air into the rest of the ship. When there was still about 5 percent of the normal amount of oxygen left in the lock, Li Fong overrode the computer and commanded the door opened. The small amount of air left in the space caused a rush out of the airlock that dragged the trash with it. Five min later the airlock was empty. A Chinese team had come up with the answer for the explosive decompression. The young engineer who had actually thought of it admitted to Royce that he thought of it only after watching Sigourney Weaver blow the alien out of the air lock in Aliens. Royce had related the story to them with gusto. So far it had turned the trick. The water situation had stabilized. They were still about 90 gallons down but use and predicted curves matched. Air was in great shape. The o2 unit worked fine while the scrubber chugged along. The fuel consumption rate was below the curve. They had cut out the return trip from the moon. The planners used a zero velocity start from the ISS after the moon visit.. So they actually had 923 mph going for them, saving some fuel over the projections. The equipment was functioning well. Still, the Unity crew was busy with various breakdowns and routine preventative maintenance procedures. The pump moving water from the toilet to the recycle plant broke down. Digger, Sergei and Watkins had broken it down and replaced the burnt bearings. The trend on the battery module finally alerted as it failed. They swapped it with a spare very quickly but Hoffman and Digger were bored and tore the battery pack down and rebuilt it. They got the Sadoway company reps to oversee the rebuild. It took six full days, but it was certified for reuse. Janice and Fong isolated a memory module on the computer and installed a new one. The monthly clean out of the ventilation system revealed furry filters filled with hair dirt and dust. They broke out the dust busters and cleaned out the filters and wiped down the ducting. Houston was pleased with the crew's ability to perform complex maintenance on the broken modules. They were managing to put modules back into service or back into the available spare parts bins. Houston was more concerned about crew morale. The second round of medical tests had shown body fat gain, loss of muscle mass and bone density. The 1/10 th g was slowly killing them. 52 days out. Speed 19,000mph. 20 million miles. The comms delay was up to 2 min 20 seconds. Sergei tried to incorporate more physical contests into the enrichment exercises to improve morale. Rosario complained to Sergei that enrichment exercises is what they did to the bears in zoos to keep them from going crazy. "Yes it is", replied Sergei. "So we are zoo animals to you"?

"Yes. Now the game is to go from the command deck to the airlock door touching every listed item with your feet, not hands! Socks only please! You can only touch the deck with your hands. Fastest wins another 100. I'll go first". Sergei moved his body up to have his feet touch the port side upper windows, the first listed item. He crouched and pushed off across the compartment. At mid compartment he doubled up and spun like a diver so his feet were now first along his line of travel. His feet contacted the radar power cabinet on its flat surface. Crouching again he pushed off towards the deck. Arms outstretched he slowed himself and used his arms to spring back towards the ladder to the o2 living quarters. He hooked an ankle around the ladder stanchion and let his momentum swing the rest of his body towards the opening of the ladder. Releasing his ankle he floated down the stairs while curling again and flipping. Hands touching and more flipping he twisted to touch down on the galley table.

Rosario and Zhou looked at each other incredulously. "No way"!

"I need to practice," said Zhou. Rosario started pushing off back and forth across the room. She found herself quickly winded and tired. "Am I that out of shape"? she puffed.

"No worse than I", Zhou said with a smile. "I may have to hit that Exercycle station a little more". Soon you could not stand watch without the cirque de sole zooming thru the command deck. No one came close to Sergei's time though. It took most of them forty minutes to complete the course. Which was the point. Sergei could do it in 33 min. Watkins accused him of cheating. "Of course I cheated. I laid out the course. I only brought three of those 100 dollar bills. I need every advantage I can get", Sergei told him. Watkins scowled while the others laughed.

Between the enrichment programs and the workout station, the crew slowly got back into shape. The bone density loss continued to be a problem. But the amount of food consumed went down and random bickering stopped. The sun became an ever smaller ball. The earth a point of light. Li's telescope provided some excellent photos back to the ship. Jupiter and Saturn became bigger and soon were the brightest lights in the sky next to mars. Li started to get some definition on the asteroid belt. The belt of rocks and debris that orbited between mars and Jupiter. NASA wanted more. NASA was also sending more personal messages. Sergei was getting twice as many as anyone. "My admiring fans", he said. They all treasured the messages. Sitting in front of the camera composing messages back home started consuming more hours. But there were still plenty of hours to sit and contemplate just how far they were from home. Three days later they hit max speed of 24,000 miles an hour. 24 million miles from home.

Video Log James Andrews 10 Aug 2022 0445

Hello, Earth Unity here. Sorry I missed yesterday's session. I got a message from home and it messed me up. Not the message itself. I loved to hear from my wife. It's just that it's hard to explain how it is out here. You are so far from home that it seems distant and removed from what I am doing. I know they have to keep on going ahead with their lives while I'm up here but it gets difficult. I missed my anniversary. Suzy went ahead and celebrated alone. She has been forced to do that twice before because of my work. That makes me feel terrible. She says she doesn't mind but I miss her at those times. I feel guilty for not being there and then angry when she takes care of something without me. Two days ago the water heater pilot light went out. She read thru the directions and re lit it with no problems. Hooray for her. But that's my job. Not that she's not capable, not that the work I'm doing here is unimportant, it's just that a man likes to feel necessary. What kind of a husband makes his wife celebrate her anniversary alone and have to do all the housework and raise the kids by herself? A selfish bastard that's who. I went into this with my eyes wide open but sometimes the price you pay to do something is a little more costly than you think at first. No questions today, I just need to wallow a bit. Out.

Launch day 630 13 Aug 2022 0223 Unity in space

Five days of zero gee had left them all sick of toothpaste food. Hoffman had broken out real steak and managed to cook them an actual meal. The real tomatoes and some lettuce grown on board helped a great deal. Half way celebrations had been tempered by a radar alert. An asteroid and a cloud of debris had shown on the return. Though it was millions of miles away and would pose no risk, it still unnerved them. Li couldn't get a good look at them from the scope. No light source to highlight them. 87.75 million miles from earth speed 24,000 mph. 578 gallons of JP 8 consumed. Now they had to flip the ship and get it into orbit. Then plan the landing. Then build the landing site. Then start the search for possible extra terrestrial life. Then launch back and survive another long stretch in space before returning to earth. So no big deal. The flip took approx 20 seconds to complete. An hour later the engines again initiated on a slow deceleration burn. The return of even the limited gravity was a welcome respite. The gymnastics returned but with less diligence. This attitude of the ship put them in a position where Mars became visible on the port side. The red planet was becoming more visible. The first pictures they took were a little blurry but clearly showed the southern ice cap. 70 days to go.

Launch day 660 12 Sep 2022 1246 Kennedy space center.

Royce was briefing the committee. There was really nothing to tell them. The ship functioned fine. The crew was performing well and hadn't killed each other yet. They were getting some good science out of the loaded experiments. 40 days to mars orbit. They had to reconnoiter the landing site and then attempt to land. Yes the computer was going to land them. No CMDR Ivanovitch would not fly the craft unless there was a problem. They had all agreed to the mission profile years ago. Yes the ratings were way down. Mostly due to the lack of newsworthy events. That was actually a good thing. Nice and boring going out and nice and boring coming back. Yes the committee would be informed of developments ASAP. Royce had had the same phone call with President Clinton. Come on, get there! he prayed.

Launch day 672 24 Sep 2022 2202 Unity in space

The constant hum of the ship had a lulling affect. Janice was at the main science station on the second level of the Einstein module. She looked up from the microscope to see Fong Li moving down the ladder. Li noticed Janice and started to apologize.

"Did you fail open"? Janice asked smiling. Fong looked

puzzled.

"Forget it," said Janice. "Just an expression I heard once. Couldn't sleep," she tried again? "Yes I could not sleep very well. I find myself getting anxious the closer we get", Fong explained.

"Me too" Janice answered. "Being on watch with Watkins for the last week or so has allowed me to get a ton of lab work done though. I find myself making excuses to get into the lab area and ignore him".

Li grunted non-committaly. "I have also had "issues" with CMDR Watkins", she said hesitantly. It was Janice's turn to grunt. Lots of nuance in the word issues.

"Anything you want me to subtly bring up with Sergei? She asked. "No please don't. I can work thru my differences with him. What are you working on"? she said changing the subject. Janice let her off the hook. She and Li talked shop for 20 min or so about the experiments the ship had going. Janice was a little taken aback at the openness of Li. She had never before spent time just chit chatting with Janice. Li had asked about Janice's doctoral thesis on biological systems. She answered gladly with an appreciation for someone who could truly understand her work. It also gave her an opening.

"You went to the Biological Institute in Beijing, right? She asked. Li told her yes. "You weren't born in Beijing though, right". Li contemplated her for a long few seconds. "No I was born in a small village outside of Gueng Jou in the south. I did well in school and was selected to go to the University. I travelled to Beijing and lived in the dorms for 5 years while I completed my programs", She sketched out the details of that period in her life.

"You must have been a little lonely so far from home in the big city"? Janice probed. In some ways it was the best time of my life. I was with very smart teachers doing the kind of research I loved and finally getting to do real things, real work". In other ways it was horrible. The competition and back stabbing was horrible". Janice murmured condolences. She knew about competition from Cal. She remembered Charles and his patience with her almighty schedule. "Was there someone special at University, she asked gently. Li looked away for a second. "There was a young man but it didn't work out". Janice let that go. Your family must have been so proud to have you in such a prestigious program. Li stared hard at her for just a second. It's just me and my grandmother. My parents are gone.

"Did you go to work after you graduated?" "Yes. In China the graduates don't go thru a US style job hunt. The government comes in and selects the students it wants in the various ministries," she said easing onto the work station table. "Then large corporations will come in and review and select candidates. Salaries and perks are on kind of a set scale based on what work you will be doing. US corporations have lately been participating in the selection process for their Chinese subsidiaries." "I was selected by ChiGeneCO to be a research biologist. I had an apartment in a beautiful building, a car and a nice salary. And I worked continuously", she confided. Janice commiserated with the notion that you have all these nice things now, but no time to use them.

"How did you get selected for Mars", she asked?

"One day a ministry official came to see me in my lab and he said that I was a candidate for the Mars program and that I would be informed of any tests or requirements. Two weeks later they hauled me out to the Gobi and put me thru hell for a month". She shuddered. "Three months later I was informed that I was a finalist and they dragged me back out to the base for another two months of training. Three months later I was in Florida at the initial briefing. It seems pretty arbitrary to me. I didn't get much in

440

the way of practical tests. Just knowledge from the sessions in the desert. And the physical training of course".

Janice grimiced at that. Li laughed. "Yes the Chinese government's notion of training includes copious amounts of running and pushups. Lui and I worked together to get thru the ordeal. Bob Royce is a pussycat compared to the Chinese government." Janice blanched at that notion. She thought Royce was an asshole at times. "However the training at NASA is light years ahead in the actual space flight training, Li went on. "I'm sorry to be loading you down with all this."

Janice deflected the thought. "Don't worry at all. We all need someone to talk to out here. The earth is a long way away. We have to be able to count on each other. I'm not talking about best friends or family but we all have to have mutual respect and care about each other in the end. I'm happy to listen any time you want to talk."

Li again took a few moments to digest this. "Thank you. I think you are right. It is just the eight of us out here. I never appreciated the danger until a few weeks ago. That micro meteor would have been the end of us." Janice remembered all too well. "Sergei says that the little reminders from the galaxy tend to focus us in."

Li smiled. "The Commander can be very funny sometimes."

"Yeah he's a real riot." Li giggled. She leaned in and asked conspiratorially, "How did you tie him down"?

"I'm an international seductress didn't you know?" Janice said confidently.

Li looked puzzled. "If any one of the three of us is an international seductress it is me." "Rose is too obvious and you are too inexperienced. "I on the other hand…"

Janice laughed and she looked to see if Li was kidding. She couldn't tell. "That's funny, Rose might have something to say along those lines."

"Maybe we should all sit down and compare notes," Li said. While they plotted out just who was the femme fatal onboard Janice was pleased that she had finally made a connection with this woman. Over the course of the next month Janice learned several interesting things from Li and from Lui about Li. She passed what she knew on to Sergei and she told him that she thought Li would never sabotage her work or take full credit by herself for a discovery. Sergei was still skeptical but glad that she had made a connection with the Chinese scientist. "It always helps when crewmates share things with each other," he told her.

Launch day 674 24 Sep 1022 0331

Sergei noted the trend line with a frown. Li Fong and Watkins were the watch standers and had brought the problem to his attention. The current draw on the 270 degree main engine fuel transfer pump was trending higher. It wasn't an alarm condition yet. The pump was simply having to work harder to get fuel into the main engine on that strut. Unfortunately that pump was outside the ship. Sergei discussed it with Watkins. "What's your assessment?", he asked. "Clogged line." came the response. That fit, thought Sergei. Some debris and dirt got into the fuel lines and was now forcing the pump to strain.

Sergei thought hard. "Lets do some what if scenarios." "What if the pump completely burns out?" Sergei asked him.

Watkins promptly said: "Bad news. We would have to shut down the 90 degree engine to keep flight profile the same. That would require working the two remaining engines twice as hard. That increases risk for both the inbound and out bound flight."

"What if we left it alone?"

"It may or may not go out before we land." "If it does go we are right back to shutting down the other engine. If it doesn't then we can repair on mars." Watkins concluded "Could we repair it underway?"

"Depends on what is really wrong. Just a clogged line? The clean out port is a pretty straight forward fix. If it is the pump itself, then that is another story."

"What are the risks of going out there?", Sergei asked.

"Standard lost in space scenario. With the ship under acceleration, the tendancy will be for the ship to pull away from the astronaut. There are hand holds and points to brace built in." "We have trained for this, Watkins reminded him. Sergei processed all this. He asked Zhou and Watkins for their recommendations. Zhou cautioned patience to wait for a hard failure. Watkins wanted to immediately replace the pump. Sergei wanted 12 hours to see what would happen. Houston was strictly letting Unity handle this. 24 hours later there was no discernable change. He decided to go for an in flight fix. The reason he gave Houston was to determine what was causing the clog. If they discovered some material in the fuel strainer, they could track it back to the source and isolate it. Maybe even clean things out when they got to mars. Sergei was worried that the lining of some bladder in the PODs was coming unglued and shredding into the fuel lines. They needed to know that. He proposed to go out and clean out the pump at the port. The whole EVA would take under two hours if all went well. Who would perform the maintenance? Zhou and Watkins immediately volunteered. Sergei was in a delicate position. He wanted to do the maintenance, but he didn't want to be seen hogging all the glory. He suggested cutting the deck of cards. Highest card goes. Fate gave him the queen to Zhou's 10 and Watkins seven. He took Hoffman as the assistant as he was the most expendable. Zhou and Watkins voiced some heartaches with this. Sergei told them that they couldn't risk two flight astronauts on one mission. Hoffman was tight lipped but willing to do his part. The brief was pretty simple: Shut down both affected engines and power up the remaining two to stay on profile. Then egress thru the Royce door and move out to the strut. Isolate the pump with the valves and open the clean out port. Replace the fuel line strainer cartridge. Open the valves. Restore system to normal operation once they were inside. At least that was the plan. They spent some time cleaning up the command section. They would have to subject the area to open vacuum to get out the airlock

445

door. They needed to ensure all items left over could withstand the rigors of space. Suiting up, Sergei and Hoffman gathered all the required tools and parts and shuffled everyone else to the equipment section. Hoffman was nervous. Houston was nervous. Sergei checked the tethers as he went to cycle the door. His head made the whoosing sound that wasn't actually there when the door opened. The exterior lights illuminated the side of the ship. They had helmet mounted lights to assist. Sergei immediately knew this would be no ordinary EVA. The bulk of the ISS was an unconscious buffer during the Unity build. This was the utter blackness of space. He'd never felt so alone. Sergei debated aborting the mission right then. Deciding to gut it out, he clipped the second tether to the bracket outside the door and swung out to the side of the ship. Hoffman released Sergei's interior tether and he didn't feel better until he clipped it into a second spot. He cautioned Georg. Hoffman now passed him his own second tether and Sergei tied him off. Hoffman grunted and was breathing heavily when he unclipped his own tether and joined Sergei outside.

"Jesus that was scary", Hoffman said. Sergei agreed. "Let's take this nice and slow." "Roger". Sergei confirmed comms with

Houston and Unity. Watkins had them on video. The pair made their way along the ship to the strut and passed the Pods mounted alongside. The profile called for twenty minutes to get to the clean out port. It took 58. Watkins kept calling for a status, but Sergei's tight "Just admiring the view" shut off the questions. Inching along the strut they got to the isolation valve and the clean out port. Hoffman shut the valve and handed Sergei the powered drive tool to loosen the captive screws. He loosened the eight screws. Even the standard joke that the manufacturer must have been paid by the screw could not lessen the tension. Sergei handed the plate to Georg. Hoffman quickly removed the old gasket and installed a new one. Sergei removed the fuel line cartridge and stowed it in the work bag. Residual fuel was balling up and coming out of the port. There wasn't much pressure in this system. The line only had to withstand 120 lbs of force. There just wasn't that much fuel going down to the engines at this burn rate. Sergei tried to keep as much of the fuel from contaminating his suit as possible. The new cartridge slipped into place easily. Sergei looked at Hoffman asking for the cover plate. Georg was white faced and breathing heavily. He tried talking to him. "Georg, hey man lets have that plate, okay." Hoffman was unresponsive. Sergei knew he was in trouble. Straining to the limit of his tether, he moved back along the strut to the German scientist. Hoffman was ridged on the strut. His eyes showed white and were unfocused. Sergei calmed his mind and entered the zone. He immediately ordered all crew members to suit up and have Watkins, Zhou and Gonsolvo, enter the Command section to assist in getting Hoffman back into Unity. Sergei eased the cover plate back out of the bag Hoffman had strapped to his suit. He moved back and installed the plate and opened the isolation valve. Wonder of wonders, the valve and clean out port didn't leak. He made his way back along the strut to Hoffmans position again. It seemed to take forever for the first face to appear in the airlock door. Watkins. Sergei ordered Tyler to egress and take up a position just where the strut joined the ship. Watkins acknowledged tightly. "Be careful to make sure both tethers are hooked in", he cautioned. The momentum of the ship wants to pull away from you." It's different than the ISS." Zhou joined Watkins along the side of the ship. The majority of sounds on the comms net was the labored breathing as the men maneuvered. Sergei kept trying to talk to Georg to get him to assist but the man was catatonic for all practical purposes. Sergei didn't want to approach too closely, so that Hoffman was prevented

448

from grabbing him and locking on. His mind went thru a basic lifeguard drowning victim rescue. He unclipped his second tether to give him more freedom. He then dangled the tether in front of Hoffmans face. The man reflexively grabbed the tether and held on for dear life. Excellent. He moved the two of them up the strut towards Watkins and Zhou. "Tyler I need you to come out along the strut another 5 feet or so," Sergei ordered.

"I, I...," was all Watkins could get out. Sergei knew that feeling. Watkins would be no help on this rescue.

"Zhou can you move around Tyler and get to the junction of the strut and the ship?" "I'll try" was the reply. Sergei watched as Zhou moved with agonizing slowness to the right position. Rose kept asking for permission to come outside and help. "Denied." "I need you inside to assist in getting us back into the ship." Sergei wasn't being sexist. At this point he was thinking that Rose could take over mission and land on Mars if the worst happened. He called up the time display. 4:32 min outside. He wasn't sure who was getting back inside that ship. Zhou made it to the proper point. Sergei explained what he wanted to do. Zhou, Watkins and Rose acknowledged. He tried to explain to Hoffman what was happening but there was no response. Sergei unclipped the tether Hoffman was holding in his hands and Hoffman's own second tether. He floated that end to Zhou. The Chinese space man clipped Hoffman into another bracket and gave the go ahead to Ivanovitch. Sergei unclipped Hoffmans first tether. They literally floated him up the strut like a piece of cargo or a tool. Watkins was himself barely functional. Rose had to clip in and come outside the door to grab Hoffman as Watkins refused to move along the ship with just one of his tethers. Rose finally maneuvered Georg into the airlock door. Sergei breathed his first calm breath in what seemed forever. Watkins followed slowly, with Zhou right behind. As Sergei slipped thru the lock and back into the ship, a cry of relief escaped his lips. Rose secured the door and Digger and Janice pressurized the compartment. Janice and Li had Hoffman out of his suit and down to the make shift medical table as soon as the lights cycled green. Silence reigned in the Command module. Sergei became aware of his own smell as soon as his helmet came off. He reported to Houston. "EVA complete. Cartridge replaced." Houston acknowledged briefly. Royce wanted an update on Hoffman. "I don't know," Sergei replied. Looking at Watkins and Zhou as they tried to regain composure, he told Houston that the crew was going to take a few hours and try to refocus. His debrief to Royce two days later was contrite. "It was my fault, Bob. Georg has recovered and we all seem to be fine, but the EVA was as scared as I have ever been. We simply weren't ready for that." "I thought it would be like the ISS and was I ever wrong!"

Royce tried to console him. "You had to make a call. And you did. Thank god the clean out seemed to have worked."

"It almost cost us four astronauts", Sergei reminded him.

"Maybe, Royce said. "We have made some changes to the protocols and scenarios based on the experience. We have you replacing the fuel cartridges on planet now." "Roger that". "Focus on the landing and the base construction, Royce advised." Sergei agreed and the ship returned to what was the new normal. Janice tried to cheer up Sergei but it was difficult. "I'm used to being fearless. Even in the cockpit, in trouble, I know there is always something I can do. Not out there." He shuddered as she wrapped her arms around him. For the first time she had some doubts about the mission succeeding. They all did.

Video Log Rosario Gonsolvo 19 Oct 2022 2323

Orbiting in three days! I think it is safe to say we are all ready to get to Mars. This has been a long trip. Despite all of the well wishes and the books and the movies and TV programs transmitted to us we have been monumentally bored. And then scared to death! The physical problems with the outbound trip are pretty bad. I think you ought to seriously consider loading up on the fuel and trying to blast out here at a higher gravity value. A quarter or better yet a half gee of acceleration will do wonders I think. Maybe I'll let you know how that works on the inbound leg. If I survive. I have been dwelling on my mortality these days. It is dangerous out here. The skin of this space ship is thin thin thin. The harshness of the vacuum of space weighs on you. It's funny. You can be told about that but it's one of those things you have to experience for yourself. I think that's what changes you. And you have to deal with that on your own. I know the guys who went on the EVA know how that changes you. I wonder how much thought you gave to having married couples come out here. Did you consider that Bob? It would definitely help to have someone to share with. Not that Janice and Li are bad friends. On the contrary we are as close as sisters. And they help. However there is just something different about a lover or husband that the closeness of sex brings. I find myself very jealous of Sergei and Janice. That closeness they share. I think about a wedding toast I heard one time: May you half each others sorrows and double each others joy. I never considered myself the marrying kind but now I find that the state of marriage has some advantages. I am trying to focus on the mission and get that accomplished but it has been harder than I imagined so far. I hope we are up to the task going forward. No questions today. Too worried. Peace.

Launch day 709 20 Oct 2022 1325 Unity in Martian space

The computer put them in geosynchronous orbit over the landing site. At a distance of less than 100 nm above the surface the features of mars were stark reality. The crew had been having increasing trouble sleeping. They had been getting incredible photos from the telescope for days. Even the ships long range camera had spotted the rover and air plant PODs on the surface. The past two weeks had been slow torture. A rash of equipment breakdowns had not really broken up the tension. Royce had noted the increasing quiet of the crew and was worried. He composed a quick coded note to Sergei imploring him to snap the crew out of the funk they were dropping into. Sergei had been receiving the coded notes with his personal messages. Royce had clued him in to Watkins but Sergei was perplexed by the statement that Watkins "probably" would not act unless he got cheated out of something he saw as his due. Probably. Well fuck Watkins. And fuck Royce. This crew was 88 million miles from earth. It was just the eight of them out here. They had to do it or it was never going to get done. They felt the weight. Even Sergei felt it. Royce wanted them snapped out of the funk huh? He was welcome to come up here and give it a go. A week before orbit Sergei called a meeting to change the watch bill. They were going to a one watch stander flight watch before landing. He put the crew through a few days of intense video training sessions on the landing site build and the science they were going to perform. Digger and Georg were distant at first but the sessions brought them around. Rosario and Janice had perked right up. Janice and Li had been doing most of the biological science so Janice had tried to get Li to open up a little. She had had some luck. Zhou had been brooding for a while and seemed to be shrunk. That was Rosario's word. Just shrunk. Watkins had always been standoffish and was even more so. Now they had to get together and land this craft. The night before orbit Sergei had ordered up a smorgasbord of the alcohol on board opened up. They had a decent meal with some chocolates and wine and alcohol. Sergei stood watch that night and tacitly ordered them to get drunk. Sergei was treated to Chinese, German, Argentinian, and American drinking songs. Watkins had started in on "one bourbon, one scotch and one beer". Which they promptly changed the lyrics to one vodka, one scotch and one fine dry reisling. Sergei played reveille as loud as possible the next morning. Each crew member staggered up to the accel couches with varying degrees of hangovers. But they also had sheepish grins. The orbiting maneuver was Newtonian simplicity. Sergei bellowed orders until Janice threatened to kill him. All crew was at stations and ready as can be. The next duty was to drop a comm satellite into orbit near them. The unit was stored in a container in the equipment section. It was autonomous once the power system was fully charged and initial nav settings in putted. The prep of the comm satellite was finished in two hours. The launch was from the airlock. This time Watkins and Sergei were tethered into the airlock as they launched (well pushed) the unit out the door. The unit immediately came to life and jetted off three hundred meters up. Solar panels unfurled while the ship gave orders for the unit to contact Houston.

Rosario relayed info to and from Houston confirming satellite functionality. The delay had peaked here at 4 min 57 seconds of one way silence. The round trip of just under 10 min called for even odd send and receive cycles. On the even 10 min periods the ship received info from Houston. Unity sent data on the odd 10 min intervals. Fuel status was 207 lbs available for landing. About seven min of powered flight to descend the 100 miles. That would mean approx 1350 gallons of fuel consumed total. The PODs would be emptied of fuel and water by tonight. The ships tank would have 2300 gallons for the return journey. The return journey was predicted to use 2000 gallons of fuel. They would have to overcome mars gravity on liftoff and they would not get a sling shot from the moon. The profile called for a larger burn rate on the return journey. NASA felt the astronauts would need the extra gravity and a shorter return journey after the rigors of the outbound flight and land work. The survey of the landing site started in earnest. Data on the surrounding area was uploaded into the computer showing hi res radar images as well as the camera shots. As much as possible the team looked at where they were to land very carefully. They spent a day taking detailed pictures of the landing site. The rover POD and the air plant were set down on the proposed spot but the mission commander had discretion to order a different landing spot based on circumstances. Houston poured over the data and declared the site green. Sergei could also call off the landing given some equipment or personnel failures. Both ship and crew had survived the journey intact in body if battered in spirit, so they would attempt the landing. The nightly teleconference/news conferences had become tortuous affairs waiting for minutes old answers to get to earth while questions travelled at them. Royce wanted to express his displeasure but Scanlon and Kat talked him out of it. They are doing the best they can and pretty well under the circumstances, Kat told him. Royce grunted acknowledgement. Bob hoped Sergei could hold them together long enough for the bustle of landing to pull them back together. The sum total of the data told Sergei the place was sat and the crew was ready. Go for landing.

CHAPTER 27

Launch day 712 23 Oct 2022 0210 Unity in mars orbit

Sergei briefed them all in the galley area. They were all suited. The landing sequence would start at 0425. If all went well 32 min later they would be safe on the ground. It was his decision to deploy the comms booster for the ground site right away. The booster and the orbiting unit would together allow for the landing site to be linked to the ship and Houston. It would also allow suit to suit comms within an approximate mile range. Sergei announced that Rosario would accompany him on the first landing party. Watkins and Digger would follow with the rigging to run down the pods from the landing struts. Watkins started to object. Sergei forestalled him. "Every single person on this crew is going to be credited with the Martian landing" Sergei reasoned calmly. Watkins had a set look to his face.

Sergei moved on doggedly. "We can't build the landing site in one day. First priority is getting the comms unit up then the bobcat. Then we move the pods down and start building. One ship watch person every day. We set the nav and radar units to standby. We have a building protocol. We will follow it." He looked at each of them in turn. "We start using the clean room equipment as of today. Dust dirt and debris is too much for our vent and scrubbers. If we are not vigilant we will choke on Mars".

Sergei laid out the schedule and the assignments in a matter of fact manner. "Some of the science experiments can be setup right away. Li, Janice and Georg will start those. Lui you have first ship watch today. The only other iron clad rule is that no one goes out alone. Questions"? There were none. "Take your positions".

An hour later the ship was ready. The crew was more ready than the ship. Houston was more ready than the crew and the people of Earth were more ready than Houston. The thrusters fired in sequence to ease down the ship. At 85 nm the ships main engines fired to slow the vertical rate of descent. Telemetry remained good. The outside camera showed the landing site as mostly sandy soil with rocks scattered around. The engines cycled up and down the power scale but never more than 1/2 gee on descent. Sergei itched to have his hands on the yoke but he knew the computer was controlling it better than he could. His only action was to keep pressing the okay button as the craft asked him to confirm various decisions it was making. At 14 nm the computer gave him three possible sites. He chose the more rocky one which was closer to the rover /air plant POD site. Watkins called out distance and fuel remaining every 15 sec. His voice was calm, almost hypnotic.

"1000 meters fuel 35 percent."

"850 meters fuel 31 percent."

"600 meters 28 percent."

"Dust on the camera."

"Thruster alarm 5-X axis- shutting down" said Zhou.

"Acknowledged," said Sergei without losing focus on the data steaming at him. The ship had lost a maneuvering thruster engine. It could lose two in total and still make the descent as long as the two were not on the same strut.

"400 meters 25 percent."

"200 meters fuel 22 percent."

"100 meters fuel 19 percent.'

"Ship rotating 20 degrees port, from Digger.

"More dust."

"35 meters fuel 15 percent.

"20 meters fuel 14 percent."

Janice watched Sergei in utter concentration staring at the screen willing the ship to touch down.

"10 meters fuel 13 percent."

".1 velocity down."

"5 meters.

"2."

Thump.

"Touch down. Engine shut down."

"Fuel 09 percent." A beat of silence.

"Houston, Zhenge he base here, Unity has landed." Sergei jauntily told the world. "Ship status engines shut down. Fuel 09 percent. One red thruster, all others green. What a beautiful view. Zhenge he over".

They talked quietly amongst themselves while waiting on the delay. A burst of static and Houston responded with. "Roger Zhenge he base we copy you on the ground and green. Fantastic job Unity crew! The whole world salutes you. Houston over".

Sergei released the crew from landing stations. They all broke for the windows and the screen displays to look outside. The alien landscape stretched out on all sides. Unity uploaded the pictures from the camera. The Martian sky was indeed a weird pinkish color. No clouds of course. The sun was a small ball the size of a pea in the sky. The Elysium plain was a mix of sand and rocks. The whole area was a giant impact crater formed a few hundred million years ago. The soil was the same reddish brown that the rovers had been showing scientists for decades. Rocky outcrops stuck up at odd angles. Due west from this position the bulk of two large volcanoes could be seen. Elysium mons and Mons Olympus. The latter the largest volcano in the solar system. It was 40,000 feet high. With almost no atmosphere to interrupt the sight line the 100 mile plus distance did not look like much. Due north was the polar ice cap at approx. 70 miles. The start of the large canal network that had captured the imagination of so many, lay east 60 miles. Closer in the bobcat pod was 250 feet away with the Air plant pod a further 100 feet beyond that. The cameras showed the landing struts sunk in to the soil about an inch. The soil had a large grain sandy quality to it that was strange to human eyes. Georg had reported that the rocks looked like remnants of the impact debris thrown up by the large meteor that created the basin.

 "Needs some tumble weeds blowin thru," drawled Watkins. Well wishes and messages poured in from earth. The crew dealt with them in a perfunctory manner. Digger and Li were setting up the clean room drop pads and the vacuums. Sergei, Janice and Rosario pulled the booster unit to the airlock and went thru the deployment procedure. They were at the airlock when Houston came back on and concurred with the deployment. They reported good connectivity with the deployed orbital comms satellite. NASA reported that the 5 X axis thruster was down by their reading and would need to be replaced. Roger. Houston also asked for a weather report. That seemingly innocent request bugged Sergei.

Watkins also snorted. Zhou reported the outside temp at -120 degrees Celsius with the wind at 16 mph. pressure at 08 milibars and sunshine for the next seven hours. The Martian day was perversely close to the normal earth day at 24.02 hours. Given its orbital tilt versus the solar system plane mars did have seasons. Late spring early summer now on the Elysium plains with summer lasting 220 days or more. The Martian year being 678 days long. It's like someone thought ahead and had us land when the conditions would be optimum. Duh. Janice asked Rosario why everyone was mad at NASA for asking about the weather. Rose explained that NASA knew exactly what the weather was. They had the telemetry data.

"NASA just wanted us to give out those fantastically cold numbers so the folks back home could ohh and ahh about how brave we are" she said quietly.

"But you are being brave going out there," Janice said.

"Yeah I know, but I don't want to brag about it", Rosario said.

"You're going out tomorrow are you any less brave", she asked?

"No, I want to go out there".

"Is it any colder here than outside the ISS", Rosario went on?

"Well, no".

"Ask me what the weather is when I'm not wearing the suit, then we can talk about brave".

Astronauts, Janice thought. Janice gave Sergei a quick kiss and set his helmet on. She embraced Rosario as she entered the airlock. She activated the airlock switch and relayed all green to Zhou. Zhou reported to Houston that Ivanovitch and Gonsolvo were in the air lock and ready to egress. Houston reported back roger go for landing EVA and booster unit relay deploy. Sergei and Rosario cycled the airlock and opened the airlock door. The red ground of mars was seven feet below them. They deployed the landing ladder from its stowed position in the airlock. The landing ladder was really two ladders connected side by side. Sergei stepped out onto the ladder and went down three of the eight steps to get to the surface. Rosario handed him the booster unit. The 18 by 24 by 12 box was bulky but not heavy in the reduced gravity. Sergei had a tether attached to the ladder more for tradition than real need. You could certainly drop the seven feet down but you wanted to do it a nice and controlled manor rather than fall. Even if that fall was going to take forever in Martian gravity. The trip down the seven feet would take 5 whole seconds. Sergei stepped to one side of the ladder and descended another step. He ordered Rosario out onto the ladder. She started down the other side of the ladder. As she came even with him, Sergei handed her the comms unit per the procedure. As he tried to take the next step down he kept coming up short. "Ah my tethers stuck on something. Can you see it Rose"?

"No I'm blocked by the unit" she reported.

"Okay let me go up one step and release it and then we get this show on the road", Sergei said starting up. Sergei stepped up and worked on the tether for a few seconds. That's no good it's looped some how". "Rose go down one step to give me some room and give me the unit than I'll unwrap the tether and we will switch places okay".

"Roger CMDR". Rosario was concerned Sergei was really stuck. He grunted and shifted position up and down the ladder and reported no joy. He struggled for 3 min. "Rose come up one step then down two when I move the tether around you. I'll keep hold of the unit for now. I need to pass the tether around it eventually."

"I can't see it Sergei. I can't see where you are stuck, she told him. I recommend that we abort this and start again."

"Hey, Rose no big issue I just need to have you down one more step and then I can swing over to your side of the ladder and get it,- okay?"

"Sure Sergei what ever you say." She descended one step and immediately knew what he had done. She looked down at her foot on Martian soil. She placed her other foot down as well. Without a word she moved out from beneath the air lock. Her breathing was the only sound. She looked at the sweep of the horizon the utter alienness of the landscape. Her breath hitched in. "Rosario Marie", Sergei's voice was soft in her ear, "tell the people of the earth what you see."

"Dios Mio its beautiful. I wish everyone could see this. I'm standing on the surface of Mars looking at an alien landscape. This is so fucking cool," she squealed. Sergei joined her on the surface. "Houston, Rosario Gonsolvo is the first human being to set foot on another planet at 0638 hours. She reports that the experience is exhilarating and that we take this step for the advancement of all human kind." Sergei and Rosario touched helmets. "I'll get you for this she said.

"No you won't I'm too fast for you. Let's set this up. Zhou how is the video feed from the suit cams?, he asked Unity."

"Excellent commander. We particularly noted the struggles you were having on the ladder." "Yeah remind Digger and Watkins that the ladder can be tricky. Houston I only have another few seconds in this report period so I wanted to make sure you saw this discolored section of sand here on this side of Unity. The sand is scorched from the engines but it doesn't look like the heat was all that intense. I think Hoffman wanted to get some samples of the melted soil. I'll collect those when we come back from the comms unit." Zhen gee He over."

Rosario and Sergei moved north of the landing spot 200 feet. The sparse gravity making for the standard shuffle hop the Apollo crews made famous. They went slowly. Sergei was afraid a fall could damage the suit. Setting up the booster relay was simple enough. Open the box, unfold the solar panel, extend the antenna and flip the switch. Easy peezy lemon squeezy. That was the real purpose of the relay unit. Any deployed remote rover would now have a boosted signal to receive commands. They didn't expect the Viking to perk up but they thought the curiosity rover was a possibility. Houston had come on the air with mixed reactions to the EVA fiasco. Houston had ordered an abort to the EVA when Sergei had faked the tether trouble. Once Rosario was on the ground they were thrilled. Right up until she cursed. Royce's comment when Rose uttered the "this is so fucking cool" line was a dry: "Roger Zhenge He base we concur on the coolness factor." All eight of them thought that was funny. Watkins and Digger were next out. They both paused to say a few words about how they were proud to be the first Americans to walk on another planet. They started the visual inspection of the ship noting some problems. It quickly became obvious that Houston could not direct or comment on things happening as they occurred. Houston reported that they were back in comms with the curiosity rover which had been thought lost 2 years ago. Royce ordered the Houston techs to remain silent unless asked to comment from Zhenge He. Now that they were there the crew had ultimate control of the mission. Houston became watchers as well. Tomorrow would see the bobcat retrieved. More fun opportunities for cussing. Houston reported sightings of tee shirts with "Dios Mio it's beautiful" emblazoned on them. Royce was relieved that it wasn't the second half of the phrase.

Launch day 713 24 Oct 2022 1101 Unity at Zhenge He landing site

Janice set foot on Martian soil and immediately started crying. She had a whole speech planned and she couldn't stop crying.

Sergei warned her that there was no way to blow your nose in the EVA suit and that she was going to be stuck with snot running down her nose. Janice started laughing. Sergei asked what she wanted to say and Janice got thru that she was honored to represent her family, friends, gender and hair color on mars. The eight of them had spent hours last night going over who was the first what on Mars. I'm the first American woman on mars. I'm the first German and by the way the tallest person ever to set foot on Mars. Sergei had ship watch today. Everyone else was going to be outside having fun. Janice and Li were putting up the four science experiments that were going to be outside long term. The first one was a seismograph would measure the Martian ground for seismic activity. Marsquakes? Hoffman and Andrews were already unbolting the top part of the rover pod. Hoffman collected the parachute and the detached heat shield which had fallen close by. Well not really close but close enough that Sergei only yelled at them for 10 min when he went by himself to get it. Besides he yelled in English how mad could he be? Watkins and Zhou continued to take down the now mostly empty PODs that would become the landing site. They were rigging them down from the landing struts. The fuel and water had been transferred to the ship. The air was in compressed gas cylinders. Lots of items inside the PODs would have to be transferred to the ship or the base but all of it would be put to good use. Sergei was kept hopping filling the airlock with tools and items going outside while other things came in to the ship. A whoop on the net indicated that Digger and Hoffman had gotten the rover out and operational. Three hours to unpack and put together was right on the predicted time. Georg put a tether strap sling around the base of the POD and put the two loose panels inside. The parachute and the heat shield also went in. They dragged the pod back gouging a smooth track. They dropped it off for Janice and Li to unpack the rest of the rover digging tools and attachments, and then they were zooming off towards the air plant POD. They just looped the tether around the POD. They didn't bother to unpack anything as this POD would be opened later. 20 min later they had the POD stored next to the landing site as Rosario laid out the boundaries. The fluorescent green paint stark against the red brown soil. Georg and James got right back to work configuring the rover to use the scoop blade. 40 min later the bobcat's blade bit into the sandy ground and started pushing the Martian soil back towards the Unity. The first 5 inches was grainy and loose before hitting the permafrost. Rosario and

Janice were using stiff 1 inch diameter aluminum rod stock 48 inches long as pry bars. Rosario punched thru the three inch thick layer of frozen ground. George was on his knees taking close up pictures as the rover scraped the ground clear and a dry ice mixture of frozen carbon dioxide appeared as a white layer. The carbon dioxide quickly dissipated, bleeding away into the thin atmosphere. James piled up the top layer of soil over the 30 foot by 30 foot landing site area. He smoothed a three foot high mound that was 10 feet long at the north end of the site next to Unity. Using the rod stock Janice and Rosario punched thru the perma frost every foot or so. James now positioned the bobcat blade near the edge of a chunk of permafrost and got underneath it. Lifting the blade broke off the chunks into a roughly foot square blocks. Georg, Janice and Rosario shuttled the chunks of frozen ground back to the berm laying them as flat as possible. They alternated between breaking up the ground with the rods and moving the chunks that James pulled up. Three hours later had the whole area was cleared of frozen ground. Sergei was calling a time check as Janice realized they had been out for seven hours now. James wanted a chance to dig into the newly uncovered ground to see if he could push it with the bobcat. He took two long swaths again pushing and piling up the dirt next to Unity. He occasionally picked up small rocks while he moved the dirt. Georg was a giddy geologist while he examined the rocks that James was uncovering. Georg kept up a running lecture about the rocks origins as they came into his hands. When Sergei called them in an hour later they had the 30 by 30 foot area cleared to a depth of a foot. Five more days of earth moving if they kept up this rate. They also had to dig the trench from the ship to the site as well as the tunnel leading down from the airlock. Then they had to clear the second 30 by 30 area and the connecting trench. Call it two weeks of digging. That was assuming one 8 hr shift per day. If they could convince James to let someone else drive, they could cut that down some. The clean up in the clean room took forever. The dirt was every where. They had to empty the dust busters into a waste can to continue vacuuming off the dirt. When Zhou was finally the last one thru Sergei and Rosario vacuumed out the clean room floor itself. Dumping the last of it into the waste can Sergei grinned at Rosario. 58 million miles to haul dirt and vacuum?

"Loved every second of it," she said. Dinner that night was a joyous affair while everyone made fun of Gorge getting on his knees to practically lick the ground. The academic realized they were teasing him when Li asked if she could get another explanation of igneous rock ejection striations on the fracture areas. He shot back that she was one to talk when she started in on microbial life possibility locked in water bearing strata. Sergei took some of the sting out of that by declaring he had never seen such a look of contentment like the one James had sitting on that rover pushing dirt around. Man has got to have a purpose James stated happily. And I think I am finally finding mine! Amen brother.

Launch day 716 27 Oct 2022 0600 Unity and Zhenge He landing site

The rover blade dug into the rock and the right front wheel dug into the dirt. They had uncovered many rocks of varying size during the dig. Yesterday they had to gang together to lift a boulder that would have weighed a ton on earth but only two hundred lbs here. Sergei James Watkins and Zhou had each grabbed a corner and heaved the rock out of the growing pit. They got it out and then moved it over to the berm to be placed on the top. They had about two feet to go and this rock was bigger than the others they had encountered. James had noted the rock edge and moved over to the other side of the hole. He continued to push the dirt up and out of the pit. Sergei and Zhou were using hammer claw ends and pry bars to outline the dimensions of the rock. An hour later Digger had completed the rest of the pit except for the rock. It was located in the back left corner of the site. It jutted two feet into the site from the edge and was four feet along the edge. However they could not find the lower edges as they kept digging down. It seemed to extend several yards under the current surface. Sergei and Zhou started persuading the rock with their hammers. Persuading in the form of hammering on it trying to break it up. Small pieces chipped off but not the big chunks they needed to make real progress. And they had been making progress. After a quick 8 hr nap. Digger had convinced Sergei to let him out again. He kept them on 8 hr shifts: Digger Rosario and Janice on one. Watkins, Li, Zhou and Hoffman on the other. He was keeping the guard duty. They were working like mad men. They had the tunnel material out and were waiting for the trench. Once that was dug they could start laying it in and sealing it. Zhou had pulled out the solar arrays for the landing site and had laid them aside on the other side of the Unity space craft. Watkins had pulled out the floor tarp that would seal and insulate them from the ground once the site was level. The POD panels were stacked and ready to be made up. The support poles and the roof panels all lay out according to plan. Now they hit this rock. They paused while they considered what to do. No jack hammer in the out load. No dynamite to blast it. Oops. They did have an option along those lines. The railgun. This did call for extensive consults with Houston. In the end they decided to blast it. The discussion was between reorienting the site to skirt the rock, but that called for extensive re-digging along the southern edge. Also the berm and trenches would have to be re-dug some. Besides it was fun to blow stuff up. Georg also recommended the explosions to expose the interior of the rock formation so he could ascertain origins. Well if science wanted the thing blown up then by all means. They moved anything they could think of away from the blast zone. The berm should protect the ship a little. The gun was at a shallow angle so it would hurl most of the material directly away. Sergei ordered everyone behind the POD stack on the other side of the lander. Fire in the hole came the call. The depleted slug hit the rock at a shallow 11 degree down ward angle. The muzzle velocity was the lowest setting the gun had. The spray of rocks was… disappointing. About a quarter of the rock disintegrated. The crew could not find the slug afterwards. Aim was adjusted and the setting bumped up and this time the debris bounced off the ship. No discernible damage. ¾ of the rock destroyed. The slug had buried itself in the back wall about 12 inches. The nose was misshaped. They retrieved it and stored it on the ship. Hammers and pry bars did the rest to shape the rock down to the level they needed. Zhou and Watkins actually gouged out rock down another foot from the rest of the dirt level. They moved dirt back on top of the rock to allow for the fabric pins to get some purchase. By the time the rest of the crew had the PODs and other items moved back into place, the pit was complete. James turned over to Hoffman and the German started in on the trench connecting the two sites. Meanwhile Zhou and Li went around the leveled pit sprinkling some boiling water brought directly from the ship. The dirt immediately froze providing an almost concrete like pad to lay out the tarp covering the site. They pinned it in place with long aluminum stakes similar to landscape fabric pins. Which they were. Once the insulating landscape fabric was laid out the three workers opened the POD with the site air plant and uncrated it. They put it in the forward corner near what would become the airlock door and shimmed it level. Next they laid out the channels that would become the footers holding the plasbond panels. Again they pinned them into the ground after applying a silicone sealant between the fabric and the channel. The whole thing was going to get a layer of spray foam insulation and sealant afterwards. The initial 10 foot wall section that joined the forward end of the site towards the ship got the first of the channels laid down. The tunnel from the airlock to the site had the flex material already in it. The reinforced material was round and about 6 feet in diameter. The tunnel headed down 8 feet and then ran along horizontally in the trench James and Hoffman had cut for approx. 30 feet. There it smacked into the new wall panels going up. One of those panels had a preformed airtight door installed. Those doors were much smaller than the ships airtight doors. The interior space would be 10 feet wide by 5 feet deep as another wall ran across the space to create the air lock. The panel on the other side of the 10 foot wide expanse had another preinstalled air tight door. The air plant was on the other side of this door. Watkins was working alone on these channels when Zhou tried to engage him in a discussion on what was the best way to proceed. Watkins rebuffed him coldly. "I don't care what you do next" he said, and walked away to get more channels. Zhou merely looked at him. He would talk to Sergei about this. Watkins had been oscillating moods over the last few days. The crew was functioning but the long trip out and the external EVA nightmare had changed them. Zhou realized that the psychological make up of the crew was very fragile this far from safety. The unrelenting work gave them something to focus on but it only masked the real divisions. Zhou hoped that they could keep it together for the next year. Meanwhile, the work must get done.

Video log Janice Lincoln 07 Nov 2022 1022

Hello from Mars! I'm taking advantage of some time on watch to make this video. We have been on mars for a little over two weeks now. We have been working like crazy to complete the landing site. Just getting here isn't enough to establish the viability of the mars mission. We feel like the site must be inhabited for a good period of time to show what is feasible. I think we are close to that day when we move into the base. It will be good to get some more elbow room between all of us. We are a little shorter with each other than I would like. Not real arguments just competing agenda's. We all want to get out and explore. I wish we would have scripted out the rover schedule a little more. It has fallen on CMDR Ivanovitch to ration the rover if you will. There have been several conflicts over who gets to go where and when. Not everyone can be pleased all the time and some feelings have been bruised. Mine included. We have worked out the tertiary and fourth level goals to get to some of the more distinctive features on mars. No sense coming 89 million miles to miss the canals or the ice caps. Meanwhile the science experiments are nearly all setup and the data is pouring in. We can't hope to look at it all. I intend to concentrate the search for possible life by a systematic approach to the samples we have taken. Dr. Li and I have consulted and we feel this is the best use of our time. Time for the question of the day. I have to get back to hauling things to the airlock so they can be put in the base. What do you think of when you look back at earth? I think how lucky I am, how scary it is to be so far away and how much I miss the earth. I also think about how fortunate I am to be here and that more exciting days are ahead! Oops got to go, they need more stuff outside!

CHAPTER 28

Launch day 729 09 Nov 2022 1902 Unity and Zhenge He site

Days of dedicated efforts had really paid off. The site was almost ready for move in. The interior was sealed off and an air tightness test conducted. The site had some small initial leaks that took two days to track down and seal up. Both sections of the site were now air tight. The decision to build both halves simultaneously was met with skepticism in Houston. It delayed the crew move into the first half by 8 days but the whole base was 12 days ahead of schedule. The site had been chosen quite carefully. The soil was sandy with few large rocks. They only had to use the rail gun on those two little shots. Both solar arrays had been setup and were now providing power to the battery/ industrial room on the "north" side of the base. The air plant was in there as well. Power lines ran thru the base connecting various vent fans and pumps. Heaters had brought up the temp to a chilly 65 degrees. The transfer of water into the air plant became a comical bucket brigade of water coming from the science station wash down sink in the Einstein module on Unity to the air plant upper chamber. The water would spill while moving from the tunnel into the airlock on the site. Sealing the tunnel material to the plasbond panels was the most challenging technical build issue. Sergei finally made a flat 6 inch wide ring with a six foot diameter out of plasbond from the 3-D printer. Slipping that over the tunnel end where it connected to the site airlock door they used liberal amounts of epoxy to glue the ring to the door. Next he placed 4 inch square hollow pipes from a plate on the tunnel wall to the edge of the ring on the outside. This wedged the end next to the door. This had solved the problem of the material of the flex tunnel coming away from the airlock door when the rover pushed the dirt back on top of the tunnel. They rigged up three more sets of the connection rings for the shorter tunnel that connected what they were calling the north and south sides of the base. The third set connected the tunnel up to the Unity airlock door. Now they could open all the doors on the ship and the site and they had a dramatically increased living space. Standard safety rules called for all airtight doors to be closed off incase something happened. It was just a matter of opening the doors to get from the ship to the base, and closing them behind you. No time consuming pump down required. All manner of items now flowed from the ship to the site. Lights, heaters, tables, cots, blankets, science experiments, food and much more flowed down. The south side air lock opened out onto a wide ramp of earth leading the 7 feet back up to the surface. The panels with the port hole windows were liberally spread out over the two halves of the base. The windows let in some of the natural mars light. The uniform grey of the insulation sealant was depressing enough. There was not much of a view from the windows. Five or six of the windows were set up on the walls and barely peaked over the dirt. The second Faraday antenna was set up over the site. The antenna took up the last available circuit breaker on the power distribution panel from the solar arrays. Sergei had Watkins and Andrews constructing another distribution panel from parts on board. The printer was making the panel itself. Once they had the panel shell the circuit breakers got wired up and more equipment could be connected to power. Janice and Li spent days hunched over microscopes searching for microbial life. Li also had her telescope set up making detailed observations of Phoebes and Demos, mars' moons. Sergei had kept everyone close to the site for the time being. They groused but assisted in setting up the science experiments. Some of those were pretty basic: take a 24 inch by 24 inch shallow box of Martian soil and stick earth seeds and add water and sun light. Wait to see if anything grows. Or even sprouts. They took a handful of seeds and took them outside and sowed the Martian soil. Add water and walk away. Wait to see what grows. In another box, mix in some earth soil and see what grows in that. In a third box take earth soil and Martian sun and see what you get. Then earth normal sun and soil but Martian gravity. They had to note down detailed observations on what was happening. They heated and froze rocks and soil and the air. They isolated chemicals from the soil and air. They observed if various chemical reactions would actually happen on mars. Take a piece of wood outside. Would it burn? How would you get a flame in this environment? They poked and prodded and gas chromatified any thing they could. They marked samples and video taped results. The crew was content to luxuriate in the extra space for a few days. The night they opened the site they all brought over some of their diminishing stores of specialized food stuffs and had a small feast. The cots in an open space were a little strange.

Six days later the crew was chomping at the bit to move out a little. Sergei appropriated the first "expedition" for himself. Digger and Georg had only taken the rover a few miles north and south to reconnoiter the general area. Now Sergei wanted to hit a major Martian feature: The Elysium canal. 60 miles to the east stood the head of the "canal". Early observers of the red planet had noted the straight line "gouges" on the surface. They made the only earth analogy that made sense: Dry canals made by unknown people. Or little green men. Higher resolution photos had shown no evidence of the canals. It was thought now that the lines the early observers saw were shadows caused by blown sand along ridges. The start of one of those ridges began 60 miles away and went north west to south east for 100 miles. Sergei was captured by the images in his head of dry canals showing evidence of a civilization desperately trying to move water around to save itself while mars dried up. He proposed a three person expedition: Himself Li and Hoffman. The rover could cover 8 miles an hour over open ground. 60 miles out and back. 120 miles divided by 8 equals 15 hours at least. Add three hours for exploration while they were there and that gave you an 18 hour time frame. Great except that the EVA suits were only good for 12 hours and the rover would need a battery charge after 10 hours. They could take the extra batteries in the solar charger packs. They could rig holders for some extra EVA suit bottles on their backs. That would extend the range by another 12 hours. They could go 18 hours without food or water but what about bathrooms? They could rig a catheter system. What equipment could they take? With the extra person it limited them to about 25 cubic feet due to space considerations. What preventative maintenance could they do to the rover to make sure it was in tip top shape? They never asked Houston for permission. They planned and debated long into the night.

Launch day 740 20 Nov 2022 0542 Zhenge He base

The predawn pink glow took some getting used to. They wanted max daylight for this journey so they were starting off before dawn. The buoy markers had been Janice's idea. They fashioned round 6 inch foam balls and painted them fluorescent green. The paint was what they had used to set out the landing site parameters. Now they made buoys to be dropped at intervals along their path. Breadcrumbs would have blown away in the wind. So would their tracks they thought. Probably not but they wanted to make sure. So Hoffman held a bag of 10 of the balls. It was huge. They had put weight in the foam with rocks. The rover had a radio location beacon that the ship was using to track them. The computer had their path plotted: 61 miles at a 082 course. That should bend them far enough North to skirt the only real obstacle in their path: Elysium mons. The volcano was average for mars at about 6,000 feet high. It did however make a ridge running north from the flanks of the volcano. That ridge lay in their path and they had to figure a way through it without losing too much time. Hoffman was dying for an hour to scout around and take pictures to see

487

how that ridge was formed: plate shift or lava flow or natural folding of the land as the mountain pushed up? Sergei was giving him 20 min. Hoffman was already begging to be left on the volcano while they continued to the canal. No way Doctor. No one goes by himself. The Venice three as they called themselves, walked out of the south airlock and mounted the rover. Li was perched precariously on most of the equipment. Sergei had said his good byes the night before. Now he just said: see you soon and slowly drove the rover east. Janice and Rosario took up stations on the command console and began feeding them updates. You are making course 087 good so bend it a little north Sergei. Roger. They dropped the first ball at the 5 mile mark. The Elysium plains were flat and relatively free from rocks. They did dodge larger boulders and the tires kicked up dirt. They were making closer to 9 mph for the first three hours. The volcano which at first was barely visible now reared up. After so much flat the mountain looked even more imposing. All three were snapping pictures. Now they began picking their way through larger boulder fields. As they slowed to maneuver Hoffman would reach out and snatch a rock up and begin examining it. Four hours in the ridge appeared in all its glory. A slanted line 70 to 80 feet high the ridge ran from out of the volcano nearly due north. Sergei now angled north to try

and find a way thru. The ridge wasn't like a cliff wall but it was

imposing. The rocks were jumbled here and there were a weaker

fracture zone had allowed rocks to break off from the main plate.

And plate it was. George had confirmed that right as they set out

to the north. He collected some samples from the base and quickly

packed them away. Li and Sergei got the geology lecture.

"This bit of rock forms a plate boundary. When the mountain rose

up because of the magma pushing up the plate rose and this edge

became exposed. I bet the prevailing wind deposited sand and

over a million years the other side of the plate has become buried. I

wish you would have let me dig for a little bit to confirm that."

"Dr. Sergei said, You and James can come back with the bobcat

blade on and dig all you want until you find that plate edge."

"Well that's not really the important thing. I just proved beyond a

shadow of a doubt that Mars has tectonic plates. We are moving

along the Ivanovitch/Fong plate boundary now."

Li and Sergei gave him a big smile. They moved on and eventually

found a spot where the rocks had tumbled down enough and the

wind had piled up enough sand to breach over the top. Hoffman

and Li dismounted and Sergei took the rover thru the Lincoln gap. Only after looking backwards did Sergei realize how lucky they had been. The ridge was higher on this side and more pronounced. Since it acted a windbreak there was not much sand on this side. Except for the little pyramid of sand spilling down from Lincoln gap, the soil was much more rocky. The ridge stood out as the rocks were 120 to 140 feet above the floor along this side. Taking video from the top Sergei could hear the gasp as Janice and Rosario saw the ridge running unbroken for several miles on either side. Nice scenery out here huh? He asked. All three mounted and Sergei carefully drove them out on the plain. The plains of Mordor. Nah. Death Valley. No good. Dragon Back Ridge. Ohh. Cool. The plains of Contemplation. No too Zen. That debate lasted a good three hours. The game of eye spy had only lasted 10 min. I spy with my little eye something that begins with "R". Is it Rocks? What else could it be? They were every where. Sergei picked his way thru making decent time. Rosario informed them that they had been out for eight hours. They were 30 min behind schedule. Rosario said that they should come to 090 and proceed another 1000 yards and they would be right where the map indicated the canal started. It took an hour of zig zagging to finally hit it. Once they saw it the three were totally perplexed. The plains were almost dead flat. Hard scrabble rock and soil together. If you stood at a 45 degree angle you could make out the narrow strip of grey sand running along what looked like a tiny mound. The mound ran straight and the narrow three foot wide strip of sand ran along on the leeward side of the mound. They got off the rover and started looking around. They dug into the mound and it was an ordinary natural rise in the land. The gray material was fairly thin 10 or twelve inches thick by three or four feet wide strip of fine pure sand. They grey color was something new. Hoffman took some and examined it under a microscope. His gasp brought over Sergei and Li.

"Please run this thru the gas chromatograph to confirm what I think."

Janice and Rosario watched the feed with interest. While the machine worked its magic, Janice called for them to replace the rover batteries and release one half of the reserve air into their suits. The replacement was accomplished in 30 min and the suits verified and each one checked the other two out to ensure the readings and o2 levels. The gas chromatograph shut off. Hoffman and Li and Sergei bent heads to observe.

"Crystalized carbon," Hoffman breathed. Sergei gasped.

Li was puzzled. "So what, carbon is one of the most basic elements in the universe".

"Yes, said Hoffman "but carbon takes many forms. Decayed plant matter carbon squeezed for years makes coal. "Coal squeezed for years makes graphite carbon when it's powdered. Coal squeezed and heated makes large crystals. Diamonds. This grey sand is powdered diamonds."

"Is that valuable? Li asked. I know that regular diamonds are but powdered? Who would want powder diamonds?"

"Lots of people said Sergei. Industrial diamonds are the fractured cousins of diamonds. There are all sorts of uses: diamond tipped saws and drills and the like. They get used to polish mirrors and lenses. They can be worth 200 dollars a carat. There is a huge deposit in Siberia that could give the world thousands of years of industrial diamonds but they are way too expensive to mine. Mars has mined and sorted this bunch for you.

"Wow. How are they formed? Li asked Hoffman.

"These are impact diamonds. When a meteorite strikes a natural carbon deposit the heat and pressure gives you diamonds. The deposit Sergei is talking about was formed 35 million years ago by a meteor in Siberia. Mars has meteors in abundance. The meteors over the millions of years have made tons of these diamonds." Gorge informed them.

But how did they get put here in a straight line out in the open? Uh. That's a good question. Lui Zhou had an answer he thought.

"Sluice Box", he said to Janice.

"Sluice Box" he said over the comms unit to the away team.

"What?" Sergei asked.

"When you mine for gold you get a sluice box to run the material over it," Zhou explained. "The sluice box contains ripples that allow the water and material to run over. The water carries away the lighter material and leaves the heavy gold piled up by the ripples. That's what this looks like," he told them. "The wind carried the material over the little mound there which acted as a ripple and it got deposited. Since the light reflects differently for this materiel the first observers of Mars saw the straight lines and assumed it meant that someone had gouged the sand. They didn't know about the diamonds," he finished softly.

Slowly that sunk in. Houston now piped in for the first time that day and concurred. Houston directed them to fill up as many containers as they could with the pure diamond dust. They had about 35 lbs of it. Sergei remembered the old maps of mars with the canal lines running all around the surface. His head boggled at the amount of diamond dust. If they brought back even a millionth of the total amount mars held, the price for industrial diamonds would plunge. So the canals of mars turned out not to be evidence of past life on mars but lines of diamonds in the sand. Sergei could be satisfied with that. He had come to see and he had seen. Now lets get on back. He could use a drink. The way back was filled with discussions of diamonds: if the dust was out there, maybe some gem quality as well? Hoffman said there might be some but it would literally be like finding a diamond in the rough. Their tracks had made it through the few hours they had been gone. Sergei goosed the speed up a little. He knew the path was good. They found Lincoln gap with no trouble and chugged up it. The sun was getting low on the horizon as they headed back along the plain. The last hour was pretty dark. The little lights of the ship and the base stood out in the darkness. Everyone came out to hail the heroes as they dismounted. Digger was sure the real hero was the rover.

"It was fine, Digger, no problems." Digger kept on checking.

"Hey James we are fine, too", Georg snorted.

"I could use a shower!" Sergei told no one.

"Let's see the magic dust, Rose demanded. Everyone was underwhelmed as the dust was poured out onto the tray.

"I thought it would at least sparkle" Rosario said.

"It does under the microscope but just looking at it is unremarkable, Georg told her.

"Okay pack it up people. Lets get inside, " Sergei ordered. The first exploratory goal was a huge success. Houston lauded them and the requests for media interviews went back up as word of the discovery spread.

Launch day 750 30 Nov 2022 1225 Zhenge He base

Sergei had promised a decision and there was no point in delaying. "Ice caps," he said without preamble. Janice and Zhou howled. Everyone else was mad.

"People we have 280 more days for exploration on this mission. There will be plenty of time for everyone to go traipsing around mars". He wanted to take the sting out of that but Watkins and Digger were upset. Since they had returned with the dust, everyone wanted to make huge discoveries. Three competing ideas had come up: a trip to the polar ice caps to see if liquid water or life

was around. Collecting samples of the ice at least. A trip to the

Viking Lander and the try to recover the Curiosity rover and Mons

Olympus. Watkins and Digger had wanted Olympus. Rosario was

pushing to recover the curiosity. Janice and Zhou wanted the Ice

caps. The disappointment of not having their own mission chosen

eventually gave way to planning the ice cap mission. Li Fong made

her case to go along on the Ice cap mission. Hoffman as well

wanted to go. The hard numbers of the length of the journey said

no. 78 nm due north the edge of the ice cap lay just at the edge of

what was possible. 19 hrs of travel there and back. With 14 hrs of

daylight available they either had to take lights or start at midnight

and begin the journey in darkness. No water for 19 hours was

troubling. Could they rig a squeeze bottle pouch? What scientific

equipment would they need? The collection boxes and the science

gear what was really keeping the number of people down. The

rover could only hold so much. The extra batteries and the lights

and gear just didn't allow for Li or Georg to go along. Since Li had

gone on the canal mission Janice was the choice for the Ice caps.

Zhou was driving and was the muscle on the trip. The prep took 3

long days. Janice and Li Fong discussed what samples would

be needed and different techniques. They opted for a grab all of it and look at it later philosophy. Hoffman had threatened all of them with bodily harm unless he got three wild card sample items. During the trip Hoffman got to look at the video at direct them to collecting samples three times. The bargaining started at 10 samples. Hoffman spent two long hours lecturing them on what to look for.

At the end of the lecture, Zhou looked at him incredulously and said: so it boils down to "look for strange rock formations" and "look for rocks that don't belong with the others"?

Hoffman blinked. "Yes."

Janice giggled as Zhou started swearing softly in mandarin.

"Georg, she said soothingly. You are the geologist we are not. You need to know why the rocks form the way they do. We will just pick them up if we see something weird. We don't need to know why. That's what we have you for. I promise to video tape all of the surroundings so you can go back and review the data in situ for the sample okay?"

The trip was delayed some days while they dealt with an air plant breakdown inside the landing site base. The base had also developed some small air leaks. Those they fixed quickly. The air plant had required almost 20 hours of repair. The heating unit for the electrolysis ended up as the culprit. It took hours to isolate and then replace but it took 12 hours to bring the unit up to full operation. Almost worse was the fact that it took another 100 gallons of pure water to begin making air again. They had retrieved some of the water from the unit but more had evaporated into the space. Sergei and Houston consulted on the water issue. Houston felt like the air leaks while small were also doing double damage as allowing water vapor out into the dry Martian atmosphere. The air leaks could be expected. The base had 6 separate air tight doors. Two operating air locks that got constant use as people cycled into and out of the ship and the outside. The plan had envisioned that the two air lock doors between the ship and the base would remain open, but that wasn't how it was working out. Basic air tight and air control training had them closing off the ship to base air lock even though it was pressurized. The constant opening and closing the doors caused vibrations which caused leaks as the sealant and insulation stiffened and cracked. They were constantly spaying new over some old sealant areas. Sergei had to resort to releasing some compressed air to keep the base pressurized. More worrying was the second replacement of the power regulator on the north solar array for the base. The ships solar array power regulator was operational but trending down. The regulator did just that: it took the uneven output from the power converter and smoothed it out so the finicky electronic equipment that used the power worked better and lasted longer. The regulator also had to have an input from the battery so it could maintain the power needed depending on whatever source it was getting the power from. Most people had no idea how nice the power grid in the US really was. You just plugged the iphone charger into the wall and two hours later the phone worked again. But without a power regulator the phone would take different voltages and currents straight from the transmission lines. Bad for the phone. The phone would not last nearly as long. Early December, before he let the ice cap mission proceed, Sergei and the Unity crew held a meeting to discuss the problem with Houston. Sergei and the crew felt like the base was running a race between the air plant and the solar array to see what could shut them down first. The options were pretty varied: They could try to fix the solar array power regulators that had failed. That would require a lot of micro circuitry repair. Houston promised to get with the manufacturer to see what could be done. Could they build new by scavenging parts together? Possibly.

Again Houston would run some scenarios to see what they could do. The ship had one more in spares and that was only predicted to last 60 days. The air plant required a full yearly maint procedure that would have them in EVA suits for the last 24 hours. The sealant was putting off some gasses that had saturated the detector for hydro carbons. Was the sealant petroleum based? No. NASA was sure of that. What about the plastic bottle? There was some kind of reaction between the sealant and the bottle they put it in to apply it. The sealant came in bulk cans from ships storage. Since they could not use an aerosol spray type system they had to put the sealant in plastic pump up bottles to get some air pressure in them for application. Had NASA tested those bottles for long term exposure? No we assumed you would use the bottle then throw it away. They hadn't counted on needing to constantly re apply the sealant. You don't know what you don't know. Pull the plug on the station? They could retreat to the ship and work from there. Yes always an option. As a public relations issue retreating to the ship was less than desirable. Watkins told them: "we busted our asses to build this thing like hell we are going to abandon it prematurely."

Sergei soothed him. "Tyler we all agree with that sentiment 100 percent, but we have to think our way through this. Here is the plan: Houston we want a full procedure on a run thru scenario for repair or scavenge build of the power regulator in three days. Tyler, Rosario and Georg, and I are all on the break down of the three old units to assemble a working spare if possible." "Baring that we will isolate to common or disparate parts that failed. We will build whatever Houston comes up with. Lui, Digger, Li and Janice will commence the maintenance procedure on the air plant. Prior to that we will inventory the sealant bottles and consolidate to make 6 or so full bottles of sealant. The rest will be disposed of. "The six will be stored in the ships hazmat locker when not in use. Remember that the air in both the ship and the base will be pumped out and replaced with new air from the compressed air bottles. We still have 5 full exchanges remaining so new air aint our problem," he deadpanned. "Depending on the fixes we will let the mission proceed. Everyone clear? Lets get to work." Oh ra!.

CHAPTER 29

Launch day 765 14 Dec 2022 2323 Zhenge He base

Seating herself Janice gave the thumbs up. Zhou was settled in and the gear all arranged on the rover. The rover looked like a family of four was going on vacation. Items looped all over it, boxes strapped everywhere.

Sergei cautioned: "slow at first. Don't hesitate to come back if some thing happens. The maps don't show much in your way until you hit the ice. "But that doesn't mean there will be smooth sailing. Careful."

Zhou nodded and switched on the single light mounted on the top of the dash board. Godspeed. They moved off into the dark, the light getting swallowed up quickly. They were leaving in the dead of the night to maximize the amount of daytime at the pole. The remaining crew would stay in contact with the rover throughout the mission. Sergei went back in to monitor the trip.

They made good progress during the first portion. Not really much to see and pretty easy going over the ground. They averaged

8.5 miles an hour. Six hours in Hoffman played a wild card.

"Okay see the small group of about 12 rocks to your right?"

Janice snorted. "There are rocks all around."

"About 3 o'clock at 20 meters, he said.

"Okay got it".

"I want you to go over and pick up three or four small ones."

Zhou stopped the rover and Janice moved out to scan the rocks so Georg could see what he wanted.

"That one, the one right next to it and the discolored one to your left. Perfect." Happy geologist.

Janice placed them in bags and labeled them then placed the rocks inside the geology specimen case. Hoffman wanted them to proceed to the small rock outcropping they had been pointing at as the only real landmark on the plain. There was plenty of sand and small rocks but nothing remotely interesting as far as Janice could see. The out crop had served as a natural landmark and they had been pointing right at it the last 30 min. Could you get bored on another planet in six hours? Kind of. Georg directed Janice to chip off two or three small chunks of the outcropping. More labeling and notations inside the case. Hoffman was writing all this down as he got the label notations from Janice. Sergei had teased him.

"We have all this noted on the tablets."

"What if the researcher doesn't have access to the tablet data?" Georg retorted. "This way he knows where and when the rocks were collected and why. I want to compare the three previous samples to the outcropping to prove or disprove that those rocks came from the same source. I think they are all debris rocks from the interior of mars thrown up by a meteor impact. In fact…"

Rosario halted him in mid lecture. "Easy big guy. You should be watching the vid, you only have one wild card left."

Georg blinked. "One? I have two. One Sergei said. You used one to have them get the three rocks on the plain and another to have them get the rocks off the outcropping. One left."

The geologist quailed. "Everyone knows that the control group counts as a single sampling unit!" Janice and Zhou had been monitoring and chimed in with their opinions. Li got them off the subject by asking what the name of that outcropping was going to be called. Point Unity Janice said. Can't be. A point is when a bulge of land juts out into a body of water. So what is that outcrop of rocks? An escarpment? A Piedmont? A heated debate started about the definitions of geography. By definition an outcrop of rocks is bedrock that is exposed. "That's what I'm trying to prove," shouted Georg to the group.

"Hey calm down we will call it Georg's rock if you want." Sergei chuckled wickedly while they teased Georg. Astronaut teasing went this way: Do it until your best friend threatens to kill you or starts crying. Then declare victory. Start on next target. When it's you as the target, grin until the next target comes up. Repeat until someone hits someone else.

Three hours later Zhou and Janice spotted the ice cap. The ground was frozen over here. As the rover rolled thru the wheels cracked through the thin frozen layer on top. Zhou stopped the rover at that point about two miles from the start of the ice cap and they dug in the soil. The thin top layer was only about a quarter inch thick. The temp was close to air temp at -123 Celsius. The layer underneath was a few degrees warmer at -109. The permafrost layer was 12-18 inches thick. Again the underneath layer was prone to white dry ice formation. They took soil samples from two different spots. Moving back onto the rover they headed to the edge of the ice. Janice got soil and some rock samples while Lui moved around documenting the thickness of the ice cap. The ice was several meters thick. Janice immediately tried heating a sample in a sealed flask. Clear liquid appeared in the flask.

Cheering could be heard in her helmet. Lui moved back to the rover and was taking sample cases and more equipment off the rover when the picture went dark in Unity. They still had data and voice from them.

Digger grabbed the mike and reported the loss to Lui. "Did you bump the wireless unit or the video cable link to the transmission unit?"

Lui looked down. "Yeah the cable got pulled from the unit when I removed the bladder. The strap cable was looped around the video cable. I pulled it right out." Sorry Digger."

"Hey no harm to me. It's a pretty simple fix but I need to be there to do it. I don't think we have that in the repair kit. Plus it's going to take some time."

Digger and Sergei consulted. "As long as we have voice and data you guys are good to go. If we lose one more item, then its drop everything and come back. You have 1 hour 47 more min to go on the ice. Proceed slow and steady." Sergei had on his mission commander hat. Sergei, Digger and Rose sat in Unity watching the blank screen as if that could restore it. 10 min later Houston noted the loss of video and then concurred with the decision to proceed. Janice had managed to find purchase and had scrambled up onto the ice.

 Lui admonished her. "Do not leave my side. I do not want you to become separated.

Good luck with ordering her around Sergei thought but did not say. Janice coolly told Lui to shove it and continued to describe the ice field for Unity, Houston and the world. "I am taking suit video so you will have that when I can upload it. I am going to walk 100 meters north to get to a clear spot and try to bore thru." I will bring an ice core sample back. Looking at the plain we can't be more than 10 meters thick. The ice has a granular crust and is speckled with sand and rocks. It looks like more north you go the more the ice has heaved and cracked and buckled. I'm not sure what that indicates." She swung slowly around as she walked north to give the video more depth of field. "Houston if you have an expert who could lead me thru this I would be much obliged. She started on the core sample. The 2 inch diameter pipe came with a drill unit and extensions. She had 15 feet of pipe. Labeling each pipe section 1 thru 5 as it went into the ground and noted that for the log in the case. Time temp lat and long went on the sample label as well. Janice went thru the buckling of the ice for the expert Houston had on hand. Houston had a myriad of questions.

They also directed her to get video from certain angles on the ice chunks to show them what they wanted. Lui had been busy as well. He had made a cargo net and affixed it to the back of the rover. The insulating tarp covered the bottom. He was pitching in chunks of ice into the cargo net. Every one was more valuable than the diamond dust Sergei had found. Water on Mars was confirmed. Atmospheric, radiation levels and gravity readings were all being noted for various logs. 10 min mark Sergei warned. It couldn't be! They just started! They tried the "Aww mom just 5 more min" trick. No joy. Janice had one ace up her sleeve. "CMDR Ivanovitch you know that bet you had with CMDR Elkington? I think 15 more min out here could seal that bet."

"8 min, Dr. Lincoln Sergei said quietly. Come home now. The street lights are on."

She packed frantically while Lui hurled chunks of ice into the net. It was bulging.

"I don't see your position moving." "We're going. It takes a min for the position to update when we first start out. I could explain it to you CMDR Ivanovitch but it's pretty technical." 2 more min passed before Unity noted the position updating. The trip back took 3 hours longer than they thought. The net slowed them considerably. Lui never once thought of abandoning the ice. They lost some mass of the dry ice mixed in with the water but most of the ice survived intact to the station. Watkins, Digger, Hoffman, Rose and Sergei waited north of the ship with lights blazing while they came in. Li had the watch. 2302 saw them stop at the garage. Digger had used the remaining panels plus some items from the 3 D printer to fashion a garage for the rover. Nothing was too good for his baby. The whole crew worked to secure the precious ice in any sealed container they could. It went into the rubberized bladders Lui had brought. They had to break it up to get it in. The precious core samples along with the soil samples went right to the science station holds on the ship. The core case plugged into the dock on the ship which started the freezing of the samples. As long as the ship had power the samples should make it to earth. As long as the ship made it back that is. The freezer system was actually pretty simple. A closed loop system of pipes went past the insulation layers and next to the skin of the ship. The ammonia inside was cooled to a frigid -35 degrees Fahrenheit. The pipes then went to a fan system which recirculated air thru a heat exchange unit. The air that came out was cooled to a nice 10 degrees. That was blown into the ice core cases and the ships frozen stores. A fairly simple system that didn't use much in the way of mechanical parts and did not require the use of the Freon cycle. Freon is very bad to clean out of the atmosphere while ammonia especially in the small amounts the system used was preferable. As long as it stayed in the pipes. The crew worked to get the other samples cataloged and stored for analysis. Janice and Li would be very busy the next month looking thru this material. Houston's first sight of the ice made the engineers assembled break into applause. Digger showed up next to the table holding the sealed flasks and the bladders filled with ice. The outsides were wet with melted water while the Co2 detector went crazy noting the increase in carbon dioxide which melted into the atmosphere inside the base. Trace levels of ammonia hydroxide and other gasses were released during the small melting that occurred. Inside the sealed units the ice slowly melted into water and whatever vapor the other gasses contained. All that would get measured and noted and studied and pondered. Digger had another purpose. He raised the container of scotch. Hey chip me off a piece?

The final haul was 87 gallons of pure H2o. Once the dirt was separated out of course. 17 precious gallons were stored away for further study. That left 70 gallons. Uh, Houston can we drink this? No! Yes of course! NO! The debate raged for a week. They were 122 gallons short on the water use curve. Not critical but projections said that they would hit the 200 gallon criticality threshold at day 892. That criticality level said to evaluate going home based on water use. They might stretch it another 30 days but they would have to cut the mission at that point. That might be 100 days short. Nearly 1/3 rd short of the planned time on Mars. Nope. Those 70 gallons gave them the cushion to make the 330 day limit. Then it was orbital parameters pushing them not controllable factors. Sergei had made up his mind just as soon as Janice said it was just water. No microbes or anything else, just water. It goes in the tanks. If he had to, those 17 other gallons might go in there too. Of course Houston and the world would have pitched a fit if they had known that they had granted Diggers wish. All eight had shared a huge glass of scotch with a chunk of Martian ice in it. Janice hated scotch and that had been the best drink she had ever had.

Launch day 812 30 Jan 2023 1203 Zhenge He base

The video screen showed the class room clearly. Janice could see Zoe Smyth in the back ground writing something down. Janice started in. "Hello Australia!" "I can see you and hear some back ground chatter so I want you to take your seats and I will start this." We have an annoying comm delay. What we do about it is talk in 10 min sections." "I talk and ask questions for 10 min and then you guys get to go for 10. Please keep a close eye on the clock and say "over" when you are completed. We have deployed Zoe's science experiment for the last month. I'm spooling up some video of the experiments."

The screen showed Janice and Li moving solids from one flask to another outside. Liquids were being transferred from one flask to another and to the solids. The results were being analyzed by the gas chromatograph. The screen went back to the classroom.

"Zoe's experiments were to look at the chemical reaction in a zero oxygen environment with reduced gravity. On earth a simple chemical reaction starts with a molecule and a catalyst." Not so on Mars." She led them thru the changing of different chemicals.

"Mars however lacks the oxygen of earth so the reactions performed differently. You can see the multiple reactions she wanted on this chart with the expected earth and mars results listed here. Unity over."

 The classroom had settled while she was going thru the power point so they had obviously heard and seen her. Zoe Smyth smiled and got up in front of the class. "Thank you Dr. Lincoln. What a thrill to be talking to you on Mars. We all wanted to say we saw the video of you on the ice at the pole and were incredibly awed by it." I know you are working on the samples so if you want to announce that you have discovered life on mars to us that would be okay!" "Just kidding. I can see the experiments and you followed my amounts perfectly so the results should be just as predicted unless physics works differently on Mars or I made a mistake." The young girl tapped on her computer. "I am sending you a power point summarizing my results and the chemical reactions shown." Zoe went thru her methodology and how she got the results in her predicted column. "I had to make up a computer program to allow me to input the different chemicals and all their associated radicals and shell values. I could not find a program to allow me to do that for Martian equivalents." She frowned. "I had to tweak the results display to get all the values I wanted to show. But here they finally are. Adelaide over."

Janice started nodding and agreeing with Zoe when she started her presentation. At the end she just stared at the little girl open mouthed. "You made the computer program yourself? Let me show you our results screen which we made with the help of a quantum computer and a NASA program and many hours of labor from Dr. Li and myself."

"By the way Dr. Li says to tell you hello and that she is sorry for not being here for this, she was up for the last 30 hours working on the samples. And no we won't be announcing life on mars today." Now let me show you our results." Janice showed a screen with the chemical values and some rudimentary chemical formulas. It was way sparser than Zoe's program. Her program allowed the user to input the different value without having to change the other variables. The equivalent was a financial program that showed you the price of a stock and the symbol only versus a program that showed you the opening price, closing price with a daily chart and historic values plus the dividend yield and all the other bells and whistles. Janice asked how long it took Zoe to input the values and get her results.

"About thirty min why?"

"It took Dr. Li and myself about three days to do this. We don't have your program but I want it. Call Bob Royce as soon as we disconnect. If he doesn't have you at Houston in one day I will leave Mars and kill him. Maybe you should be up here and I down there!"

The last month had been a blur to find a microbe. Or a fossil of a microbe. The hard science had really started in earnest. Christmas and New Year passed with a minor nod to the holidays. Best to keep working and not dwell on what you were missing. The growing experiments had yielded results. Martian soil was too alkaline to grow plants. What about lichens? Or algae? Certain simple plants liked extreme environments. They now attempted to grow earth lichens on mars. Algae were encouraged to grow in Martian soil with a stream of water running and the UV light set to mars setting. They could not setup a similar experiment on mars the atmosphere just wiped away the water. The temp was too cold. Nothing could grow now. They tried cold water algae and ice blocks. That worked. They could get things to grow in controlled conditions which proved life could be here or may have been here. They just didn't have that proof. Houston wanted another ice expedition. Sergei was working on that. They had come up with a fix on the solar array. They had made some adjustments to the current power regulator and had scavenged two of the broken regulators to make another. The back ground radiation was too much for some of the more sensitive electronic circuits. They shielded the current unit and its twin on the other array. Projections now said they would be fine with what they had. Sergei, Watkins and Zhou had all swapped out the damaged thruster on strut number two. They had some spares but Watkins wanted to try to repair the damaged unit. Sergei did not want solid rocket propellant inside the base structure. They shelved that idea. Now they were bugging him to let them go to the ice cap! Sergei put them off by having Digger and Hoffman totally tear down the rover and inspect/repair any faults. That bought him a week. In the end he couldn't say no to Houston and the crew. Watkins and Digger went. They returned with another 100 gallons of water but many more rock and soil samples. Plus two precious ice cores. They had also been five hours overdue. Sergei had words with both of them. Digger and Watkins went sullen when given the reprimand. Janice had found Watkins three days later coming out of the cleanroom. He was bruised and rushed by her without a word. She found Sergei holding his hand and breathing hard.

"What happened? she asked.

"Nothing, Sergei told her. "Tyler wanted some instruction on command technique and I gave it to him."

"Did that instruction break your knuckle?"

"No but I hurt my wrist. Hey that reminds me aren't we due for a round of physicals?"

"Yes we are, but don't change the subject. Janice asked him with real concern, "What's wrong with Watkins?" Sergei laid out his knowledge of Watkins activities and Royce' suspicions." Janice was livid. "He killed Brad?"

Sergei said, "That's what Royce thinks." I've been getting coded messages from Houston since we launched." They don't think we are in danger but no one knows for sure." Sergei was glad to be sharing this, but he warned Janice to let him handle Watkins. She reluctantly agreed. "And no sharing with Rose, Sergei warned. Oh joy. Janice couldn't believe that Sergei was holding onto this information.

"What could I do?" he asked her. "Tell everyone and risk Watkins going off and killing us all?" "Let it lie, he told her.

She looked at Sergei helpless. The Earth got further away.

Days later Li and Janice were discussing the latest round of physicals. The results were disturbing. Bone loss was high. Muscle mass had decreased for all. You simply could not subject the human body to 300 days of $1/10^{th}$ gee and expect their to be no consequences. They went over the results with Sergei. No one has cancer or broken bones-yet. But we are all suffering the effects.

"We are going to pay for this back on Earth," Li said.

"We were briefed about the physical problems before the mission," Sergei replied. "Yes but that didn't have the reality of this. We are all going to have long term effects from this." Li concluded.

"None of us is going to make 80," Janice chimed in. "We can combat the bone loss with the shots but we need to double the exercise time and the UV lamp time. We are just not producing enough vitamin D. I don't think an enrichment program is going to work for this." Sergei said he had to try. "I know EVA suits are the hardest physical thing we do. Maybe I can come up with something for that." "What, an EVA suit marathon?" Janice asked.

"No but close."

The end of Feb saw Sergei announcing that the crew needed to work on the EVA suit walking skills. Future mission astronauts would need to know what the limitations of the suits were in a non rover capacity. The closest geographical feature to them was a small impact crater about three miles away. Sergei proposed that seven of them go out to the crater carrying equipment make some observations and take samples and then come back. He estimated a seven hour trip. They would leave tomorrow. One person would have to remain with the ship for safety and in case the rover was needed. Watkins had the duty. He seethed at the perceived slight but Janice knew that Sergei had planned this in response to the test results not as a punishment to Watkins. She thought. Sergei had shrugged. "Someone has to stay back, he drew the short straw that's all."

 Bright and early the next morning saw them setting out southwest to the crater. M1203S by its designation. Rosario wanted to have the first person to reach the crater get to name it. She shuffled ahead two or three hops. Carrying the tool box made that awkward. Hoffman was already puffing twenty min into the walk. They all were when a halt was called twenty min later. Sergei estimated they had come halfway. Watkins confirmed their position with a vocal sneer. The group sat on the equipment boxes and recovered. "You know what I like about Martian weather, Zhou suddenly said. "Its very predictable. I like that."

Janice was suddenly consumed by giggles. Rosario and Li joined her immediately. The ladies laughter made Sergei start in. Hoffman and Digger chuckled. Zhou was totally perplexed.

"What? It is very predictable. The same day after day after day." That set all six of them off. Gasps and wheezing laughter filled the comm net.

"I see no reason," Zhou started.

"Stop, stop!" came the plea from Janice. Suddenly they all seemed to come to their senses and get themselves under control. A second of looking at each other and that set off a second burst of intense laughter. The cathartic release lasted another minute. Digger complained that the giggling made his sides hurt more than the walking program. Hoffman nominated Zhou as the lead comic for the half way night entertainment festivities.

Zhou started to object, "I see no reason to.." Li broke in and rattled off a string of Cantonese. She lectured him for two min straight. At the end Zhou ruefully accepted the half way night festivities honor. As the group started off again, Digger sidled up to Li and asked helmet to helmet. "What did you say?"

Li grinned. "I told him to shut up and say yes."

"All that for shut up and say yes," Digger teased. "Cantonese is a very complex language."

The crater mission was a success in that they all made it to the crater, looked around, collected samples and made it back safely. It was even a bigger success in that all seven complained of soreness for two days afterwards. In pairs the crew ranged far and wide around the ship. They had some minor suit issues but overall the suits performed magnificently. The science mission went on at the same pace. Janice and Li alternated between collection and analysis. Sergei complained that they should have found the microbe by now. "The single celled organism has had ample time to morph into to a little green man by now", he jibbed. "Are you sure you know how to work this thing" he asked pointing to the microscope. Janice told him it wasn't like looking for a needle in a haystack. It was like looking for a needle of a particular length, a particular diameter and eyehole size in a haystack of other needles. "Don't you have wrenches to turn? Get out."

Half way night was very subdued. The physical and emotional toll was telling on all. They ate and drank and sang songs but

522

even the comedy styling's of the great Zhou failed to pull them out of their funk. Royce brought his concerns to the committee. Coded messages flew back and forth to Sergei. The month of March was absolute rock bottom for the crew. People barely spoke. The media sessions were pure tedium. The constant pressure and work was grinding them down to the nub. Sergei confided to Houston thru the video log that he had doubts about his ability to get the crew back to earth safely. People made plans.

CHAPTER 30

Launch day 882 10 Apr 2023 0100 Zhenge he base

Two days of hard bargaining had led to this. Rosario and Zhou were heading out to try to retrieve the curiosity rover. The season was turning. Late summer. They could only count on about 13 hours of light now. The curiosity rover was a mission goal and if they were going to attempt it now was the time. The diligence of the weekly EVA suit maintenance had either paid off or betrayed them depending on how you looked at it. Two suits had been put out of service during the procedure. The helmet joint rings were a major vulnerability. The inner lining of the suit was complicated and had hard wired connections and they had replaced those on numerous occasions. The ship carried multiple linings sized for each individual. The outer lining was tough and durable and could be repaired. Those also had spares and had been used. The joints were a repair part. However the helmet was not getting good seals on two of the suits even with spares. The rings looked fine. The helmets looked fine they just couldn't get an air tight seal. Uh oh. It affected Digger and Hoffman. Hoffman had joked that great minds think alike. Big giant head sizes was more like it. Coincidentally, those two had spent the most EVA time. Not unexpected to have breakdowns but it left them with one functioning spare each. Sergei did not want to make them stay in the base or on ship. Sergei had Watkins making new rings on the 3 d printer. The spares in supply were not quite large enough to make a good seal. That repair to get the new rings in place could take two three weeks. If it even worked. Houston was working on alternative solutions to the problem with the suit manufacturers. So Digger was removed from the curiosity mission and Zhou took over. Digger was angry about it. Sergei let him be. Curiosity lay stuck in some sand some 62 nm distant to the south east. The Viking lander lay just 5 nm north of that position. The rover had been commanded to try to make it to the Zhenge He site but had become bogged down. Now they wanted to try to tow it back. The curiosity vehicle was much bigger and heavier than the bobcat rover they sent. It was also much faster. Zhou and Rosario had tools and parts and batteries to try to strip away what they could and to slap new wheels and batteries on. They also had a quick software update to let the Curiosity respond to driving commands. If they had time NASA had asked them to visit the Viking site and retrieve some items. Rosario and Zhou had four extra air

bottles each. This mission might take some time. They planned on

36 hours but Sergei thought they might need as much as 48 hours.

They only had 50 hours of air. The catheter and drinking water

systems had worked okay but this was pressing it. They left

quietly, with little fan fare from Unity or earth. The two made

good time at first but slowed considerably as the terrain got

rougher. Viking had set down inside an impact crater and the

whole area was much more affected by meteors than the Elysium

plains were. Janice monitored their position with Hoffman. No

wild cards for this trip. Rosario had taken to reaching down and

plucking rocks up while they drove past. She would hold them up

and let Georg see what they were. If he said no then she tossed

them back. Drive by geology was the term they came up with. Just

two miles north of the rover and another three miles west of the

Viking site the long odds of hard driving caught up to the rover.

The area was actually smoother and less rocky than what they had

been experiencing. Zhou had goosed the speed to make up some

time. He moved left to avoid a small rock sticking up and hit a

patch of loose sand. The front wheels of the rover dug in a bit

lowering the front end. The smaller rock was really a larger rock with a small portion exposed. The tip of the rock caught the main cross brace of the front axle. The jarring hit threw everything not tied down forward. Zhou and Rosario were belted in. The battery packs were mounted but the impact had knocked them up from the brackets holding them. They tore loose as the rover bucked and halted. All picture telemetry and data ceased immediately to the ship. They were way out of suit range. Sergei and Digger re ran the tape several times before deciding that the power outage was caused by the wreck. James said that he thought it would take 35 min to get the batteries back connected and make sure the system was recovered before the connection could be re-established. If that was the problem. 57 long minutes later, video and data were restored. Rosario was looking back at the rover. Zhou was at the front end and equipment was strewn around. Sergei and Janice blew sighs of relief. Digger immediately asked to see the damage. Zhou and Rose had strapped back in the batteries and repaired the cable to the video/data transmission unit. The main problem was the axle. It was bent slightly.

"Define slightly?" said James.

"See for yourself." The rover was jacked up so the front was off the ground. In front wheel drive mode the wheels turned but the wobble was evident.

"Not good."

"Can we straighten it?" Lui asked.

"No way, James told him. "We have a spare axel in the repair kit. Get the wheel puller unit from underneath. You have to reassemble the jack stand. The duct tape is in the tool box." Digger led them thru the procedure. Pull the wheels, pull the axel, put the new one on. Getting the axle out of the turning gear transmission box was the toughest. It had to run thru and it was bent enough to require coaxing. Rosario had taken advantage while the rover was being repaired, she took some equipment over to the curiosity site. Sergei gritted his teeth but said nothing of her going off by herself. The smart car sized vehicle was stuck in a small swale in the land. Wheels buried up to the axel. Bad day for mars rovers she thought. Setting two of the sadoway batteries on the top she rigged up an input into the curiosity power system. The external charge port was still operational. Power came on instantly. She next connected a tablet to the control module. She cleared the wheels as best she could with the small shovel. Well the garden trowel was what it really was. 45 solid min of effort later she held her breath. Commanding the curiosity rover to ahead slow she pushed on the back. The wheels spun but found some traction. The rover slowly pulled itself up the small rise and out of the swale. Whooping, she let the rover continue forward while she put her gear on top. We're coming on back she crowed to Zhou.   Two hours after setting off she rejoined Zhou at the rover repair shop. The bobcat was back in some semblance of action. Lui and Rose shifted to get the curiosity up to speed. They muscled the front(?) end of the vehicle up onto two equipment boxes. Stripping off the wheels they put them on top. The new axel went thru the transmission. The old rover had been built and launched in 2010 time frame. Each wheel had an independent drive. The new axel tied two wheels together and didn't have tie rods attached. The wheels didn't have to steer the thing just roll free and provide a little help. Digger and Hoffman had great plans for this little beauty when they got it back to base. Pimp my rover. That was for later first they had to get the thing back. Shifting ends they put the other axle on. Adding to the battery total they connected more in series to provide more power. Rosario began stripping off some of the old science experiments. The old batteries joined the growing junk pile. The two were loath to leaving anything. You never knew when something could be useful. They had a garage right? A garage was supposed to be full of old junk. Five solid hours left them exhausted and tired. Changing out emergency air bottles was little daunting. The little caravan left for the Viking site at the 20 hour point. The dark was haunting. The 3 mile trip took almost an hour. They stopped at the edge of the crater with Viking sitting offset from the center in their direction. The light from the rover barely reached the 250 meters to the lander. Zhou and Rosario called it a night at that point. They wanted 4 hours of sleep but Sergei gave them 5. Rosario confided to Janice that her catheter bag was full. Lots of sloshing. Eeww. The crater rim proved to be no large issue. They proceeded to Viking and started pulling items off. NASA wanted the trench digging tool and the samples stored in them. Viking had caused some controversy in 1976 when it examined some soil and seemed to show life. NASA wanted that sampling boom. Plus the soil. They also wanted soil samples from around the site to compare. As she moved off to complete the samples Rosario noticed the difference in the sand as she moved higher on the crater rim. She discussed this with Houston. The sand looked smoother and different than the surrounding territory. It looked for all the world like those pictures of the African savannah when the dry season hit. Viking looked like it was just outside the edge of the last pool to dry up in the wilting heat. Rosario expected to see the wildebeest skull bleaching white in the sun. She shook her head at the thought and kept moving rocks and soil into the bags. Lui reported that he had the last of the items NASA wanted off the lander. They both posed in front of the lander like tourists. Gathering the booty they trudged up the crater slope. Now they had to get back. Bone tired, the journey back quickly became a night mare. Zhou kept driving into danger zones and the curiosity was a lead weight being towed. The time kept ticking by. Houston was calling Sergei with urgent requests for him to look at the clock. "I see the damn clock he muttered. Rosario and Zhou were trapped in a no mans land. Approx 15 nm from the base. They desperately needed a few hours sleep. They had been gone 38 hours. At the rate they were going it would take them another 7 to get to the base. If they didn't make a mistake and drive into a crater or huge rock. They had 12 hours of air left. Maybe. The physical exertion was making the oxygen use higher than modeled. If they fell asleep for too long, they would run out of air and that was that. Okay time for some big picture perspective. Sergei called for Rosario and Lui to stop the rover.

"Why?" came the confused reply.

"Rose, Lui look at the course and speed made good over the last three hours" Sergei told them. You are wandering left and right and you are not making good time. About four miles an hours. Let's think this thru." "I want you to unhook the curiosity from the bobcat.

"No!" came the immediate reply.

Sergei kept his voice light but firm. "Hey you guys have lost perspective. We don't have to get the rover back in one mission. You guys have done the bulk of the work. Nice job. Why don't you unhook and head on back here. You get a good shower, some chow and rack time and then you can come back out and pick up the curiosity with no trouble at all." He hardened his voice. "You two are way more valuable than any old car. Now I am ordering you to unhook and head straight here. Got it?"

Zhou and Gonsolvo saw the correct path through the fog of fatigue and their fixation on accomplishing the mission.

"You bet, Sergei," Rosario said. A hot shower sounds good to me. Unhooking now."

They dropped the curiosity and started back straighter and faster to the base. Janice was keeping a running course update to Lui to keep him on the right vector. All was fine for about 23 min. Janice alerted Sergei as the indicated speed slowed down. Sergei came on and tried to be light hearted.

"Hey Lui, you can't be late for dinner you need to goose that speed a bit. Rosario's voice came on a little weak. "Shit, Sergei. He could hear the panic.

"The damn batteries are dying!" Crap.

Lui came on. "Sergei we used up too much battery life pulling the rover. Shit."

"Relax," commanded Sergei. "I want you to listen to me very carefully. I need you to remain with the rover. Whatever happens: stay right there! I'm coming to you. I won't have position data on you when the batteries go. I can't afford to have you wandering around out there. I'm bringing air to you. Acknowledge."

"Sergei we... " the signal petered out. Voice data and pictures faded. Sergei bolted for the EVA suits. "Watkins!" he bellowed. Wriggling into his suit Watkins appeared on the command deck. "Get into your suit he commanded. Take an extra air bottle for yourself. Get the position from Janice. I need you to bring two batteries for the rover. Follow my tracks! "Got it?" Watkins tightly acknowledged the order.

"No." Janice cut through the discussion. You are not going out there."

"I have to."

"How in the world are you going to find them? She asked. It's dark. There are no direct tracks left to get to them." Hoffman, Li stared at them, processing the emergency.

He looked at her and paused pointing. "Look at the display.
 Remember the crater we went to a while back? M1203S? The one where we all lost it when Lui made that joke?

"I remember."

"When we were there I remember looking out and I could see the top of Mons Elysium from there.", Sergei told her. "Look at the rover position. Its on a direct line between the crater and the mountain. Once I get to the crater, I position my self looking at the mountain and then walk straight at it. Easy peezy lemon squeezy.
 I'll have four air bottles. If I can't find them in 12 hours it won't matter any more. Then I'll follow my own tracks back. He paused putting on the helmet. "I'll be back, Sophy. Count on it."

He left the clean room for the air lock. Janice watched him go as Watkins struggled to get into his suit. Hoffman and Digger came in with the batteries for Watkins. The load was bulky and would slow him considerable. Sergei voice came hard and controlled as he moved out with a rapid hop shuffle. The air bottles looped over his back in a net bag. Sergei was in the zone calculating odds as hard as he ever did in Vegas. "Tyler, you take it easy out here. You have the far more dangerous job. If I get lost, you drop those batteries and head right back to base got it?"

 Watkins acknowledged. Royce came on the line as Sergei started to move out of suit range. "You sure cowboy?"

"You bet, Bob. Be seein you."

He had to wait an agonizing hour at the crater for the sun to come up enough to see the mountain in the distance. He figured he was eight or nine miles from Rose and Lui. Somewhere along this path. As long as he kept true. He had a compass on the suit display. He set that to 000 relative while he watched for the mountain. Once he set that 000 into the suit compass it would always be 000 relative to him. Give or take 10 degrees. 10 degrees over a nine mile distance. Possibly three miles of error. Suit comm range was just under a mile. All these thought kept running thru his head. He also had hoped to see Watkins come trudging up to the crater while he waited but he knew Watkins had a bulky load that would slow him. The predawn light gave just enough glow to see the top of the mountain. Here we go. Setting off as fast as possible Sergei tried to pick out local land marks to try to run at. He also kept looking behind as long as he could see the crater to keep himself lined up. Land mark to land mark he kept that up for 3 hours. He estimated his travel at 5 miles. Hop shuffle step. Hop shuffle step. Repeat. Again. The rhythm lulled him. 2 more hours. Shit, he hadn't taken a sip device. He had no way to get water into himself. Plus he had to pee. He knew he was fatigued and that tired people made poor decisions. "Rosario! Lui! He shouted into the empty Martian landscape. Shit. He thought: six miles traveled maybe more. Another hour of travel and he was getting more desperate. He was pointing right at the mountain but he could be just outside of suit range. He kept shouting for Zhou and Rose without hearing anything. Another Hour. Eight miles he thought. He paused gulping great breaths and calling for the two crewmates. Nothing. Crushing despair. Batteries. Two people dead for batteries. Not yet! He started up again. Hop shuffle step. He almost missed it in his haze. He saw a flash of white grey where there should only be red brown. 300 meters to his right. Veering off, he quickly came up to the anomaly. A sample case. Tracks all around. But stamped into the Martian soil was an arrow pointing almost due south. A giant whoop escaped him. He followed the arrow calling out for Lui and Rose. 10 min later he heard a voice on his suit comm answering his calls. "Not so loud we are trying to sleep." Lui. What a fantastic sound!

"Hold on, I'm coming."

"Take your time, Rose said. I think we have 30 min of air left."

10 min later he found the two back at the rover. Without preamble he passed over the air bottles and checked them over while they gratefully breathed in stale compressed air. A 12 hour supply of stale compressed air.

"That was damn smart putting out the debris field for me to find."

"Your last comm faded but Lui and I heard you," Rosario said. "I knew you would come," she kept saying. Hugging him thru the suit. "The debris field was Lui's idea. He figured you would have to be dead reckoning to find us and that the best thing to do was make ourselves bigger."

Lui said, I" put the debris field at a mile and a half or so around a 270 degree arc."

"The arrows were a nice touch," Sergei said.

"We had faith Lui grinned.

"Whats the plan? Rosario asked.

"We should follow my tracks back a little ways. Tyler Watkins is following them with batteries for the rover. I don't want him to give up and turn back."

"Lead on Mcduff!" Rosario said.

They found Watkins a little over two hours later. Rosario and Lui profuse in their thanks to him. The batteries installed, the rover perked right up. The roar and crying from Houston and Zhenge brought smiles. Let's get home.

Launch day 927 22 May 2023 1802 Kennedy space center

Bob Royce was in the VTC with the President. "We overreached," he admitted. "The 330 day mission was too much. We should have had them start for home a month ago. As it is it will take them 20 days or so to seal the site and prep the ship for liftoff. They have given everything to this mission. I want them home before we lose someone. I'm particularly worried about Tyler Watkins. He stopped making entries into his video diary a few weeks ago. My conversations and messages to Sergei indicate he is sullen and withdrawn. Madam President the crew has vindicated every ounce of faith we have put in them ten times over. Hell it will take 5 years to pour over the data they bring back. I don't think we can expect a eureka moment on the question of life. I'm recommending to the committee we bring them home early with liftoff on day 955. That puts them on a 127 day return trip. Figure 3 days recuperation on the ISS, home on day 1085. That gives us a date of Oct 28 2023. 3 months early." Royce concluded.

"Good. That takes them out of the election cycle politics," Clinton said. "Can we do anything to Watkins to make him play nice on the trip home?"

Royce hesitated a moment. "We could have his brother send up a little message. Something like we are worried about you and we want to see you soon."

Clinton grunted. "We can't kill him or his brother. Too high profile for that. We can't even prosecute him for what he did."

Royce was not pleased. "They killed Brad Elkington."

"I know, I know," the President considered. "Trust me. There are ways of getting to him once he is back. Hey we got Al Capone on tax evasion. I wonder if Tyler has been scrupulous in his taxes."

"Didn't Obama get into trouble using the IRS as a cudgel?" Royce asked.

"Nixon was the real asshole," she said. "Have you ever listened to the tapes? Chilling to hear the President talking so cavalierly about ruining people's lives." She held up a hand. "Don't give me that look Mr. Boy scout. Watkins is a murderer. Okay, Bob talk to the committee. And have Watkins brother make that message. Lets get them home."

"Yes ma'am."

Launch day 932 27 May 2023 1108 Zhenge He base

Sergei re read the coded message from Royce. Watch Watkins. Duh. The message he had received from his brother a few days ago had been a surprise to them. Tyler wasn't getting many family messages. Plenty of hero stuff from the press though. He had given a somewhat rambling interview with CNN the other day. Sergei had to step in and make some sense of what he was saying. After the near miss everyone calmed down and was waiting on the end of the mission. The collection and experiments had continued but everyone knew NASA would pull the plug early. Meanwhile they kept working doggedly. Digger and Hoffman had taken advantage and expanded the garage. Movin on up! A two car garage. And shelves for storage! They had a fine old time ripping apart curiosity. Stripping it down to the frame and combining bobcat parts they had made a true beast. More rugged, the curiosity had better speed and range than the bobcat. Once they put an interface unit and some antennas the thing could hold an amazing amount of gear. Georg had gone an orgy of sample collecting. After the message from Royce, Sergei found him working and asked him how many lbs of rocks he thought he had.

Georg replied, "I don't know 125?"

"You have 402. Four Hundred? In mars weight?"

"Yes." "I have 2 tons of rocks on board?" "Yes, you do."

"Uhhm. Maybe I can sift thru to only take the necessary rocks."

"Your limit is 435, earth weight. Its really a volume problem too." Sergei confided in him. "Choose wisely Dr." "A little bird told me we might not be long for this planet."

"Really?"

"Yes. I got a message from Royce. They are talking about bringing us home in 22 days or so. I expect the announcement tomorrow."

"Okay, Sergei will do." Sergei went around to the crew and

told them the impending news. He expected most to be ready

Watkins and Digger however were another matter. "We have one

mission goal left," Watkins said. "Mon Olympus."

"Come on Tyler. That's a fools errand. You know that's just a

plant the flag on the tallest thing around mission. No real science,

Sergei tried to reason with him."

"They wouldn't have assigned it if they didn't see value," Watkins

doggedly said.

Digger agreed. "Besides that's the mission I'm supposed to lead,

Watkins' whine cycled higher.

"You've led countless collecting missions here, Sergei told him.

"You've done fine work. Saved fellow crew mates. Lets not go

off half cocked on this because its there mission. Please."

Tyler slowly relented. Even Digger admitted that the mountain

was too tough to get to anyway. Sergei left them feeling uneasy.

Wandering to the Einstein module he looked for Janice and Li. As

he found them, the pair blinked at him from the science stations.

They listened silently to his info. Leaving? Okay, whatever, let me

get back to my work. Okay geeks carry on. Sergei hoped they

noticed when the ship blasted off. Lui and Rosario were in the

galley area when he found them. Holding hands. Just sitting

touching hands. Oops. He loudly coughed. "Are you decent? They both smiled. Lui and Rosario? Okaay.

Sergei started in with every argument he had ever heard against him and Janice. "Don't you two know astronauts are the worst people to fall for? How could you possibly carry on a relationship with someone you work with every day." "Well I'm not going to stand for any of that "I'm mad at her so I'm not working with her" stuff I can tell you that." Sergei lectured.

Lui and Rosario just smiled and nodded along. "Well you can also bet I'm not making any special watchbill considerations in 22 days when we blast off this rock." That at least got thru. "Okay now that you've come up from playing kissy face, we have some work to do." Royce expected whining when he officially broke the news the next day. Calm acceptance from the crew. Damn you Sergei he thought. Always stealing my thunder. "So anyway prep site for sealing and ship for blast off. Launch day 955." Godspeed."
They were going home.

CHAPTER 31

Launch day 940 04 Jun 2023 0922 Zhenge He site

"Look over that list carefully. I want to leave as much stuff as possible but I would hate to say Uh oh, I left it at base." Sergei had them all packing and moving.

Moving sucked. They could not call any friends over and promise pizza and beer to help either. Experiments? Stay or go? Janice and Li discussed the fact that they may need the actual experiment more than the data results. Some got packed up carefully and some got shoved onto the tables that would be staying. Sergei held a ceremony burying lots of trash near the site. He hoped that some future explores gave him a pass on leaving the planet a little dirty. He wondered out loud how long their tracks would be around. Rosario had a little squeeze bottle with her she placed a foot in the sandy soil leaving a perfect print. She bent down and squeezed water out of the bottle over the print. The ground instantly absorbed the water and freezing the soil preserving the print. She held up the bottle which was now frozen. "There are seven more on the table inside with the water heated. You have about two min to make the print and put the water on it." The other seven followed suit. The foot prints were next to the art sculpture Rosario had setup up as part of the NASA contest. Along with Ray Bradbury's ashes. The CD and the silver plate were also mounted along the small mound of trash that had been built up. The dump and a monument next to it. Perfect. Janice thought. She looked around the landing site. The Martian landscape was alien and subtly hostile. Maybe it was because on earth the atmosphere interfered with the visual view. The air tended to blur things to a soft smudge. Not so on mars. The lack of atmosphere meant that everything was in stark visual clarity. All the sharp edges of the rocks, all the contours of the land. There was nothing SMOOTH in site. No wind or rain to knock off the rough edges. Mars kept you on edge. She wouldn't miss that part. She felt satisfied by the work she had done. They had succeeded in establishing the concept of space built craft and that a landing site could be constructed. The search for life continued but they were making discoveries every day. She had years of lectures and study ahead of her. She wasn't sure how she felt about that. The focus required to get thru all that was pretty large. Her time as an astronaut had made Janice into a different person. She was way more aware of the world and her part in it. She regretted that Charles and Danny had not seen her accomplish this great feat or had benefitted from the changes. She felt Sergei move up next to her. "Daydreaming?" he asked.

"Just taking a good long look. People are going to ask what it looked like."

"They have months of video footage and still pictures."

"Yeah but people always want another persons description of a place." Sergei grunted agreement.

"Are you sorry we got cut short,?" Janice asked.

"Sorry? I'm relieved as hell. We got everyone here safely and we made some fantastic advances in space travel. Think about it. You and I are casually having a conversation in a space suit that doesn't weigh 224 pounds. We got into the suit in 15 min and we can stay out here for 12 hours with as much freedom of movement as someone wearing heavy work gloves. Do you think Story Musgrave would have liked that? We are talking on a communications network that Neil Armstrong would have killed for. You have more computing power in that tablet hooked onto your chest than NASA had for the entire Apollo program. Hell, you have thousands of times more computing power. We have travelled further and longer than any other astronauts. And not just by a little. We went millions of times further than anyone else has ever gone. Our rover traveled further in two days than all other remote rover vehicles on any planet or moon put together." Sergei paused looking around. "One of those many thousands of samples that you, Li and Hoffman have been collecting will contain the remains of a living organism, I'm sure of it. So I'm not really upset that we got cut a few months short. Now we just have to get back without killing each other and we are home free."

"Killing each other?" Janice asked.

"Yeah some members of the crew are a little miffed at me."

"Tyler?" "Yeah. Digger as well but not as much."

"Screw them."

"Not that easy, sweetness. We need them. We aren't home yet. As soon as we dock on the ISS I may bust Watkins one in the mouth but for now, we all play nice."

"You really don't like him huh?"

"You have no idea, Sergei said. Lets get back at it. We should be ready for seal up in the next two or three days."

Launch day 942 06 Jun 2023 1459 Zhenge He base.

Rosario was setting the last of the protective covers over the comms booster relay unit. It was staying put of course, but NASA wanted to make sure it was still operational for Mars 2. They were openly planning a longer mission now. As she worked to install the cover she saw Watkins Digger and Hoffman moving to the garage area. They were each burdened with gear. Everyone was totting that barge lifting that bale.

Sweet Lui was standing command watch. She smiled. That man had depth. She was so blind. It had taken a near death experience for her to see the qualities the man possessed. Slow asphyxiation was a horrible way to die. Rosario was scared enough to start to panic in the rover.

Lui had calmly placed both hands on her shoulders and said "Look at me. We are not going to die, but we are in danger. We have a chance but we need to stack the odds in our favor. We cannot panic." She gulped and nodded.

"We are dead if we don't use our heads, Lui continued. Now you know CMDR Ivanovitch. Put yourself in his head. What is he thinking right now?"

Rosario got a grip on her fear. Lui's calm eyes had done that.

Think like Sergei, think like Sergei. She was ashamed to admit even to herself the first thought was: Hey baby I'm Sergei Ivanovitch lets make love! No. Sergei was a brash asshole but he was a deadly poker player. And brave. He knew odds and angles. He would gut it out and keep coming. Stack the odds was what Lui said.

"Sergei said he was coming out to us. That means on foot and carrying oxygen," she mused out loud.

"Yes said Lui.

"How is he going to find us? She asked perplexed. If I know him he was out the door ASAP." "But he would have a plan right?" "Yes he would." Rose told him.

"There are no direct tracks from the ship to us for him to follow right? What about tracks to a known place and then to us?" Lui reasoned. Yes.

They pulled up a map on the data pad. "Where are we?" she asked.

"Right here Lui pointed. "What's near us?"

"Nothing is that close. That crater is over to the west. The ship is North West. Mons Elysium is over to the east. Sergei could only dead reckon, right?" Lui asked.

"Yes. Hey, Look at this." Rosario traced the straight line from the crater to the mountain peak. We are right on this line."

Lui lit up. "Rose, he said quietly, that is it." Sergei will walk that line. But there are problems for him. He can wander. The suit compass is not that accurate. Once he loses site of the crater he will have to go land mark to land mark." "He could miss us by three miles, maybe four."

"You are saying it's impossible, Rose said her hopes sinking.

"No just difficult."

"Sergei can do difficult" Rosario said to him.

"We need to help him as much as possible."

"How?" she asked.

"We need to be bigger."

"Taller maybe?"

"No. Bigger."

Lui laid out the plan to spread out sample cases or anything they could at a mile and a half distance. Lui had taken some pieces of equipment and other items: nets and tarp and tools and started walking out. Rose followed for about ¾ of a mile until she could just see the rover. Lui had then continued on until he either lost suit contact at another ¾ mile or lost site of Rosario. He placed

down the gear and stamped in the arrow pointing back at the rover.

They he then started an arc walking back to Rosario and back out

after transcribing a few degrees. He kept dropping things and

stamping arrows. When he ran out of items, he took to just

stamping arrows. It took almost three hours to set out the items.

Returning to the rover they had settled down.

"How long? Rosario whispered.

"Six hours give or take."

"How much air do we have?"

"Seven hours. Again give or take, Lui answered

"Look at the map. Something you said abut tracks kept running

around my brain. Sergei and Hoffman and Li went to that canal

out to the east right? They came right back to the ship from there.

Those tracks are what 5 miles to the north? We could run straight

north and intersect the tracks and then follow them back to the

ship, right?" she said hopefully. "Triangles. Lui said dejectedly.

"You are perfectly correct in your thoughts but we would have to

walk two sides of the triangle between us and those tracks and the

ship. In seven hours we might be able to go 12 miles." Its 5 miles

to the tracks but another eight or nine to the ship. We can't

make it. We couldn't have made it if we started on that the second
the battery went out. If we had communications established Sergei
could have started out on that line of tracks and then we could have
started on our end at met but there was no way to coordinate that.
Odds." "Sergei is our best hope, he told her. "We have done all
we can to stack the odds in our favor now we wait."

"Okay. They were silent for a long time.

"Thanks, Lui."

"For what?"

"You calmed me down. Made me see there was one thing we could
do to help ourselves and now its just a waiting game. I can accept
that. It's the helplessness that gets me."

Another long silence. "Any regrets Lui? If Sergei doesn't get here
in time."

"Regrets he said slowly. "One. Cowardice." "I spent the last 18
months working with the smartest, most beautiful, and exciting
women in the world and its only now sitting here with her possibly
dying that I have the courage to tell her that. I regret being a
coward."

Rosario was stunned. "I had no idea. Why didn't you say
something! I always thought you were cute and mysterious."

"You are a wild woman. It can be a little intimidating watching you turn heads. I am a hopeless little moth next to your flame."

Stunned. Rose turned to him. "From now on no more inscrutable Chinese stuff okay? When we get back to the ship you have to tell me these things okay?"

"When, not if?"

"Yes when!"

Lui was silent for a minute. "Rose."

"Yes."

"Inscrutable Chinese is a little racist."

"Now we get to have our first fight!"

Working on the comms unit she smiled at the memory. Lui still needed to be whipped into shape but he was good raw material. As she straightened, Rose saw the curiosity rover AKA the beast move out of the garage and take off full speed to the west carrying Watkins Digger and Hoffman. Click.

"Lui! She screamed into the suit! Where are those three going in the rover?"

Lui asked what she meant. The rover feed was not showing up.

"Watkins, James and Georg just took off in the rover," she told him.

"I have a visual said Lui, I don't know."

"Call Sergei! Call the rover! They are doing something stupid."
Returning to the ship she found Sergei, Janice, Li and Lui all
clustered around the command display.

"What's missing Sergei was asking. "They have batteries and
plenty of air. Only a few sample cases." Li said. Shit. They are
trying for Mons Olympus. Oh shit. An hour of discussion led to
this: Unity and Zhenge He base had developed voice and video
issues down to Houston. Data was spotty. Rosario was working on
it. She threw the switches cutting off Houston. Sergei and Janice
were taking the bobcat after the three idiots. "Why, Li asked? You
can't catch them and you can't force them back. They deserve
what they get for disobeying orders."

Sergei just shook his head. "They are my responsibility. Even the
screw ups are my fault. I need to be there to pick up the pieces.
The feces will hit the fan. Watkins attracts it like a magnet." I need
Janice to help me drive. Zhou, you have command. If we all die
take off as soon as feasible and tell them it was my decision. Li be
ready to take injured personnel. Sergei grabbed a suit repair kit and
a spare helmet as he left. They had two water bottle feeds and

a larger catheter bladder. Air bottles, batteries and some med supplies rounded out their load. Driving out Sergei followed their tracks. He had comms and data back to the ship. Sergei gave up following the tracks as it became apparent that Tyler was drifting North in his movements. The men in the beast could not see the top of Olympus. Not yet. But very soon they would see it. It may take them two or three hours to get to a point where they could see it. Once they did it was simple, just point straight at the biggest thing in the solar system and press the pedal down. The beast could haul the three of them at approx. 11 miles an hour. Sergei was limited to about 8.5. Sergei had a small hope that the three would turn on the video data link to see if they could get a position out of Unity. Zhou was under strict orders not to give them vectors to the mountain. He also hoped that they might stop once the sun was down. The three would not have visual bearings on the mountain. They could keep up running on suit compass but their course would wander around a little. Sergei could overtake them if they stopped. He had no idea of what he would do if they overtook them out on the plain. About 6 hours in Sergei had a good visual on the mountain. He figured the beast was approx 2 miles north on a roughly parallel path. He also seriously considered turning back. He discussed it with Janice.

"Look at this plain! Sandy firm soil. Only a few craters to move around. In the beast they can traverse the 120 miles in 13 or 14 hours. Another 12 climbing up the slope. Plant the flags, take some pictures and return. Follow the tracks home." EPLS. Easy Peezy Lemon Squeezy.

"Then why are we out here Janice asked. "We turn around. They come back conquering heroes and we claim it was a ship decision to go cloaked in secrecy because we didn't want Houston overriding us!"

"Because deep in my gut I still feel that they are my responsibility and that Tyler will muck it up somehow. Sergei told her. "I think the easiness of this plain might make him even more reckless and the other two more trusting of his line. I have to try."

"Okay. But you better work on what you are going to say to Watkins to convince him to come back."

"I'm working on it believe me."

Sergei angled more to the north hoping to run into their tracks.

 Now that the mountain was visible they were just driving at it and he was no longer making up ground. No, he thought, not making up ground, I was just not losing ground at as fast a rate as I was. Now they were pulling ahead again faster. They saw the tracks as they came over a ridge. He came up in the rover and kept the tracks about 10 meters off his right side. Stopped to swap rover batteries at midnight. Janice had been asleep for four hours. The light showed the tracks swerving a little now. Hell he thought they could be at the mountain now! He didn't think so. He figured the beast was an hour or more away while they had six or seven hours to go, in the dark. Dawn was about five and half hours away. Watkins wouldn't try to climb the mountain in the dark would he? That was a bet Sergei wouldn't take even with the zone. He woke Janice with the admonition to wake him if she saw them or four hours passed whichever came first. He dropped off immediately. His dreams were of flight.

Launch day 943 07 Jun 2023 0553 Mon Olympus

A jolt of the rover snapped him awake. Sergei took in the scene in a glance. Sun up, 0554. Heading north east. Terrain much rougher here. She let me sleep. The beast was about a mile ahead and above and stopped. He could make out one figure. Mons

Olympus loomed over them. It had filled the sky at sunset. The reality of a 40,000 foot volcanic cone hit him like a ton of bricks. Sergei had climbed Kilimanjaro. 5895 meters high. 19,000 plus feet. It had taken him five days for the trek. Arduous but no real mountaineering. This mountain was a monster. It menaced the plain. Two Kilimanjaro's would still be shy by a half mile. Janice was staring at it grimly. Sergei looked at her. "Morning dear!" She grunted. "I hate that you are a morning person. No one should snap awake and see that and be chipper." Sergei got serious. "Fill me in."

"I debated waking you but I figured you needed the sleep. I think we really started climbing last night. I just couldn't tell it in the dark." Janice gestured to the shelf ahead. "Either they have good maps or they got blind lucky. We hit the edge of the mountain last night and got onto a lava field plain that we could move up. There is actually some soil. We hit the real edge of the mountain about 40 min ago. They turned north east and followed the edge until they could broach up on that lava field ahead. I can see the rover and one person but I can't tell who. We are not quite in suit range but soon." She fell silent.

"Okay Tonto great job! Bring us near the rover but not up on that lava field. Another two min and they heard thru the suit comm: "Hoffman here. Who is in the Bobcat over!"

"Georg its Sergei and Janice can you read me."

"Sergei, Hoffman babbled. Thank god." "They made me Sergei I swear. I tried to back out but they had me captive I could not have gotten back. I just wanted some samples." Hoffman rushed all that in out in a burst.

"Georg. Calm down, Sergei said quietly. "Where are Tyler and Digger?"

"They left about two hours ago. I can see them right at the base of the mountain face right there!" "They wouldn't come back and are out of suit range."

"Is the rover stuck, Janice asked as she pulled to a halt at the edge of the lava field. The beast was up on the field where they had piled sand up the three or four meters to make a ramp similar to the natural ramp at Lincoln gap.

"Yes it is stuck. That idiot Watkins thought he could drive all the way to the mountain face. We made it about 30 feet as you can see. I can't get it by myself but now that you are here we can get the rover out and go home. "What about Digger and Tyler," Sergei asked seriously. "Fuck them! Hoffman shouted. I never should have listened to Tyler." He said that you were keeping him from an assigned mission. That the incident with Rose and Lui had made you scared to try anything even remotely risky. Digger was less enthusiastic but still he agreed. I just wanted samples," Georg repeated.

"But you didn't tell me what they were planning did you?" Sergei asked.

"It seemed so easy at first. We cruised here are even though the rover got stuck we made it in good time. Then they left..." he trailed off.

"You mean to tell me that your mission commander left you here with the only available means of return disabled and no way to fix it?

"They didn't say anything about the rover they just wanted to get to the mountain," Georg whispered. Tyler kept saying it was his mission and he had to complete it. Then they left me here."

"What would have happened if we hadn't found you and they don't come back," Sergei asked brutally.

Georg quailed even more. "Sergei I'm sorry, I didn't think. I should have come to you with this I know that now. But you are here and we can get the rover clear and head home.." again

Georg pleaded.

Janice turned to Sergei. "What's the plan?"

"You and Georg get the rover clear. I'm going after them. I think Digger is as ready as Georg to come home. I just need him to see the errors of his ways." "How much air did they take?" Sergei asked.

"They just took one fresh bottle each. They thought no more than 3 hours there and then three back came the answer.

"Do not come after me Sergei warned Janice. Janice agreed after some "debate" on the subject. You owe me for this," she said.

"I believe that," Sergei said. He swapped out a fresh air bottle himself and debated what else to take. He had fashioned a rock axe out of a sample hammer and a round rod. The ever present duct tape binding them together. He took a small suit patch kit and a med pack. More air? Too bulky. He might have to climb. The stick could help him climb and serve as a makeshift weapon. He set off, picking his way thru the lava field. Some wind blown sand had worked its way in here setting up areas where the going was easier. Other wise he had to step from rock to rock using the stick as a tripod for balance. He kept slipping and flailing. He didn't want to fall on those rocks. The suit was very tough and could stand some punishment. God knows they had been diligent in the repairs and maintenance. Seeing if the suit held integrity after failing on lava rocks even in 1/10th gravity was a test he didn't want to take. As he closed on the mountain face he could see a figure up about 300 meters. He was moving up towards a flat protruding rock formation that looked like a balcony. Tyler Sergei thought. He is going to plant that stupid flag on the flat area sure as shit. Where was Digger? He should be in suit range. "James Sergei called. "Tyler!" A burst of static in the suit. Just on the edge of range. "CMDR Watkins come in, this is CMDR Ivanovitch." Another burst. "DR Andrews this is CMDR Ivanovitch come in."

"Too late Sergei," a voice crowed. Tyler. "I'm almost up there. Almost complete"

"CMDR Watkins I read you. Where is Dr. Andrews?

"He's not here," Tyler said strangely.

"What do you mean not here? Where else would he be? Sergei asked.

"He's gone," Watkins said it like he had just realized it. "Gone.

"Dead."

Sergei processed this. He skipped over the rocks a little faster.

"CMDR Watkins I am here on scene and I am taking over this mission." Sergei had reached the slope face and had started up. It wasn't a cliff face just a steeply sloped face with larger rocks jutting out. Sergei used the rock hammer stick to hold onto rocks and lever himself up. He found a rhythm and found he could make good progress this way. His announcement that he was assuming command of the mission had Tyler howling. "I am in command you asshole! NASA should have never put you in charge in the first place!"

"Never the less Dr Hoffman please put into the record that CMDR Sergei Ivanovitch led the first expedition to the slopes of Mon Olympus. We place this flag for the benefit of mankind to implore them to keep reaching new heights."

"Nooo!" The guttural voice was animalistic. "That's what I get to say! You prick! You were never better than me! It was Royce's fault. And that black bitch!" The hate Watkins held in poured forth into Sergei's ears. "I should have taken care of you too!" Watkins grunted.

"Me instead of Brad Elkington?" Sergei said quietly. Watkins howled at this. He was gaining on Watkins. Tyler had three different flags in his hand and a net bag over his shoulder. He

was 150 meters above Sergei and 50 below the flat area. The sound
of Brad Ellington's name whipped Watkins around to face Sergei.
He squawked a little to see how fast Sergei was over taking him.
"Elkington was another who didn't deserve to be ahead of me. He
was cheating to get better team scores while I was left to drag
along the rest of the rejects." Sergei's stomach churned. Tyler was
way beyond help. "CMDR Watkins Where is Dr Andrews?" Sergei
put all of his years of command in that voice.

"Andrews is dead against that large boulder to your left. He died
when he could not keep his air in his suit." Tyler laughed a little at
the image in his head.

Sergei turned to spot the body against the ground. Moving over he
found Digger dead of decompression. He was not a pretty sight.
Sergei felt a stab of pain guilt remorse and rage. By god Watkins
this is the last death at your hands he swore to himself. He resumed
his climb still taunting Watkins.

"Thirty three percent of your command already dead. Not too
good Tyler. That has to go in the official record." Taking away
Watkins perceived glory was the only weapon he had. "CMDR
Watkins I order you not to proceed to Andrews Rock. I will plant
the flag to claim this victory."

"No No NO NO NO came the chant. Sergei tried to put on a burst of speed and it almost killed him. The rock hammer lost its grip on the rock and he nearly rolled down the mountain. That would be fatal he was sure. "Almost almost almost almost came thru Sergei's head set. "CMDR Watkins you will stand by for court martial for the deaths of CMDR Brad Elkington and Dr James Andrews." Tyler was at the junction of the face and the protruding rock. Screaming at him incoherently. The bench area was not a seamless transition. To get to the flatter area of the balcony the climber had to traverse around a bulging section of rock on the left. Sergei could not see if the right side was easier. Watkins was struggling to move around the rock holding the flags and the net bag on his shoulder. Sergei was only 10 meters behind and preparing to grab Watkins ankle when he moved out literally hugging the rock. It was an impossible spider man feat in normal gravity. In the $1/10^{th}$ gee of mars it was possible just hard on the arms. Sergei scrambled up to just below the bulge when Tyler flung himself flat on the slightly tilting rock face in triumph. Sergei used the hammer stick to move out onto the transition rock. He heard Watkins mumbling in triumph as he went thru his prepared speech. Sergei tried one last gambit. He swung the rock stick up to catch the rock higher above the flat face. He would then pull himself up and away and around the stupid rock and onto the balcony. Once there he would kick the living shit out of Tyler Watkins. End of story. He played the card as it came out of the deck. He swung out and said: "Hey Tyler don't use any of my lines in your little speech, I copyrighted everything!" His feet hit the ground and he looked over at the flag and had one split second to think; That looks awesome with the view and the flag! Wow."

Then Tyler Watkins moved out from the rock face and shoved him as hard as he could with both hands. Oh shit! Sergei knew he was dead. He flew back out into open air. Well flew in the relative sense. Tyler had imparted a lot of back wards momentum to him and he had 2 to three meters of open air below him. A thought flashed in his mind: Sergei Ivanovitch you are the best low gee gymnast in the world. The best out of eight he thought in reality. Fuck me. Twisting, he doubled up and spun as quickly as he could. He kept his knees flexed and slightly apart as he braced for an impact that he knew was coming. It still shocked him and threw him off as he tried to absorb all of the imparted momentum. He spun off the face of the mountain down ward and tumbling. Watkins swore in rage and glee. "See ya fucker!" Sergei continued the slow motion come apart by bouncing off the mountain on his hands. He felt the arm of his suit brush by the rock face as he went. Uh oh. He was wind milling his arms in a futile attempt to gain control of his fall. He did manage to stop most his rotation but that just put him 30 feet in the air failing slowly to the ground. So he only had rotational speed and time for four cartwheels before striking the ground again. This time both feet hit closer to the same time and he was able to kill almost all of the momentum. He skidded. Hopping five times down the slope to regain control. He stopped at the base of the face about 375 meters from where he started. He turned back to face the balcony. As he swung he saw three things thru the sudden haze in his vision. The figure of Tyler Watkins standing on the balcony. Sergei couldn't see his face but he imagined Watkins was slack jawed at his miraculous not death. The second thing he saw was the small jet of air coming from his suit arm in a thin white stream. And he saw an angel walking towards him. Wha? Blackness.

CHAPTER 32

Launch day 950 14 Jun 2023 1002 Zhenge He base

Houston was on them about the launch preps. "CMDR Zhou you are in command of this mission since the incident on Mons Olympus." Royce was lecturing again. "I know you are short handed with the deaths but you must complete the launch preps by 955. That means a test firing tomorrow. You may need time to replace an engine if necessary. Plus you have to ensure fuel transfers and get the Nav system calibrated."

Lui breathed steadily and squeezed Rosario's hand. Li looked on from the other chair. He assured Royce they were working as diligently as possible but they were heavy hearted. Royce nodded. "They were good men," he said. I know you will do your duty. Houston out. "How in the world did Sergei deal with that man all those months? It's like dealing with your angry mother in law and a substitute teacher all in one."

Rosario giggled. "Ask him," she said pointing. Sergei lurched up the stairs followed by Janice, to the command deck and into an accel couch.

"Royce? he's easy, just ignore him."

"You look good Sergei are you sure you don't want to take over?"
Lui asked.

"I still have head aches and dizziness. Plus look at my arm! She
lopped off a huge chunk of flesh!" He raised the bandaged
frostbitten arm. Hoffman had heard the commotion and tentatively
stuck his head in. "If I'm intruding I'll go back down."

"No no, said Sergei, we might as well have this out. Come up."
Georg sat down. "Okay who wants to know what happened?"
Sergei asked.

Li spoke up first. "I want to know why you went with them Dr
Hoffman."

Georg immediately looked guilty. "Bad judgment I guess. I wanted
more samples. I thought Watkins was as competent as Sergei in
leading an expedition. I was gullible in the extreme. I'm very
sorry."

Sergei held up a hand. "Dr. I'm okay with you. Sometimes we trust
people we shouldn't. You certainly saw reason when we were on
the mountain and that counts for something. You saved my ass
when I was hurt, thanks." Georg recovered a little. Rosario started
in next. "Sergei what happened? I have had bits and pieces but

not the whole thing." Sergei related events up until the angel.

"That's when I passed out." Janice spoke up. "I guess that makes me the angel. Hoffman and I started after Sergei about 20 min after he set out. He never looked back once!" Sergei muttered something about another one who never follows my orders. "We heard the whole exchange with Watkins on the mountain. He was certifiable at the end." What made you think of taunting him?"

"Only thing I could think of to get him to slow down and fight me."

"Which he did by promptly beating your ass," Janice teased! Georg spoke up. "I will NEVER forget the sight of you going down that mountain. It was like the enrichment games we played!"

"It took forever for you to fall down." Janice said, "and you did fall down. Practically at my feet. You looked at me and passed out from air loss." I dug into the repair kit and got a patch on and swapped out bottles we brought." Georg then took you out to the rover."

"What did you do Janice?" Li asked.

"I went after Watkins, she said grimly. "He was raving about being the leader and having conquered the mountain." She shivered remembering the scene. Watkins looking down on her, shouting he was on top of the mountain. She shouted back: "Shut the fuck up! Sergei is alive and I'm coming up there to rip off your head you psycho asshole."

"Sergei's alive?"

Janice picked up on that. "Yep still alive and in charge. Not like you." And you are certainly not on top of that mountain. You have miles to go."

Confused, sounding like a kid. Miles to go?"

"Miles to the top. Can't you see it?"

Watkins had turned and whimpered at the site of the mountain.

"That's the top. Janice sneered at him. "You better get going. That's an ORDER." One whimper was all and Watkins started climbing up. He was crying and apologizing until out of suit range. Janice figured his body at the 2000 meter level.

"I killed him, she said into the stillness.

"He killed himself Sergei said flatly.

"And Digger?" asked Lui?

"I'm sorry about Digger, Sergei said. I found him dead of decompression. I think he just fell in the lava field and Tyler never helped him," Sergei related. "He just wanted to explore that's all. I think I could have talked him back home but it was too late."

571

Hoffman took over, "We couldn't get both of them back to the rovers. Janice had Sergei in the beast and I took the bobcat." Hoffman finished. Rosario addressed the elephant in the room: What do we say to Houston and the reporters.

Sergei said flatly, "The same lie we told Houston. We decided to mount a mission to Mons Olympus and personnel died and were injured. The flag was planted on the mountain by CMDR Tyler Watkins who deserves great honor for that act. Unfortunately he ran out of oxygen and we were unable to retrieve the body. Dr James Andrews was accompanying CMDR Watkins and he perished from a tear in his suit on the lava field. The same kind of tear that injured CMDR Ivanovitch." "We were unable to retrieve Dr Andrews body as well. Mons Olympus will serve as the headstone for these two great Earth heroes."

Over the next few days the Earth bought their story but not Royce. Zhou was in charge while Sergei recovered from his injuries. Zhou polled everyone: assignments for the launch prep. Groans. Back to work all. Plenty to do.

The group rallied for a final effort to put the landing site in order and get the ship ready for the return flight. As they sealed up the site Sergei was the last person thru the hatch. Unity

had more in the way of open space from equipment removed but

much more in the way of storage cases strapped into any corner

they could go. Home.

Launch day 955 19 Jun 2023 1809 Unity

The liftoff from Mars was smooth as silk compared to the violence

of an Earth launch. The six mars astronauts sat four and two.

Sergei and Zhou next to Rosario and Li. Janice and Georg

occupied the back two chairs. It was a happy exhausted exhilarated

sad crew that left mars after 231 days of exploration. Two of their

number did not make the return journey. They were still coming to

grips with that. Royce wanted to schedule an in flight debrief. He

wanted their impressions of the mission and the base and the ship.

What worked what bugged you what helped you? Should we go

back? He had them all scheduled in the next month. Please write

down the impressions now. They had much publicity to do. Unity

only made six mars orbits. The ship soon bent over the top of mars into the gravity well and picked up a few hundred mph as a parting gift. The long slide home began. Sergei had them in 8 hour watches 2 2 and 2. He and Janice. Li and Hoffman. Rosario and Lui. They swapped the bunk arrangements by tacit agreement. Janice thought Li and Georg started sleeping together out of boredom more than anything else. The flight profile called for 127 days to return. The good or bad thing about the return journey was the increase in gravity. They were going to get .45 gee on the way back. Even a two week period of half a gee. They spent days trying to get ready. The tick up from .1 to .25 was noticeably tough on the muscles. Man that cup is heavy. They had to learn to move around the ship again. Maybe it was the stress of the engines but the ship had a rash of equipment failures. The common theme was power supplies. Three bad power supplies. Radar 3D printer and the nav unit. Sergei and the crew discussed it. The units were common. Same power supply. Same type and model number. Houston also did not believe in consequences. Turned out to be a bad manufacturing run. One more installed in the air scrubber unit that was preemptively replaced and two more yanked out of stock. Only six left. There were sixteen of those power supplies on the ship. Another worry for Sergei. The level jump to .3 gee started producing sprains and strains. Sex started to require some effort.

The first weeks passed with no real problems. Janice got them thru

the next series of medical tests. Too early to see if bone loss was

repairing itself. More ostio shots. More uv lamp time. All six

seemed to need less sleep. Four hours was about the max anyone

could get. It was not uncommon to see the four off watch crew

group at the science stations to work thru the mound of samples.

Even though Sergei was not a scientist by training he could mount

a slide with the best. They often teased each other. As they worked

thru the rock samples, Rosario would remind Georg that drive by

geology was going to be taught in class in his school in Germany.

Gone from Mars barely 20 days and it already seemed like another

lifetime ago.

Video Log Sergei Ivanovitch 20 Jul 1507

Hello Earth. This may be one of my final submissions for the

video logs. Not much left to say, I think. I intend to use this to

give you my impressions of the mission. I think it's a qualified

success. Anytime you have some deaths it can't be a total

success. I am still dreaming of that ledge with Watkins. And the vision of Digger laying on the Martian soil. I think I will carry that around for a while. Still, we did accomplish all mission goals. More than that I hope that we have re-fired people's imaginations as to what's possible. We have made some advances in technology since the Apollo program. Mars Mission just shows what man is capable of if differences are put aside and we really go for it. I hope this ship comes back in good shape and we send another crew out to stay even longer. I think you have to look at boosting fuel loads to make higher gravity available on the whole flight. Maybe you can have a new exercise machine that actually works. The shower/toilet/recycle system needs to be redone. I recommend a POD shot with whatever system you design. Maybe three if you need to hook them together. You can build three copies. Mars base, Unity and the ISS. You should look at new technology to line the inside of the Mars base. The sealant to seal the cracks is a good first step but now there needs to be some kind of large wall sized lining to keep the air/heat in and the cold/vacuum out. I never slept really comfortably in the base. Even the ship was a little cramped. Speaking of cramped the rovers worked fine. I also recommend someone way smarter than myself come up with ships activities. Watching movies and TV works for some people but not driven goal accomplishing types. Crew make up and morale. Bob you need to be more careful selecting the crews. Some of the training can be about conflict resolution and personal skills. I'm not saying these guys don't have to be astronauts but they need different skills to survive a long voyage. They still need to be able to break down electrical and mechanical components and put the modules back into service. Those kinds of basic skills will be better served than how to turn a wrench in space. I think we focused on that because no one knew if it could be done. Now that we know I think we need to dial back a bit on that and work on some of those fundamental systems like the power distribution system. And the plumbing systems. Sure as shit the pump down to the recycling plant is going to burn up and some bearings will need replacing. But it's the mental that needs to be worked on. There are just so many things we never got around to saying. Even now I wrestle with the fact that the only reason I ordered Tyler Watkins to follow me out to the rover with batteries to rescue Lui and Rose was that I thought we would need the rover to recover the bodies. I haven't spoken to them about that. I still wish we could have gotten Tyler and Digger home. That's my fault. I have to live with that. I didn't kill them but I did have to leave them behind. I'm not sure everyone feels that way. We don't speak about it. We should try. Sorry, that's about all I can think of. Thanks for trusting me with your ship Bob. Sergei out!

Launch day 989 24 Jul 2023 2207 Kennedy Space Center

The light from the office shown into the hall way. John Scanlon walked into Bob Royce's office to find him reading a thick report. What are those he asked tiredly? The summaries of the debriefs I did with the Unity crew. Anything interesting? Yes, the crew requests us to invent a local gravity machine that will instantly adjust the gravity to whatever they want. Oh and a toilet that actually works in low gee. Might get the first before the second Scanlon laughed. Royce went on, with more seriousness. They do have some good suggestions. Better and more cameras and telescopes integrated into the ship. More general purpose tools. Three small rock chisels was not nearly enough. We do need to get a decent septic situation up there. Some different training. As head of the committee that's going to be Tatiana's worry now Scanlon said soothingly. That announcement is not coming out for six weeks Royce said. Yeah lots of things staying under the surface. He pulled a file from his briefcase. Thanks. That made dealing with Mathew Puring easy. He has cancelled his press conference for Tuesday. Royce opened the file to look again at the photo. None of the Unity crew knew of the suit cam video back up system. NASA had felt like the possibility of the astronauts just turning off their cameras was a distinct possibility. They had rigged a backup that allowed NASA to turn the cameras on remotely. Royce had ordered it on almost as soon as the Unity crew reported the "outage". The video was automatically uploaded when Sergei and the rest returned to Unity. The photo he was holding was from Sergei's helmet cam. You could see the Mars Unity Mission flag on the edge of the rock area. The vista was stunning, with Mars laid out below the mountain. But in frame to the left was another figure. The camera had caught Watkins a pace from Sergei. His face was visible in the helmet as was his name tag on the front of his suit. Not the best photo of Watkins but he was recognizable. Also recognizable was the hate twisting his features and his arms pulled back to shove Sergei off the plateau. Royce hoped to god this photo never reached the light of day. The new deputy director for CIA clandestine operations and his assistant had delivered the file themselves. Bob wished Raven and Kat good luck with all sincerity. Putting the photo away and the file in his safe, Scanlon asked how the Unity crew was holding up. Very well all in all. We just have to get them back safely. Then we have to get them thru the media frenzy and I can finally get some sleep. Scanlon paused at the doorway. The committee is announcing Mars 2 in three days. There is even talk of Europa after that. Don't you want in on that? Royce looked stricken. Oh god no! Scanlon chuckled all the way down the hall. Royce thought about where mankind's exploration of space would head next. Now that mars was possible and the diamond dust had been found Royce was betting that soon a consortium would put together an exploration of the asteroid belt. That fabled pure gold asteroid was out there waiting. More importantly to the consortium, the pure REE asteroid was out there. REE. Rare Earth Element. More valuable than gold in the manufacture of modern electronics. I'll bet Sergei ends up designing all that equipment he thought ruefully.

CHAPTER 33

Launch day1001 14 Aug 2023 1325 Unity in space

Setting down the stylus she was using to mark off samples in the tablet system, Li Fong straightened up slowly. She checked the sample number and the collection data. She ran another test. Looking back under the microscope she smiled. 5 for 5. Excellent. She walked, really walked forward to the airtight door. Ducking thru she carefully swung the rest of her body thru the hatch. She had to be very careful. Li had banged the shit out of her knee a week ago. Gravity sucked. As she approached the galley table she saw Rosario and Lui with Sergei and Janice. Oh good. She continued forward and called up the ladder to Hoffman.

"Georg please come down for a second!" George came down and asked what was up. Li Fong from Chengdu China calmly told them that life had existed on Mars. The wide grins and questions from the others were what she expected. Janice rushed down to see the sample while Li answered questions. The sample was one the Rosario collected from the Viking lander site. Li shook her head. The lander missed it by about 40 feet.

"I think the water collected in that crater and it lasted long enough for the single celled organisms to flourish. The results still need to be peer reviewed but it should stand up to the rigor.

Sergei congratulated her on the discovery. Li shook her head. I'm just the person who looked at the slide. Rosario collected it. Sergei you mounted the slide after Janice sliced it up. No the credit goes to the whole Unity crew. All eight. Janice returned to say she completely agreed. How do we break it? As a crew.

The six of them gathered and called Houston. Janice asked for Royce, Scanlon and her favorite chemist in conference. Royce and Scanlon had a clue. They had a huge group of engineers and officials in the VTC. Zoe Smyth bounced up and down in mission control center in Houston. Janice took over.

"Roger. We see you Zoe good day! I need you to confirm a chemical signature for us."

"More alkaline,?" she asked.

"No something challenging. Kennedy you please confirm as well.

"Roger Unity go ahead."

Janice sent the data. 1 min 12 seconds later the data arrived at Kennedy and Houston. A gasp immediately in Florida. Janice watched Zoe. She looked and checked and checked.

"Organic?" Janice she asked.

"Yes Zoe that's what we got." "But..."

Janice thought what would Sergei say? "That's right kid! Life on Mars!" The applause and tears said it all. Li smiled. 5 mission goals 5 completed sat. She would deal with the government wrath when it came at her!

Seventeen straight days of media interviews would make anyone crazy. Unity refused to answer the big question: what does it all mean? It means that life can exist in areas where we used to think it was impossible. Is of God dead? God is tougher than that. Did life on Earth begin on Mars? Impossible to say. Is it safe to bring back living organisms to earth? Uhh yes because the stuff we are bringing back is fossils not actually living organisms. Ad nauseum. 63 days down 64 to go. Half a gee gravity was making them heavy. However the exercise regime was paying off. Muscle tone was up, thin gaunt alien looking features were way down. The earth was growing in the window.

Launch day 1031 13 Sep 2023 2312 Unity in space

Sergei and Janice had just started the mid watch. The topic quickly came around to what they were going to when they returned to earth. Janice said she was going to go back to the FDA. Sergei laughed at her. "Sweetheart you could run the FDA." "You could teach."

"Maybe. What about you?"

"Either motivational speaking or professional poker."

"Royce wants you to help Tatiana for Mars 2."

"Nah. Grace doesn't need me looking over her shoulder."

"You think Grace is going to be mission commander for #2, Janice asked.

"She better be. I left a note for her in the landing site."

"A note?"

"Yeah I found something I wanted her to have."

"What?"

"You'll find out when the rest of the world does. Why don't we just go on permanent vacation when we get home?" he said changing the subject. "The earth is going to want to talk to us. I say we just pick a random nice house, walk in and say we are the mars heroes feed us!"

"Right. Us." she said seriously.

"Man did the o2 level drop?"

"Ha ha. I'm serious. What happens to us?"

Sergei looked at her."I don't know. Janice, things are going to be crazy when we hit earth. Famous! Heroes! The greatest explores since Cook! Hell the greatest ever! Every newspaper, TV show and University is going to want us! They'll give us anything we ask for."

"What do you want Sergei?"

"I want you to be my wife, he said. It won't be any fun unless you are with me." He waited. Janice smiled. "Yes," she said.

"I'm going to want a small traditional wedding," he said.

"I thought the bride got to plan her big day."

"I'm a totally traditional guy. We Russians have amazing traditions."

"Okay. I guess we will make it up as we go along." She told him.

"Okay with me."

"Lets wait a year or so to have the ceremony Janice said. I want to let the hoopla die down. "Okay with me."

Lui wandered into the command deck. He found Sergei and Janice kissing at the console. He coughed to get their attention. "It's too late to win the pool for having sex on the command console. Rosario was insistent."

Launch day 1055 27 Oct 2023 1345 Unity in earth space. ISS

The thud of the grappling arm grabbing Unity went thru Georg Hoffman. He was relieved anxious scared excited all at once. It was over. The hard part anyway . Or maybe the easy part. He was ashamed of what had happened with Tyler but long talks with Sergei convinced him he didn't harbor any ill will. Janice might be another matter. The rest of the crew was inclined to give him a pass, so he was getting over those terrible hours. Now he had to get

thru the rest of his life. It took forever for the airlock to cycle.

Grace Adler was the first thru and met them in the equipment deck.

She threw Sergei a crisp salute and then a massive hug and kiss.

Welcome home!!! More people came thru the airlock door.

Camby. Larson. Edminton. Larionov. The ISS had three capsules

docked. Dragon, Orion and Orel. The crews were up to start

service on Unity. Sergei could see the PODS on the platform. Hugs

kisses smiles. Someone new to talk to! "Get your stuff. I'm taking

you home in Orion tomorrow!, Grace told them all.

"We've been packed for days, Zhou laughed. The chatter in the

Einstein module was a little deafening. Everyone wanted to talk to

everyone. Mike Camby grabbed Sergei and softly told him that he

was to take Watkins and Andrews personal effects personally.

"We made two markers and left them at the landing site, Sergei

reminded him. "One of Diggers hats is there and one of Watkins

Florida gators t shirts. The rest is packed and sitting on their

bunks."

"Thanks said Camby. How do you feel Sergei, he asked.

"Tired, scared proud, anxious a little of everything I guess Sergei

admitted. It was a fantastic mission. It was way harder than I ever imagined. It went as smoothly as we could have wanted and still two people died. You know what keeps running thru my head, Mike." "What's that?"

"What if I had just let them go on the mission when they had asked?"

Camby shook his head. "Can't be playing what if games, Sergei."

"You are the commander and you made the call. What would you say to Grace if she would have come to you with the same offer?"

"I would have told her no. You should see that mountain Mike. It's too big. It just keeps going up and up and up. I predict that we will lose way more than two astronauts on those slopes before it all said and done."

"Mallory", was all Mike Camby said to him. "Yeah, too true."

The mars astronauts had a hard time sleeping in the ISS that night. As tired and exhausted as they were home was shining on them from the window. The planned "reintroduction" period went right out. Get them on the ground!

Launch day 1056 28 Oct 2023 1507 South Atlantic Ocean

The Orion crew capsule bobbed in the ocean 100 miles north and east of the island of Exuma in the Bahamas. The helicopter crew was being extra careful putting in divers and securing the craft. Transferring the mars crew was pri I. As Janice slithered into the small raft she couldn't help but feel the weight dragging at her limbs and lungs. This isn't going to be fun. Kat Williams was in the helo. They were heading directly to Kennedy after a quick stop on the GHW Bush, CVN 88. A quick hand shake a quicker shower and a change of clothes and off again. Janice wasn't sure the helo blades had stopped turning. The flight to Kennedy was wonderful, just breathing in all that warm moist air. Kat was going over the schedule. Very light she said. "Meetings with the families and Bob and then a reception for the official welcome from The President, Vice president and the committee." Oh and the President of Russia. The Premiers of China, Germany and Argentina as well. The UN Secretary General was there. And the heads of state for the rest of the G20."

"Are you kidding me? We will pass out 20 min into that circus," screamed Sergei.

The rest voice similar thoughts.

"We have made arrangements. We have you in couches. You just have to sit there and smile pretty and people will circulate around you. If you feel bad we can wheel you right into the medical wing. Speaking of which the next three days are in the hospital. After that we just have to figure out some loose ends and we will be all finished with you."

Loose ends Rosario thought. That didn't sound like fun.

As the helo touched down at Kennedy Georg Hoffman could see a huge crowd waiting for them. A squadron of six wheel chairs waited to take them from the helo to the bus. Sergei was the first off and waved away the chair. Stepping out carefully, he waved to the crowd which roared. Bob Royce shook his hand and mouthed something and smiled at him as Sergei grinned. He waved again and moved off to the bus, shaking hands and receiving well wishes the whole way. Rosario was next out and she too waved away the chair. Georg was kind of sad at that as he was feeling some definite aches, but once the precedent is set, you had to go with the flow. The ever popular Rosario was blowing kisses to the crowd as they showered her with affection. She was a natural as well. Janice was little more subdued as she got off and greeted the crowd. Zhou followed and grinned madly as he went over to greet some of the training personnel and some of the other mars candidates that were lining the short route to the bus. Scores of people were capturing the moment on phones. Hoffman just had time as Li went out the door to take out his tablet and started the video. He held up the tablet to capture the wild scene as the normally staid, jaded NASA folks went all out welcoming Unity home. Stepping off the bus he shook hands with Royce who told him how proud he was of him and that the whole world was proud as well. Georg was overwhelmed. He hoped he mumbled something intelligent as he shook hands or just touched people who were straining just to get near him. Wow that is heady. He saw the bus ahead and saw the rest on board leaning out the windows waving madly to the crowd. As he boarded the bus he noticed Tatiana Medvedev on it already and she didn't look happy while Janice looked smug as hell. I wonder what happened there. Finding Li he sat on the next seat and asked if she was okay.

"Yes, she said just look at those people.' "Crazy.

 Whats China going to be like he wondered? He also wondered what he was going to do with Li. He thought that maybe their affair was over. Neither had any attachments to anyone here on earth but there was nothing holding them together. Loose ends he thought. Leaning out he barely noticed the look Royce was giving him.

Lui Zhou could barely lift his head. Four hours of meet and greet had left him exhausted. It was wonderful to see his family. His mother and father were beaming. The Premier and Chairman of the Party Wei ze bo, had been effuse in his praise. The integral part that Zhou and Li had played in the discovery of life on Mars was a triumph for the people of China. Only a slight tightening around the eyes when Zhou had said the whole world had triumphed. It was pretty obvious Li was going to catch hell for not announcing that she had discovered life but giving the credit to the whole crew. Her grandmmother was not in attendance tonight and she looked scared. Zhou noticed that Georg Hoffman was holding her hand and trying to comfort her. Lui tried to run as much interference as he could. The Unity mission showed exactly what could be accomplished if China were to join forces with the rest of the world and not try to go it alone all the time. The Premier had looked at him and nodded. Too much? Too little? Who knew. Zhou had only been out of the chair once. To stand to shake the hand of Rosario's father. Her father knew instinctively what that gesture had meant. As he gripped his hand Gabriel Gonsolvo had looked him in the eyes. Zhou met him stare for stare. Gabriel had nodded and smiled. Releasing his had he looked at his beautiful beaming daughter and said, "May you be happy together." Rosario had been in tears since. All of her pictures with the various heads of state looked funny with her eyes all blotchy. Sergei was deep in conversation with Vice President Julian Castro. The recent polls had him well ahead of the Tea Party Candidate or the Republican. Since the official split in 2015, the Republican party had been dwindling. Just 15 percent of registered voters now identified as a Republican. The Tea Party could boast a 25 percent slice of the electorate. But the real winner of the great schism as it was coming to be called was the Democratic party. They had 55 percent of the vote. A bare majority but a majority. This election promised to be a new kind of election. None of the candidates were going to spend much time in the state of Iowa. That small state didn't matter anymore. The super Tuesday states now held the most sway in who would win the nomination. Large states like Texas and California now started seeing actual rallies instead of just fundraisers. Clinton had capitalized in 2016 and 2020. Castro was hoping to parley the new unified direction of the world by attaching himself to the astronauts. In fairness the Republican Party candidate was here as well as the Tea Party rep. Janice took great delight in reminding the Tea Party guy Ted Cruz that he had voted to cut off NASA funding five times. The President came over with her grandchildren as Cruz left . Sergei kept producing a rock out of the pocket of his flight suit. Every time a child or an adult for that matter saw the rock come out of his pocket it was like a magnet for their gaze. "Would you like to hold a little piece of Mars? he would say. Young and old alike became Mars converts holding that rock. Sergei had made up 5 different stories about where the rock came from. Every one a little more dangerous. Clintons grandkids ate it up with a spoon. She smiled down at them as they peppered Sergei with questions.

Janice admonished him. "People will not always be mollified with rocks she said. I can't believe you can manipulate people with a little rock, she said.

Sergei replied, "yeah you know me always bending down and finding rocks and stuff. For instance look at this other rock I found up on Mars". Sergei reached into another small pocket and produced a crystal about the size of a marble. He held it up to her. Janice looked at it stunned.

"Yeah some people are just mesmerized by the site of a rock from Mars. He twirled it in his fingers making the crystal catch the light.

Janice stared rapt. "Is that what I think it is?" 'Yep." "Where... she started Why..."

"I found it in the M1203 crater. I found it the night I went after Rose and Zhou. I waited in that spot an hour. I just looked down and there they were. I got this one because it looked real sparkly. The much bigger cousin to this rock is now a paper weight holding down that note for Grace Adler. The map is pretty clear about where to find the diamond pipe."

Sergei pocketed the rock with a flourish as more people approached.

"You left Grace Adler a treasure map to a diamond mine on mars?"

"Did I say treasure map? I did not. It's a map. And there is treasure. And she does have to figure out one clue."

Janice squawked. "You are going to make her figure out clues!!"

"Nah I'm teasing about that. I figured we found so much stuff she should get credit for some things as well."

Epilog 8 Nov 2024 The White House

It turns out the tradition of holding a wedding at a friend's house in Russia means that you can ask your friend the President Elect to have the wedding at his new house. So a small intimate affair was being held for 450 guests at the White House for the wedding of Sergei Ivanovitch and Janice Lincoln. The cooler weather was no problem as it was clear. The guests were still buzzing at the new discoveries from mars: diamond pipes and living bacteria on the ice at the pole. Wow. Mars 2 was just 35 days into its 400 day mission on mars. Sergei thought that having popup emergency shelters for expeditions was cheating. He was already starting sentences with: In my day we only had… The new UN ambassador from the United States gave away the bride. Bob was resplendent in long tails. Lui and Georg and Mike Camby served as groomsman. A hugely pregnant Rosario, Li and Zoe Smyth were bridesmaids. Brad Elkingtons little girl was the flower girl. His son the ring bearer. And what a ring it was. Five carats of flawless mars rock. Two more 1.75 carat stones adorned the brides ears. Sparkly. The drinking and dancing kept up for long hours. The picture of the six of them together was soon flashed all over the world. Sergei congratulated the new explores in residence at The National Geographic Society. Li and Gorge both blushed. "They offered so much money it was obscene!" Li said.

"Plus we get to do more cool stuff together," Georg observed. Fantastic. Sergei and Janice only got three bites of dinner as well wishers congratulated them. It took two hours but Sergei noticed something a little off about the well wishers. All night long women kept coming up to Janice and congratulating her and handing over envelopes. She kept stuffing them in a small bag at her wrist.

"What tradition is this," Sergei asked? "Are they giving you advice for the wedding night?" he joked.

"Nope." Tatiana Medvedev approached the couple. She kissed Sergei and then Janice and wished them well. She then handed Janice 10 100 dollar bills and walked away. Janice smirked and shoved the money in the bulging bag.

"Whoa, she gave us a thousand dollars as a wedding gift? Sweet."

"No, Janice corrected she gave me a thousand dollars."

"Why?"

"She paid off the bet. 10 to 1 that we got married. She was down for 100 dollars."

"That's what these women are doing? You had a bet that we would get married? I can't believe you would do that! Outrageous. Half that's mine."

"Bullshit."

"Hey whats yours is mine and all that, right, he whined.

"Nope this is hazard pay for having to be married to you."

"Now that hurts." Taking her in his arms. "Hey, you want to play some poker tonight?"

The End